S

As I went down the narrow hallway to the music room, candles flickered in the gargoyle-shaped wall sconces, half lighting my way. At the end of the hallway, I got out the key. The lock seemed rusty, but finally I heard it tumble.

The door scraped as I pushed it inward, then a flash of lightning illumined the shrouded furniture and the cobwebs that hung from the chandelier to the corners of the room. I gave a shudder, somehow sensing unseen dangers. But the memory of my mother and her haunting music drove me on.

Then another flash of lightning lit the silhouetted garden beyond the glass French doors. Terror rushed through me as I suppressed a scream. Outlined on the edge of the terrace before me was the hooded figure of a man . . .

ISLAND OF LOST RUBIES

PATRICIA WERNER

ZEBRA BOOKS
KENSINGTON PUBLISHING CORP.

ZEBRA BOOKS

are published by

Kensington Publishing Corp.
475 Park Avenue South
New York, NY 10016

Second printing: August, 1992

Printed in the United States of America

For the real Eileen

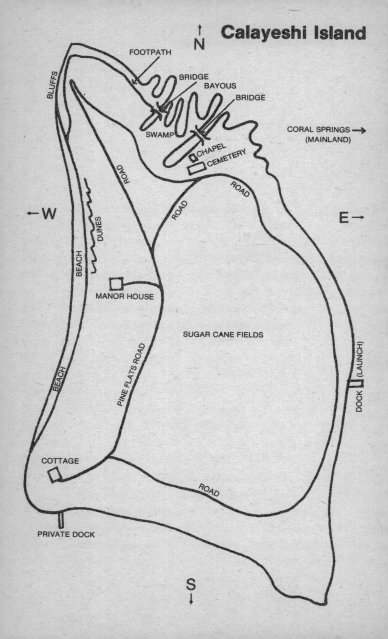

Prologue

October, 1885

The rain beat on the canvas top of the four-seated carriage, as the last of the Blakemore servants got in. The stinging drops pelted in the little girl's face as she huddled in her blanket.

"We must hurry," said her nanny to the driver. "The child's got a fever as it is. I can't have her out in this wet."

"She's going to get more wet in the boat," the driver shouted from the front seat. "With luck we'll get to the mainland before the hurricane hits."

It seemed to the nanny that the hurricane was already upon them. The wind was already a fierce, rising, shriek, but she simply pulled her ulster farther around her face.

Realizing that they were about to leave, the little girl suddenly sat up and stared at the door to the house behind her. *My dolly. I can't leave my dolly.*

She slid out of the seat and into the drive, hastening on her small legs up the steps to the portico, across the slick, gray marble, and into the house. She had left her dolly on the seat in the foyer when they were getting ready to leave. She reached for her dolly on the chair, then turning, she looked into the room beyond, where her cousin was turning a knob on the wall and opening a small door. He must have sensed he was being watched and turned, staring at the child.

"What!" he said. Then muttering an oath, he strode hastily to where Erin stood clutching her dolly and pushed her roughly aside.

"Stay there," he ordered, then stepped out into the rain. From the doorway, she could see him on the steps, one hand cupped around his mouth as he shouted, "Go on, I've got her. We'll come in the other boat."

Nanny looked back in wild-eyed fright, but the driver jerked the carriage forward.

The others disappeared behind the gray sheet of water, and Erin looked up as her cousin strode back to the house, wiping mud from his boots on the door sill. He picked the girl up and took her into the formal parlor across the hall and set her on the green velvet sofa, her slicker dripping onto the polished wood floor.

"Wait here," he said. "We'll take my boat. You'll meet your nanny on the mainland."

He left her where she started to tremble, huddled in the corner of the sofa, pressing her dolly to her face. Her forehead was so hot she started to cry, and the rest of her was so cold. But soon Cousin was back, and he picked her up, carrying her to the door. Then he covered her face with her hood and splashed through the mud puddles to the waiting buggy. Once settled, he slapped the horse's reins, and they headed through the hissing, lashing water toward the dock.

had known, I mean, my mother, and now my father. And of course the little casket that had been entombed for my sister...

Chapter 1

September, 1899

Calayeshi Island. I could never say the name without thinking of the white sand dunes on the gulf side or the mangrove swamp, where the spread of exposed tree roots broke the wave of tropical storms. There should be nothing odd about returning to the barrier island where I was born, but I had been away several years, and even the news of my father's death might not have brought me back so suddenly had not circumstances conspired to hasten my return. I knew that I could not get here in time for his funeral, even though I left New York shortly after sending a telegram to my aunt that I was coming home.

From the steam launch that ferried passengers to our island, I could see two figures waiting on the boardwalk above the dock. The sole passenger, I sat in the shade of the vessel's striped awning gazing at the two on shore. One I knew was Riggin, our driver, but I could not guess who the other might be.

The white sands of the shoreline came nearer and the sea oats that grew in the dunes bent and waved in the warm September breeze. The two figures on shore came down the weather-beaten steps to the dock, one shuffling, the other taller one walked slowly, surveying the scene before him, his jacket slung over his shoulder. Sunlight glinted off the stranger's fair hair, and I could see that he was young, broad of shoulder and quite tanned from the sun. The sea breeze billowed his white shirt, and his stance as he waited for the launch held a certain confidence.

We were very near now, and I waved. Riggin lifted a hand in greeting, then the ferryman cast the line around the piling at the edge of the dock. Riggin came along the dock and when the ferryman had opened the hatchway, Riggin offered a hand to help me to the dock. Then he cleared his throat and turned halfway toward the blond man coming slowly towards us. "This here's a friend of your cousin Richard's."

He had come closer now and smiled at me, the curious expression I had noticed giving way to one of courtesy.

"Gaius Amundsen," he said by way of introduction. I could see now that his eyes were blue, his chin angular, and the blond hair had a natural wave that reminded me of a Greek hero. I smiled at the image, and he responded to my smile, for his eyes lit then he bowed in front of me.

"Your driver is correct. I knew your stepcousin, Richard at college. It is a pleasure to meet the lovely Miss Blakemore." Then on a more serious note, he said, "And may I offer my condolences for your father's untimely death."

I forced a smile. "Thank you." I suppose one could call it untimely for a man of fifty to meet with his end.

10

The grim thought flashed through my mind that there were far more Blakemores buried on the ancestral island than there were living, for besides Richard and myself, there were only his mother Lettice, and his sister Nannette left.

"Your father's body was interred day before yesterday," said Gaius, offering an arm to lead me up the dock. "I happened to arrive just after the funeral. I didn't know of course, otherwise I would have postponed my visit."

I took his arm, for after the dipping and swaying of the launch and the strangeness of returning, I was feeling a bit unsteady. Some mechanical part of my mind made the correct responses, while the rest of me gave way to the powerful feelings of nostalgia always associated with a place where one has grown up.

"No need for that," I said to his protestations about his untimely appearance here. "Of course I knew I would not get here in time for my father's funeral."

"Your aunt Lettice has instructed me to bring you to the cottage. Richard was called to another part of the island at the last moment."

I hesitated, and he turned to face me as my arm slipped out of his. At the mention of Richard's name, I realized my disappointment that he had not come to meet me. Though he was five years older than I was, I had not seen him since we were children, and I was curious about how the years had changed him.

"I believe you have inherited the manor house," Gaius went on, chattering to put me at my ease, no doubt, although in actuality he was the visitor. "Still Lettice, that is the family, thought you would be more comfortable with them at first."

I had tried to convince myself that it would be best to stay in the manor house that had been built a hundred years ago by Blakemore ancestors and had now passed to me, my father's only heir. But the place had never been a happy home. After the death of my sister, Erin, when I was a child of six, my mother could not look at me without thinking of the small casket symbolically entombed in the family vault, for Erin was drowned in a hurricane, and her body never found. Grief-stricken, my mother, Helen Blakemore, died of pneumonia, a year later.

Gaius watched me carefully, his jacket now hanging through one crooked elbow, his hands in the pockets of his white duck trousers, as if aware that I was sorting out my thoughts while we stood on the dock.

Then he said gently, "Except for the staff, Lettice indicated that you would be alone at the manor. Wouldn't you like to be with the family at the cottage? It seems your cousins would enjoy your company."

I reached up to remove my straw bonnet so the island breeze could cool my damp temples. "I suppose you are right."

He smiled as if I had indeed given the right response. "I do hope, though, you'll not deprive me of at least a glimpse of the ancestral manor house I've heard so much about. When it's convenient, of course. I've a great desire to acquaint myself with all the landmarks on the island."

I turned my gaze away from him and took in the low bluffs and the tangled foliage that lay farther to the north. That way led to the swamp and the old bridge, probably now rotted from lack of use. I was starkly aware of all the reasons I had seldom returned home since leaving for boarding school in New York at the age of twelve. And yet I knew that the longer one stayed on the island, the better attuned to it one became, and I could already feel it beginning to claim me.

I shook myself and said, "It's all right. We can stop there first. I'll need to inform Henrietta of my arrival." My father's housekeeper was very close to him, and I believed she would be hurt if I did not go there first.

Riggin dropped back to bring my luggage and Gaius touched my elbow as we began walking toward the wooden steps. "I do hope we can be on a first name basis. Richard has told me so much about you."

I nodded to Gaius, anxious to get out of the late morning sun, for I could feel my blouse sticking to my back. I wore a dark brown bengaline traveling suit, and in this semi-tropical setting, the weight of it dragged on me. I carried my bonnet, ribbon trailing, as we climbed the wooden steps and followed the boardwalk over the dunes to the phaeton, waiting on the road. Riggin hoisted my trunks into a wagon he had brought and started off, so I was left with Gaius, who got up to drive the phaeton.

I settled myself beside him, and he picked up the reins. The matched pair of dun-colored mares knew the way home, and so hardly needed any driving.

"What brings you to Calayeshi Island?" I asked Gaius.

He gazed at the grasslands we passed, dotted with cabbage palms at intervals.

"Call it self-indulgence if you like. I'm on holiday for a month from my father's shipping firm, and Richard used to talk about the place, when I could get him away from his books, that is."

I knew next to nothing about Richard's terms at college, for by then I was busily involved in my life at boarding school. Thoughts of school and of what it had led to brought a fresh pang of embarrassment to my heart, for I was not yet over the betrayal done me by my best friend, Millicent Van Nuys, and the young man I had foolishly thought I might one day marry.

But in order to take my mind off myself, I gave Gaius a bright smile. "You must tell me how you and Richard met at school."

"I would be glad to." He flashed me a grin. "I'm glad you are only stepcousins, for you must be less likely to share Richard's moodiness."

"Do you find him moody?"

Gaius laughed. "He was at times, but we did get on all right. He could never turn down the challenge of a good arm wrestle."

We followed the road through the pine flats while Gaius chatted and I half listened. Apparently he and Richard had met in athletics and found themselves quite equally matched.

"But what of your life, Eileen? Did you enjoy New York society?"

I had once enjoyed life in a Fifth Avenue mansion at the invitation of my erstwhile friend, Millicent and her family. But I was afraid my expression must have been sardonic when I said, "The last year was a round of parties and of exploring the city. But at last, I grew tired of it."

"And will you find Calayeshi Island less boring, what with the responsibilities of your inheritance?"

I puckered a brow. "You can hardly compare an island to a city. And my father did very little in the way of agriculture. He leased most of his land to tenant farmers. His other business enterprises may not need my interference. I haven't yet decided what to do about the house."

The lawyers had informed me that my father had tidied up his financial affairs, and his investments had left me an income. Still, I hoped there would be some work to do, for I hated to sit idle.

We turned into a lane where the foliage on either side had been cleared except for the rows of live oak with branches tangling overhead like long black fingers rounding over us to form a leafy tunnel. Then I saw the manor house, half hidden among trees choked with Spanish moss. Gray pillars supported both the balcony and the upper roof, and the six-over-six paned windows seemed dark, for sunlight failed to penetrate the heavy shade here. We pulled into the hedged drive, and when we reached the steps, Henrietta Stafford, the housekeeper, opened the door to us.

Gaius helped me down and I climbed the stone steps. For a brief moment, I felt I had moved back in time and was seeing the familiar portico not as I was but as a young girl dressed in a traveling costume and leaving for boarding school. Even Henrietta's round face seemed not that much older, with only a few tell-tale age lines about her eyes and chin. And the hands that reached out for me were more veined.

She bustled toward me, dressed in her black satin uniform and crisp white apron. "Welcome home, Miss," she said. "I didn't have much time to get the place ready for you, what with the funeral. But of course I knew you'd be coming. I was sorry to see him go, poor man."

"It's all right, Henrietta. I've been persuaded to stay with the family at the cottage."

The relief in her gray eyes was evident, and I wondered if there were some other reason I should know that she didn't want me to stay there.

"Can't say as I blame you," she said. "And I'm sorry you're returning home on this sad note." She lowered her head.

"Thank you, Henrietta." I introduced her to Gaius, and she curtsied a little, intimidated somewhat I thought, by his golden looks. Then I led the way in.

The foyer was dark and cool, and though it was a relief from the heat, I shivered slightly. As I turned into the parlor, memories overcame me. I remembered how my father used to sit in the overstuffed leather chair with his feet on the ottoman. As I stood staring at the corner of the room, another image filled my mind— that of my mother kneeling down in front of him, a smile on her face. Then the image was gone.

Gaius examined the room, the flocked wallpaper, the heavy damask, fringed drapes, and the wooden clock with its painted columns resembling marble. The hands on the face had stopped at a quarter past three, and no one had rewound it.

"Your father must have had good taste," he said.

"Yes," I said, running my hand over the smooth walnut of a side table, the fringe from the lampshade swinging as I brushed it. "I suppose he did."

Gaius looked at me curiously, as if assessing my reactions to being here, and I suddenly wished I were alone. His fascination with the place annoyed me, under the circumstances. Then he crossed to me, smiling gently, and I chided myself for feeling so

16

impatient. He did not seem insensitive, rather my own nerves were on edge.

"It's a lovely house," he said. "But I can understand your reluctance to look at the rest. Perhaps we should go."

"No. It's all right. We'll go upstairs, just for a moment." I turned and left the room, pausing at the foot of the stairs, my hand on the newel post. Looking up the long, straight, heavy, mahogany banister, another image came to me. I recalled sliding down that smoothly, polished banister, my skirt flying up over my drawers. Richard would catch me before I hit the post.

"When I was little . . ." I started to recall the incident, but I realized the memory would mean nothing to Gaius. My words trailed off, and we started up.

For the last several years, I had put my life on Calayeshi Island in the back of my mind. Still I was surprised at the force of the sensations that assailed me as I passed along the runner that led first past my father's rooms, then past the nursery where Erin and I had spend our early years. I paused and reached for the door knob, but it wouldn't turn.

"It's locked," I said.

"What's in there?" Gaius asked.

"The nursery." I shrugged and went on toward my bed chamber. The door creaked a little on its hinges, but we stepped across the parquet floor to the oriental carpet in the center of the room. It seemed very familiar, though I had not slept here in some time. The coverlet and pillows on the four-poster were fluffed up as if Henrietta had prepared for me to stay here.

Gaius was running his fingers over the inlaid veneer

on the oak mantle when I glanced over my shoulder and saw the door move inward by itself. Then, my hand on my heart, I glanced down and saw the white cat.

"Goodness, that gave me a start. I guess I'm a little jumpy."

"Understandable," said Gaius. "But what is this?"

The white Persian cat came into the room and blinked his large, round, green eyes at us. For a moment, I had the odd sense that we were the intruders.

"It's only Pericles. He's lived in the house for as long as I can remember."

"He must be quite old," said Gaius.

"Yes, and rather strange too. That is, he's not really very friendly."

"Ah," said Gaius, bending down and holding out his fingers for the cat to sniff. "Perhaps he is the spirit of one of your ancestors. They say the spirit can come back, you know."

I gave him an uneasy look, for that very thought had occurred to me in the past, though I had never said so. Pericles ignored Gaius but stared at me, his full, brushlike tail moving slowly across the floor.

"You are right," I finally said to Gaius. "I don't want to stay here. This is more a place of the dead than the living."

Gaius rose and held the door for us, turning his smile on me. Again I tried to convince myself that he was not being deliberately inconsiderate. It was not his fault that the cat had startled me.

"Thank you for indulging my wish to see the house," he said when we were downstairs. "It must be trying for you. It's only that your ancestry fascinates me, and I am intrigued by all old places of this sort. I hope you will forgive me if I seem overly curious."

"It's all right," I said, trying to sound cordial. "Perhaps you'd like to see some of the family relics— some other time that is."

His expression became more serious and he looked deeply into my eyes, his look searching my expression intently. "I would be entranced if you would show them to me."

I had to turn away to take a deep breath.

I told Henrietta that we would be leaving, and she squeezed my hands. I saw her lip tremble and realized that she must miss my father very much.

"I'll be back in a few days to see about things," I told her, determined to appear competent and under control. "In the meantime, I'll be at the cottage."

I gave the manor house one last glance and climbed into the phaeton. There was enough breeze to cool us now, for the wind had picked up, and the air felt heavy with rain. The road to the cottage curved past the fields of sugar cane that the tenants worked, then the foliage grew thicker, where the ground had never been cleared. We drove northward and eventually I could see the bluffs where I had often strolled to watch the sea birds and the fishing boats out from Coral Springs. I pointed out a bridal path to Gaius.

"Do you ride then?" he asked.

"Yes. We always kept stables."

"Perhaps you will show me your island on horse-back? When you are ready of course."

My island. Well it was partly so now.

The cottage was a two-storied, many gabled frame house with white pillars supporting the roof of the verandah that surrounded the house on three sides. As we turned into the drive, the front door opened, and my aunt Lettice came out to the verandah.

Though twice my age, she had lost none of her patrician beauty. She looked radiant and self-composed in her gown of white lawn, trimmed with a deep flounce. She lifted a parasol to protect herself from the sun when she came down the steps to greet us. I could see that though there were a few more lines in her triangular face, there was a serene quality in her hazel eyes that I had not noticed when I had last been to the island, five years ago. Her hair was still a shimmering black, though now touched with gray.

I thought I should be lucky to look like that twenty years hence, for though I had a good complexion, and people often commented on my gray-green eyes and rich brown hair, I sometimes speculated as to what I would look like when older. For my mother had died so young, that I had no one with whom to compare myself. But now here was Lettice, still lovely, and I was glad.

"Welcome home, Eileen," she said as we kissed on both cheeks. "I am sorry the circumstances are not more fortunate."

"Thank you Lettice. It's good of you to let me stay here on such short notice."

"I would not think otherwise." She squeezed my hand and we looked into each other's eyes for a moment as if seeking the link with a part of the past we had both shared. Then she tilted her head in the direction of the house, and we went up the steps and through the front door, which led directly into the formal parlor. I noticed new wallpaper with its broad floral print above the heart of pine wainscotting.

"Have you redone the house?" I asked as Lettice led me up the stairs.

She smiled when we reached the landing. "I wanted something to do this last year." I followed her along a short hallway past the necessary room, with its shiny faucets and porcelain, claw-footed tub. Then she led me to the guest room. It was small but bright, with white lace curtains on the window. The bed faced diagonally into the room from one corner with the closet across another corner.

"The room is lovely, Lettice. I shall be very comfortable here."

She sat in a spindle-back chair by the window, and I dropped my bonnet on the bed beside me. I ran my fingers through the curls that had trailed from my coif, which had come quite undone by now. We spoke of my father's funeral, and then began to talk of other personal things. I began to wonder about Richard, for I had not seen him since I was twelve and he seventeen. When I had last visited the island, he had been away at school. Since then, he had taken on running the island estate for his mother, as well as managing the rest of his family's business interests.

"How has it been for you since Richard took over managing the estate?" I asked Lettice.

She smiled easily, glancing out the lace curtains to the lawn below. "It has been pleasant. Some might find it too quiet, but for me it has been like a long needed rest."

"I'm glad."

"Since Jasper died . . ." She hesitated then faced me directly. "You know of course that ours was never a happy marriage."

"I was too young to know such things," I hedged.

She gazed out the window again and I could see that she seemed to want to talk. I was flattered that she felt she could confide in me.

"He brought me here when I was a young widow. Richard was six, and Nannette barely one year old." She sighed. "Jasper and I were never blessed with children of our own. I know Richard and Nannette tried to please him, but he started to change when the children began to grow up. I believe he was an ambitious man."

I had always suspected that their marriage was not happy, and I knew that Richard and Nannette were not close to their stepfather.

"Did he not do well with his sponge-fishing boats?" I asked. Jasper had owned two sponge-fishing boats and employed several fishermen to hook the natural sponges that grew in abundance in the gulf waters.

"He might have, if he had not incurred the enmity of those who came to the area to compete with him." I knew she was thinking of the horrible night when his boat went up in flames, and he on board. She shook her head regretfully. "It was not necessary. There would have been room for all."

"It was a terrible accident." I hated for her to dwell on it and sought to change the subject.

I rose and walked to the window, parting the lace curtains to gaze at the lawn below. Both my father and his cousin, Jasper, had died before they passed the age of fifty. I shuddered to think it was some sort of curse that might hang over the island. But no. Father's fate and that of my cousin Jasper must have been each his own, for my grandfather had lived to be seventy-five.

Lettice's expression was one of concentration as she looked down at her hands in her lap.

"What do you think of Gaius Amundsen?" I asked, turning from the window and wanting to change the subject.

The thin lines of her brow creased to a frown. "He seems pleasant enough, but . . ."

I said nothing, allowing her time to gather her thoughts.

"Our way of life must seem slow to a young man like that," she finally said. "He does not know our ways."

Then she focused on me. "How does he compare to the young men you met in New York society?"

I pulled the corners of my lips upward, but I was afraid it must have appeared more of a smirk than a smile as I said, "He's not unlike one of them . . ."

"So there was someone?"

I nodded admission. "His name was Ian Menasce." I wanted to tell her how his smile could light a room; how he made heads turn. But I only said, "I rather misunderstood his intentions."

I shrugged, fingering the lace tatting of the curtains. "He used to call at the house where I lived with Millicent's family. I spoke to him alone several times, and I thought we were in accord with one another."

Then I shook my head, running my hand along the damp curls at my temple. "I could not believe it when his engagement to Millicent was announced. She had told me nothing."

"And so that is when you left?"

"Yes. I knew there wasn't time to get here for my father's funeral, but I had no more reason to linger in

23

New York."

"My dear," Lettice said, a look of concern into her her eyes. "How awful for you to face that disappointment on top of your loss."

I lifted my chin. "I suppose I'm rather over Ian. I think mostly it was my pride that suffered."

Lettice gave me an understanding half smile.

"As to my loss, well, I hadn't seen Father in so many years . . ." I paused, then said. "After Mother died, well, I suppose Father and I were not close."

She set her shoulders in that way I had so often seen her do. It was a gesture that said one became resigned to one's life and accepted the responsibility one was given. "It's regrettable that the Blakemores were not closer. I suppose we all grew so used to being alone here."

"But you have Nannette and Richard."

"Nannette spends much of her time on the mainland." She rose and stood beside me at the window. "Richard keeps to himself."

"Yes."

My stepcousin was head of the Blakemore family now, and I wondered how he carried that weight. Suddenly I felt very anxious to see him, to find out how the years and experience might have changed him, and whether he would see similar changes in me. I grinned to myself. Surely he would, for I was twelve when he last set eyes on me.

"I'll leave you," Lettice said, rousing herself. "You'll want to rest and refresh yourself before dinner."

"Thank you, Lettice. And thank you for"— I shrugged, not finding the words—"everything."

She came to me and squeezed my shoulders, smiling. "And I am glad you are here. We will have many womanly talks." She left me then.

Riggin brought up my luggage, and I changed out of my wrinkled traveling clothes, splashing water on my face and arms from the porcelain sink in the necessary room. The afternoon heat caused me to drowse, and I lay on the bed and gave way to comforting sleep, telling myself I would wake in time to dress for dinner.

Chapter 2

Late in the afternoon, I awoke and saw that the sun was low. It had been so long since I'd seen an island sunset that I dressed and went downstairs. I wore a green and white striped silk that seemed to float cooly about me as I slipped out of the house and went along the path to the dunes.

The sky had turned pink with streaks of blue, and the water below was metallic blue-gray. I stood at the top of the dune where tall sea oats gave way to sand that fell away suddenly to the long, smooth beach below. I watched the red disk of the sun drop from a blue and purple cloudscape until the deep fiery red burned between the sky and sea, then sank toward the rim of the darkening waters below, bathing the sky in its red glow. Then I returned to the grassy meadow and walked along its edge, near the woods, turning when I had reached the far side, to look back.

At the western edge of the meadow, against the red backdrop, walked a figure, elbow crooked, and I knew at once it was Richard. Dark hair fell across his tanned brow and touched his white shirt collar. He wore a tweed, belted, sporting jacket. And though he was some distance away, I felt as if my spirit rushed across the distance to him, though he had evidently not noticed me.

Perched on the leather glove covering his hand was a large red-tailed hawk, and I saw that he spoke gently to her. The wind ruffled her brown and white feathers and she danced on his wrist, talons circling the gloved fist that held her. I was fascinated by the sight and stood watching, as he removed the hawk's hood.

She shook her leg, and he stroked her throat and breast with his finger. Then she raised her wings and rose, a dark silhouette in the blood-red backdrop of sky, and I felt as if my spirit rose out of my body to fly with her. She flew into the sun, lost for a moment in the red glare. Then the wingspread coasted seaward, circling back toward the land. She passed her master once and circled again, hovering, waiting for her prey to fly out of its covert.

A disturbance in the nearby trees caused a flock of sparrow to rise, and the hawk dropped quickly, claws half-closed to strike her prey. The sparrow fell, and the hawk dove after it, following it to the ground. Richard walked toward her slowly as she fed. When she was finished, she fluttered again to his outstretched hand.

I crossed the field toward them, and the hawk fluttered her wings as I came up to them. Then Richard hooded her so that she sat docily as he stroked her with a feather. I could see up close the sharp claws and their gripping strength, and I wondered at the communication that passed between hawk and master. But then she rested, wings folded and smoothed.

"Hello, Richard," I said, as soon as he could hear me. "It's good to see you."

He finally turned his gaze on me. "Hello, Eileen," he said, with only a hint of a smile in his eyes. The curiosity in his expression made me suddenly self-conscious, aware of the changes in both of us since we'd last seen each other.

"You look older," I said.

Though he was five years my senior, he had experienced his sister's and my girlish teasing when we were children, but standing before him now, I somehow could not relate to those childhood antics. He was tall and had filled out. There were a few narrow creases across the plane of his forehead as if he concentrated a great deal, and he had the same fine, straight nose as Lettice. I remembered how I used to find his eyes menacing when his heavy brow bone shaded them. But now as he tilted his head back, the light caught the translucent green-gold of his pupils.

He allowed himself a conservative smile and said, "I am older, and so are you."

What I meant was that there was a commanding presence about him, a few character lines also at the corners of his eyes and a jaw that seemed more firm, even though he was only twenty-five. His voice was much as I remembered it, but deeper and firmer. Still there was gentleness in the way he spoke.

I stopped smiling and touched his arm. I felt his muscle tense as he lowered his eyes then said, "I'm sorry about your father."

"Thank you."

There seemed little else to say, and we began to walk along the path toward the beach. My breath was shallow, and I sensed that he too was withholding his words, not wanting to rush the expression of his feelings.

"What a noble bird," I said, looking at the hawk on his wrist. "I didn't know you took time for sport."

"A diversion from work. She is a passage hawk, caught in the wild and therefore more difficult to train, but more powerful than those taken from the nest."

"But you have tamed her," I said. "Does she like to be petted?"

"Only by her owner."

I nodded, and though I longed to run my hand over her feathers, I did not attempt to touch the bird.

Only a faint pink glow remained above the darkness that descended quickly now. The water rushed to shore beyond the dunes where we paused, looking at the stretch of sky with gray clouds fading into the darkness. I could sense Richard's energy, akin to my own, as we silently communed with the beauty and mystery of the windy island.

"Have you come back to stay then?" Richard asked. We followed the path as it wound back toward the woods on the other side of the meadow.

"I don't know. I did leave New York in rather a hurry."

"Would you like to talk about it?" His voice was softer, touched with a certain melancholy I had not known in him before.

Suddenly New York seemed very far away. As I had expected, life on the island had begun to draw me into itself. Looking at Richard, I suddenly felt that society life as I had experienced it in the Fifth Avenue mansion was rather meaningless. But I went on by way of explanation.

"I had a season of parties. There was a"—I paused,— "a young man who used to call on us. Only I soon learned it wasn't my attention he sought, but rather those of my friend, Millicent."

I knew there was a trace of bitterness in my voice, but I

did not attempt to hide it. Perhaps more than being hurt by Ian, I was irritated at having been duped by the two of them.

He looked at me inquiringly, and his gaze warmed my cheek. "Were you very disappointed?"

I stopped to face him. "I thought so, but being here makes it seem different."

Richard lifted his chin, and again I could see the muscle along his jawline. We stopped where tall sand pines rose above us, while all around us clumps of saw palmettos hugged the ground. The breeze from the beach just barely reached us, and Richard stood next to me, catching a spiny palmetto leaf in his right hand. As he gazed at my face, I was reminded suddenly that we were children of the island, and therefore were perhaps more like each other than either of us could ever be like anyone else.

It was growing too dark to see, and so we turned to go. "I believe I'll go to the manor tomorrow," I said. "I need to sort through things there and see what needs to be done. Your friend, Gaius, has offered to help me."

"Gaius?"

"Yes. He seems to want something to do."

"I see."

When we reached the mews, Richard opened the little door to the hawk's cage, placing her on her perch. He removed his leather glove, shut the door on the mews, and we continued walking toward the house.

"Richard," I said, thoughts of the manor conjuring up old family memories. "Do you remember how we used to hide on the balcony and try to listen to our fathers talking in the study?"

"I remember. Mostly when they raised their voices

in argument."

"I suppose I was too young to understand what they were speaking about."

"Whatever makes men argue. Or perhaps your father never really forgave my stepfather for your sister's death."

Jasper had been with Erin the night she died. Both Richard and I knew the story well.

"I suppose Father could not help the remorse he must have felt," I said. "But I remember your stepfather's grief as well."

I unconsciously put a hand on Richard's arm as I spoke. "I know he tried to save her, but it was a mean storm and the boat capsized. He said he dove after her but—" I suddenly choked on the words, surprised at the surge of grief I felt. My sister had died many years ago, and I thought I had grown used to the loss. I supposed being here had suddenly brought it all back.

Richard stopped and took my hand, raising my fingers to his lips and kissing them gently. I felt his compassion wash over me, and I tried to smile and changed the subject.

"Find the jewels, that was our game wasn't it?" I gave a half-choked little laugh.

"Yes." His grip loosened and I extracted my hand.

The family jewels. Rubies set in two gold bracelets, a necklace and brooch. I had never seen them, but they had been described to me so many times I started to believe I had. They had been in the family for generations, brought here from England at the turn of the century. But the jewels had been missed a few months after Erin died. My father had gone to the safe to take out some documents. I do not know what made him look in the jewel case, but when he did, he saw that the jewels were gone. I remember his terrible anger and distress. He notified the local police. Not satisfied with that, he hired a private investigator to question everyone on the island. The police watched carefully, but the jewels never came on the market. Some thought the thief had drowned trying to leave the island, and that the rubies now lay at the bottom of the gulf.

"I suppose we took our game seriously, thinking our parents would be pleased if we actually did find them," I said.

"But we never did. No one did." I felt his sidelong glance. "The search was quite thorough."

"Yes, you are right. It was just a childish game we played, trying to find the missing jewels, wasn't it?" I said.

"Yes."

It was too dark to see his face, but as we walked toward the house, I had the feeling that he was still watching me.

Chapter 3

We went in to dinner, and I did not speak to Richard privately again. It was a joy to see Nannette, who had come back from taking some medicine to one of the tenant farmers' wives. We were determined to renew our friendship at once.

Nannette was the same height as I, but her hair was darker than mine, like her mother's, and she wore it in springy curls that touched her shoulders. Her brown eyes had the same flecks of gold in them as Richard, but hers held the serene quality I had seen in her mother's, though Nannette's eyes sparkled with mischief when she laughed. I was pleased to see that she still had the joie de vivre I remembered in her.

At dinner, she said she had had many proposals from young men she had met on the mainland, but she had turned them all down, much to Lettice's chagrin, for she planned to see the world before she married. I was secretly amused and wondered how she intended to accomplish this.

Everyone seemed to make the effort to keep the dinner conversation light. Gaius and Richard talked about the sports they had played together, but I was surprised to notice a certain tension between them. I could not understand it, for I thought they were friends, and not rivals. But by the time we left them to their port, Gaius had Richard smiling at some amusing incident at the expense of one of their former professors.

Nannette was ready with plans for the next day.

"Why don't we take a buggy and drive to that little mossy glen at the north end of the island near the cemetery?" she said. Her look sobered respectfully. "You might like to put a wreath on the vault."

I appreciated her thoughtfulness, for I had wanted to visit the vault where my father's body was entombed, and we agreed to rise early for the outing.

After helping Nannette and Lettice clear the table, I expressed appreciation of the meal to Lettice's cook and housekeeper, Martha, who likewise bid me welcome.

I was walking along the hall afterward, when I heard Gaius's voice behind me. "You must be weary from your kitchen labors, Eileen. Would you like to sit down?"

I was not sure I wanted any company, but I didn't mind the idea of resting my feet. "All right," I said.

"Why don't we go in here?" We were near the study and went in.

I crossed to the windows and looked out. It was nearly dark, but I could still see the royal palms lining the gravel drive, bent slightly as if tired of holding their leafy tops so erect. I seated myself beside Gaius on the settee facing the windows.

"Is everything all right, Eileen?" he asked, turning to me, his blue eyes filled with a look of compassion.

"Why yes, of course." I supposed he was asking if I were holding up all right after my father's death.

"I am glad." Then he faced the windows again and

straightened the sleeve of his jacket. "I don't mind telling you that I feel as if I've known you longer than only a day."

"Why do you say that?"

He glanced down at me, and I thought his tan cheeks darkened slightly in embarrassment. "I know it may be the wrong time to say this, and I hope you will not find it inappropriate, if I tell you that I hope you will allow me to get to know you better."

His remark startled me, and I did not know how to respond. "If you wish," I said.

My remark must have encouraged him, for he had turned back to look toward the windows and said, "You know I am fascinated by Calayeshi Island, and you are so very much a part of it. How fortunate you were to have grown up in such a place. Did you take for granted the pastel sunsets? Clouds sculpted for your pleasure over the blue horizon?"

I was surprised to hear him describe it so eloquently. "Everyone takes for granted the place where one grows up," I said, thinking again of the past. "Yet I always knew it was part of me."

"How lucky you were. Of course I would say so, having grown up among smoky factories up north. Not that I'm complaining. My father owns his business and taught me how to continue so as to make a profit. But to be able to run along beaches, to fish and play in these blue waters whenever you wish. How idyllic that all seems to me."

He looked at me intently again. "Were you and Richard close as children?"

I was surprised at the suddenness of the question, but I answered, "No, we weren't. That is we played together

35

when my cousin Jasper brought his family to our house on rare occasions."

He laughed gently. "Childish games I suppose."

"Well, of course. Hide and seek, and find—" I stopped. For some reason I did not want to speak of the other games that had so occupied us as children.

"Yes?"

I smiled. "Scavenger hunts. You know how children like to hunt for things."

"And a fascinating place it must have been for that sort of game. What sort of things did you look for?"

"Sea shells, bird feathers, thimbles, pennies."

"Of course. Did you often win? No wait. Let me guess, now that I've met you all."

He rose circled the settee as if seriously weighing the idea of Richard, Nannette and myself playing together as children. Then he stopped in front of me and rocked once on his heels.

"Richard must have won, didn't he?"

"He sometimes did."

Though I was only entertaining him with conversation, I found myself going on, seeing the pictures in my mind as I explained how our games sometimes ended. Before I realized it, I had told him more than I had intended.

"Sometimes Richard took things home with him afterward." Then I pressed my lips together, realizing I had said too much.

A crease formed between Gaius's brows as he listened to this part.

"You mean things that he had won in the game?"

"No." I bit my bottom lip and glanced at the wood slats of the floor. "I mean things that weren't part of the game." Then I glanced up.

Gaius looked puzzled, making me feel obligated to explain. I felt flustered. "I didn't mean to say that. You mustn't—"

He smiled and sat down next to me again. "Of course I won't say anything you wouldn't want me to repeat."

I stumbled on, feeling obligated to finish what I had begun. "He took other things more valuable."

"Such as?"

I shrugged, wanting to get off the subject, feeling a little irritated at Gaius's coaxing. "Sometimes plates, silver."

"And did he keep them?"

"No. Jasper, Richard's stepfather, always sent them back with a note of apology.

I had said more than I had meant to, but Gaius's curiosity had caught me off guard. It was unsettling. His solicitousness made me want to please him for some reason, yet I was not obligated to do so except that he was a guest in my cousins' house.

"Hmmm, yes I wondered if that were a childhood trait," he murmured, as if to himself. Then, as if remembering my presence, he said, "I'm sorry. It's just coincidence that you mention it."

I frowned. "Why is that?"

He took my hand in his, exerting a slight pressure on it. "I would never have mentioned this, it seems too petty. But when we were at school, Richard and I shared rooms."

"Yes?"

"Well, I would sometimes find things missing. Small items, a pen, a book, once my change purse."

"And did you find them?"

"I did. Usually on Richard's dresser."

A sensation of nervousness overcame me, and I exhaled slowly. "He took them?"

"I'm afraid so." Gaius squeezed my hand once, then let it go.

"Nothing really important," he went on. "And when I found the things and pointed them out to him, he usually didn't seem to remember picking them up. On more than one occasion he claimed that I had loaned him the items. Of course it was perfectly all right for him to borrow my things. I just preferred he ask me first."

A look of pity came into his eyes, as he said, "That is, if he even knew he took them."

A tremor passed through me and I felt suddenly stifled. I found it difficult to believe that Richard actually did things like that. When he took things as a child, I had always thought he considered it part of our games.

I would ask him about it. Perhaps he had simply become absent-minded. I knew he had studied very hard at college and perhaps simply paid less attention to other trivial details. I did not want to believe that our childhood games had somehow become perverted in Richard's mind as he grew older.

The thought made me feel slightly queasy, and I rose. There had been too many upsetting events in the last few days, and I did not want to dwell on another unpleasantry. Gaius must have sensed my discomfort, for when I rose he stood with me, looking down at me out of his clear, brilliant, blue eyes.

"I'm sorry. I don't know how our conversation turned to such matters." His own look was one near regret, but with a light of hope mixed in. "Eileen, you must believe the last thing I want is to upset you in any way. It is

38

rather the opposite . . ."

"It's all right." I tried to put on a congenial expression. "I just need some time alone. I believe I'll retire and rest."

"Very well. But please allow me to be at your service when you decide to go to that old mansion of yours. It would please me if I could make myself useful."

I left him there and went to find Lettice, who assured me that she didn't need me downstairs anymore. Then I sought the privacy of my room, where I got out of my gown with some effort, undoing the many hooks and eyes by myself. I stood for a moment in my camisole and petticoats, letting the breeze from the open window cool me.

Then I bathed and slipped into a light cambric dressing gown. White cottons and cambric were more practical in this sultry climate, I decided. I refused to go about in the heavy black silks and satins usually required for mourning.

My mood was solitary and a bit self-pitying. I was troubled by what Gaius had said, and then I had not yet recovered from the unexpectedness of leaving New York, and coming here to decide what to do about my future. For that was the crux of the matter, wasn't it? What would I do now? I could live here of course, but I wondered if I would find any reward in an existence that at times might be too quiet for me. I had a desire to make myself useful, to live an active life.

The interchange with Gaius had left me unsettled, confused me about Richard. Something had happened when he had taken me by the hand in the mews. Was it only a moment of needed comfort and understanding based on our mutual past? Certainly a cousinly affection would be natural under the circumstances, but I wondered if I had begun to build a fantasy about my handsome older cousin. And yet I also suspected that my disappointment in Ian had sent me on the rebound, ready to seek sympathy where it was offered. It was certainly too soon to be able to think logically about matters of the heart, I told myself.

I laughed inwardly at the situation, for I had never considered myself a femme fatale. That was more Millicent's appeal than mine, and perhaps that was why I had lost Ian to her.

The air was refreshing after the night's rain, and the leaves on the trees seemed greener. Nannette looked cool in her cream colored faille trimmed with green bows, and I wore a white batiste gown trimmed with blue ribbons. We packed a picnic lunch and took the phaeton, which she drove expertly. As she told me about her life these last few years, I felt warmed by the renewal of our friendship, for we were the same age, and I hoped we would have much to share.

We chatted all during the drive to the north end of the island, and we stopped in the little glen where lay the cemetery for all the families on the island. I got down, and lifted out the wreath I had brought.

I opened the gate and walked through the grass, passing between the ancient plots. The air was still here, and I paused a moment, contemplating the quiet place where all the Blakemores were buried, as well as many of the tenant families. I swallowed the lump in my throat and looked up at the vault, built only in the last generation and housing the remains of the Blakemores I had known; Jasper, my mother, and now my father. And of course the little casket that had been entombed for my sister, Erin. I placed the wreath on the door.

Behind the cemetery was a stone chapel, and I considered going in and sitting for a while to meditate, but I did not feel that it would bring me comfort at present, and so I turned and walked back to the gate, emerging into the dappled sunlight of the road and climbed up to the phaeton again. We drove for a while and sought a clearing where we could spread out our blankets.

Our picnic was a sumptuous feast of chicken, celery, macaroni pudding, pickled crab and cheesecakes. Our stomachs full, we lay back on our blankets. I was not interested in sleeping, however, but when Nannette's eyelids had drooped shut, I sat up and said, "I think I'll take a walk, if you don't mind."

"All right," she said, and then closed her eyes again.

The woods were peaceful, and I let my heels sink into the sandy soil that was covered by a layer of pine needles. My thoughts were stilled, and I was content to listen to the cry of the cicadas and to the rustle of leaves.

I was about to turn back, when I heard a twig crack behind me, causing me to draw in my breath. Richard emerged from behind a tree, and I breathed again. He walked softly toward me, carrying his sack coat, his collar unbuttoned.

"Richard, you startled me. I thought it might be Nannette. I left her napping on our picnic blanket."

"I'm sorry. I didn't know there was anyone else here." His gaze settled on my face, and I laughed at my nervousness. His eyes took in my features, as if trying to convince himself that I was the same girl he used to have to put up with when his family came to visit, which was not often after Erin's death.

"Come," he said, smiling a little. "Walk a little way with me. I've left my horse by the road."

I fell in step with him, and we walked for some time in silence, following a path that widened between the pines.

"What was Gaius talking to you about last night?" he asked.

I was about to answer when a screech beside me caused me to jump, and Richard caught my arm. A branch swayed near my head, and a scarlet macaw opened its curved white beak and screamed threateningly again.

My hand was on my heart even though it was only one of the pair that my father had brought here when he had envisioned putting in a bird sanctuary.

"Goodness. He gave me a fright."

"It's only old Samson."

"I know. I remember."

I reached out a finger to see if Samson would let me touch his feathers, but he screamed again and moved on the tree branch, turning his head sideways, viewing me with the small dark eye on the right side of his head. I admired his red, yellow, and blue feathers, then we walked on, and Samson fluttered away, presumably to find his mate.

Standing next to Richard under the pine branches, I felt a sense of belonging, and when we stopped, I found myself staring at the set of his shoulders as he tossed his coat over a tree limb. Something about his nearness stirred me unexpectedly, drawing me into the small circle of light and shade that held us there.

I breathed deeply and turned, taking a few steps toward the trees with gray moss trailing in places for more than a yard and touching the ground here and there. There was something moody and dark about its gray presence in the pervading green.

Richard must have known my thoughts, for when he came to stand next to me, he said, "The Indians tell of a girl killed by their enemy during her wedding ceremony." He reached toward the moss. "Her mourning family cut off her hair and spread it on the limbs of the oak tree under which she was buried."

I nodded, for I too knew the legend. "Her hair blew from tree to tree, finally turning gray. It endures as a tribute to those not fated to live out their love."

He must have felt something of what was passing between us. For the line of his lips relaxed, and his eyes, which searched my face, lingered on my mouth. He reached a hand to touch my face, and I felt as if a coil wound up in me unsprang. He looked into my eyes, and a tiny thrill ran up my spine, but my heart was pounding so hard, I couldn't move. The light and shade played on his eyes, and I was again struck by the gold that seemed to glow from behind the dark green pupils.

"Richard," I whispered the half question, as his fingers gently touched my cheek, my ear. I felt a sense of yearning that I had not known before and did not quite understand. At the same time we both must have realized that we were very near the spot where Nannette was waiting. Neither of us spoke for a long moment, and then he reached for my hand.

We walked back to the clearing slowly, and just before we rejoined Nannette, he reached up and brushed a twig from my hair.

"I'm glad you've come, Eileen. You will be good for the island."

My voice stuck in my throat, and I could hardly explain to myself what had just happened. But I nodded mutely. Then I heard a rustle of leaves and Nannette appeared, grass and leaves tangled in her hair.

"Why Richard," she said, smiling at her brother. "Have you come to surprise us?" She glanced quickly at my face, and I wondered if she could see my blush.

Then Richard said laughingly, "I didn't trust you two to find your way home. I thought you might need an escort."

"Oh Richard, you know we couldn't get lost in these woods. Why we spent our lives as children exploring them."

"That was a long time ago," he said.

We packed the lunch basket and were soon on our way. Richard drove, his horse tied behind, and though I occasionally glanced at his profile, we did not speak alone again until we reached the house. Nannette took the basket in, while I accompanied Richard to the stable where Riggin took charge of the horses.

I had been about to tell Richard what Gaius had said to me last night, only the macaw had made me forget. Now I remembered and was determined to bring up the matter. Feeling myself flush in embarrassment I said, "Richard, when we were young and played our games at the manor, do you remember the things you used to take without mentioning them to us?"

I laughed, trying to make it sound light. "That silver plate from the dining room and the figurines from the parlor. I always wondered how you got away with them."

We had reached the back steps to the house, and he paused, looking at me curiously. "No," he said, his brows drawn into a frown. "I don't know what you mean."

44

Chapter 4

I stared at him blankly, feeling suddenly disoriented. I remembered my father cautioning us not to mention the missing items when Jasper's family visited, since the items had been so promptly returned. Undoubtedly Jasper had disciplined his stepson, and it would be impolite to mention it. Father must have thought it best to drop the matter. I could almost hear his voice now, telling me so.

Realizing I was standing there, mute, I struggled to get out an explanation.

"When we played our game, your family would leave and then Henrietta would miss things. But one of your servants always brought them back with a note of apology."

"A note from me?"

"No. I think the notes were from your father."

His eyes suddenly darkened, his brows still knotted. "I never stole anything from your house."

"Then who—"

He lifted an eyebrow and placed a hand on the porch railing. "I would remember if I had taken anything. I swear I did not."

He moved closer to me now, gripping my arm so hard it hurt. "Eileen, you must believe me. I would never take anything from your house, never."

I swallowed, the anger in his face frightening me. "All right, Richard. I believe you. You're hurting me."

He loosened his grip, but still held my gaze.

"It was just some silly mistake," I said, trying to catch my breath.

He watched me a moment longer, as if assessing my sincerity, then he turned to go in, as if he were still angry with me.

I did not know what to make of him. I wanted to believe him, of course. But his reaction had been so extreme. I had heard of people who took things and didn't remember it. Could Richard be likewise afflicted? It was horrible to contemplate, and a sudden feeling of grief mixed with pity overcame me. I went up to my room, avoiding seeing the others, so that I could be alone.

Nannette offered to accompany Gaius and me the next day when I went through my father's house, and indeed I appreciated her company. Perhaps having Nannette and Gaius with me would help me face the cobwebs of the old house.

After breakfast we met in the foyer. Charlie, Lettice's stable boy, had brought the phaeton around, and Gaius climbed in front and drove while Nannette and I seated ourselves in back. We took the road past the sugar cane fields, and I waved to some of the farmers as we passed, for they must have heard I had returned, and they waved back. Then we entered the wood, where the road was dappled with shade from overhanging oak and pine.

46

Nannette chattered on about some friends she had met on the mainland, and Gaius gazed at the scenery until we came to the fork in the road and slowed.

"The way to the mansion is to the left," I said. The horse shook his harness as if impatient to be on his way. But Gaius asked, "What lies the other way?"

Nannette and I exchanged quick glances, for we had been that way only yesterday. Then I said, "That's the way to the chapel, and there's a path that leads to the cemetery."

He nodded. "I should like to see the chapel, some other time." Then he slapped the reins and we moved on.

Finally the road came out on the grasslands again, then we came down the oak-lined drive, and as we stopped in front of the house, a curtain in the upstairs parlor moved. Henrietta must have seen us drive up. In a moment, the front door opened to us.

I told Henrietta that I'd come to look over my father's things and work on the household accounts and that Gaius and Nannette had offered to help me.

"Very well," she said as we passed into the foyer. "I locked up the accounting ledgers myself. I'll bring you the key in the study. Will you also be going to the upstairs rooms?"

"Yes. We'll stay through lunch and return to the cottage before supper."

"Very well."

She departed, but not before she cast a questioning glance at Gaius over her shoulder. But he was busy examining the pink satin, upholstered, oval-backed chairs that sat in the four corners of the foyer.

We went to the study, and I pulled back the drapes and opened the casement windows to let in some air. Gaius made a tour of the room, his eyes trailing over the bookcases, the polished oak mantle. He paused in front of a picture of my mother and father and gazed at it for some moments.

"Your parents," he finally said.

"Yes. That was taken shortly after they were married."

"I can see the resemblance," he whispered softly. He let his gaze wander over the portraits and daguerreotypes, small photographs of Erin and me as children, Jasper and Lettice, dark hair cascading down her back.

I left him to his explorations, and when Henrietta brought the key, I sat down at the desk and withdrew the accounting ledger where my father had kept a record of all the expenses for the household.

"Eileen," said Nannette, interrupting my thoughts. "Do you mind if I take Gaius upstairs? If you don't need us here, that is."

"All right. I'll work here for a while and join you later."

"What shall we do for you? After all, we're here to help."

"You might go up to the attic and see what is up there. This might be a good time to get rid of useless pieces of junk that may be a fire hazard. If you don't mind climbing around a musty attic, that is."

"An excellent idea," Gaius said, smiling good naturedly. He removed his jacket and rolled up his sleeves. "After all, we've come to work, haven't we?"

I was glad the other two found it entertaining to go through the house on their own and soon lost myself in the ledgers again. For I wanted to learn how my father had managed the estate. Outside the light grayed and when I looked up just before noon, clouds had darkened the sky. When I heard the muffled thunder, I knew a storm was on its way. I sat for a moment looking out, remembering the many tropical storms that passed this way, for we were well into the hurricane season. Most storms, however, were not damaging, and when I was young, I had rather enjoyed the hard, driving rains and the falling dark clouds.

When Henrietta came in and announced lunch, I sent her up to find Nannette and Gaius. I went up to freshen up, and in ten minutes we met downstairs in the dining room. It got so dark that Henrietta had to light the kerosene lamps so we would have light to eat by.

"Did you find anything interesting in the attic?" I asked after we were seated and Henrietta had served us piping hot stew.

"Yes, rather," said Nannette. "There is a trunk of some old dresses of your mother's." She seemed to gauge my reaction, then decided to go on. "Out of fashion, but you ought to look at them, Eileen. With some alteration, some of them might do. Gaius was rather taken with an old shotgun we found."

"Oh?"

He had taken a swig of port and set his glass down, patting his lips with a napkin. "I would enjoy puttering around with it, if you don't mind. There's no rust, and it ought to be a simple matter to clean it."

I knew old weapons could be dangerous and warned him to be careful. "I think my father used it to shoot poisonous snakes that got near the house," I said. "What else did you find?"

Nannette glanced at me. "The rocking horses were there. I'd forgotten."

"Yes, so had I."

I was silent for a moment, and I think Nannette was unsure of the wisdom of having reminded me of them. Speaking of family relics brought twinges to my heart, but I had expected it and had tried to prepare myself. Facing the past had to be done if I were to go through the house as I'd planned. I could not allow myself too much sentiment, even though my feelings seemed to belie such rational thoughts and run away with them at times.

I explained to Gaius, "The rocking horses were my sister's and mine. We got them for Erin's second Christmas, when I was four. I'll never forget the way they looked under the tree with red ribbons around their necks."

Gaius was watching me carefully, but I smiled. "You mustn't mind my talking about Erin. I've lived with that loss for so long I've little grief left. Only regret for a young life that wasn't allowed to live to her prime."

Nannette nodded in accord, evidently relieved at my attitude. I believe she understood how I felt, for she and I were the same age, and even she must have remembered something about Erin.

I thought momentarily about my brief conversation with Richard yesterday, when I had choked on words about my dead sister. But I attempted to shake myself out of the somber mood. A crash of thunder startled us all, and then the rain began beating on the windows in earnest.

"A good day for working inside," said Gaius. "What do you intend to do this afternoon?"

"I suppose we might go through my father's belongings," I said as we were finishing our stew. "There were some things he wanted Richard to have. I should be able to find them."

We went up to my father's rooms after lunch, and as I entered the sitting room, I realized again how much of a mystery my father had become to me over the years. Perhaps he had shut himself off from people when my mother had died. Or perhaps because I had been away at school, I never really got to know him. I felt a momentary loss that I had not tried to be closer to him, but what does youth know of such things? It is only in retrospect that we discover so many might-have-dones.

But I attempted to shake off the introspective feelings and proceeded to my task. We began by sorting through the closet, setting aside a few good quality items for Richard. Nannette helped me decide what to throw away and what to hand down to the servants. Gaius spent some time studying my father's pipes. He particularly admired one of the Turkish Meerschaums, and I said he might have it.

He seemed quite pleased. "If you're sure you don't mind."

"No," I said. "I'd rather see these things being enjoyed by those who will appreciate them than mouldering here."

About mid-afternoon, Gaius came to Nannette and me where we were looking over the books Father had kept in his sitting room.

"I've developed a thirst," he said. "Wouldn't you ladies like a cup of tea?"

"Good idea," I said, rising to reach for the bell pull.

"Don't get up," he said. "I've a need for a stretch. I'll go down and find Mrs. Stafford myself. Kitchen's in back, isn't it?"

"Yes. We can have tea in the front parlor." I wiped a

hand across my damp brow. "A change of scene would do us good."

"Agreed."

He took himself off, his step light, and I could tell that he actually seemed to enjoy poking around the old place. I shook my head and shrugged. But as he said, there wasn't much else to do for entertainment on such a rainy day, and he seemed fascinated with our family history.

Nannette and I finished and stood. I walked to the windows overlooking the front lawn. The storm had not abated, and the overgrown branches seemed to bend further to the ground. The wind howled about the house. It would be supper time in a few hours, and I began to wonder if we could get back to the cottage. We certainly could not travel in this downpour.

Nannette went downstairs, and I stayed behind to tidy up the bundles we had placed on the settee. I heard a footstep behind me and thought Gaius had returned, but when I looked up, no one was there. The door moved silently on its hinges, and when it shut, I jumped. There was a presence in the room with me, I was sure.

Then I heard it. A high pitched howl of wind rushing through some crevice of the house. I realized I was gripping the arm of the settee where I knelt on the floor. It had been years since I had heard that sound, but I had not forgotten it. It used to wake me up at night, and then my nanny had to come and comfort me.

I used to hear the whisper of the servants after storms like this one. It was the cry of the child who had drowned on a night like this and the moaning of her mother searching for her, they said.

I shuddered, knowing it was only the storm making me think these thoughts. But I rose slowly, as if not wanting to make any noise. Still I had the distinct feeling I was being watched, and I turned to look behind me toward the windows and gasped.

Pericles stared at me unblinking from the window seat. I took a deep breath. Only Pericles. He must have brushed the door when he entered, causing it to slam. The storm and my imagination had gotten the better of me. Still I had the feeling that the cat did not like me, staring at me the way he did with his widest green eyes and snub nose, his glossy white ruff standing out from his stocky body.

Lightning flashed outside but the cat remained where he was, unmoved by the storm. Most cats would run and hide from the lightning and thunder. Why did this one remain so unaffected, as if he enjoyed the storm's menace? I backed out of the room, telling myself it was silly to feel so disturbed.

In the hallway, I smoothed my hands on my skirt and went downstairs to the parlor where the tea things were laid out, feeling a sudden relief to be in the presence of the others.

Nannette poured me a cup, and I sat in the corner of the faded green velvet sofa. Gaius was holding his cup where he stood looking out into the rainy late afternoon.

"If this keeps up," he said, "you might want to stay here. Even if the rain quits, the road is likely to be mired. I wouldn't want to try it after dark in the phaeton."

"I had thought of that. If only we could get word to Lettice. I wouldn't want her to worry."

"I think Mother will understand," said Nannette.

"If you are concerned that Lettice know what's become of us, I'll ride over on one of the horses," Gaius said. "It would not be so difficult on horseback, it's only the wheels of the carriage that I'd be afraid of on the road. That is, if you ladies wouldn't mind staying here alone. In the morning, Richard and I could ride back and fetch you."

"We could send Riggin," I suggested. "He knows the roads better than you."

Gaius grinned at us. "But I am the younger, stronger man. It would be unsporting of me to send him out in this. Besides he might be needed here. And your Henrietta would worry about him. I can't have three worried ladies on my hands, now can I? Besides I would find a ride exhilarating after digging in these musty closets. But we have a few hours. Let us wait and see if the storm passes."

We worked another two hours, going through closets and drawers, then sat down to a dinner of turkey soup, sirloin of beef, stuffed mushrooms and asparagus.

Afterward, Gaius stuffed his trousers into a pair of my father's high rubber boots and asked Riggin for a horse. He promised me that he and Richard would return for us in the morning.

"I can drive the phaeton myself," I argued as we stood in the foyer, the damp wind blowing in from the partially open door.

"But the roads will be rutted, and trees may be down. And if you should overturn the phaeton, you wouldn't be able to get it righted by yourselves. Don't worry. I'll deliver your message, and we'll be here bright and early in the morning."

I saw him out and watched him mount the big black horse my father used to ride. He turned and flashed a smile at me, then rode off into the night, the horse's hooves splashing in the mud. I closed the door and stared at the chairs with their slightly faded pink, oval, satin backs, one in each corner of the foyer, thinking that Gaius Amundsen reminded me of someone, but I could not think who.

The evening wore on as Nannette and I sat in the parlor trying to read. I felt restless, however, and soon put my book down. Nannette must have sensed my uneasiness and suggested we find some activity.

She cocked her head to one side, thinking. "I know. Why don't we go to the music room? I always used to love it there when . . ." Her brow puckered, and her words drifted off.

"I know," I said, smiling. I did not want Nannette to be afraid to mention things from the past because she was afraid they might upset me. I wanted her to feel free to talk of anything she wanted to.

"Mother used to play when we were very little," I said. "So you remember that?"

She nodded, her curls bobbing prettily on her shoulders. "I was only there two or three times, but I remember very clearly. She was beautiful, sitting there, her long fingers touching the keys. I loved the music that came out." She looked at me hopefully. "Do you think we could?"

"Open the music room, you mean? It was locked up some years ago. I suppose my father didn't want to be reminded."

"Oh." Her face fell. I didn't want to disappoint her however, and I admit my curiosity was piqued. It was the one room we had not been too, for I had thought it best to begin by going through the rooms my father had more recently used.

I sought Henrietta in the kitchen and asked her for the keys.

She gave me a strange look as she repeated, "the music room? But it's been locked up all these years. Are you sure you want to go in there?"

"Why not? We can knock down cobwebs and remove the shrouds. Nannette wants to play the piano. Of course it will be out of tune by now."

She frowned but fumbled with her keys and handed me a long dark one. Then she gave me some candles to take with us. I thanked her and returned to fetch Nannette.

"I've got it," I said, showing her the key in my palm. "Shall we go?"

She seemed to brighten up at once. "Oh yes."

The music room was located in the west wing. We moved along the narrow hallway, seemingly made narrower by the heavy carpenter gothic paneling on either side of us. Candles that Henrietta had lit for us flickered in the gargoyle-figured wall sconces, half illumining our way. At the end of the hallway, I got out the key. The lock seemed rusty, but finally I heard it tumble.

The door scraped as we pushed it inward, and we held the candles we had brought with us aloft, so we could see. Then a flash of lightning outside illuminated the shrouded furniture and the cobwebs strung from the chandelier to the corners of the room. I gave a shudder, somehow sensing unseen dangers. I turned to suggest we forgo the idea, but Nannette's eyes glittered in the candlelight and she pointed to the piano standing on its rounded legs by the set of French doors that led to the terrace. Beyond were the formal gardens, now gone to weed from lack of care.

Then another flash of lightning lit the silhouetted worlds beyond the glass French doors, and terror rushed through me, as I suppressed a scream. Nannette clutched my arm at the same instant, dropping her candle, for outlined on the edge of the terrace before us was the hooded figure of a man.

Chapter 5

Nannette shrieked, and my heart leapt into my throat. Her fingers were wrapped around my arm, but I scarcely felt the pain of her grip. The thunder crashed about our ears, and then a second flash lit the gardens, spilling light into the room itself.

The second flash frightened me as much as the first, for now there was no one at all on the other side of the French doors, only the trees with their claw-like branches. I stared at the space where the figure had been, wondering if I had been mistaken. But the image was too clear in my mind for me to doubt, and Nannette had seen something too.

Another more horrifying thought seized me as I stood there rigidly. No human could have appeared and disappeared so quickly. Surely that idea was absurd, yet Nannette stood trembling beside me, her terror as great as mine.

"What, who, was that?" she asked in a voice modulated unnaturally high.

I struggled to get a hold of myself. "Well, it could have been Gaius. He only left a quarter of an hour ago. Or perhaps Riggin is outside securing anything that might blow off in the storm."

But I knew my explanations were weak. Gaius would have taken the road in the opposite direction. There was no reason for him to be in the gardens. And I did not really think Riggin would be out now.

I tried to persuade myself that it must have been Gaius. Perhaps he had gotten lost in the storm and had circled back. There was no one else about, I was sure.

Nannette's hand shook, and now we had only one light. I hastened to put the candles we'd brought into the wall sconces and light them.

I thought the candlelight around the room might help quiet our imaginations, but on the contrary, the flickering flames only cast an erie glow on the cobwebs that strung across the chandelier and reached to every object in the room, deepening the shadows in the corners.

But even in the erie, uneven light with the rain pelting against the windows and the lightning flashing at intervals, I could see that Nannette's original impulse had been a good one. This room had been closed off for too long. I would restore its use.

I felt almost as if my mother watched me as I crossed the room to the piano that stood on its squat legs, the music stand above the keyboard outlined against the glass of the French doors in the light of the storm.

The dust was thick, and the keys more gray than ivory. But I pressed a key, and the hammer struck a broken string. I tried other keys, and it soon became apparent that most of the strings were rusted or broken. Still, I decided I would have the piano restored. The instrument would remind me of my mother, and somehow I felt that in this room, of all rooms, I would want her spirit to dwell.

But I had forgotten Nannette, and I turned to see her gently lifting dusty shrouds from the furniture. The shrouds had kept the sun from the satin upholstery, and at least in the faint candlelight, the loveseat and matching side chair looked to be in good condition. Some polish would take care of the dark stained mahogany trim.

The project excited me, and I could hardly wait to get brooms in here and knock down the old cobwebs. The gilt frames on the mirrors were badly tarnished and I would have to ask Henrietta's advice on cleaning them.

The lightning and thunder had moved off, but the rain still beat steadily. We wouldn't be able to enjoy this room tonight, for there was too much to do.

"It will be a lot of work, but I want to put this room to rights," I said determinedly.

Nannette looked uncertain about the possibilities. "It is a musty old place, isn't it? But it would be wonderful if you wanted to do something with it."

"I think I'm up to the task." I knew the prospect of bringing life back to a house that had had so little life in it for so many years would be a challenge. But already my eye roved over the dark spots on the flocked wallpaper where moisture had ruined it. Paint peeled from the woodwork.

"You must help me with the task," I said to Nannette. "You said it was your favorite room. Wouldn't it be lovely to have it the way it used to be?" I tried not to see the cobwebs, but to envision people seated around the room listening to the tinkling piano.

Nannette gave a quick little nod. "I'll help you, Eileen. It could be fun." Then she wrinkled her nose. "I suppose we'll have to clean the room first."

I smiled. "Well, Henrietta will help us with that." I supposed Nannette might not like the really dirty part of the work, she was perhaps too romantic for that. But I didn't mind sweeping out the old dust, letting sunlight in on mouldering furniture, washing away old soot.

I glanced out the French doors again. The outlines of trees were only faintly lit by distant lightning now, though the wind still howled about the house. The image of the figure we had seen before still made the back of my neck tingle, but I tried to persuade myself there was a rational explanation for it. Still, I was ready to leave this wing of the house.

We found extinguishers on the cypress mantle above the fireplace and put out the candles I had lit, their smoke mingling with the cobwebs until the only two lights were our own, though as we moved toward the door, our candles reflected eerily in the mirrors at either end of the room.

We shut the door behind, but I did not lock it. I wanted the rooms in this house unlocked so that people could come and go as they pleased.

We extinguished the candles on the wall sconces as we proceeded back up the hall, leaving darkness behind us, and I must admit I felt relief when we came to the main hall and the warm glow from kerosene lamps in the parlor.

We carried our candles upstairs, and as I had expected, Henrietta had lit a fire in the guest room for Nannette. The coverlet was turned down for her on the four-poster, and I thought she would be quite comfortable. Still I lingered in the cozy room. We chattered about the house as if delaying parting. But I finally said good night.

"Sleep well, Nannette. I'm sure the storm will be over in the morning."

Her eyes were still rounded as she glanced toward the shuttered windows. "Yes, it will pass, like all the others."

In my own room, I got into the night dress Henrietta had laid out for me, quickly brushed my hair out and got into bed.

But I tossed and turned, trying to get used to all the old sounds of the house and the storm. Would the incessant wind never stop howling? I turned over for the twentieth time, it seemed, thinking I might be better off getting up and perhaps going down to the kitchen for a cup of chocolate. But I knew Henrietta would have gone to bed, and the thought of going about the house alone in the dark was not appealing. It must have been in the wee hours of the morning that I finally slept.

When I woke, all was quiet. Henrietta had come in and opened the louvered shutters, so that now fingers of sunlight reached across the floor. My limbs felt heavy after the fitful sleep I'd had, but I roused myself and went to the window, pulling back the curtains to see what the storm had left.

There were some branches strewn about the grounds, and some burlap had blown toward the house, probably from the tool shed, but I could see no real damage from my window. I would dress and find Riggin to see how things had faired.

Nannette was down by the time I entered the breakfast room, and Henrietta had made eggs, sausage, potatoes and hot rolls.

"Good morning," said Nannette as she poured herself a cup of hot coffee from the silver urn. "Did you sleep well?"

"Not very. The storm kept me awake. And you?" I moved to the sideboard to dish up some eggs.

She shivered. "This place is creepy. The wind howling around the corners of the roof like that. It gave me bad dreams."

"Well, the storm is over now," I said. "Things always look better in the daytime."

I wanted to convince Nannette and perhaps myself as well that the manor house could be a normal place to live. I don't know exactly when I had made the decision to restore normal life to the place, but by now I was swept away with my determination to do so.

"I'll speak to Henrietta about the music room directly after breakfast," I said.

"I suppose Richard and Gaius will be coming for us."

I had almost forgotten about that. "Yes. But I'm not sure I'll go back to the cottage just yet."

"You can't think to stay here alone?" She looked at me with huge eyes, as if I were mad to consider it.

I bristled in self-defense. "Why not? It *is* my home. I might as well live in it while I work on it as I intend to."

She was immediately apologetic. "I didn't mean—"

"No, no," I said, with a small laugh. "It's all right. I suppose it does seem strange, but you see, Nannette—"

But my explanation was cut off by a thundering knock on the door, and after Henrietta went to get it, I heard Gaius's and Richard's voices in the foyer as they scraped muddy boots and discarded their riding gloves. They came in with much bluster, and my eyes flew to Richard's.

He started towards me, then stopped halfway, hands on hips, as if seeing me assured him that all was well. Then he turned to his sister.

"I see you two fared all right, tucked away here in the storm." Brightness returned to his brooding eyes, and I flattered myself that he was concerned about us.

"Ah, breakfast I see," said Gaius, crossing to the sideboard. He rubbed his hands together in anticipation of the warm food, and both men took plates and helped themselves.

Richard took a seat across from me, and Gaius sat to my right. They ate in silence, starved, I supposed from their early morning ride.

Then Richard's eyes found mine again, and I wished suddenly we were alone. I had the sudden fantastic notion that we both shared a fondness for quiet breakfasts, lingering with quiet talk over a cup of steaming coffee. But Gaius's boistrous talk and Nannette's chatter spoiled the illusion.

"Had quite a ride last night, I did," said Gaius between mouthfuls.

I had neglected to ask him if he had gotten back all right, let alone whether it happened to be he on the terrace.

"The horse was frightened at first, shied at every branch that waved in our path, but soon enough she must have sensed the direction we were headed, put her head down and pushed homeward. Got there in time to stop Richard here from heading out in the wet to find out what had happened to us. Met him mounted in the drive."

I glanced at Richard in surprise. "You were coming here?"

He frowned. "I was afraid you'd got caught in the phaeton on the road. I knew if you'd been overturned you'd need two men to right the thing."

I was secretly glad that Richard had been concerned

enough to come after us. Then I remembered the awful specter we had seen last night. I turned to Gaius.

"Did you find your way easily enough? I thought I saw you from the windows in the music room about half an hour after you'd left. I thought perhaps that in the storm the horse had circled back."

He shook his head, swallowing a forkful of eggs and wiping his mouth on a napkin. "No. Kept to the road we did. Though like I said, the horse shied once or twice."

"Then it wasn't you," I mumbled.

"Wasn't who?" Richard's sharp tone made me look up.

I felt flustered. I had thought surely this would be the explanation. My fork clattered onto my plate. Richard was staring at me, waiting for me to explain.

"We went to the music room last night," I said. "Nannette thought it might be a good idea, and I did too. I want to restore it to use."

Richard shot his sister a quick look of disapproval, then returned his gaze to me. "You seemed to pick an odd night to open rooms that have been locked for thirteen years."

I reacted defensively, the way I had with Nannette. I was getting tired of people telling me what I should or should not do with my own house.

"There was little else to do," I said.

Nannette looked miffed, and Richard continued to send disapproving glances her way, but I imagined that as her older brother he had developed a habit of chastising her for her girlish pranks. However, I did not consider exploring the music room a prank.

"Where is this music room?" asked Gaius, leaning back in his chair, evidently satisfied with his breakfast.

"It's in the west wing. The gardens are behind it."

"Well, I didn't come across any gardens on the way home last night, that's for sure," said Gaius, tossing his napkin over his plate.

Richard stared at Gaius as if assessing his answer, and the expression on Richard's face caused a ripple of nervousness to pass through me.

Nannette said what I had been thinking. "If it wasn't Gaius then, who was it?"

I shook my head. But Nannette's imagination began to take hold, and in her usual outspoken way, she said, "You don't suppose someone was *trying* to frighten us, do you?"

Richard got out of his chair and moved to the sideboard for more coffee.

"Don't be ridiculous, Nannette," I said. "Who would want to do that? And besides no one knew we were going to the music room until you suggested it."

In the silence that followed, I realized what I had said. I looked up to see Gaius staring at Nannette, a look of speculation on his face. Richard was gauging her reaction too, and then she seemed to comprehend the import of us all staring at her and opened her mouth in mute protest.

I tried to ease the tension in the air by a laugh. Surely we were letting things get carried away. Richard sipped his coffee from where he stood, and I said, "It must have been Riggin or one of the tenant farmers. There's no one else it could have been."

"It could have been me."

Now we all looked at Richard. He set his cup down and walked around the table again, confronting all of us.

"Gaius here saw me on horseback. How is he to know I hadn't already ridden over here, passed through the gardens and returned?" He raised an eyebrow at Gaius as if issuing a challenge.

Gaius, rubbed his upper lip with his finger, considering. "Quite right, old man. You could have done that. I hadn't thought of that."

"Oh stop it," I said, dropping the side of my hand on the table rather firmly. "Richard would hardly ride out in the rain unless he were coming here to find us, which he did not do. I think we should forget about it." I cleared my throat, taking on a more commanding tone, remembering my new position as lady of the manor.

"I will inquire of Henrietta as to who else from the island might have ridden in last night to seek shelter from the storm. There can't be anything more to it than that." I rose.

"Well then, it's settled," said Gaius his marked good humor validating my decision. "Shall we all return together? The road seemed rather more passable than I had imagined when Richard and I rode over."

Nannette seemed relieved to have the subject changed and started for the door. I moved around the table to the window where Richard was standing.

"I believe I'll stay here," I said. I had forgotten the others, but I wanted to know what he would think of my plans.

For a moment I thought his expression softened as he looked at me, and then he raised his voice to a mocking tone as if he wanted the others to hear.

"You would stay here alone to sweep out your dusty rooms and be troubled by specters."

Gaius and Nannette paused at the door, and even I was horrified that he continued to joke about it. I turned to face out the window, disappointed that he had not understood my intentions.

My thoughts about Richard troubled me deeply. I was still confused about our earlier argument and about all that Gaius had told me. I truly did not know what to think, and I drew steady, even breaths, telling myself that this would all be sorted out in good time. I wanted to be fair to Richard, and some conviction deep within me still made me want to get to know him better.

Perhaps it was only my sense of loyalty to the past. Truly, I did not know how I could feel nostalgia for a past that was as grim as ours, but I seemed to be drawn to it more and more. Perhaps that too was why I wanted to remain in the house. I wanted to spend time in these rooms, to think, to remember, to perhaps unlock some secret of the past. Yes, it was my fate to dwell here now, I was sure of it, and no amount of taunting from the others would make me change my mind.

Gaius had gone out. I could hear them chatting in the hall, and I turned and walked with Richard slowly across the room. Left alone with me, he was gentler when he spoke.

"You are determined on your course?" he asked, turning to face me.

His eyes were clear as he looked into mine, and at that moment I knew he was not unbalanced as Gaius had led me to think. I felt a small swell of joy in my heart. I wondered if Richard wore a shield around himself in public as if he did not want anyone to get close to him. Did he lower that shield a little just for me?

We were standing so near that I could see a reflection of myself in his eyes, and I smiled. "Yes. I am rather looking forward to the work. And Henrietta will be with me."

One dark eyebrow came down in a frown, but he could see there was no changing my mind. "I have some matters to attend to today," he said. "But I shall come back after dinner to see how you are getting on."

I was more than pleased. "That would be wonderful. I'll wait supper for you."

He shrugged acceptance. Then he glanced around the house and across the foyer to the doors that had been slid back to reveal the parlor. Perhaps he too wondered what I would find as I tore into the house.

Nannette had fetched her cape and donned her boots, and she came into the room. "Coming?" she asked.

"Richard will come with you. I've decided to stay here and work. Please tell Lettice I'll return to the cottage in a day or so. It's just that I'm enamoured with putting my ideas to work. I can't stand the thought of being idle now that I've decided what to do."

Nannette looked doubtful, but nodded. "All right then. We'll see you when you're ready." She came up and pecked my cheek with her lips." She started back to the door, then she brought herself up, wrinkling her brow.

"Oh, I forgot. I did say I'd help."

But I could see her mind was on other things. "Never mind that. You can come back when you've run out of other things to do. I'll manage quite well with Henrietta's help for now."

"Well, if you're sure."

I smiled brilliantly, as if there were no more exciting prospect in the world than redoing the house. "I'm sure."

Richard took my hand and hastily raised it to his lips. It was an endearing gesture, and I was touched by it.

Then he dropped my hand and without wasting any more time, he went to fetch his gloves.

"Let's be off then," he said.

I saw them all to the door and watched them get settled in the phaeton. Nannette waved to me, Richard picked up the reins, and they were off. I watched them jostle down the bumpy road, then I went back in.

After changing into a serviceable gingham dress for work, I headed for the kitchen to find Henrietta, who was clearing up the remains of our breakfast. I could see that just from serving breakfast for four, there was quite a bit of work, to say nothing of the preparation. It reminded me that during my father's last years, life must have been very quiet. With only my father to take care of, she and Riggin must have managed, but if I were going to turn the house upside down and then perhaps have occasional guests on top of that, two servants would hardly be enough. I decided to put her mind at ease about it at once.

"Henrietta," I said, idly picking up a dish towel and refolding it. "I must look into the matter of hiring more help. I've decided to redo some of the rooms, and they'll have to be cleaned first. Do you know anyone on the island who might want to come in days?"

She stopped her work long enough to tuck some gray hair back under her cap, and she nodded.

"I think I do. There's Sally Goodsel. Her family's hard workers. Always paid their rent on time from what your father said. She'd be the right age, and I'm sure her mother'd be appreciative of the extra income."

"Good. If you could send for her, I'll speak to her. If she seems suitable, she can start right away. And I'll help too. I'd like to get this place looking less gloomy as soon as possible."

"As you wish, Miss. But you shouldn't be doing the dirty work. You want to save your pretty hands."

I stretched out my long fingers before me. Would Richard notice if I kept my hands soft and smooth? Then in embarrassment as if Henrietta had read my thoughts, I put my hands behind me.

"I'll wear gloves then for the heavier work."

"Yes, Miss."

"Oh, by the way, Henrietta. Did anyone call here last night after Mr. Amundsen left?"

She opened her eyes wide at me. "You mean in the storm?"

I know it sounded half cocked, but I really had to get to the bottom of the figure Nannette and I had seen in the garden.

"Yes. I thought I saw someone outside, but I assumed it must be Riggin going about the place to secure loose shutters or bringing in the lawn furniture."

She shook her head, looking at me curiously. "No, Miss. Riggin was here in the kitchen with me once the storm blew up really steady. And no one would venture here in that weather. Are you sure you saw someone?"

I stacked the dish towel I had folded with the others on the work table in the center of the room. "No, perhaps I was wrong. You know how your eyes can play tricks on you. I suppose it was no one at all."

I gave the towels a final pat and went to the broom closet, not wanting Henrietta to think I was at all concerned. I reached in and pulled out a broom with a long handle.

"I'm going to begin by getting at the cobwebs in the music room. When you're finished here, bring two pails of water, one soapy, and some rags, so we can start removing the soot."

"Yes, Miss. You'll be staying here then?"

"Oh yes, I forgot to tell you. I promised to return to the cottage in a few days, but in the meantime I'm quite settled upstairs. Oh, and Mr. Blakemore is returning for supper. We'll dine about eight."

"Yes, quite. It's nice to be makin' a meal for a man again," she said. And with that, she began to bustle about. I could see that in spite of the extra work, Henrietta must enjoy the idea of Richard's taking a meal here. I grinned to myself, and began to hum a little tune, swinging the broom ahead of me as I took off down the hall.

"Specters be gone," I said to the narrow hallway in the west wing, brandishing my broom. For no logical reason, my heart was light. I was not afraid of stirring up family ghosts. They had lain too long in these dusty corridors.

Chapter 6

I succeeded in knocking down most of the cobwebs, then Henrietta came, and we washed soot from the woodwork. She was right. I wasn't yet used to such hard work, and by the time we had swept out all the corners, my limbs cried out for a rest.

In the afternoon, Sally Goodsel came, and I saw her in my father's study. She was a thin, shy girl with a rather large mouth, which she kept stoically shut unless spoken to, but she assured me she was quite strong. After all, she had carried milk pails and water from the well all her life. We agreed on her wage, and I sent her to Henrietta. Then I wrote a letter to Sally's mother confirming the agreement and had Riggin take it over.

I was tired, but once started on the music room, I didn't want to stop. I took such pleasure in seeing each layer of grime removed, imagining how it would look when I was finished. There were at least two more hours before I had to change and freshen up for dinner, so I decided to return to the task.

We moved the furniture onto the terrace, and Sally and Henrietta took the oriental rug out to the grass to beat it. I started beating the dust from the upholstered furniture. When I had done all I could with the side chair, I rose and gazed at the weedy garden before me. Again the image of the hooded figure the night of the storm came to mind. I hated questions without answers. *Who had it been?*

The wind came up again at the end of the day, and when I walked around the house to look down toward the beach, I saw that dark clouds had crept across the pink hues and murky white of the early evening sky, like bruises where the sun had faded.

"You'd better come in," I called to Henrietta and Sally. They finished rolling up the carpet they were working on and I helped them drag it back to the terrace.

"It looks like it might storm again," I said. "We'd better get all this inside while we can." And we wrestled the heavy furniture back inside.

Even though Henrietta grunted and groaned, neither she nor my new maid complained about the heavy work. I smiled inwardly. I supposed if it was good enough for their mistress to do, it was good enough for them.

I sent them off to the kitchen where Henrietta had a roast turning on a spit, then, giving a satisfied look around the room at what we had accomplished that day, I went up to clean off the dirt and dress for dinner.

As I donned a quilted robe and made my way down the hall to the necessary room, I silently thanked my father for having installed modern plumbing in the old mansion. I stepped out of my robe and turned the porcelain faucet handles so that the water soon filled the tub with warm water to which I added a generous amount of bath crystals. The bubbly, soapy water looked inviting.

The wind rose, and once I stopped my splashing, thinking I heard that unnerving high-pitched shriek I had heard the other day, but it was much fainter, and I knew it was only the wind. I was not afraid of spirits tonight, I told myself bravely, as I drained the soapy water and rinsed myself off with fresh water. Richard was coming tonight. I was so very excited about the fact that we would actually be able to dine alone.

I toweled myself dry, and then donning the robe once again, went along to my room. I had asked Sally to come to me. Undoubtedly, she had no experience as a ladies' maid, but I would teach her how to do up my hair.

When I entered my room, I saw that Sally, now dressed in a crisp black muslin uniform, a bit too big for her, and a neat white apron, had laid out the dress I had told her I wanted to wear.

"I see Henrietta found you something to wear," I said, admiring the girl's efforts to behave properly.

She nodded, standing gawkily before me, not seeming to know what to do with her hands. "My mum can take it up to fit me. Henrietta says it's never been worn, even though it's more than a decade old."

"Yes," I said thoughtfully, walking around her. "It was probably bought for a maid my father meant to hire but never got around to. In any case, I'm sure your mother can make it fit you perfectly. For tonight it will do admirably, and the apron looks very crisp and white."

"Thank you ma'am."

"Come," I said, moving to the vanity. "We haven't time to waste. My cousin, Richard Blakemore, will be here by eight to dine." I handed Sally my brush. "I would be grateful if you could get these tangles out of my hair."

Sally held the brush clumsily at first, but I showed her how to follow through on nice long strokes, and soon she had the feel of it. From the pleasure that lit her large boned face, I thought she was enjoying the task.

"That's enough now. I'll need your help with the curling iron. Use that pad to pick it up, it's hot."

It was a little awkward showing her how to do the coils, and I was so enjoying myself that when I again glanced at the clock on my dresser, I widened my eyes in horror. It was straight on eight.

"All right," I said to Sally. "I can finish by myself. Run along now and tell Henrietta to let me know the minute Mr. Blakemore arrives. I don't want to keep him waiting."

"Yes ma'am." She backed away, lowered her bony knees in a curtsy and ran out the door. I grinned. I wondered if she thought that just as one did in the presence of royalty, she was not to turn her back on me.

I was feeling quite gay again, and I knew why. I tried to give myself a stern look in the mirror. *Don't be so foolish over Richard. It's bound to lead to trouble.* And the reprimand did bring back the other sobering thoughts. Getting re-acquainted with my handsome cousin was one thing, but I had to learn if his mind was touched.

Somehow the very notion that there might be something wrong with him angered me. Anger, I decided was a better emotion than pity. And the alternative, that he was actually some kind of criminal, or worse, that he had been the man in the storm in our gardens was too horrifying to contemplate.

When all was said and done, I fell back on my old resolve that I would find out the truth. The truth, whatever it was, would not hurt me.

Only a moment after Sally had left, it seemed, came a knock on the door.

"Come in," I called, and then Henrietta entered,

looking ill at ease and wringing her hands. "What is it?" I asked.

"There's a gentleman to see you, Miss."

"You mean Mr. Blakemore."

She shook her head. "No, ma'am. Mr. Blakemore didn't come. The gentleman says his name is Mr. Menasce, though I'm not sure I'm pronouncin' it rightly. He sent up his card."

I stared at her aghast. There must be some mistake. Ian Menasce was in New York, engaged to be married to my erstwhile friend, Millicent Van Nuys.

Nevertheless, Henrietta handed me an engraved card with Ian's name printed in script. I stared at it stupidly, hardly knowing what to think, feeling I had been suddenly transported out of time and place.

"Are you sure?" I asked Henrietta, who bobbed her head.

"Then you weren't expecting him?" she asked.

I shook my head mutely, then I lifted my chin. It wouldn't do to reveal my feelings to Henrietta, so I tried to regain a semblance of composure.

"This is a surprise, but yes, I was acquainted with Mr. Menasce in New York. Please tell him I'll be down directly." Then I pressed my lips together, staring at the card again. "But there's been no word from Mr. Blakemore? I expected him to arrive by now."

"Oh yes, Miss, I almost forgot, what with this other gentleman arriving instead. Mr. Blakemore sent along this note." And she handed me a square envelope, which I tore open quickly.

Inside was a folded note with Richard's scrawl. *Since this gentleman claims to be a suitor of yours, I thought it would be in bad taste to come this evening. You will undoubtedly wish to speak to him in private. Yours, Richard.*

I clenched my jaw in irritation, then raised my eyes to Henrietta. "Thank you, Henrietta. It seems Mr. Blakemore will not join us. Rather, I shall dine with Mr. Menasce. I shall come down in a moment."

She nodded and hurried out of the room.

Ian here! I still could not believe it. I was stunned.

But standing here would do no good. I glanced hastily at myself in the mirror and left the room. Feelings of curiosity and nervousness mingled in me. I could think of no logical explanation for this. Had Ian and Millicent argued already? But even so, that would not explain so lengthy a journey. Unless . . . unless, Ian had decided he cared for me? Somehow after all the distance I'd put between us, the idea seemed foreign to me. I had not given Ian a thought since the day I arrived and told Lettice about him. So much for a broken heart, I thought with irony.

However, I picked up my skirts, raised my chin and marched into the parlor to greet him. He was standing with his back to me, and I could see that he wore the same fine cut of clothes I had always admired about him. His blonde hair was clipped neatly over the ears, and when he turned, I saw the flowing white cravat, tied perfectly at his neck.

"Ian," I said, looking into his sparkling hazel eyes. He lifted his sandy colored brows in pleasure and flashed me a smile, showing even white teeth. Then he crossed the room and reached for my hands.

"Eileen, you look radiant. Let me look at you." He seemed sincerely glad to see me, and I grasped his hand in welcome. Then his brows wrinkled, and he shook his head.

78

"I know you must be surprised to see me. But you must believe me that I have not had a moment's peace since you left. I fear there's been a terrible mistake."

"Mistake? I don't understand."

"Please, let us sit down. I've much explaining to do."

"Very well." He started to lead me to the sofa, then I remembered my manners. "Would you like some sherry?"

"Thanks, I would. I rode straight here from your cousin's. Richard was kind enough to lend me a mount."

The corner of my mouth jerked back at the mention of Richard's name, but I let my questions wait. Henrietta had filled the crystal decanter of sherry, and I started to pour two glasses, but Ian stopped me.

"Allow me," he said, pulling the stopper and filling the glasses that sat on the tray.

Sipping the warm sherry helped calm my nerves, and I sat on the sofa. Ian followed me and sat beside me on the edge of the seat, half turned in my direction.

He tilted the glass, then looked at me earnestly. "You see, there was no more between Millicent and myself than friendship. She is a nice enough girl, but I'm afraid our parents rather had designs on our relationship."

I stared at him, taking another sip of sherry. "Go on."

He set the glass down and took my other hand in his. "It was you I came to see all those times I called at the Van Nuys's house. Of course Millicent was sometimes there, and I knew you and she were friends."

He shook his head. "I'm afraid her mother had ideas of her own and refused to see things as they were. Before I knew what had happened, her father had spoken to my father, and then my mother came to me saying that the marriage had been all arranged, that they knew I had

79

made calls to the Fifth Avenue mansion, and that they were very pleased with my choice."

He dropped my hand, picking up his glass again and getting up to refill it. "Of course I did not know how they'd found out, that I was calling on you, I mean, for I had not told them. But you see it was all a mistake. They thought I was calling on Millicent. By the time I found out what had gone wrong, it was rather too late. Our families had reached an agreement."

I frowned in irritation. "Then you went ahead with the engagement because you were a victim of circumstances. Is that what you're telling me?" I decided I would have another glass of sherry myself, for what I'd drunk so far was not enough to numb the irritation I was beginning to feel.

A hopeless look came into Ian's eyes. "What I mean is that there was that tea. I had to attend, otherwise Mother would have disowned me. I thought I would have a chance to straighten it all out. But instead, my father announced our engagement."

"I know," I said irritably. "I was there."

"Yes, so you were. I was rather shocked, of course. Could do nothing about it in public like that. By the time I got to speak to Millicent in private, she admitted she was rather confused about it all herself. She thought I rather liked you, but then her father had told her I had asked for her hand, and then she didn't know what to do."

"Well, she certainly didn't come to me."

"You didn't give her a chance."

I had crossed the room again. Reliving that dreadful scene did nothing for my humor, and I wasn't sure if I was still angry with Ian and Millicent for their deception or at the very least at their inaction, or if I was annoyed for another reason. I had come here to forget about them, and it seemed as if I were doing a rather good job of that, and now here was Ian to remind me of it all.

Realizing that Ian was waiting for me to respond, I turned back to him. "I hardly know what to say, Ian. I had put this all behind me. If you're no longer engaged to Millicent, then I am sorry. I mean, I'm sorry there's been a misunderstanding. I—" I swallowed. "I mean I just don't know what to think now. So much has happened since then."

His face fell. "I can understand your being angry." He shook his head. "But I couldn't let you think the worst of me. I had to find you and apologize."

I nodded in acknowledgement, though I was still astonished that he had traveled all this distance just to see me. "I accept your apology." *Belated as it is,* I wanted to add. But I tried to be civilized and simply said, "I can understand your not wanting to make a scene at the time."

He looked up hopefully. "Yes, that's all it was, you see. But by the time I could talk to all the parties involved, you had left. Just like that. I could hardly believe you'd gone so quickly."

"Yes, I did leave rather quickly. But you see I had also just received word that my father had died."

"I *am* sorry about that."

"Thank you."

He squared his shoulders. "Well, then that's settled."

I blanched. "What is settled?"

He looked flustered. "That it's all a mistake. I'm not engaged to Millicent." He chortled. "Rather angry, my father was at first, you know, but I made him see it my way."

"Ummm."

81

"Then I told my parents that the only decent thing to do was to follow you down here and apologize."

"Well, you've done that."

"Yes, I have. So you see I'm a free man now." He started towards me, and I was afraid he was going to take my hand again, so I turned toward the dining room.

"Let's go in to supper. Henrietta will not want to have to keep it warm forever."

"Ah yes, supper. And I am starved. Got down here yesterday, but couldn't cross to the island until today, because of the storm."

"Oh, you were in Coral Springs yesterday?"

He had followed me into the dining room and held my chair for me. "Yes, anxious I was to cross too, but I found a comfortable bed at the inn."

"So you spent the night on the mainland."

"Did so. Glad I was to see the sun come out this morning. Finally got the launch across in the afternoon. Then I walked along the road until one of your local farmers saw me and carried me on his wagon up to the house. Seemed I'd got to the wrong house though."

"Yes. My cousins live at the cottage, and the tenants wouldn't all know that I'd taken up residence here. So you met the Blakemores."

"Indeed. Your cousin, Lettice was quite gracious, and Nannette is quite a fetching girl. I must say, this, er Richard seemed a rather serious sort. Not too friendly, I didn't think, but I soon found I had a great deal in common with his friend, Gaius Amundsen. He offered to join me for a ride tomorrow. Said he'd show me a bit of the island."

"He did, did he?" Not so very long ago it was Gaius who was being shown about, now he was playing host?

"You're welcome to stay, of course, Ian, since you've made such a long journey." I realized it sounded rather formal, and my welcome must not have been as enthusiastic as he would wish it to be, but I was still not over the surprise. Nor could I sort out my feelings.

Being honest with myself, I knew I didn't care for Ian the way I thought I had while I was in New York. I had to admit that being home put things in a different light.

I appeared to concentrate on my roast, keeping my eyes downward for fear my expression would give away my thoughts. I knew it was more than the fact that Ian just didn't seem to fit in these surroundings. It was embarrassing, but I was beginning to see that my heart had not really been his in the first place. I suppose that when he first paid me so much attention I was swept away. But how much of that experience had been the excitement of a season of parties and dances and being promenaded about by a dashing young man?

It all seemed rather shallow now. I managed to glance up and smile at him pleasantly. For all I thought I knew him well, I could no more imagine being married to him than I could to a total stranger. I felt stiff, unnatural, and it was an effort to keep up the appearance of enjoying myself.

I studied my peas again. How different from the way I had felt the few times I was alone with Richard, the way we seemed to understand each other's feelings, even though I could not be sure just what was in Richard's mind.

I took a deep breath and swallowed some water.

"I'll have Henrietta make up a room for you."

"That would be delightful. I had hoped you would ask me to stay." His cheeks tinged pink. "After the way we parted, I wasn't sure what kind of reception I'd have here. But I wanted an opportunity to see you again to," he hesitated over his words, "to assess your feelings for me."

Then he rushed on, changing the subject. "I've brought my sketch pad with me. I thought since I was coming to an island I might get a chance to do some sketching. That is if you asked me to stay."

The way his words tumbled out amused me, though I tried to keep from showing it. Perhaps I did not need to worry so much about Ian's broken heart. It looked as if he would be solaced by a few weeks riding and sketching scenes on the island.

"You can stay as long as you like, Ian. Make it a holiday."

He slapped his folded napkin across his thigh. "How good of you. I accept the invitation."

I rose. "Shall we take coffee in the parlor?"

"Of course." He jumped up quickly to take my elbow, and I led the way. Now that the awkward part was over, I found it easier to engage in conversation with Ian. We discussed old friends, and he made me promise to write Millicent saying I forgave her, for she was quite troubled about the whole matter.

I agreed to do so. What use was there in holding a grudge over something I no longer cared about? As Ian and I jumped from one subject to another, I realized that there was a lack of depth about him that I had not noticed before. The thought made me introspective. Had I just not noticed it? Or had I changed so very much since my return to this island?

I told Ian of my plans for redecorating the house and he seemed to approve.

"I've started with the music room." The sore muscles in my arms told me just how much work I had done. "It was a joy to sweep away all those old cobwebs. We've removed most of the soot, but I'm not sure what to do about the tarnish on the gilt frames. You wouldn't know . . ."

He looked at me curiously. "Don't your servants know what to do about such things?"

I shrugged. "There's only Henrietta. She's both housekeeper and cook right now. And I just hired a girl as maid today, but she's completely without experience. I suppose Riggin might know."

"Riggin?"

"He serves as handyman and driver." I cast Ian a teasing glance. "I'm afraid I haven't the staff of a Fifth Avenue mansion." Then more seriously, "my father didn't have many needs. And after my mother died, he seldom entertained. But perhaps I will change all that."

I yawned. "I'm afraid I am rather tired, after all that heavy work."

He looked shocked. "You don't mean to tell me you're moving furniture and scrubbing floors yourself?"

I blushed in spite of myself. "As I said, the house hasn't had much care in over a decade. I can hardly sit by and watch a middle-aged pair of servants past their prime and a clumsy new girl without any training to do it all. I prefer to be involved myself."

He held his hands up in a gesture of protest. "All right. all right. It is your house, Eileen. I didn't mean to offend."

I jerked my head sideways in acknowledgement. I was being rather defensive I knew. But my muscles hurt, and I was anxious to go to bed.

"But you can't be planning to work so hard every day, I hope?" he said.

"Why not?"

He looked at his feet. "I had hoped you'd accompany me tomorrow morning. Show me the grounds. I had thought I'd sketch you, if you didn't mind, of course."

"Sketch me?"

He looked up as if he already had the sketch in mind. "It would be rather good, don't you think? A picture of you in your natural surroundings."

"Well yes, I suppose it would, but I had planned . . ."

"Oh, plans be damned. Give me a morning anyway, and I'll let you go back to your blessed sweeping in the afternoon."

"Well, I suppose I could do that. All right." It would be rude not to show him about, I suppose. But then I remembered that Gaius had said he would do that, and mentioned it.

"Oh, him. Well it was sporting of him to offer, and I suppose I can ride out with him the next morning." Then he came closer, helping me to my feet. His look was sincere and he gazed into my eyes. "I really would like to spend the morning with you though, Eileen."

I could not refuse him since he was my guest. "All right. I'll pose for you."

"Good. I'll let you pick some idyllic spot." He stepped back, examining my hair, my profile. "Some place that brings out the wildness of nature in you."

His choice of words seemed strange, but if it would amuse him, I would allow him to sketch me. I suppose my muscles could use a morning of rest before I went back to my self-appointed tasks.

Ian wasn't sleepy yet, so I left him and went up. I

closed the door on my solitude gratefully. Then I managed to get out of my dress, put on my dressing gown and sat down to brush my hair.

It was then that the disappointment sank in. When I had last been seated here I was expecting Richard, and I remembered how I had felt. Being with Ian had been nothing but an obligation, and it made me impatient. It seemed I would have to wait until I saw Richard again to explain what had occurred. He might suspect the worst.

Then I put the brush down heavily on the vanity, grunting as I pulled myself up and went to the bed. I didn't even know if Richard spared any thoughts for me at all. And there were still those other strange matters to resolve.

Chapter 7

I suppose that I hoped Richard would appear the next morning, but for what reason, I asked myself. He had business to attend to that was no doubt more pressing than seeing to the goings on in the manor house. I tried not to be disappointed, therefore, when I entered the breakfast room, dressed in a white high-necked blouse of eyelet and lace and plain dark green foulard skirt and found Ian helping himself to boiled eggs, fresh bread and honey from the sideboard.

"Good morning," I said.

"Good morning, Eileen. I hope you're ready for our outing."

"I suppose I am." I walked to the sideboard and took up a plate. I was ravenously hungry after the exertion of yesterday and with the prospect of hiking around the island today, I knew I would need my energy, so I took generous helpings.

We made pleasantries as we ate, but I could not help my eyes drifting to the door every once in a while, as if I were expecting someone. Finally we finished, and I went to fetch my parasol in case I needed it against the sun. Riggin brought the phaeton around, and we set out.

This time I told Ian to turn the phaeton to the north. I hankered to visit the bayous at the northeast part of the island, though I was not certain how far the road would go. As I remembered, that end of the island had gotten quite overgrown. There was an old bridge through part of the mangrove swamp that I thought Ian might find interesting.

As we drove north, the island rose slightly, and instead of gradual slopes down to the water, small bluffs rose above the rocky beach. The pounding of the surf at high tide had eroded some of the bluffs, weakening the topsoil in places. We were always cautioned as children, not to go exploring there, but to stick to the safe, well-worn foot paths. But that was when they were kept cleared, and I was almost sure they had fallen to disuse by now.

The road grew rougher and the branches grew closer to the road, as we progressed northward and deeper inland. I began to think we oughtn't to have come this way, and suggested we turn back. But Ian was fascinated, and we could just now see the old bridge ahead.

"Just a little farther," he said. "The light here is interesting. I would like to see how the swamp winds about, just past the bridge."

He reined up, and we got out, for the horses could go no farther. He tied them to a branch where they could nibble at the grasses, and then he helped me over some branches fallen in the road, overgrown here. We made it to the bridge, but I could see that the wood was rotten. Some of the planks had fallen away, and I could see through to the swamp water below.

Nevertheless, Ian was fascinated with the place and insisted on trying the bridge.

"Don't go out there, Ian. It's liable to collapse with

your weight."

"Hmmm. Perhaps." He tested it with his foot and found that the support on the left seemed strong.

"If you could just sit here," he said, indicating the edge. "You could lean on this part of the railing. It's really all right as long as you don't push too hard." He shaded his eyes with his hand and looked at the angle of the sun, which had climbed above the tangled foliage.

Then he held out a hand to me. "Come, I'll show you where to step."

I was wary of his plan, but he seemed so determined on the setting that I held out my hand and let him pull me to the spot where he wanted me to sit.

"Now here, hold onto the railing. Just be careful of splinters. Sit there."

I lowered my legs over the edge. reasoning that the water wasn't very deep here. Still I didn't trust the wood completely. Ian walked back carefully, and then stepped off through the weeds along the solid bank. With every step he took I felt more vulnerable, and I hoped he wouldn't go too far.

He finally found a spot and sat down in the weeds, opening his sketch pad before him. He flashed me a smile, and then studied the setting, exotic as it was, with the walking mangrove roots that grew above the water line.

"Turn a little sideways so I can get your profile," he called to me, and I turned and leaned gingerly against the beam supporting the railing above, and though it creaked a little with my weight, it seemed to support me.

I took a deep breath and sighed. The morning was quiet, the air not too humid for once, and there was just the hint of a wind touching the tops of the trees. As I sat there I could hear bird calls and glanced upward to see the huge pelicans sailing on their outstretched wings. I had always been amazed at how those ungainly birds with such huge beaks looked so elegant in flight.

We were quite secluded. It was a pleasant morning, and I tried to relax. I could hear Ian's charcoal sketching furiously on his pad, and wondered how long I would have to sit there.

The sun finally made my eyelids droop, and I closed my eyes, daydreaming. I envisioned some of my plans for the house, then thought of Richard, wondering when I would get to speak to him again. Thoughts of Gaius too kept interfering with my pleasant daydreams, casting a tinge of some unnamed threat, that I wanted to turn aside.

When I fluttered my eyes open the shade from the opposite bank had begun to creep toward the middle of the swamp and the shadows of the trees now reached out onto the bridge toward where I sat.

Quickly I turned my head to seek Ian, fearing for a moment that he had gone and left me here. But no, he was sprawled on the damp ground, head supported by his elbows as he frowned down at the marks on his page. I moved forward, my limbs stiff from having been in the same position for such a long time.

I hauled myself up carefully, but even so, my skirts caught where the rail had split, and I had to balance gingerly and lean over to remove it. Standing up I felt dizzy, and struggled to regain my balance. By the time I was stepping toward the embankment, Ian had stood up and was brushing himself off.

"Tired of sitting?" he asked.

"My limbs need a stretch," I told him, relieved when I reached solid footing. "Did you get what you wanted?"

"It isn't too bad. But perhaps we should try another setting."

"May I see?"

He flipped the pages of his sketch book open, and I saw now that he had made several sketches. I was surprised at the likeness, and at the way in which he had handled the surroundings. His charcoal strokes were firm and sure, and though I had seen some of his work before, these had a flavor about them that fascinated me.

"Why Ian, they're very good."

I saw now why he had insisted that I sit on the bridge. He had carried the lines of my pose through in the lines of the wood in a most interesting way. I wondered if my hair, which had come loose, really looked as wild as he had made it seem in the sketch, for he had given my tresses the same wild, tangled quality as he showed in the branches of the trees.

In the last sketch particularly, he had elongated everything, and some of the aerial roots seemed to reach right out to the bridge to where I was sitting, as if long fingers were trying to drag at me. The sketch made me shiver.

"What an active imagination you have," I said.

He eyed the last sketch critically. "Yes, something about the place made me draw it that way." He looked up at the thick woods about us, and with the sun now more westerly, it seemed as if the shadows drew in towards us.

"This is an odd place," he said. "Rather creepy feeling, would you agree?"

"Yes, I suppose it is. No one comes to this end of the island anymore since . . ." I hesitated. I was not sure I wanted to talk about the unpleasant past, but Ian urged me on.

"Since what?"

Perhaps it was the way the mid-day sun hit his face, but I thought there was something macabre about his expression, and I drew in a breath. I knew that many people had a morbid curiosity about mysterious happenings, and it seemed as if the island's many secrets were beginning to affect Ian as well.

I swallowed and took a few steps back through the grass toward the road, and Ian followed me.

"My mother was found dead not far from here," I said.

"Oh, dear God, I am sorry. I didn't know how she died."

We were back on the road, and I turned toward the phaeton, but Ian paused, studying the thick forest about us. Then he brought his attention back to me. "I'm sorry, Eileen. I know you told me she did not live long after your sister died, God bless her soul."

"Yes."

I had turned away from the small footpath that led through the forest toward the bluffs at the furthermost tip of the island. I had thought I would visit the spot sometime alone to meditate. But I did not think I wanted any company with me when I visited the spot where my mother had been found.

I tried to brush these gloomy thoughts aside, but Ian had already seen the path and started for it.

"What's this? Where does this lead?"

I had no choice but to follow him. "It just goes to the bluffs above the beach."

He had plunged onward, pausing to hold branches aside so they wouldn't tear at me. The trees were thicker here, and the woods quite dark. I tried to still the irritation I felt that Ian should drag me through these woods now. But the reasonable side of my nature made me think that perhaps if I were to visit the bluffs, it would be smart to do it with an escort. I had not come this way in a long time, and could not be sure what menace I might meet with in terms of animals or snakes. This last thought, made me shudder, and I stepped gingerly, thankful for my high-topped boots.

When we came round the bend and the trees opened out on a level plateau above the water, I breathed a sigh of relief. The forest ended suddenly, and we stood on the high ground, with the surf beating on the rocky beach below.

The sun seemed blinding after the darkness of the forest, and I was again struck with the contrasts of the island. The wind lifted my hair off my shoulders, and I gazed at the brilliant blue waters, but even in the warmth of the Indian summer day, a cold shudder passed along my spine. I was reminded for no apparent reason of Erin's death in the waters on the other side of this island, so long ago.

I shook myself, trying to push the thought aside. I supposed it was natural, standing on the spot where my mother was found to think of that other death, the one that drove my mother to her own failing will to live. Then a strange new feeling pulsed through me, one that I had succeeded in pushing to the back of my mind for years, and I did not know why it surfaced now.

I had still lived. Why had my mother's grief over her youngest child made her forget that she still had a daughter to care for? I tried not to think badly of the dead, but I remembered hating her for her grief; for the way she walked about the island as if in a daze, no longer aware of my own existence.

Ian turned, and I was brought back to the present. "What an incredible view," he said.

Indeed it was. Vessels at sea were clearly visible from here, two fishing boats, tiny from this distance. The lowering sun made the sky a china blue, and the splashing waters its equal. It was beautiful and wild, and that must have been why my mother was so fond of coming here.

Ian was gazing at me. "Is this where she was found then?"

"Yes. She too found it beautiful to come here."

Indeed, if I were to commune with this spot, I preferred to remember my mother as she had been when she came here to admire the scenery, not the fact that she had died here.

"Where?"

The question startled me, and I stared at him with wide eyes. Why did he have to know?

But I pointed, and as I did so, the scene rushed up to meet me as if the past replayed itself. I had been with Richard and my father at the time. We had been in the wagon, helping my father haul cypress wood back to the house, when we had taken this detour.

I remembered as clearly as if it had happened yesterday. My father, knowing that Mother liked to come here, had gotten down from the wagon and followed the path along to the bluffs, while Richard and I had waited in the wagon. Richard had tried to entertain me by naming birdcalls, but when my father did not return, he decided to go after him. I did not like the dark woods, and so had climbed under a burlap sack in the back of the wagon to wait.

Then I heard shouts and popped up. I remembered the terror, holding my ears as sudden cries and noises mingled as if the birds of the forest were answering the horror and shock in Richard's and my father's voices. Something propelled me from the wagon, and I stumbled down the path to this spot, not understanding what had happened.

Father held my mother's lifeless shoulders in his arms, and Richard was trying to drag him away.

The memory overwhelmed me, and I felt weak, unaware that I was holding my ears and murmuring, "No, no."

"Eileen, what is it?" Ian's voice penetrated the haze of pictures floating in my mind.

"I—" but I felt like I might faint, and Ian put his arm around my shoulders, guiding me to a grassy spot next to a tree at the edge of the clearing, so that I might sit down.

"Here, rest awhile, Eileen. Goodness look what I've done." His face looked white, and I knew he felt sorry that he had brought me here. He babbled on.

"I got so carried away with poking into all the enchanting parts of this place that I've had no thought for your fortitude at all. Do forgive me, dear Eileen."

He slumped down in the grass, and I rested my back against the tree for support. He fanned me with his sketch pad, and I began to recover.

"It's not your fault, Ian. I'm afraid I'm not a very genial hostess."

"Good heavens, don't worry about that. I'm afraid I've been inconsiderate again. Dash it all. Having you out in this heat and bringing you to places that remind you of such awful things. How can I make it up to you?"

The pallor of his cheeks and the way his mouth turned down in self-abnegation made me want to laugh. That horror and humor could mix so incongruently must mean I was becoming victim of some sort of hysteria.

I exhaled a deep breath. "It's all right, Ian. Let me rest here a moment. I shall recover, I assure you."

"Do you want me to help you back to the carriage. Perhaps we should go back to the house."

"Yes, in a moment, but there's a breeze here. If I could just sit here for a while."

Indeed the sun warming my face and the breeze from the water was doing a great deal to restore me already.

"If you say so." He hugged his knees, straightening his back to look around.

"I believe I'll just close my eyes," I said, so doing.

"Very well," he said, and I could hear him getting up. "I'll just have a look about, while you rest."

When I opened my eyes, Ian was gone. I rubbed my eyes, thinking that yesterday's efforts must have tired me more than I'd thought, for I could hardly keep my eyes open today. I shook my head. My muscles would just have to get used to what I intended to put them through, for I had never thought I was cut out for a life of leisure.

I rose and stretched, succeeding for the moment to forget the reminders of the spot where I was. But I must find Ian, for I really needed to get back. He could explore on his own and sketch to his heart's content without me on another day.

I started back on the path to the road thinking perhaps Ian had returned to the phaeton, though why he would do so without me I could not fathom.

I stopped once, thinking I heard a twig snap behind me, but when I turned, no one was there. I hurried along the shady path, my grogginess completely gone now, as my senses came alert. The woods seemed more dense, and I had to push aside branches that Ian had held for me when

97

we'd come the other way. I had to cross the bridge again and did so carefully, and I was relieved to come out at last to where the horses were tied.

But Ian was not there. I stood for a moment in perplexity. Then a loud screech made me jump, but as I saw the branches above me shake I realized it was only a red-tailed hawk.

"Ian," I called out, but my voice seemed to die where the thickness of the trees began. "Ian," I tried again, this time louder.

But the only answer was the caw of a common crow. Suddenly I shivered. Could something have happened to him? I tried to tell myself that he had just wandered off in that absent way of his, drawn by an interesting setting, or wanting to know what some half hidden form might be.

I should have told him it wasn't safe to wander about on this part of the island. Then I wondered why I thought that, and I felt my thoughts running away with me the way they did when something had frightened me. I gave a little choking cry, real fear seizing me now. There seemed to be enough natural hazards, to say nothing of the odd sensations that there were also unnatural ones present, to make me lose my senses very rapidly.

Grief, fear and anger all seemed to mingle in me in turn, and before I knew what I was doing, I turned and fled back down the path toward the clearing, this time hardly stopping for the branches that tore at my clothes and scratched my face.

"Ian," I choked as I ran. "Where are you?"

A hissing sound made me stop in my tracks, my heart pounding in my chest. The trees seemed to close in on me, and I collapsed in a heap of tears. I couldn't seem to locate the direction the hissing sound came from.

"No," I whispered to myself. Then louder I tried to call, "Is someone there?"

The hissing sound came again, right behind me and I rose. I was sure I heard a footstep this time, but I couldn't see anyone. It couldn't be Ian or he would call out. Who would be here following me?

The terror built in me, and I thought my head would burst. I momentarily lost my sense of direction, and I was no longer sure whether I was heading for the clearing or for the road. But it didn't matter. I wanted desperately to get out of these woods.

I ran on, certain I was being followed. *What had happened to Ian?* Perhaps my screams were not loud enough for him to hear me, but my breath was coming in great gasps, so that I didn't have the strength to cry out.

Then suddenly, I was on the road. There was the phaeton. I ran to the horses, trying to talk to them through my gasps, so they wouldn't shy. Shaking, so that my fingers fumbled, I untied the reins, pulled them around, then climbed up on the driver's seat.

I hardly spared Ian a thought that I might be leaving him to his own fate. The overpowering menace that I could not name was so strong that my only impulse was to flee.

Then finally, the horses picked up speed and I was tearing along the narrow road, ducking when the branches of the trees seemed to thrust at me as I passed. Still I raced on, as if whatever it was that had frightened me was still pursuing me.

We came to a fork in the road and veered left. I was too confused to realize that I should have gone the other way if I wanted to get to the house. This way led to the beach.

Finally, the road widened, and the trees seemed to

grow farther back at the side of the road, and I slowed the horses to a trot. I was breathing hard, and while I was not absolutely sure of my safety, the branches were farther apart here, and the dappled sunlight on the road comforted me.

I slowed the horses to a walk, and then drew them up to where the trees opened at the side of the road, and I could see the water beyond. I sat there, panting, and the horses snorted. I stared at the calm blue waters and a thin veil of clouds that floated above like watery vapor.

My heartbeat still pounded from the exertion, but as I waited for my pulse to return to normal, I examined my surroundings. It seemed quiet, and yet I still had the odd sense I was not alone, and my pulse quickened again. Was I going crazy, or was someone really following me? *Show yourself*, I silently willed. I could fight an enemy if I could see him, but I could not fight a presence.

Suddenly the hairs on the back of my neck stood on end, and the hiss came from directly behind me. I turned and dropped the reins as I screamed.

Pericles, the cat was leaping toward me, claws outstretched. I put up my arms to ward off the short, strong legs and long, sharp claws, and the horses, frightened by my scream, reared in their harnesses.

Suddenly I was caught in a tangle of sharp claws and leather reins. The cat's howl and the horse's whinnies mingled with my own screams, and I felt the phaeton jerk forward as I tumbled off the seat.

I saw blood where my sleeve was torn, and still the horrible cat clung to my dress, my hair. I fought to keep it away from my face as I fell to the bottom of the buggy. Then with strength that came from terror, I threw the thing off, saw the white fur disappear over the side, as I huddled in the floor of the fast moving vehicle.

I grasped the seat and reached frantically for the reins, but they flew behind the horses, out of reach. My hair was in my eyes, and I tried to pull myself up, then the horses took a turn too close to a tree that leaned over the road, catching the corner of the buggy and tilting it. I felt a sudden thud as I was spilled over the side. The horses screamed as the buggy jerked them, twisting, to a halt. They reared, hooves flying out in front of them, and as I hit the ground on my side, I felt the breath knocked out of me.

Then everything was black.

Chapter 8

I was first aware of a throbbing pain that seemed to engulf me. Other colors seemed to swim in the darkness, and I didn't seem to want to wake up. But my eyes opened and blurred figures hovered over me.

Then I heard my name. Someone was calling me, and as the shapes above me began to come into focus, I realized I was not alone.

I knew Richard was there before I could see him clearly. I could feel his hand clutching my shoulder, and he was saying my name. Then I felt something cold on my forehead and temples, and then the water trickled toward the corners of my mouth.

"Ohhhh," I groaned. "Richard," I sighed feebly.

"Eileen, lie still," he said. "I can't tell how badly you're hurt."

He had clutched my hand, and I held on, finding comfort in having him there.

"I—I fell," I managed.

"Shhhh, don't talk."

But I was coming around, and the uneven ground where I had fallen was uncomfortable, and I tried to rise. Richard caught my shoulders in his arm, and held me against him

"Richard," I said. "The horses bolted. The cat scared them." I turned my head from side to side, resting it against his shoulders. The pain was still there, but I felt somehow better, cradled as I was in Richard's arms. letting the balm of his nearness soothe me.

He brushed my brow with his lips. "Don't try to move," he said. "I've got to get you to the doctor."

"Hmmm. Where's Ian? We were out sketching. I mean he was sketching, then I . . . I couldn't find him. Ohhh." Words were too difficult.

I felt Richard's grip tighten ever so slightly. "You were with Ian?"

He was silent for a moment, and I opened my eyes to see him frowning into the trees. He glanced down at me, and I saw the harsh look of his mouth as it was drawn in concern. His eyes were dark and shaded now, and I drew in my breath at his intense expression, but then his eyes softened with concern, and as the blood began to rush into my limbs, my heart seemed to thump louder.

He held me gently, as if he were still not sure how badly I was hurt, but I thought now that I was rather more shaken than injured except for the bump I could feel forming on the back of my head.

He must have thought about possible injuries at the same time, for he laid me down gently again, then ran his hands down my arms and sides checking to see if I had hurt myself anywhere else.

"Can you move your arms?" he asked.

I nodded and bent my elbows. I attempted a smile. "Fingers too, see?" I said, wiggling my fingers. He caught my hands and kissed my fingers, and the earlier feelings I had had rushed through me again.

He closed his eyes and opened them again. "I was so afraid you were . . ."

He let it trail off, but I swallowed. "You thought I might be dead." The thought frightened me, and I pinched my lips together thinking I had had a close call.

Then I moved my head from side to side. "No, I'm all right." I winced. "Well, almost all right."

He felt my temple and head gently with his fingers, and when he came to the bump at the back, I winced again. His face had an ashen color to it, and I realized he had been truly frightened.

Then his fingers paused on my mouth, and I moved my lips against them. For a moment he held me there, and he opened his lips as if he were about to say something, but then he hesitated. Instead, he looked down into my face and I felt as if I were drowning again, staring into the translucent eyes where I could see my own reflection.

"Richard," I murmured, not knowing why I spoke his name. He dropped his gaze to my lips, and I felt his fingers move in my hair. The blood pounded in my ears as his lips moved closer. Emotions churned in my breath, and the throbbing spread through me as I gasped for a quick breath before he kissed me.

His kiss drew me in as if he were drawing breath from me, and my arms went around his back as he leaned over me. Dizziness mingled with the pain, and heat that began within my breast flooded over me. I clung to him tighter, feeling vulnerable and frightened, yet drawing strength from the feel of his arms around my bruised body, yet frightened too of what we were doing.

I was aware of my aches and pains, but also of sounds around us, of the water beating on the shore, not too distant, of movement in the branches behind us.

Richard kissed my jaw, my temple, then he took a slow deep breath.

"Can you sit up?" he asked.

"I think so." My breathing was still labored, but he helped me sit, and now the pain where I had hit my head was more intense. He rocked back on his knees to support me.

"I can stand if you help me," I said.

He pulled me up, and my legs were wobbly, but I think my weakness came more from the ordeal than from physical injury. I was sure I would discover a few bruises on my limbs and derriere, but nothing seemed to be broken.

Then I looked at Richard, remembering the wreck the horses had made of the phaeton. I was not fit to ride, and I did not know how we would get back.

"How did you come here?" I asked him.

He pointed to the shore beyond. "By boat. I brought the skiff."

My mind began to form questions, but I was too muddled to ask them. And there was still the mystery of where Ian had gone.

Richard put his arm about my waist and we walked gingerly toward the boat. I was feeling better, but having him help me down the gentle slope was reassuring after what had just happened.

Richard helped me into the small boat, and I sat in the middle as he shoved off, then climbed in. As we left shore and Richard took up the oars, I glanced up and saw Ian emerge from the trees.

"Ian," I cried in surprise and waved.

He stared at us, his sketch pad in his hands, but Richard made no attempt to turn the boat around. And so

I watched mutely as Ian's figure receded on the beach.

I did not need to ask Richard why he kept rowing. Obviously he blamed Ian for leaving me alone and therefore thought the accident was his fault.

But finally I gathered my wits and said, "the phaeton is broken. Ian will have to walk back."

Richard smirked. "If he likes to wander in the woods so much, he can find his way back to the house easily enough. Or he can hitch a ride with one of the tenants."

I was half amused by Richard's answer, and wondered if he were actually jealous of Ian. I knew I was flattering myself to think so, and I tried to keep my expression sober.

I glanced at the water beside us where Richard splashed the oars. I did not know exactly what was happening between us. I knew I was no longer in love with Ian, perhaps never had been. And I was somehow so in accord with Richard. I was drawn to him, and yet frightened of him at the same time. That is, I was frightened of the things about him I did not understand.

After a while, he stopped rowing and let the current carry us around the southeastern tip of the island.

"I'll take you to the cottage," he said. "Mother will insist on sending for the doctor."

I felt my head gingerly. A doctor was probably not necessary, but I did not protest.

Richard was frowning in concentration, and the boat rocked gently.

"How did the accident happen?"

I had forgotten that in my first incoherent moments, I had probably not explained very well how I had come to be thrown from the carriage. Then another thought struck me.

"You didn't see it then?"

"If you mean your accident, no, I didn't. It was lucky I saw you when I rowed past." He clenched his jaw, and I saw a flicker of something that looked like anger in his eye. "I don't mind telling you I was frightened. I almost rowed past when I saw someone lying prone on the road above the beach. When I saw it was you, I was afraid—"

I was touched at the emotion my accident had stirred in him.

Then he looked at me again. "You said something about a cat."

"That's right. It was Pericles. You remember the old white cat that hangs about the mansion."

He cocked his head. "Yes. I hadn't seen that cat in a while. I had forgotten about him. But how could it have been Pericles, so far from the house?"

"I don't know."

"Are you sure, Eileen? Might it have been some other animal. The woods are full of wild creatures. You might have mistaken something else for Pericles."

"No, I am sure it was Pericles."

Richard paused, assessing me. "I see. And you say he frightened the horses."

I nodded, shuddering as I remembered how frightened I had been. How could such a small animal as a cat cause me so much fear? I hesitated to mention the feelings I had associated with Pericles, for fear Richard would think me strange.

"I heard a hissing noise," I began. "I thought someone was following me. Then when I turned, there was Pericles leaping from the seat up to me. He attacked me. I must have lost control of the horses then, and I fell."

107

Richard said nothing, and his gaze disturbed me. Perhaps he was wondering if my memory had been rattled in the fall. Or perhaps he was trying to understand why a house cat would attack me in the woods, several miles from the animal's domain.

He had a point there. I did not think a house cat would wander so far from its habitation, even Pericles, but then I knew nothing of the habits of domestic felines.

"I know it sounds odd."

I had to tell him what I was thinking. It might sound mad, and I would hesitate to express these thoughts to anyone else, but I had to let Richard know what was in my mind even if he rejected my notions. I looked up at him.

"Richard, do you believe that spirits come back to haunt us?"

Instead of mocking me, he turned pensive and took up the oars again, for we had to make the distance to the small private dock that served the cottage. When we were approaching, he again lifted the oars.

"I am not as skeptical as some when it comes to the notion of spirits."

I should have felt glad that we shared this belief as well as the many other things about which we seemed in accord, but the import of his statement made me feel suddenly cold.

"Then you have considered it?" I asked him.

"Spirits?"

I nodded.

"I have had a sense that some of them are tied to a place and do not go on as they should."

I gripped the gunwale with one hand, feeling a sense of curiosity mixed with fright. It was almost as if he had spoken the truth, and when confronted, brought a strange sense of relief as it peeled away part of the mystery surrounding it.

My voice was so low when I spoke that I was surprised he heard me, but the wind must have carried it in his direction. "Someone then haunts this place? Is that what you think?"

He tilted his head to one side, looking toward the island as if idly surveying its features.

"I am not sure. Perhaps one of our family is very unhappy and has stayed in this place until something is put to rights."

"A troubled spirit?"

"Something like that."

I could not begin to know how to react. I could see how the many tragic occurrences on the island might trap a spirit here, but this was the first time I had seen it in quite the light Richard put it in. Something needed to be put to rights. What could that something be?

"Then you believe someone or more than one person has been wronged?" I asked.

He looked directly at me, and the sun reflected in his eyes causing that glow that seemed to come from behind the pupils. "There are the missing jewels to begin with."

A fish jumped out of the water next to us, splashing water into the boat. I swallowed.

"But the investigators assumed the thief made off with them. They could be anywhere by now. Wouldn't they have been sold on the black market?"

"So we were told."

I stared at Richard. Was this what had been on his mind that made him seem so distracted? Had he been contemplating these old family mysteries, perhaps even calculating possible answers. What else had he been harboring? Suddenly I had a deep desire to know all that he was thinking. I was drawn towards the mysteries as a moth to flame, irrationally perhaps, but there is nothing like an unanswered question to make one drop all other thoughts and seek that answer.

"Richard you must tell me what you have been thinking."

"You are awfully avid to sort out puzzles for someone who has so recently been the victim of an accident."

I blushed. "I was winded, but I don't think it has affected my ability to reason."

A hint of a smile played in his eyes as he pulled the oars again. "I will get you to the house first. Lettice will put you to bed. Time enough to discuss these matters later."

I felt he was patronizing me, but I didn't argue. Though I felt suddenly apprehensive that in Lettice's busy household there would be little time for me to speak with Richard alone.

"You will promise to talk to me then, about these things I mean? Perhaps I can help you puzzle them out."

I was leaning forward and perhaps making a fool of myself looking so hopeful, but Richard's amusement left him as he seemed to think once again of the serious consequences of the danger that had beset me.

"I tell you this much, Eileen. If there is a threat on this island, whether spirit or human, I will get to the bottom of it. I will see that no more harm comes to you."

I felt a flutter in my chest and took his words to mean that he did care for me. The feelings warmed me. He held my gaze as he rowed on, and I settled back on the seat.

The small inlet at the back of the cottage came into view, and Richard rowed under the branches that drooped over the water, steering expertly. We hit ground, and he leapt out, then dragged the boat further up the beach.

I stood and reached for him and he half lifted me over the side, holding me until I found my footing in the sand. For a moment we stood together, and I enjoyed the feeling of his strong arms supporting me.

He looked down at me as if he too wished we could dally in the shade of the heavy oaks and mangroves. Already I felt the fire that seemed to burn deep within me when he looked at me that way. I was embarrassed by my own feelings, but becoming more emboldened by the intimacy Richard and I seemed to experience when we were alone.

Somehow forgetting his earlier declaration that I must be taken to the house and seen to, his arms went farther around me, and I reached up to encircle his neck. He bent to kiss me, and the want I experienced was excruciating. Pain or no pain, all I seemed to need was Richard. Richard's arms encircling me, Richard's breath against my ear. Richard's body next to mine.

I knew it was not right. I would never be caught throwing myself so blatantly at someone in the New York society I had just left. I thought I had learned the rules of courtship there. But see where they had left me? I had been mistaken by the actions I thought had meant a young man held affection for me. Perhaps because of that debacle, I was more willing to let my feelings run rampant when it came to those Richard aroused in me.

He pressed his lips against mine and moved his body nearer, and all my thoughts turned dizzily on the pleasurable sensations I was experiencing. We were children of the island. Living close to nature, we seemed to take on its wildness. I knew with certainty that I could not explain my actions to anyone else. What I did with Richard was between he and I alone. It was as if we had entered a secret world, ours alone, for no one else to share. And it brought me feelings of pleasure and rightness that I had never experienced before.

I felt his body harden, and his kiss became more demanding. His hand moved to my bodice, cradling the curve of my bosom, and the fire that had smouldered in the core of me leapt into a burning flame. I could not stop myself from wanting more. Thought was cast aside.

"Richard," I gasped, when his mouth left mine to seek the base of my throat. I arched against him, loving the feel of his mouth on my skin, of his fingers on my throat. "Oh, Richard," I sighed, wanting these sensations never to end.

We became a mass of whispers and moans, and I felt I would swoon in his arms. He paused, pressing my head against his shoulder, still caressing me.

"I will hurt you if I am not careful," he said. "Your bruises."

But I could feel nothing, and feared he would stop what he was doing and take me to the house. My grasp around him tightened. "No, Richard it doesn't hurt anymore. Not if you're with me."

He smiled down at me with a teasing look that reminded me of times we had played together as children. "I am to kiss your wounds and make them better then?"

I smiled back at him in complete understanding and joy. "That is exactly right. No doctor can do for me what you are doing."

A look of mock horror came into his eyes. "I should hope not. In fact I will stand guard while Doctor Sutcliff treats you. If he finds you as tempting as I do he might lose control of himself and violate the Hippocratic oath."

I laughed suddenly at the vision of old Doc Sutcliff bending over to kiss me. The man must be old enough to be my grandfather.

Richard kissed me once again on my brow, and I settled into his arms comfortably. The sun was crawling toward the western horizon and we watched silently as nature painted her brilliant pinks and blues on the sky's great canvas.

I felt Richard move as if to go, but I sat down on the warm sand, still not wanting our time together to end.

"Let us just watch the sunset from here," I said.

He looked as if he were about to protest, then joined me on the warm sand. I felt him watching me as I stared out at the azure blue water. Then I felt his fingers trace my temple gently and felt his breath on my ear as he leaned over to kiss the base of my neck.

"Eileen, I cannot resist you. How did you grow up to be such a tantalizing young lady?"

I smiled, realizing an answer was not called for. And when I opened my lips to speak, he put a finger on them. "No, do not say anything." And he kissed me again.

His arms came around me, and he lay back on the sand, pulling me across his chest with him. I clung recklessly to him, my skirts tangled in his legs, as I absorbed the warmth of him. My tongue mingling with his as we tasted each other. This was what I wanted. I could not help it if it seemed brazen. I trusted Richard and believed that I was as free to be with him as I felt. The rest of the world need not know.

He turned on his side, his hand caressing my bosom, exploring the outline of my waist and hip, and the dizzying sensations overcame me once again. Perhaps I was too reckless and did not know what I was doing, for my own hands were wandering over his body as if they had a life of their own.

"Eileen," he whispered hoarsely. "You are too tempting. You do not know where this will lead."

The buttons of my torn blouse had come undone and his lips were pressed against the rise of my bosom. He was right. Some part of my mind warned me that all my foolish justifications would not protect me if I did something I might later regret. I was inexperienced in sensual matters, letting my feelings be my only guide. But I was not completely ignorant. Richard and I might commit an act that would be irreversable. I had to force myself to stop before it was too late.

Feelings and sense warred with each other now, as I tried to command my hands to withdraw from his waist, tried to turn my head aside from his moist kisses.

Then his words, spoken low in my ear, caused the sweet sensations to plunge even deeper into flame. "I want you, Eileen," he said. "It is dangerous for me to want you so much. I'm not sure I can trust myself with you."

I rolled on my back, trying to pull my bodice together, panting for breath. His advances stopped also, and we lay apart. I sat up, hoping the breeze from the water would help clear my head, waiting for my pulse to begin to slow.

I hated the circumstances, feeling a sudden deep anger that such pleasure could not continue. I hated a rational world where one must align actions with expectations and restrictions. But I summoned enough inner strength to convince myself that I need not throw everything away in one moment of impulse.

I counted to ten as my pulse started to return to normal. Then I smoothed my hair and arranged my clothing, even though lace had been torn off in my battle with Pericles. I looked down now in embarrassment. Confusion replaced passion. I did not want to look Richard in the eye now, for fear of what he would think of me.

But he would not allow me to hide my eyes from him. He stood before me and I saw the hand that reached down to help me up. When I got to my feet, he lifted my chin, forcing me to meet his gaze. He smiled at me, and my fears vanished.

At the same time I felt something I had not experienced before. Richard had a certain wisdom that was seeing him through. I did not know where he had acquired it or when he had gained it, but it was there. I felt in that moment that I could trust him. That he desired me was evident, but that he was also concerned for my welfare warmed me beyond the thrill of sensation we had just shared. I silently thanked him for that look of reassurance.

He tucked my arm through his and we started up the beach. This inlet was seldom used, for most boating was done now from the dock on the eastern side of the island, where the launch had brought me. But from here, there was an overgrown path through a stand of pines to the garden at the back of the cottage. We struggled through the weeds, and then Richard led me to the opening in the hedge. Then we were on the shell walk that lined the garden.

Chapter 9

Lettice must have seen us approach, for as we neared the house, she came out to the back porch and down the steps to meet us, reaching for me with great concern. Yet she seemed somewhat relieved that I was with Richard.

"Good heavens, what's happened?" she asked, seeing my torn blouse and scratched face and arms. "One of the horses came home dragging her harness, and Ian came back leading the other one. We thought something dreadful had happened."

"I'm afraid I had an accident."

"My dear, are you all right? At least it seems apparent that you can walk." She glanced from me to Richard as if seeking assurance that he had found me unharmed except for minor bruises, and I sensed her relief merely from the look she exchanged with her son.

"It was lucky I came around just after she was thrown," he said. "She was winded, but I don't believe she has broken anything."

"Thank goodness for that. Let's get you upstairs in any case, I'll have Doc Sutcliff look at you."

"I don't think I need a doctor, Lettice really."

But she insisted, just as Richard had predicted.

We went through the kitchen and up the stairs to the guest room where I had slept the first night I was here. Lettice made me strip down to my camisole and drawers, then went to get a pan of water and cloth to bathe my scratches and dress them.

Now I could see the bruises that were forming on my left thigh and arm. The cuts on my head and face were little more than surface scratches, and Lettice soon had them bathed and dressed. Then I put on a dressing gown and sat back against the pillows on the bed.

"Lettice really, I don't need all this pampering. I simply took a fall, but I don't think it's made an invalid out of me."

She gave me a patronizing look. "I am glad you are made of such sturdy stuff. But I want you to rest here until the doctor gives you a bill of health."

I half chuckled. "If you insist. But I think I would know by now if anything were broken."

"Perhaps. But you said yourself that your ankle still hurt you. I'm sure the doctor will want you to rest."

She put the medicines and cloth on the dresser and came to sit on the edge of the bed. Just then there was a knock on the door, and without waiting for a reply, Richard entered.

I was glad to see him again so soon, for I had wondered if he would make himself scarce, once we returned to the house. But he strode into the room as if he were very much the master of the house and my welfare as guest was foremost in his mind. Again I saw the look that passed between Lettice and him, and then they both fixed their attention on me.

"Now," said Lettice. "Tell me about this accident."

I relayed much of what I had told Richard, leaving out

117

my suspicions that any sort of supernatural forces had anything to do with it, for in this setting, such ideas seemed absurd. And Richard seemed concerned about a menace of another sort.

"I've just come back from the stables," said Richard when I had finished. "The harness had been tampered with at the point of the break. I could see where the leather had been cut."

My eyes widened as I stared at him. "Someone cut the harness? Are you sure?"

He nodded slowly. "I suspected it, but I couldn't be sure until I saw for myself. Two horses do not so easily come out of their traces at a collision with a tree. There had to be a weakening of the leather."

My throat constricted as I gazed first at Richard and then at Lettice. Finally I found my tongue. "Why would someone do that?"

Richard turned his back and paced to the window, looking down at the lawn outside. Lettice leaned forward, patting my hands.

"We don't mean to frighten you, my dear. But what Richard means is that someone wanted that accident to happen."

"To me?" My voice was a high squeak.

"I know it isn't very nice. And I hope it isn't so, but it does appear that way."

My jaw clenched. I had had the notion before that someone on the island meant me harm, but I could not understand why. I had not done anything to anyone that would precipitate some sort of evildoing. It made no sense.

I shook my head. "I don't understand."

"Neither do we, dear," said Lettice. "But we hope to

find out. Richard has promised me he will get to the bottom of this."

So that explained the knowing glances between mother and son. They knew there was something evil going on here, and they had decided the evil was aimed at me. It was incredible. Again I asked, "Why me?"

But there was no answer. Instead Richard turned from the window and threw me a worried glance. Then he spoke to his mother. "I'll be downstairs if you need me. I have some work to do in the study."

She nodded. He paused by my bed and I looked hungrily into his eyes. He rewarded me with a gentle smile, but the look in his eyes was distant, and something pulled at my heartstrings. Already I felt him slipping away from me. I could not quite explain my perception. But it was as if sometimes Richard were completely himself and gave all of himself to me. But then he would slip off into his own world where I could not reach his thoughts. Then I felt lost, foolish and confused about what I dared hope was growing between us.

But I had no more time to contemplate it, for he left me alone with Lettice. I sighed, closed my eyes and lay back on the bed. It had been a trying day to say the least, and I knew Lettice would allow me to rest.

By the rustle of her skirts I heard her rise. "Under the circumstances I think it will be better for you to remain here. At least until we are sure you are safe."

I opened my eyes again, my feelings mixed. I appreciated her concern for me, but I resented not being able to return to my own home. For the longer I was on the island the more attached I became to the old mansion. I do not know what its hold was on me, but it was my home, and somehow I felt I should be there. However, I knew Lettice would brook no argument since I had experienced this most recent mishap.

Perhaps she was right. A few days at the cottage might restore my energy. For my muscles were still not quite used to the efforts I had been putting them to at the mansion.

"All right. I'll stay for a few days. But I must get back before long. There's so much to do, Lettice. I shall have to tell you of my decorating plans."

My eyelids were drooping, and even as I spoke, my head fell back against the pillow. "I think I'll just doze a while," I mumbled.

"A rest will do you good. And when the doctor comes, I'll bring him up."

I nodded, and she tiptoed out. Then I turned my head into the pillows and slept.

Doctor Sutcliff pronounced me fit and announced that he could see no sign of concussion. "Just winded by the fall, I'd say. Though you were a very lucky young lady," he said.

I was sitting up again for his examination, as he had appeared just before supper. He praised Lettice's ministrations and left a sleeping draught in case I needed it.

"She has a very strong heart," he said to Lettice, who was permitted to sit in on the examination. He straightened and removed his stethoscope from his ears. "Very steady heartbeat."

His words embarrassed me, for I knew how that heartbeat had fluctuated only very recently.

But I smiled prettily. "Thank you, Doctor. Then I

have not injured myself seriously."

"Nope. A few days rest to let those bruises heal, and you'll be fit to be up and around again."

If he meant a few days bed rest he did not know of my innate restlessness. I shrugged. I might agree to ease my activities for a few days, but I did not mean to stay cooped up in this room.

"Don't worry, Doctor," said Lettice. "We'll take care of her."

"See that no more harm comes to her," he said as he snapped his black bag shut.

"I'll see you out," said Lettice, and she led him out of the room.

I watched the door shut behind them, only then realizing the strangeness of his words. *Let no more harm come to her.* What more harm could come to me? Had Richard and Lettice already told him that they suspected that my accident had been planned? I could not help the nervous feeling that made my stomach turn over.

When Lettice returned, I had difficulty maintaining my calm demeanor. Now that I had rested, the whole incident was beginning to seem more unsettling to me, but for some reason I did not want to discuss it with her.

I allowed her to fuss over me, fluffing the pillows and smoothing the covers. Then she straightened, tucked a whisp of hair behind her ear that had come undone and stood, looking absently over the room, hands on hips. I sensed she wanted to talk, but I hoped she did not want to delve into serious subjects just now. My head was starting to ache from the strain of what had just passed.

"It should be pleasant weather in a few weeks," she said. "What would you say to having a party the last weekend of next month? We would invite young people

121

from the mainland and it would be your official welcome."

I bent my mind to this new train of thought. It seemed an odd time for Lettice to be thinking of entertaining, but then perhaps it was not so odd. Perhaps she wanted something more festive to take my mind off the supposed threat behind my accident.

"I think that would be very nice, Lettice," I agreed. "If it would not be too much work for you."

"No, I think it is what we need. And since Gaius and Ian are our guests, it will give them something to look forward to."

"Yes, of course." Lettice was nothing if not a good hostess.

She turned a gentle smile on me. "Speaking of Ian, if you're feeling up to it, he wants to see you. Poor young man. He was quite distraught over losing his way in the woods. He said that when he finally found his way back to where he thought he had left you, you had gone. Then after walking along the road for a while, he came upon the broken carriage, and saw you rowing away with Richard."

I couldn't resist the amusement that came to my mind thinking of Ian getting lost. I supposed that was like him. I had not realized he was so absentminded when I had known him in the city, but then, when he had lived at home everything was taken care of for him, and he knew the way to his haunts quite well. Here, he seemed so captivated by the island that he could be led off and lost in no time. So that explained why he had not answered when I had called to him.

"Yes, I'll see him," I said, sitting up on the pillows and moving about agitatedly.

Now that I had had my nap I was ready to get up and be about the house, but Lettice and the doctor seemed determined to keep me a prisoner of this room, and I struggled to behave myself at least for now.

She smiled, smoothing her long fingers over her skirts. "I'll send him to you then."

With that she left, and in no time at all I heard a knock on the door.

"Come in," I said, and Ian entered.

"Eileen, I'll be dashed. When I heard what had happened, you can't imagine my remorse."

I tried to keep from smiling too hard. As I had more opportunity to observe Ian, I was beginning to see that it was like him to make some blunder and then to come rushing in to apologize later. I sighed. I could not remain angry, especially when he humored me so. But he was going on about the accident.

"If I had not wandered off to see where that path led on the other side of the road this would never have happened. I am completely to blame. How can you ever forgive me?"

He drew up a chair and sought my hand, looking into my eyes with the most contrite expression.

"It's all right, Ian, I don't blame you."

Then a thought struck me. "But tell me, on your walk, did you happen to see a white cat anywhere in the woods?"

"A cat?"

I nodded. "Yes. There's an old white cat that inhabits the, um, island, and it was he that frightened the horses."

Ian drew his brows together and shook his head. "I didn't see any cat, though I must say from the sounds of bushes rustling where I walked, I can imagine there might have been many creatures hiding themselves from the view of pedestrians such as us."

"So you heard something?"

He shook his head slightly. "I'll admit to you that it was an eerie feeling. I did not mean to wander so far away from the road, and I must have lost track of time. When I tried to get back I did not know which way to turn. I knew there must be creatures in the woods thinking I was a fool. It was a relief to at least come out of the trees again. Then when I couldn't find you I was doubly depressed. I felt sure something had happened, and then when I learned that something had happened . . ."

His words gushed out like a babbling stream, and I gestured that he need not explain further. But I was interested in one thing.

"Did you have the feeling you were being watched in the woods then?" I asked.

"Yes surely. As I said I imagined every pair of eyes from the deers to the hawks and some things much worse."

"But you saw no white cat and no one else." My words were spoken more to myself than to him. For I still had not resolved how Pericles had come to be in that part of the woods. I surreptitiously studied Ian's expression as he resettled himself in the chair. My train of thought was an odd one, and I was tempted to dismiss it as improbable. I really had no reason to believe that Ian himself had anything to do with my accident. I shook my head to myself. No, I did not think Ian capable of cutting through the leather harness, transporting the white cat to the woods without my knowing it and then letting it loose just as I was driving away.

I gave a little shiver and reached for the coverlet rolled

up at my feet. Ian bent to help me.

"Poor Eileen. It has been too trying for you. Will you let me make it up to you by waiting on you hand and foot until you are quite healed?"

I met his gaze with rather a bit of irony. I hardly thought such solicitation was necessary.

"Thank you, Ian. But I will be all right." I thought for a moment. "But I will let you know if I need anything done for me. You may be able to help me with some small errands after all."

"With pleasure. I will await your command."

I was not sure what errands I might have for him, but it was just possible that I could enlist Ian's help without him knowing it. If I could not roam about the island by myself looking for clues to the mysteries that we seemed saddled with here, I could send emissaries. It was only a half-formed thought at that time, but I knew there was some logic to it.

I told Ian I was tired, which was not true, and that I desired to rest. He was only too anxious to leave me to recuperate, taking my hand in his again most humbly.

"I shall let no one bother you then. We shall miss you at supper."

I supposed I would have to have supper in my room alone, but it would give me a chance to think. I thanked Ian and sent him away.

As the supper hour approached I could feel my stomach rumbling in anticipation, and just as I was about to reach for the bell pull to make sure I had not been forgotten, a light tap sounded on the door, and Nannette entered carrying a tray with several covered dishes.

"Oh I'm glad to see you're up," she said. "Everyone else has had their turn with you so I was determined to bring you your supper. How are you feeling?"

"Quite crochety if you want to know the truth. I don't think these minor aches and scratches merit my lying in bed all evening. Everyone's trying to make me out for an invalid."

She smiled in understanding, then as she placed the tray over my lap so that the legs supported it on the bed, she gave me a frank look.

"The truth is, Eileen, everyone was so frightened of what happened to you, that they are all being overly concerned. I think we are all so thankful that nothing worse happened, that everyone's overreacting. I don't mind telling you the atmosphere is rather charged downstairs."

She uncovered the steaming dishes that Martha had prepared, but I was less aware of the delicious aroma that came from the wholesome food in front of me than I was of Nannette's intimation that she preferred escaping the tension in the dining room and being with me while I ate.

I frowned in concern. "Then they *are* overreacting."

I had not planned to share my suspicions with Nannette as I had with Richard. But I could not ignore the sense of uneasiness everyone seemed to have.

"I cannot see what there is to be afraid of," I said. "Accidents happen."

But Nannette was not taken in by my nonchalance. "I'm not sure what to think. In any case, I'm glad Mother persuaded you to remain with us for the time being."

I sighed. "For the time being."

I picked up my fork and started in on my supper, finding that I was ravenously hungry. Nannette paced nervously about, and I remembered that she had said she did not plan to eat with the others.

"Would you like some of this?" I offered. "I cannot do justice to such huge portions."

She considered the food, but shook her head. "No thank you, you should eat as much as you can, it will give you strength. I can eat something later downstairs."

"After the others have left the table?" I eyed her curiously.

She lifted her shoulders as if she could not explain her actions. Then she tried to smile at me. "Poor Ian. You left him in quite a state."

"I left him? I'm afraid it was rather the other way around."

"You mean his getting lost in the woods." She shook her head in amusement, and I thought I detected a sparkle in her eye. "He does seem rather awe struck by our island. How different it must be for him from the society of the city he's used to."

"It is different, I'll grant you that much. But he must pay more attention to what he's about. He doesn't know all the hazards of the island."

I'm afraid my annoyance with Ian's flightiness showed, but Nannette seemed quite entertained by thoughts of his doings.

"Well, perhaps since you're laid up, I can take him in hand. It might be amusing to wander about the island with someone who has an artist's eyes. That is, if you don't mind."

I raised an eyebrow in speculation. "Of course I don't mind. If you mean to inquire as to whether I have any feelings of affection left for Ian, the answer is no. I have quite disabused myself of the notion of romance with him. I feel more maternal toward him, if anything. He does seem to need some looking after. But I don't have the inclination to follow him about the island. So feel free if you wish to do so."

She brightened, and I began to wonder if Ian was going to make another conquest here. "I think I shall enjoy that," she said.

I wanted to warn her of Ian's fickleness in case her heart was in danger of warming to Ian's charm.

"You must be careful, however, Nannette. I'm afraid Ian Menasce is not the most reliable of persons. You may find him amusing, but I'll warrant there's not a serious bone in his body."

But she laughed at me. "I can give him his due there. But don't trouble yourself. I'm not in danger of falling in love, if that's what you mean. It's just that I like entertaining companionship, and there has been so little fun on the island."

I supposed I could understand her feelings. Nannette had perhaps more need of brilliant conversation and diverse activity than she would get by living here. One had to be especially tuned to nature and able to enjoy solitude to thrive on an island such as this. Gifts that I was beginning to believe I still had. But I could see that Nannette was still too unsettled for that.

Speaking of fun, I told her of the party that Lettice had suggested, and she was immediately enthusiastic. She had met many of the young people from the towns on the mainland and would like nothing better than to have them here for some end-of-October festivities. We agreed to work on plans tomorrow. We spent the remainder of an hour chatting idly, and I did not bring up any of the more ominous thoughts that Lettice and Richard had discussed with me.

She lifted my supper tray to take it away, and I found that on a full stomach I was more tired than I wanted to admit. Everyone seemed to prescribe sleep, and perhaps they were right. To lose myself in sleep for the next eight or so hours might be the balm I needed both for my aching body and my troubled mind.

Nannette lit the kerosene lamp by my bed, and I slipped down in the covers glancing at some of the novels she left on the corner of the night table, But I was not sure I could interest myself in any of them.

Then she took the supper tray from the bed and bid me good night. She promised to glance in to see if I needed anything more before she went to bed herself. But I assured her I didn't and was glad for the peacefulness that descended on me as she left the room.

There was so much to think about, I didn't know how to sort out my thoughts. None of them fit into neat categories that I could understand. I thought back to my reasons for coming to the island, and tried to recapture the feelings I had in the launch the day we approached the dock. But whatever expectations I had had then seemed to have become submerged in the actualities of what had happened since I had arrived.

I had not expected to meet Gaius Amundsen before that day, and I still did not know how he fit into our lives here. Nor should he necessarily have a place except for his strange relationship with Richard, which I did not understand.

Now that I had time to think about it, I wondered why Gaius was here. He and Richard did not seem to be that close, and in fact I wondered why Gaius had chosen to spend his holiday in such a place.

Gaius's facination with the old mansion and his intimation about Richard's character were just as curious as the improbability of Ian's fascination with the island from an aesthetic point of view.

And then there was Richard's quiet suspicion that something was not quite right. I had not bargained for all these disquieting thoughts when I had decided to come home.

I should be frightened, since Nannette and Lettice seemed to fear that something more dreadful might happen to me. I was not sure whom to believe nor whom to trust. But the oddest part about it was that somehow these notions did not disturb me in a way I might have thought they would. Did the island have some deadly curse or an unanswered mystery that lured us all to an unsuspecting doom? I should be frightened of being here. I should consider leaving the island, but somehow I knew I would not do that.

Was it only because this way my home and that something about being here nourished a need in me that I was not aware of until now? Or was it simply the lure of whatever sinister forces existed here, the source of which I was driven to find out? Whatever the cause of my motivation and determination to remain here I could not know.

But the thoughts and images that swam in my mind were connected in some way that I could not yet fathom. I knew with certainty that I belonged here. It was my destiny to walk the ground my family had walked, to commune with a place that had belonged to Blakemores for three generations, going back to a time when the island was shared with Indians.

Then a different thought intertwined with the others as I began to drift off to the plane of sleep. Was there truly someone who did not want my presence here? And in what ways would that being make it known that I was not welcome?

Chapter 10

The next morning I felt much too well to stay cooped up inside, so I dressed and went down to breakfast. Five faces looked up in surprise as I entered the dining room and all almost simultaneously gasped out, "Eileen."

I smiled and nodded greetings all around, and for a moment I had the odd sensation that I had caught them all talking about me, for they seemed so shocked that I had appeared.

Ian and Nannette broke off from a conversation at the far end of the table to look up at me. Lettice half turned in her chair at the head of the table nearest the door. Richard eyed me speculatively from over his cup of coffee, and Gaius, whom I had not seen at all yesterday, beamed at me and came over to take my arm, pulling me into the room.

"How are you feeling?" asked Gaius. "I have been pestering our hostess to death with questions about your misfortune yesterday, but I was away from the house until supper was served last night, and Lettice instructed me that under no circumstances were you to be bothered."

We reached the buffet, and I extracted my arm to take

a plate and serve myself.

"I appreciate your concern, but I'm quite all right today."

Lettice came over to examine the bandage, still taped to my forehead. Then she gave me an assessing look, but the look I returned to her must have told her that I was not going to be coddled today, and so she gave me no lecture.

"I will change those dressings," was all she said and then poured herself another cup of coffee from the urn.

It still seemed as if they were all staring at me, and I felt awkward as I carried my plate to the table, sitting opposite Richard, who said nothing.

"I really am feeling much better," I said by way of a general statement for them all. "None of you need concern yourselves on my behalf."

I heard muttered acknowledgements, and then I concerned myself with eating my breakfast. Ian, who had evidently finished, rose and came to stand by my elbow.

"I must say I am pleased that you look so well, Eileen."

Glancing up, I saw that he looked rather tongue tied, and I wondered if he were concerned that everyone thought the accident was his fault. But Nannette came to his rescue.

"I'm going to take Ian boating this morning," she said. "I think perhaps he won't get lost if I'm in the boat beside him."

"Hmmm." It was the first sound I'd heard from Richard. He was giving his sister a very instructive look. "Stay away from the shoals at the north end, Nannette. And don't go too far out. If there's a storm, the skiff is extremely hard to handle."

She wrinkled her nose at her brother. "There isn't

going to be a storm," she said, though surely she must be aware of how quickly storms could blow up in these skies. There was no guaranteeing that just because there were no clouds in sight in the morning, that they wouldn't form later in the day.

"Do be careful," I threw in, feeling I suppose solicitous toward Nannette and Ian, neither of whom were the type to take many precautions when an adventure challenged them. But I knew that Nannette was used to the island and could surely take care of herself in its elements.

"Well then, we'll be off." Ian nodded to Lettice, who dipped her head in acknowledgement, and then he and Nannette made off.

Richard rose as well. "I'm afraid I must go myself. I've promised to advise Jason Hebridge about the sugar cane. If you will excuse me, Mother."

He went to kiss his mother's cheek, then he stood and faced me. "Cousin, I do hope you'll not strain yourself today."

I felt my face warm as I looked at him. After what had passed between us so recently, I felt embarrassed to be talking to him in a room full of people, as if they could all read my thoughts. I risked a glance at his eyes, and though he met my gaze, there was none of the intimacy in them that I might have expected. He seemed very much in control of his demeanor, and although it made it easier to deport myself in a proper manner for the benefit of the others, I could not help the disappointment that sprang up in me.

Was I being foolish to hope that Richard's actions in public would demonstrate some sort of declaration of affection? My own feelings were too new even for that, and I knew I was being silly to contemplate such notions. I merely nodded my acquiescence to him and returned to my food. I glanced up again just before Richard left the room and saw what passed between Gaius and him.

Gaius was helping himself to another warm bun from under a linen napkin and without looking at Richard said, "Don't work too hard, old man. And don't forget that game of chess you promised tonight."

Richard said nothing but raised his chin, something like a warning in his eyes. It made me pause with the fork half way between the table and my mouth, but then Richard turned and was gone.

I chewed slowly, again fearing that I did not really know Richard's mind as well as I would like to, but now was not the time for contemplation. I looked up at Lettice, who was folding her napkin and trying to hide her disapproval that I was up and about so soon.

"I do hope you'll not try anything too strenuous," she said. And I could read her unspoken thought that I should not return to the manor house today.

"I promise not to do any work, if that is what you mean. But I do need to get some exercise."

"Perhaps you will allow me to accompany her, Lettice," said Gaius. "Since I have been deprived of Eileen's company of late I should be only too happy to drive her out wherever she wishes."

I did not miss Lettice's look of apprehension as she flashed him a look, but she seemed to force her features to remain under control. "It is up to Eileen," she said.

I was not sure I wanted to spend the day with Gaius, but since everyone seemed to think I needed a chaperone, I agreed. "I would like to visit my father's grave," I said, only lighting on the idea at that instant. "I

135

should cut some fresh flowers for it."

Lettice's look softened at the notion, and I could see that she approved. "You'll have to take the wagon, of course. It will be some time before the harnesses for the phaeton are repaired. And I want Riggin to look it over for any less obvious damage the wreck could have caused."

"I can handle the wagon," said Gaius. "I've had much practice at driving." He turned to me. "Whenever you are ready."

I scooted back my chair and went upstairs to put on my high-topped boots. I picked up a straw bonnet to protect my face against the sun, and then went down again. I went to the garden and picked some stems from one of the Golden Rain trees. The bright yellow flowers and the reddish seed pods would add color to the wreath I had taken last time. After fashioning a bouquet, I went to meet Gaius, who waited for me in the entry hall. He held the door for me, and we stepped onto the porch.

The smell of lilac assailed me, and I took a deep breath, realizing how much I needed to be outdoors again. Lettice had planted the bushes in front of the cottage for late bloom.

The air was not so heavy today, and there was a warm breeze coming in from the gulf. My heart lightened, and in the bright sunlight, all of my earlier concerns seemed almost to vanish.

Gaius helped me up to the seat of the wagon then came around and sat beside me and picked up the reins.

He clucked to the horses, and we were away. He seemed to have no need to speak as we rolled along the road past the pine flats on our left and the sugar cane fields to our right, and I was just as glad to ride in silence and gaze at the fields and the palms in the distance.

When we came to the fork in the road, we took the one that led to the cemetery, and I wondered if today I might ask Gaius to leave me alone for a while in the chapel, for I thought that now I might be able to meditate.

The trees thickened around us, and soon we were rolling along under the live oak branches and the Spanish Moss that entwined above us. Then I could see the headstones and the gray granite of the family vault beyond. We reined in and Gaius helped me down, then tied the horses.

I pushed open the gate to the little cemetery and walked between the graves, noticing again how many of them were overgrown. I would have to mention it to Lettice. Surely she made sure that Riggin kept up the appearance of the cemetery.

I paused before I got to the family vault and felt a curious atmosphere settle around me. The sky overhead was becoming just slightly overcast, but it was very quiet. I heard none of the usual bird cries. All the creatures of the wood seemed curiously still.

Gaius joined me but kept a respectful distance. He must have realized I would be lost in my own thoughts here, and so he studied the inscriptions on the grave stones, walking softly along the gravel path behind me as I slowly approached the vault.

The wreath was just as I had left it, and so I merely added my bouquet to the center of it, tucking the stems under the wreath so the flowers would not blow away. I sent up a quick prayer and then stepped back.

I was still aware of the curious feeling that had enveloped me here, and I found myself wanting to explain it. It was nearly the same feeling I had when I was in the bosom of Richard's family. I had always thought that if spirits remained around their graves to haunt intruders it would be a frightening experience. And I truly did not know whether or not my family's spirits roamed this part of the island, but I had the oddest sensation that if they watched me it was with love, perhaps yearning, but not malice. If I voiced my thoughts, I wondered if Gaius would think me mad. For who in their right mind would come to a grave sight to find peace and restfulness?

He smiled beneficently at me, and I broke our silence.

"It is quiet here, is it not?" I said, gazing at the headstones on either side of the path.

"It is. Does your family visit these graves often?"

I cocked my head. "I wouldn't know, but I've not heard them mention it." The question pulled a memory suddenly forward, and I did not mind sharing it with Gaius.

"My sister has a memorial casket here, you may have heard. Her remains are not here, but we symbolized her death with the burial of a small casket."

He nodded solemnly.

"Richard's stepfather, Jasper, used to visit the grave quite often after it happened. He could not forgive himself for her death."

Gaius narrowed his eyes in puzzlement, and his jaws tightened, as he most likely tried to piece together snatches of the account he may have heard about how my sister died. I found myself narrating the event again as I took slow steps on the soft grass between headstones.

"The rest of us had gone on holiday, you see. I can never forget the big hotel on the Halifax River, where we stayed. But at the last minute, before we left, Erin took sick. She had a fever, and so my mother didn't want to risk having her travel. Jasper was also delayed by business and planned to join us in a week's time. He offered to bring Erin if she was better, so mother left her in the care of our nanny."

Gaius had followed me, his head bent as he concentrated on my story. I stopped, unsure of why I felt such a need to unburden myself of this memory, but Gaius glanced up and nodded in understanding, urging me to continue. So I looked out toward the woods again, but in my mind I saw the scene of my sister's death as I had so often imagined it.

"There was a hurricane, and everyone on the island was warned to evacuate. There should have been enough time. Apparently Erin slipped out of the carriage just before it left for the dock. She wanted her dolly. So the others left and Jasper brought her himself later. Everyone in the first boat made it safely. But," I paused, choking suddenly on the words.

Gaius had come nearer and reached out to put his arm around me to comfort me, but I did not encourage it. I struggled to finish the narrative.

"Jasper had Erin in a small row boat. They were caught in a current, and then capsized. He went down several times where he thought he had last seen her, but he never found her."

The tears had welled up in my eyes, and this time when Gaius pulled me gently against his shoulder I did not resist.

"A horrible way for a child to die," he said, and I thought his own voice was hoarse.

I shook my head, wiping away the moistness with my fingers. "It was such a long time ago. I don't know why I should become so emotional about it now."

He patted my shoulder. "It's understandable. One death reminds us of another, and being in this place . . ."

I swallowed. "Poor little Erin. She was such a tiny girl. I shall always cherish her memory."

"Of course." He glanced away, and I straightened, fearing my histrionics were making him uncomfortable.

When he saw I was again under control, he offered his arm so we could stroll back to the path.

"You say Lettice's husband came to this place often," he said.

I nodded. "Poor Jasper. I wonder if it had anything to do with the bitterness he seemed to feel later on."

Gaius looked down at me. "What bitterness?"

"Oh, he seemed rather distant from everyone. Hard to get to know. But then maybe I am prejudiced. You see my father and he argued, and so we did not see a great deal of Jasper and his family."

"But surely he was not such a hard man if he felt so much remorse over the girl's death."

"Yes, that is true."

We were silent for a moment, and Gaius turned to the vault as if thinking of something. "You say he came here often to pay his respects."

"Yes."

Only then did it strike me as being odd that Gaius was so interested in Richard's stepfather. I remembered how interested he had been in everything about our family, and puckered my brows. I wanted somehow to get at the reasons behind his interest in all that happened on Calayeshi Island, but I was not sure how to form the question.

"Did Richard speak of these things at school?" I asked him.

He looked at me and blinked, as if my question had jarred him back from his reverie.

"Richard? Oh yes, he did. Some, that is. But you know how it is. A person tells bits and pieces of his family's story, and the listener is left to fill in for himself what has happened in between."

"But why do you find our family history so interesting. Do you not have similar stories of your own? I mean, perhaps not so tragic, but a family heritage?"

I was afraid I was being rude, but Gaius was not offended. He tucked my hand in his arm and led me back along the path to where the wagon awaited us.

"My family is not very interesting, I'm afraid." And that was all he had to offer on the matter.

We got in, and I turned to give the cemetery one last glance. I had not gone to the chapel, but I decided that I would wait and go when I was alone.

We started off and again lapsed into silence. I was a little surprised, for I had found Gaius more garrulous on the other occasions he had accompanied me. He seemed thoughtful today, but I dismissed it as being the effect of having just visited the graves.

We returned to the house, and Gaius asked me if I would like to take a walk on the beach after lunch, to which I agreed.

I rested a little before luncheon, and then Lettice, Gaius and I lunched on fresh caught smoked mullet and garden vegetables. Lettice commented that she would be busy planting now for her winter garden.

Gaius and I excused ourselves and left the house,

walking along the path that led past the near field toward the dunes where the sea oats grew. We stopped to watch the fishermen in their boats casting their nets to catch the mullet that had gathered in bunches getting ready to school.

The tangy salt air filled my lungs, and I explained to Gaius that the early fall months were when net fishing was at its best.

"The amount of fish that can be caught in these waters is limited only by what can be sold," I said.

"Then is the island entirely self-sufficient?" he asked.

"We get a lot of things from the mainland. The fishermen sell dressed fish to the housewives on the mainland, and the farmers make their rounds here and in Coral Springs with wagons of fresh vegetables and cuts of beef. But we get our dry goods from the general store. We used to go over once a month for staples like flour, sugar, coffee and that sort of thing. And of course we rely on the mainland for all the hardware. There's a very good blacksmith in town."

"Did you go to school there as a girl?"

I smiled at the memory.

"My father taught me to read. He was a very great reader, and he once said that when I learned to read, the knowledge of the world would be at my fingertips. Erin and I always hoped that father would teach us everything, but after Erin died, I had to go to school."

He smiled at me. "And so how did you get there?"

"By the time I was nine I was fully capable of rowing to Coral Springs. I used to tie up my little skiff at Mr. Malone's private dock. Then I left my oars on the porch of the house to keep them from being stolen or in case the boat sank. The school house was east of town. Miss Jordan taught all eight grades."

He looked in the distance, as if seeing the scenes I described.

"Were you frightened on your first day?"

"I was rather scared. I hadn't seen very many other children until then, except for my cousins on occasion. But when I arrived at the fenced-in yard and walked through the gate, a girl came down off the entrance porch and told me her name. Eulalia Hodgson became my best friend."

"Ah, so you were not alone."

I had thought Gaius merely humoring me as I talked about my upbringing here on the island, but when I glanced at him he seemed to have a rather intent expression on his face. However, I rambled on about those early days at school.

"Miss Jordan hardly knew where to put me. I could read and write and spell my name, but I had never been to school before. She put me with the tiny tots in first grade. Next day I was in second grade, and I finally ended up in fourth grade. I had to catch up on the things I hadn't learned at home, and I think I did rather well. My biggest problem was arithmetic."

"Arithmetic, yes. And did the other children come to accept you?"

"I suppose they did. Some of them thought me a bit strange for living on an island. The boys played baseball after lunch, and the girls played house in a saw palm patch with orange crates and pieces of discarded china." I smiled. "I remember thinking it was a bit dull."

We had walked some distance along the beach, and a

143

flock of gulls ran along just ahead of us. I pointed to where a little blue heron stood very still, its gaze fixed on a certain spot. Then with a quick stab of its long beak, a minnow that thought it was well hidden in some sea grass became heron food.

Gaius paused, shielding his eyes from the sun and looking out toward the gulf.

I remember how, as a girl, I had enjoyed half drifting, half paddling on the incoming tide to the point where the tide rushing in flowed over the grass flats just beyond where we stood. All the sea life would be searching for food. I could almost hear the snapping sound of the shrimp and the splashes where the lady fish fed on the shrimp. I had learned to distinguish the snorts and grunts of channel bass, but my favorite sound was always the whoosh and tail splash that signaled the bottlenosed dolphin.

I remembered the treasures that Erin and I sometimes found on the beach, for the sea washed in many gifts. Once Erin and I had found a broken oar from a ship's long boat, the name of the ship on the blade. I always wondered what had happened to bring in that broken blade.

One time we came across some bricks from the low tide, which father had said were no doubt ballast out of a ship. We found heavy chain and the blade of a machete, and it made me ponder the many ships that had gone down in the gulf over the centures. Old Spanish artifacts were often found in these parts.

As if giving life to my very thoughts of treasures, Gaius began to scan the shells at our feet. He had paused a few steps behind me, causing me to turn. He bent down and picked up an oyster shell that had been dried by the sun. I watched as he turned it over in his palm and then applied his fingers to opening it.

He knelt by the water and, casting the shell away, he rinsed what he had found. Then he rose and I gasped, for he held between his fingers a perfect pearl, small but lovely.

Chapter 11

I stared at the small treasure between his fingers, my lips half parted.

"How beautiful," I said.

"Please take it," he said and handed it to me.

I gazed at the tiny lustrous object with a rainbow of iridescence. Then I looked up at Gaius. I had searched for colorful shells on this beach countless times as a girl and had often come up with wonderful treasures, but never something as lovely as this. It made me wonder all the more about Gaius and his curious link to our island, and I had the strange notion that somehow his destiny had led him to this pearl.

"It is lovely," I said. "Thank you."

"Perhaps you will have it set in a piece of jewelry," he said.

I rolled the pearl in my hand. "I don't know. It is so wonderful the way it is."

We returned the way we had come, and when we entered the house I heard Ian and Nannette's voices coming from the hall. Evidently they had just returned from their outing. Nannette practically bumped into me in the hallway as I was going upstairs to change. I showed her the pearl, which she admired with wide eyes, agreeing that neither had she ever found such a beauty as this. Then she began to chatter about her day.

After dinner, we all gathered in the front parlor. I had changed into my green silk gown for dinner and taken care with my hair. I was beginning to feel rather light-hearted and joyous again, and when Nannette, Lettice and I joined the men in the parlor, I was pleased to see that Richard was there. He and Gaius were sipping port, and I felt my usual apprehension that Richard was going to ignore me, or else leave us all to entertain ourselves.

He had been polite but withdrawn at dinner, only commenting on the bees one of our tenants would soon move to winter quarters, after extracting the summer crop of honey.

As I entered the room, he caught my eye, and I thought I saw a hint of pleasure light his eyes as he glanced at my low-cut bodice and silk flowers trailing from my waist. I felt the urge to cover my exposed shoulders, but the pleasure I felt as he looked at them made me move even more boldly to the love seat where I arranged myself. His eyes dwelled for a moment on the shadow the kerosene lamp above my right shoulder cast on my decollete, and then his eyes rose to my lips and eyes. And then he looked away.

I too turned my head to study the backgammon board unfolded at my left. For I did not want the others to notice the rosiness in my cheeks or the blush that surely must be coloring my skin.

The thoughts Richard's glance stimulated in me were most shameful, and yet I was powerless to fight them. As

I surreptitiously watched him as he, Gaius and Ian began a game of cards, I knew that it was more than just physical attraction, I could not explain it, but it was as if Richard had some hold over my soul, that was frightening as well as exciting.

I tried to pretend I was listening to Nannette as she carried on about her day, out sketching with Ian. He was showing her how to make the broad charcoal strokes, and she went to fetch the drawings she had made, which I had to agree were not half bad for a beginner. But my mind was elsewhere the whole time.

Lettice asked me if I would play the piano, and I rose to take a seat on the small round stool. I remembered many of the pieces I had played on the Van Nuys's piano in New York, but I wanted to avoid playing anything that would remind Ian of that time. So instead I turned to the sheet music that lay on the music stand and selected a familiar ballad.

When I lifted my head, I saw that Richard was watching me from his seat at the card table. The look in his eye was curious, and I hastily looked away. Was it going to become more and more difficult then to dwell under the same roof with Richard? It made me more determined to return to the manor house and take up life there. No doubt there was much to sort out about my feelings for Richard and his intentions as regarded me, and there were the other unanswered questions that only time would explain it seemed.

I concentrated on the keyboard then, and after a rousing rendition of "Oh! Sussanah," I announced that I was ready to go up.

"I believe I'll return to the manor house in another day or so, Lettice," I said. "I'm anxious to see how Sally

Goodsel is getting on under Henrietta's supervision. And I need to look into ordering the new upholstery and wall coverings if I am to get the place into decent living condition."

She looked doubtful, but reached out to squeeze my hand. "I hate to see you go alone," she said.

"I won't be alone. As I said, Henrietta and Sally are there."

I noticed that conversation had fallen off in the room, and everyone was staring at me. My next words were spoken in a rather loud voice in a reactive defiance I suppose.

"After all, it is my own house. I am not going to live in fear of being there."

I happened to glance at Richard when I said it, and noticed his lip jerk back, but whether in annoyance I could not tell. However, he said nothing, but walked to the cabinet to refill his glass from a carafe of brandy.

Ian glanced from Nannette to me, and clearing his throat rose. "If you would like me to accompany you Eileen, I would be only too happy to . . ." His look was solicitous, but I could tell his heart was not in it.

"Thank you, Ian. But I would prefer to be alone. There will be things I need to decide for myself, and I would not be a very companionable hostess."

He looked relieved, and rocked slightly on his heels, hands in pockets. Before anyone else could offer to help me, I said good night and left the room. Lettice followed me out into the hall, calling after me. I turned.

"The Coral Springs clambake is day after tomorrow. Perhaps you'll stay here at least until then."

I was about to protest when I saw Richard watching me from behind Lettice. I suppose I looked for some sign from him. I may have imagined it, but I thought I saw by a slight lift of the brow and anxiousness of expression that he too wished me to remain here.

"Very well," I said. "I'll stay here until then."

As I climbed the stairs, I half hoped there would be the sound of masculine footsteps coming behind me. I reached the top, where I could just hear the voices drifting up from below. But no one came to say a hushed good night at my bedroom door.

On the first weekend in October, the town of Coral Springs held its annual clambake. Everyone was invited, and on Sunday we all rowed over for the festivities.

We walked from the docks to the campground where large green and white tents had been erected at the edge of town to shade the mouth-watering corn on the cob, potatoes, clams and crabs that were roasted over the red-hot stones covered with seaweed. Everyone had brought a covered dish, and the long tables groaned under the weight of sweet potatoes, mashed turnips, salads and casseroles.

We spread blankets on the ground and ate.

"I've never eaten so much in my life," said Nannette, setting her plate aside and lying down in the dappled shade that played over our blanket.

"I hope you've saved room for dessert," I said. "Lettice will be insulted if you don't sample her peach cobbler."

Nannette gave a groan. I too had done my share and was feeling quite full. Just then I saw Ian come back with a second helping. Nannete sat up at his approach, making room for him.

"Ian, how can you put away so much food?" she admonished.

"I don't often have the chance for such delicious food," he said and winked at both of us.

To round off the feed there was hot coffee, tea, fresh rolls, bread and butter pickles and homemade ice cream, cakes and pies. In the afternoon there was a baby-judging contest. Baby buggies were decorated with colored paper flowers, and the little toddlers were dressed in their finery. Small girls were allowed to push the carriages while the beaming mothers looked on.

The sack race had begun when I took my mug of coffee and walked a little way from the tent, looking over the field next to where we picnicked. I walked through the knee-high grass, enjoying the feel of it brushing against my skirt and petticoats.

I could hear someone brushing through the grass behind me and turned to see Gaius, who had stepped away from the crowd and had followed me. He had slung his beige linen sack coat over his shoulders, his white shirt sleeves rolled up over his forearms.

Holding my straw bonnet against the strong breeze, I watched him approach. The peaceful setting soothed me, and I had put away any worries that might have been crowding my mind during the week.

"So," I said, when he had come nearer. "What do you think of the local hospitality."

He grinned disarmingly and rubbed his stomach. "I have no complaints." We walked a little way through the field toward the road, then stopped and watched nature and the others having a good time at the picnic.

"So you are anxious to return to your improvements at the manor house?" he asked.

151

"I am."

He sipped his coffee, gazing off into the distance. I followed his gaze, not wanting to look him in the eye. I had been keeping my distance from Gaius, and though I had not forgotten his surprising declaration of feeling soon after we had met, I did not want to encourage him in that direction. He seemed to be following my thoughts and reached casually for my hand, linking it through his arm, forcing me to half turn toward him.

"Eileen, I hope you consider me your friend. I perhaps overwhelmed you by being too candid when we met. I know it was foolish to hold out hopes for you. But I hope you will not try to avoid me and that you will let me be your companion in the idle moments when you want for nothing more that conversation or someone to pass the time with."

I struggled for appropriate words. "I appreciate your kindness, Gaius."

His look clouded slightly. "I can see that perhaps your heart is not under your own control." He shook his head. "It is too bad that such matters are so often not simple."

His comprehension of the situation surprised me, and I raised my eyes cautiously to him. "I'm afraid you may be right. It is not simple."

"If you don't mind my speaking frankly," he said, "I can see that there is something between you and Richard. I would not interfere under normal circumstances. The oddity of it is that I care about both of you very much, and I am worried for you."

I turned my head away. "I do not expect you to understand. You—" I paused, afraid my words would sound blunt. But I had to tell Gaius how I felt. It would be no good otherwise.

"You are an outsider, Gaius. There are things we are heir to on the island. Outsiders could not feel as we do."

He jerked his chin up and looked outward toward the water across the road again. "That is what I am afraid of."

Something about his words bothered me, but I laughed nervously. "There is nothing to be afraid of. There are things about the Blakemores that even I do not understand."

"Perhaps I could help you understand if you wanted to tell me."

I sighed. "I would like to. But it would not be fair, you would gain nothing by it."

"I would gain by it if I were to help you unburden your thoughts."

"I appreciate your concern," I said. "But I'm afraid there's nothing you can do. Really."

He turned to me. "You are in love with him then."

"Perhaps. I don't know. Something binds us. Perhaps we have some destiny to carry out that we are yet unaware of. Perhaps it is the curse of the island and its mysteries."

He looked at me intently. "Its mysteries?"

I shrugged. "The missing jewels. My sister's and my mother's deaths."

"You do not think the deaths were accidents?"

I paused. "I am not sure. They were a very long time ago. Perhaps we will never know."

He frowned. "The past is done. You and Richard cannot undo it."

I shook my head. "I'm not sure. Sometimes I long to know the truth, and I do not know why. I suppose I can never know what was in my mother's mind before she died or what happened to the jewels, or why Erin had to die. But sometimes I feel as if part of the reason I came back here was to find some of the answers."

He gripped my shoulders, forcing me to look at him. "Eileen, you will drive yourself mad with these questions. You can never know any more than anyone else can. It is already driving Richard mad. I cannot stand by and let you come to the same fate. Can you not let it rest? You have a life to live, you must get away from the island's shadows."

I glanced at his hands on my shoulders and he let go of me. "You are foolish, Eileen. You should go away from here. The island cannot be good for you if all it does is conjure up your ghosts."

I stiffened. "I have nowhere else to go. What family I have left is here."

"*I* could take you somewhere else. I will inherit a business. You know how I feel about you. You do not have to stay here if you do not wish it. Not if you will let me take you away."

He had moved closer to me again, and I trembled at the intensity of feeling behind his words. I knew that a great deal of what he said was perhaps true. But I could not simply run away from everything I had found here since I had come back.

My head fell forward, and he pulled me toward him. I felt confused, grateful for his concern, and guilty that I could not return his feelings. Perhaps he was right. It would make things simple if I went away with him. But I knew in my heart that what I felt for Gaius was not enough. At best I could only offer him friendship, and that might even have been enough to build a marriage on if not for one thing.

I had tasted passion. I was not foolish enough to think that passion alone was enough to live on. I knew that two people had to build a relationship on a foundation of understanding and trust, and I might never find all of that in Richard or even expect him to find it in me. But I could not make a commitment to Gaius or any other man until I knew that the passion I had felt for Richard no longer tempted me. I could not marry one man while yearning for another.

Perhaps my passion would die as I grew older, if it were not fanned by the flames of love. I could not know, but I thought it would be better to waste away unfulfilled than to live out some hellish compromise. The truth was that in my heart I was committed to Richard, whether or not the words had been spoken.

I lifted my head to Gaius and sighed. "I am sorry. I cannot do what you ask me to do. I wish that I could, and I am honored that you care for me. And that you care about Richard as your friend."

I stood back and looked him in the eye. "And perhaps you are right. I am foolish. But it would be even more foolish of me to tell you I could do something I cannot. Until I succeed in answering these questions for myself, I would not be giving all of myself to anyone who wanted me, and I could not ask a man to accept anything less."

He lifted his chin, the exasperation still in his eyes. "Forgive me for losing my temper."

"I think I can understand your losing your temper."

"It is because I care deeply about you."

I shook my head sadly. "It seems we are all trapped by our feelings."

He squared his shoulders and his expression turned philosophical. "I believe one can control one's feelings if

155

one works at it patiently."

"I do not think you are wrong. Certainly a person can master his feelings, and I shall strive to do so. But I cannot promise anything."

He threw back his head in resignation, and I again wondered at my own impracticality. Many women would settle for such an offer, and what had I in the world except a derelict mansion and tenant farmers that may or may not have good crops depending on nature's whims. If I stayed on the island and never came to an understanding with Richard, I might age quickly, and hard work might kill me before my time. But still, I could not ask Gaius to wait until I sorted out my feelings for Richard.

I did not mean to hurt Gaius, but I had to turn his attentions away from me. "You are a strong man with much life to give," I said, trying to smile at him. "You must go on living and find someone else to love."

He did not answer, but rubbed his chin with one hand as we began to walk back toward the gathering, and I felt the regret that flowed between us.

We reached the perimeter of the picnic grounds. Gaius turned and looked at me sadly, then he settled his shoulders and walked away.

No sooner had I returned to the tent, than I saw Richard standing near one of the poles that supported the striped top, hands in pockets. We glanced at each other and then away and I felt the nervousness begin in me the way I always felt when we were together in a crowd. Somehow the intimacy that we experienced when we were alone translated into a feeling of tension when in public. It was as if we were afraid to look at each other, for fear others could read our thoughts. And yet, part of me said that if we felt passion for each other, why not let the world know. Why were we so hesitant to let those feelings show?

A horrid thought crossed my mind. Was it because Richard had no intention of lasting feelings? Was what passed between us when we were alone a fleeting nature, not to be acknowledged by public announcement or the sanctity of marriage? I stared at the pastries on the red-checked table cloth in front of me, certain that my face was red from embarrassment.

Was I really being foolish as Gaius had suggested? If so, and Gaius was still prepared to offer me marriage, then I was doubly a fool. I might let Richard have his way with me and then be left with nothing.

The sinking feeling in my stomach made me feel worse than I had before. I took deep breaths, trying to still the runaway thoughts, but I had circled the table, and Richard came to stand beside me.

As soon as he looked at me, my hesitations fled, and I felt myself warmed by his nearness, as I always was. He reached up to brush a crumb from my cheek.

"Are you enjoying yourself, Eileen?"

I nodded, swallowing, thinking feebly of the thoughts I had had, only a moment before.

"Are you?" I finally asked.

He shrugged, glancing over my head and over the crowd. "It is pleasant enough. But I weary of the conversation. Come, walk with me."

We strolled to the edge of the park and along the road by the water. Richard said very little, and I felt unusually tongue-tied. Somehow the magic that I always felt between us when we were in secluded spots on the island did not quite flow between us today, and I wondered if I had made him angry. I did not have long to wait, however, before he spoke what was on his mind.

"I notice you have been spending quite a bit of time with Gaius. Do you find him that entertaining?"

I pressed my lips together. Was Richard perhaps jealous? "It means nothing, believe me." I exhaled a breath. "He did hint that he had feelings for me, but it is nothing. I am not interested in Gaius Amundsen, if that is what you want to know."

Richard frowned down at me as we walked on, and what he said next surprised me. "I only say this for your own good, Eileen. I think it best if you are not alone with him in the future."

"Why?"

He lifted his chin. "I cannot say. But I do not trust him entirely. I would not trust him with you."

I had to hide a slight grin. Was that it then? Was Richard worried about me losing my virtue? But then my cheeks flamed in embarrassment. Perhaps Richard was already ashamed of what had passed between us and was trying to tell me I should be more careful when with other men. But there was no likelihood that anything like that should pass between Gaius and me. Hadn't I just told him so?

However Richard's words did give me reason to contemplate my actions of late.

"You've no reason to worry," I said lamely. But then some attempt at self-respect began to make me feel angry.

"Why do you say such things about Gaius? Did you not know him at school? Isn't that why he is here?"

"I do not know why he is here."

His words were sharp and made me draw in my breath. I stopped in the road and made him turn to face me.

"Richard, I must know something. There are things

going on here that seem to defy explanation, not the least of which is your friendship with Gaius. If I must say so, he is equally as suspicious of you. I have noticed that the two of you are not close. Why then did he choose to visit our island for his holiday? Why did you invite him?"

"I did not invite him."

I supposed I had expected a more detailed explanation. I felt Richard was holding something back from me, and I felt frustrated by it. Why the hooded expressions, the reticence in our conversations? I was tired of having him deal out little morsels of his thoughts like crumbs from a plate. Did he think me incapable of understanding his deepest reasonings and feelings?

He must have sensed my irritation, for he took my arm and pulled me forward with him. We nodded to passersby. To most of the townspeople out to enjoy the day of fun and relaxation, we probably looked like an ordinary couple out for a stroll. No one could sense the emotion churning in my breast. Life in town looked so simple, so regular. Everyone knowing what they were doing. But it was not so for me. And Richard did not seem disposed to put my mind at ease.

Finally we passed into a lane where a single house sat tucked among the trees. We went a little further on, approaching the sea grass of the bayou. We paused where a low hanging branch from a giant oak offered a seat, and Richard steered me to it.

I sat, while he propped his foot on the branch, leaning on the trunk for support. He took a deep breath, gazed out over the water for a moment, and then finally brought his attention back to me.

"Very well," he said. "I'll tell you what I know of

159

Gaius Amundsen."

Until then, the day had been so pleasant that I had almost forgotten all my forebodings. It was so pleasurable to feel part of such a pleasant community with no other purpose than to enjoy the day and to sample the delights that all the housewives had outdone themselves to bring.

But looking at Richard as he stared off into the distance, the sun catching that odd phosphorescence in his eye, my spirits settled back into a level of contemplation that I had been used to experiencing since I had been home. We were no ordinary family with an ordinary past. I clenched my jaw slightly. Not that I had not realized that before, but seeing our group in the midst of the other townspeople, I realized unhappily that there was something that set us apart. It was not wealth or social status, but some innate secret, some horror that prevented the others from truly opening themselves up to us as friends. For as cordial as the townspeople were, they kept a distance from all of the Blakemores. A polite respect that none of us seemed to break through.

Nannette came the closest with her vivaciousness. It was as if she alone refused to acknowledge that the Blakemores had any special heritage or any memories to drag on our frivolity and well-being.

I felt the resentment boiling upward. Surely other families experienced tragedy and death. How many generations did it take to lay the dead to rest and get on with life? The world did not wait on ghosts of the past, no matter how they cried out to be acknowledged.

But my thoughts were turning morbid, and I wanted Richard to communicate to me what was on his mind. I leaned back against the rough bark of the tree and tilted my head up to him.

"Go on," I said. "You were going to speak of Gaius."

He looked at me almost as if he had forgotten my presence and my words reminded him that I was there. He shrugged and lowered his foot from where it had been propped up on the limb where I sat. He lounged next to me against the tree.

"Yes. Gaius Amundsen. There is not much to tell. He claims his family owns a shipping firm in New York."

"Claims?"

"I never met his family, and I've seen nothing to indicate whether or not his story is true."

"How strange."

"We met at school, and I suppose he seemed a nice enough chap. We rowed together on a team, and he always seemed ready for a chat in the evenings just to get away from the books."

"Then you must have gotten to know him rather well."

"I am beginning to see that I did not." He looked at me strangely. "It was only an illusion."

"But you shared rooms, didn't you?"

"Yes, in our senior year. Still, I would not say we were close."

I pressed my lips together, wanting to raise the issue of Gaius's accusations again, but not wanting to upset Richard by doing it. Still, I could not let the opportunity pass.

"That was when," I hesitated, glancing at Richard, "when Gaius said you sometimes took things. But I know you said it wasn't true."

I saw Richard's jaw thrust forward, and a spark of anger kindle in his eye. "I did not take things as he so unkindly puts it."

His words puzzled me. "What do you mean? Did you borrow them then?"

"No. You see I wondered about Gaius even then. I admit I rifled his letter box a time or two, trying to see where his letters from home came from. He may have noticed."

"That's all?"

"Yes of course." He looked at me sharply, causing me to stammer.

"Then . . . that . . . that must explain it."

We sat in perplexity for some moments. Then Richard turned his face to me, and the corners of his lips lifted slightly. His look was clear and direct, and it made my heart lift.

"Come now," he said, reaching for my hand. "It is not right of me to spoil such a lovely day with such morbid thoughts. I am only being overprotective of you. I meant only to tell you to watch yourself with Gaius. You can not be sure of his intentions."

Any more than I can be sure of yours, I wanted to say, but did not. Instead I only met his gaze as my heart pumped harder within my chest, and I was again aware of the many things that bound me to Richard, though I wondered if any of them could be considered love.

He drew me off the tree limb, and we walked slowly back to the road. I suppose I was disappointed that he did not take me to some more peaceful isolated spot, and I was disappointed that he did not seem to want to dally longer in my presence. Though I could sense a warmth in the hand that held mine until we reached the road, none of the passion that had flowed between us before was present.

The thought sent me into an equally unreasonable

depression. Perhaps I had been foolish to expect more from him. Perhaps the desire we seemed to feel for each other was a passing thing. Richard, being a man of the world, would know of such things. I was fortunate that I had not let things progress any further between us.

Of course I was his cousin, not some attractive face that he might meet somewhere, spend a few hours doing what he would and then forget. Perhaps it was for the best that we had both struggled with our feelings that day, putting them aside when temptation seemed too much to deny.

Yet I dared hope that out of that passion would grow something more enduring. Richard's stoic demeanor at present gave me no reason to hope for such a thing. I suppose I was beginning to feel rather sorry for myself, even if the more rational part of my mind told me that this was for the best. And of course I could blame my actions the day of my accident on my rattled state of mind.

Perhaps Richard would never come near me again in such a manner, recognizing that in my right mind I would not have behaved so. I did not know whether I experienced relief at the thought or disappointment.

We both put on our most social expressions to rejoin the group near the tent. The games and races were over, and we threaded our way back to the blanket. I saw that Ian and Nannette sat near our picnic basket, their heads bent in a very deep discussion. They were not aware of our approach, and when I finally stepped onto the blanket, they both looked up guiltily, and Nannette's cheeks turned crimson.

I had never seen Nannette blush. I glanced at Ian, who could not meet my gaze. Nannette began to fuss with the picnic things, making spurious conversation.

"There you are," she said. "We've packed everything up as Mother thought it best if we left while it is still high tide."

She glanced quickly at Richard, and I wondered if I imagined it, but there seemed to be some meaningful communication that passed between them, though what it could be I did not know. I could have taken Ian's guilty look to mean nothing more than that he had been caught flirting with my cousin.

I had tried to let him know that where he put his attentions did not matter to me, since there was nothing between us anymore, and I would have thought that had there been anything serious developing between Nannette and my erstwhile flame, she would have come to me to confide, as she had been so used to doing when we were younger.

But I had the strange feeling, ever so brief, that what happened at that moment was something else entirely, even though I could not name the feeling nor its source.

However, I reached for my bonnet, which I had left lying on the blanket and said, "then I will find Lettice so we can go."

On the way back I sat next to Ian in the boat, for Gaius and Richard rowed, while Nannette and Lettice sat in the bow. I watched the two former college roommates apply their weight to the oars, and as their forearm muscles strained and the tiny droplets from the oars occasionally sprayed our faces, I could see that they were well-matched as oarsmen.

Gaius Amundsen, I thought as I watched him pull with large, sure strokes on the undulating water, *what is it you want from our family?*

Chapter 12

I was determined to return to the manor house, and so after the picnic I had Riggin drive me over. Henrietta welcomed me and reported that Sally Goodsel was doing rather well, though she was still clumsy with utensils and tools she wasn't used to.

They had scoured the music room and the hallway in that wing, even polishing the gargoyles on the wall sconces in that narrow corridor. I found that being back here revitalized my enthusiasm for my project, and we began talking of wall coverings.

I could see that Henrietta had been troubled by the news of my accident, and I did my best to reassure her that it was nothing, and that I was quite fit now.

I could not tell if Sally was glad to see me or not. When I sent for her to find out how she was progressing, she came hesitantly into the room, her eyes round. I felt as if I were some freak, the way she stared at me, and I could not imagine that the small scab that still showed across the corner of my brow merited such fascination.

"What are you looking at Sally? Surely I have not changed so much in the short time I was gone."

She dipped her head. "I'm sorry, Miss. It's just that I

heard what happened to you. Scared the daylights out of me it did."

"What? That the carriage wrecked in the trees? Surely you've heard of such accidents before. I'm afraid I simply lost control of the horses."

She chanced a look at me, though her head was still lowered in an attitude of humility. "Beggin' your pardon, Miss. It wasn't the wreck that was so frightful. It was the way it happened."

I stiffened. So the gossip had spread already. I sometimes wondered how it was that events that occurred in places like this somehow became known, and interpreted before one could announce the fact oneself. But the grapevine that existed, especially in isolated places such as this seemed to be the most effective method of communication we had. Though in some instances, such as this one, the rapidity with which the story had flown about troubled me.

"And what have you heard about the way it happened?"

She looked out from under her eyelashes at me again as if afraid to tell me the version she had heard. I had tensed slightly, for I knew instinctively that there must be something awful about what she was going to tell me, and yet as mistress of the manor it was my duty to ferret out idle gossip and stop it from spreading.

"Come, tell me what you've heard. I must know what the talk is among the servants."

"You won't punish me for bein' superstitious?"

I could feel the hairs on the back of my neck tingle, and yet I was determined to keep our conversation light.

"Well, perhaps we all have our superstitions, but you must tell me yours, so I can help you understand if they

166

are not founded on reason."

It sounded wise, and I wondered if I could live up to such a lofty sentiment. I motioned for her to step closer.

"Come over here Sally, so I can hear what you have to say."

She seemed to gain more courage and crept forward. "It's just that they say it was something odd that frightened the horses."

I twitched my lip. "Well, I suppose it was. It was the cat that frightened them, if you want to know."

She nodded slowly still looking at me oddly. "The white cat."

"Yes, Pericles. But it's not so odd really. He's been here many years. Why he must be nearly eighteen years old."

But my bluff wasn't fooling her. She knew as well as I did that the odd thing about it was that the cat had been so far from the house and her next words confirmed it.

"But it's a domestic cat, least that's what Mrs. Hodgson says."

I knew Hodgson was one of the tenant farmers.

Sally went on. "And a domestic cat don't roam so far in the woods."

"Perhaps not. Unless someone brought it there."

I clamped my mouth shut. I hadn't meant to voice this suspicion in front of a servant. I could just imagine how the talk would fly now. But apparently my idea was nothing new. For Sally eyed me.

"'Xactly right. That's what she said."

"I see."

I didn't quite know how to form the next question without unnerving the girl further, and I was having difficulty remaining in control of the situation, when it was she who seemed to have all the information I wanted.

"And tell me," I asked. "Are there any rumors about why anyone on the island would want to cause such an accident?"

Her cheeks flared with color and she bit her underlip, refusing to meet my gaze. I walked nearer, touching her chin with my forefinger so she would look at me.

I arched an eyebrow at her. "I see there is. Well, you'd better tell me then." I lowered my hand to my hip and waited.

Tears seemed to form in the corners of her eyes then, and to my surprise, she began to tremble.

"Don't be afraid, Sally," I said. "Tell me what is on your mind."

"It's just that I'm afraid you'll be angry with me," she blubbered.

"Don't be ridiculous. I can hardly be angry with you, if you have a warning for me that might be for my own good."

She swallowed and seemed to try to raise her chin.

"Who do they say might have caused such an accident?"

She looked at me quickly then said, looking at the floor, "Master Blakemore."

I dropped my mouth open, hardly knowing what to say. A slow nervous agitation began in my stomach that turned into anger, nearly making me tremble, but I tried to keep my voice normal.

"And why do they say that?"

"He was the one who brought you back, wasn't he?"

"Yes. Luckily he was rowing nearby, and saw me lying on the ground and came to my rescue." *Richard would never harm me,* I wanted to cry, but I kept my decorum in front of the girl.

"That's just it, Miss, you see. He happened to be there, so he might have brought the cat with him."

"Oh that's preposterous. Why would he do such a thing?"

She shook her head. "I don't know, Miss. It's just that he's taken that cat with him before. I've seen him."

Now I stared at the girl. My defense of Richard crumbled at this new piece of information, and my words lost some of their authority.

"You've seen Richard with the cat?"

She nodded. "Twice. He had it in a box beside him in the carriage like he was takin' it somewhere."

I swallowed. "I see." I wiped my hands on my skirt and stood. "Thank you, Sally, for what you've told me. But don't worry. I'm sure Master Blakemore meant me no harm. I'm sure there's an explanation as to how Pericles came to be in the woods." And I was determined to find out what it was.

She looked at me uncertainly.

"You may go."

She hurried out, leaving me in this new quandry. It was shocking to think of Richard carrying the cat away from here. Where had he been taking it? I tried to tell myself there was a logical explanation, and I would ask him about it the first chance I got.

If Richard had taken the cat away, how had it come to be back here after my father had died? I shivered and rubbed my arms together. No one had seen Pericles or thought about his whereabouts since the day I took my fall. I glanced around the room nervously as if fearing to see him appear suddenly. But there was no sound of soft paws on the pine floorboards or the sight of a long tail

169

swishing across the rug.

Had Pericles found his way home after scaring the horses that day? Or was he still out there in the woods? Somehow at the moment I did not care to know.

In the evening I turned my mind to other matters and spent a few hours perusing mail order catalogues. I lost myself in bronze hardware, hinges, keyholes, and drawer pulls. I would have to inventory the rooms I planned to redo to see which hardware needed replacing. It soothed my mind to let my eye roam over the intricate designs on the bronze pieces that had been cast in plaster molds lined with wax.

I knew that other metals were also used in the so-called lost wax casting process. My father had once told me that it was more expensive to use cheaper metals because they had to be replaced more often. Therefore, I was not tempted by the advertisements of Geneva bronze, which was merely iron made to look like bronze. I ran my finger down the page as if I could feel the raised figurative designs on the drawings of doorknobs and locks. If I ordered any of these pieces they would be the true bronze.

I also considered what I might do to modernize the manor house. I would have to ask Henrietta if all our bellpulls were in working order. The catalogues showed the more expensive system of speaking tubes. There was no possibility of using electricity on the island unless I installed a generator, which I could not afford to do at present.

That thought made me consider my father again. He had always seemed the kind of man to want to experiment with all the new inventions. Had he not built a generator on the island because it was too expensive to be practical, or had he simply preferred the use of kerosene and beeswax candles? I decided that it must have been the impracticality of installing electricity that had prevented him from doing so.

Likewise, he had never put in gas pipes to light and heat our rooms, and the island had no gas works, but I was glad it did not. The homes in New York that were lit by gas got filthy from the soot that covered the ceilings, and all the upholstery, carpets and drapes had to be taken outside to be cleaned every year. I could see why Father had kept the manor without these modern conveniences, for though we had less light, there was far less work required to clean all the rooms than if we had used gas.

Instead of gasoliers, my father had put in hanging kerosene lamps, and in the main rooms downstairs, kerosene chandeliers hung from the ceilings.

But perhaps someday when we could afford it, I would install electricity. I imagined these rooms lit by the sparkling, clean lights that, once installed, were not at all unsightly as long as the wires were well hidden.

At least my father had had forethought when it came to the necessary room, for he had put in the modern conveniences of plumbing. In the upstairs necessary room was a china basin set in marble and a metal-lined wood encased bathtub. I thought that in that room I would have to repaint the wainscotting and select new wallpaper to put on the upper half of the walls.

We had two water closets, one upstairs and one down, with sturdy porcelain toilets, wooden tanks and pull chains. I did study the lavatory furnishings in the mail order catalogue, marking off items such as the nickel tumbler and soap holders, and kerosene wall brackets that I might need. I would pay attention to the design of these items, making sure that they coordinated with the geometric or floral patterns I might select for curtains and wall paper.

By ten o'clock, my eyes were drooping, and my lamp had burned low. I got ready for bed and finally extinguished my light.

I had had such a peaceful evening, that I should have slept well, but I tossed and turned instead. A dog howling somewhere kept me awake, and a ward's heron flew over, giving its harsh call. And as the wind came up, the creaks and moans of the house disturbed me.

But though I slept badly, I rose as the light was just barely visible through my drawn curtains. And though I had not slept well, still I experienced a sense of vigor, for in spite of the strangeness that seemed to surround me, I was excited by the prospect of being mistress of my own home, even one as unwieldly and full of old memories as this one.

I thought for an instant of how much warmer a place it would be if I had a family here, but I would not let myself dwell on such a thought. For any such thought made me think of Richard and set the dormant warmth in me to flame, and I could not be distracted by those wayward notions of mine.

And so I rose and dressed in a practical calico gown and went out to the kitchens to find that Henrietta and Sally had the place bustling. Henrietta dished up a platter of bacon and grits for me, and I poured fresh milk from the pitcher and tore off a piece of bread hot from the brick oven we used for baking in the hearth.

"I think I shall select wall covering for the music room

172

and the west wall," I said between bites, blotting the melted butter that had smeared at the corner of my mouth.

Henrietta thought she had a sample book from which I could order. In order to overcome the darker, moodier look of the room, I planned to select one overall paper in an attractive repeating pattern, then a plainer paper for trim above the chair rail and a complimentary ceiling paper. With the dark woodwork that was already in place, I thought it would create a pleasing effect. Then after having the piano repaired and replacing the ivory keys that were broken, I would brighten that room with melodies.

My spirit seemed to infuse Henrietta and Sally, and I got them moving to their chores with alacrity. We would do the initial cleaning, inventory and ordering. Riggin could take care of repairs to broken or cracked plaster and do any carpenter work as well as replace fixtures, but I supposed I would need to hire someone who was handy with hanging wallpaper.

I had tasks to occupy me throughout the day, stopping only for nourishment at one o'clock. I had barely noticed the covering of gray clouds that moved across the sky, as if God were pulling a shade over the sunlit blue dome above. The hall upstairs, where I worked was quiet, and soon Henrietta passed behind me to light some lamps for me to see by. Then she returned downstairs.

I was humming to myself and then suddenly stopped and turned, for I thought I had heard a tread on the stairs. But there was no one in the hallway. I was near my father's sitting room and went in. As soon as I stepped into the room, my skin prickled, though there was nothing that should have frightened me. It was more a sense of uneasiness such as I had felt when I'd been alone in this room before.

However, I straightened my spine and passed through the sitting room to my father's bedroom. I eyed the conservative print of mauve wallpaper with its repetitive oriental birds. While it blended with the heavy carved bedstead with its towering headboard, the massive marble-topped dresser with built-in, full-length mirror, and marble-topped nightstand, I found the effect of the room with the heavy tufted coverlet and dark carpet to be stultifying.

I was not sure I could bring myself to redecorate the room, for it reminded me so much of my father. Not that I approved of the morbid habit some people had of leaving rooms of the deceased as they had been while the person was living. In such houses, it was as if one expected the dead to return and take up the hairbrushes or shaving kits left exactly where they had been. This house had enough reminders of those who had gone on without leaving these rooms like a mausoleum.

In that spirit then I might see what I could do to brighten this room. Yet I found as I surveyed the furnishings and decorative motifs, I could not concentrate the way I had been doing before. My thoughts remained scattered, and I could not organize them into any sort of plan. I shook myself where I stood in the center of the room near the foot of the large bed.

It was almost as if I had lost the ability to think as I wished in this room, as if someone else was directing my thoughts. The notion was unsettling, and I was about to give up and return to my own room.

I had half turned to see my own reflection in the tall mirror that hung in its frame above the dresser, next to the door. The light from the lamps in the hall flickered into the room casting gloomy shadows around me.

Then my hammering heart seemed to stop beating and my gaze froze on a shadow in the shape of a skeleton hand that I watched in the mirror as it rose slowly behind me, fingers outstretched, as it reached in an arc over my head, moved across the wall and down again on my other side.

I gave a blood-curdling scream and clapped my hands over my mouth. I turned around to stare at the wall behind me, but the shadow was gone.

I seemed frozen to the spot, not knowing what awful specter had caused that shadow. From the way it had been reflected in the mirror, the shadow had to have been cast by something in the hallway. I knew I should go and see what was there, but my feet would not move me. The fact that it had been the shadow of a skeleton hand frightened me too much.

Then I heard running steps on the stairs, and this time they were human. Henrietta burst into the room with Sally right behind her.

"Good heavens, Miss Eileen, what's happened? Are you all right?" She rushed over to me, and I grasped her outstretched hands and tried to speak.

"I'm . . . I'm all right. I had a scare that's all."

She drew me to the bed and made me sit on the edge. "Sit down, you are white as a sheet. Sally, go get the smelling salts."

"No, it's quite all right, Sally, I shan't faint."

Henrietta was fanning me with my apron, and her own face was pale. Sally stood with her back to the wall, her eyes round as they usually were when she was frightened, and I noticed that she too was trembling.

175

I started to ask them if they had seen the arm and hand of a skeleton, but evidently they had not, otherwise they would have said so. I hesitated to tell them of this new occurrence, for fear that there were just too many odd things that were going on in this place, so my mind raced to conceive an acceptable truth that was not too horrifying.

I gulped air and began to breathe more normally. Meanwhile, my pulse slowed to a more normal rate. "It was just a shadow, actually. I overreacted."

Henrietta frowned. "A shadow. What kind of shadow?"

I fumbled for an explanation. "It was probably a trick of light on that wall." I pointed. "I was looking at myself in the mirror when the shadow passed behind me, in a sort of arc. And I jumped."

She looked at me, then at the mirror. She took a few steps away as if considering what I had said. Her conclusion was the same as mine had been.

"Then the shadow came from something in the hallway."

I had regained control over myself enough to notice that Sally was quaking where she stood, and though I was still frightened myself, I did not want to say too much in front of the girl. I composed myself long enough to dismiss her.

"I'm quite all right now, Sally. You may go."

But she stood dumbly where she was, her eyes wide. "If it was in the hall," she finally stammered out. "I don't want to go out there alone."

I tried to give a nonchalant laugh. "Now Sally, I believe I was mistaken in what I saw. It was probably just the flickering of light from one of the lamps that went out

MORE PASSION AND ADVENTURE AWAIT... YOUR TRIP TO A BIG ADVENTUROUS WORLD BEGINS WHEN YOU ACCEPT YOUR FIRST 4 NOVELS ABSOLUTELY *FREE* (AN $18.00 VALUE)

Accept your Free gift and start to experience more of the passion and adventure you like in a historical romance novel. Each Zebra novel is filled with proud men, spirited women and temptuous love that you'll remember long after you turn the last page.

Zebra Historical Romances are the finest novels of their kind. They are written by authors who really know how to weave tales of romance and adventure in the historical settings you love. You'll feel like you've actually gone back in time with the thrilling stories that each Zebra novel offers.

GET YOUR FREE GIFT WITH THE START OF YOUR HOME SUBSCRIPTION

Our readers tell us that these books sell out very fast in book stores and often they miss the newest titles. So Zebra has made arrangements for you to receive the four newest novels published each month.

You'll be guaranteed that you'll never miss a title, and home delivery is so convenient. And to show you just how easy it is to get Zebra Historical Romances, we'll send you your first 4 books absolutely FREE! Our gift to you just for trying our home subscription service.

BIG SAVINGS AND FREE HOME DELIVERY

Each month, you'll receive the four newest titles as soon as they are published. You'll probably receive them even before the bookstores do. What's more, you may preview these exciting novels free for 10 days. If you like them as much as we think you will, just pay the low preferred subscriber's price of just $3.75 each. *You'll save $3.00 each month off the publisher's price.* AND, your savings are even greater because there are never any shipping, handling or other hidden charges—FREE Home Delivery. Of course you can return any shipment within 10 days for full credit, no questions asked. There is no minimum number of books you must buy.

suddenly. Here, I'll show you."

It took some courage for me to step into the hallway, but I was determined not to fall apart before the servants. I had to satisfy myself that nothing was wrong, and now that the two others were with me, I had a modicum more bravery than if I had been alone.

Of course the eerie feeling that something had caused the skeleton hand made me tremble inwardly, but my instincts told me that right now the important thing was to reassure Sally. For if she feared something macabre, it would spread to the entire island, so well aware was I now of the gossip chain. For the sake of the island's economy, I could not risk frightening all the tenants off the island.

Already, anger was replacing my fear. Anger at whoever or whatever cast its shadow over the manor house. My new emotion braced me to confront whatever evil lurked there, for some part of me knew instinctively that if the source of evil was confronted head on, it dissipated. That it was effective only against helpless victims. But when ferreted out into the light of day, there could be no contest.

Of course my philosophical view did not completely erase the nervousness I felt as we stepped into the hall. I looked for some dark specter to reach for us all and to squelch the life from us. But nothing of the kind happened.

We stood in the hall, Henrietta's expression doubtful and perplexed as mine must have been.

"You see," I said in a rather loud voice. "There is nothing here."

Sally's eyes darted along the hallway and she shrank back against the door. Then she raised an unsteady arm and pointed toward the dark end of the hallway that led toward some of the guest rooms we had not yet opened.

Out of the shadows came Pericles, creeping softly along the hallway, his tail curving slowly back and forth. I drew in my breath, my skin crawling as I reacted in preparation for another attack. But none came.

Pericles sat before us blinking, I thought, with a malevolent look in green eyes that suddenly, frighteningly, reflected the yellow light from the lamps.

Chapter 13

"You see," I said, refusing to let Pericles intimidate me. "It is only the cat."

But Sally only stared, her jaw hanging open. I faced both she and Henrietta squarely, refusing to let whatever superstitions existed about this cat overcome me and cause havoc in my house. Pericles did not look particularly friendly where he sat, but neither did he look like the embodiment of an evil spirit. Still Sally stammered, staring at him where he sat wagging his tail.

"That cat." She pointed. Still, I tried to allay her fears.

"Yes, I'm sure I just saw his shadow and thought it was something else." I knew that it was impossible for a cat to make a shadow of a skeleton hand, but I did not say so.

Henrietta looked at me sideways, and I believe she knew what I was trying to accomplish.

"Come along Sally, now that we've settled this we must leave Miss Blakemore to get some rest before supper. We haven't time to be standing about the halls staring at this pesky animal, for he's no more than that."

Then she said to me. "I can have Riggin get rid of the cat if you like, Miss. It seems it has been a troublesome animal."

I imagined Riggin drowning Pericles or shooting the cat in its head and I shuddered.

"I'll think about it Henrietta. He seems harmless enough at the moment."

She looked doubtfully down at the white animal now licking his paws. "If you say so, Miss."

She gave me one more look, narrowing her eyes slightly as if speculating as to what was on my mind. I had not noticed the sharpness of her gaze before, and though her knowing look probably came from the fact that we were both trying to calm Sally Goodsel before she ran out of the place and refused to set foot in it again, I thought I saw a brief flash of cunning in my housekeeper's eyes that I had never seen before. But it might have been attributed to my imagination, for I was still rattled.

However, I sent them on their way and went along to my own room to rest and sort out my thoughts while I changed for supper.

Once in my own room, I closed the door. I glanced at the keyhole, wondering if I should lock it, then shook my head, once again fighting the ubiquitous threats that seemed to pervade this place. I gritted my teeth and walked to the center of the room. I would not live in fear.

I sat down at my dresser, shaking in spite of my resolve to appear calm before Henrietta and Sally. A skeleton hand. I had not imagined it. How then had it come to be? There was no skeleton risen up from some grave walking about the house. The very thought struck enough terror in me to cause me to grip the top of my dresser with both hands for support.

No, it had been some sort of illusion. Another possible explanation occurred to me. Someone very much alive might have created the illusion to frighten me. But who?

There was no one in the house except for Henrietta, Sally and myself, and perhaps Riggin from time to time. Had someone else come here and hidden themselves? If so they might still be here.

I finished dressing for supper and, summoning my courage, decided that if there were someone in the house that I didn't know about I should at least attempt to find them.

I stepped out into the hallway and with great trepidation I walked past my father's rooms once again and came to the next door, which had been my mother's bedroom. We had already opened this room and had aired it out. Still, my hand hesitated on the doorknob. But I made myself swing open the door, which creaked on its hinges.

The room was dim, as the evening light without was fading. But nothing sprang out at me. I didn't know if I had the courage to enter and look in the tall wardrobe that stood to one side of the room, but I made myself do it. Some of my mother's gowns still hung there, and I remembered Nannette's comment that I should consider altering some of them for myself.

I glanced at the four-poster and dropped to it, looking under the bed. There was nothing. I rose, left the room and shut the door behind me. Quickly I made a search of the guest rooms at that end of the hall, and though some of them were still musty, with shrouds over the furniture. There was no threat either human or supernatural, and neither did I have the sensation of uneasiness that usually accompanied my suspicions of another presence near beside myself.

My instincts told me that whatever the threat had been, it was gone now. I was relieved of course, and yet troubled that I had not solved the mystery of who or what had caused it. But I raised my chin and marched down the hallway toward the stairs whispering aloud, "Whoever or whatever you are, you have not bested me yet."

Nannette surprised us the next day with a visit. She had come wearing a checked gingham work dress and announced that she wanted to help with the work.

"Oh come now, Nannette," I said after greeting her with a hug. "You cannot mean that. Have you run out of things to do at the cottage so soon?"

She gave a shrug. "They can do without me. Gaius and Richard went hunting, and Ian decided to row over to the mainland. I decided you and I hadn't had a chat in a while."

I pushed some of my stray hair back behind my ear. It had come loose from my coif, for I had been busy in the house since just after the sun rose.

"If you mean it, I'm sure I can use your help. I'll show you the wallpapers I've selected for some of the rooms. I could use your artistic eye."

She smiled. "Good."

I led her into the study where I had catalogues spread over my father's desk along with my notes and plans. She surveyed the headquarters of my industry and shook her head.

"My goodness you are serious about this, aren't you?"

I chuckled. "Yes. I suppose you could say I never do things in half-measures. But I haven't offered you any refreshment. What would you like?"

"A cup of tea sounds tempting. I don't mind if we get it ourselves. You've probably got poor Henrietta running her legs off."

I laughed, realizing how refreshing it was to have Nannette's company. I was truly glad she had come.

We made our way out the back of the house and along the dogtrot to the kitchen and, lighting the stove, I put on the iron tea kettle. We gossipped away while the water heated, and then I poured boiling water into the china teapot so the tea could steep. I told Nannette of the plans for the house, refraining from mentioning any further threats. Neither did we bring up the night we had seen the horseman in the storm.

I soon noticed, however, that underneath our chatter there was a sense of strain, as if we both wanted to seem carefree and gay, but in reality did not feel that way.

"And so you are determined to stay here, Eileen?" she finally asked.

I nodded, placing my hands around the teapot, absorbing some of its warmth. "This is my home after all. The longer I am here, the less I can imagine living anywhere else."

"Hmmm."

She nodded in agreement, but I noticed the shadow that crossed her eyes. I felt my reserve melting and suddenly wanted to confide in Nannette. I had kept all my innermost thoughts to myself for so long that I suddenly longed to unburden myself. To each person I was associated with here I was only able to reveal a part of myself, and I realized how comforting it would be to be able to talk with someone frankly, holding nothing back.

Perhaps it was Nannette's ingenuity that made me sense she was the person I could do this with. I knew that Lettice wanted me to confide in her, but at times I hated to add to Lettice's burdens by telling her my troubles.

And there was still a sense of distance between myself and Lettice that I did not feel I had bridged. It was as if she, herself, held secrets in her breast that she would not share with me.

No, Nannette's live and let live attitude seemed far more suitable for me. Her hopefulness might be able to shed light on the dark places in my mind and dismiss old superstitions. I told her about the skeleton hand shadow.

"I suppose not everyone agrees that I should stay here," I began.

She frowned, glancing at me sharply. "You mean because someone is trying to frighten you away."

I nodded. It was no use pretending with Nannette that the strange events that had befallen me were merely accidents. I leaned forward, my words almost a plea.

"Nannette, can you think of why anyone would want to frighten me?"

She studied me seriously for a moment. Her words surprising me. "I am not sure."

"What do you mean?"

She glanced around the kitchen as if to see if anyone else were listening, then she leaned forward slightly.

"There's something strange about this place, Eileen. I don't see how you can stay in it alone."

"You mean that you too think some malevolent spirit is causing these disturbances?"

Her brow wrinkled slightly. "Well, they say that a spirit can inhabit a place, particularly if it isn't happy."

Her words made the hair on the back of my neck stand on end, for the same idea had been in my thoughts.

"You mean that there's some reason for the spirit to remain here."

She nodded.

I shook my head. I had considered the possibility, but

if spirits were haunting Calayeshi Island I had no way to know who they were. There had been no real consistency to the strange occurrences I had witnessed, and for some reason I had a hard time believing the threats were from supernatural causes, and I told Nannette as much.

"I can't explain it myself," I said. "But I think I would know if my mother or father or even if poor Erin were trying to tell me something. They are my own flesh and blood, and I think I would know if they were trying to communicate with me. And I can think of no reason why my own family would harbor malice for me." I shook my head slowly. "No, I'm afraid of something worse."

I raised my eyes to her and saw that her face had lost some of its color, her mouth twitched slightly, and a doubtful expression filled her eyes.

"What are you afraid of?" Her words were spoken timidly, unlike the Nannette I was used to.

I hated to say what I thought, but I felt that Nannette would not be so easily put off the island by rumors of evildoing. She had the island in her blood, the same as I.

"Someone means me malice."

She seemed to shrink into her chair. "You mean someone who is here now."

"Yes, it would have to be."

I watched her as she seemed to consider the idea. It became apparent to me that the notion was not new to her, but that I was making her confront the possibility, whereas before she could hide her fears in notions of ghosts.

"But who?" she asked, her eyes pinched.

I shook my head. "I don't know. Neither can I fathom why." I put down my teacup. "Nannette, you've been at the cottage more than I. You must tell me the truth, as hard as it might be. Has anyone told you they did not

185

want me here for any reason?"

She dropped her gaze, but shook her head. "Not really."

I stiffened. Something in her answer made me think there was more to this than she was admitting. I reached for her hand, making her start.

"Nannette, think. Has anyone dropped a hint, even if they did not mean to say it directly? I know it sounds preposterous that any of your family or even Ian or Gaius for that matter would want me off the island. It makes no sense. Neither does it make sense that any of the servants or any of the tenants would want me gone. Surely everyone can see that I mean to improve life here. No one would benefit by my going."

"Yes, of course," she said, slightly breathless as if agreeing too readily. "It cannot be anyone like that."

I leaned back. "Then it has to be a phantom or else someone who is hiding, some unknown menace?"

Suddenly, I felt frustrated by this useless speculation and rose to pace in front of the kitchen table. An uncomfortable thought pushed itself into the forefront of my mind. I had been trying to ignore it, but since I had resolved to confide in Nannette, I might as well say it. And besides, she had the look about her that she wasn't being completely honest with me, though I truly believed that her reticence was born of a concern for my well-being, not out of any wish to lie.

"Some say," I said, "that it is not safe for me to be alone with your brother. Do you think so, Nannette?"

She winced, and I could see the indecision in her eyes. I felt the nervousness that seemed to unsettle my stomach.

"What is it, Nannette? You must tell me."

Her face reddened in embarrassment, and I felt a new fear. Perhaps my growing affection for Richard was obvious, and she wanted to warn me not to make a fool of myself.

"Tell me, Nannette."

I had lost my patience and felt the whine creep into my voice and instantly shut my mouth. But my insistence had won out, and she finally explained herself, though what she said did no more to put me at ease.

"First you must tell me something, Cousin."

"What do you wish to know?"

"I don't mean to pry, Eileen. But I admit I am worried about Richard. I thought I sensed that you cared for him. Is it true?"

I cocked my head in admission. "I had thought I felt a sort of rapport with your brother. I don't mind admitting it. I hope I have not been foolish. I do not know if he feels the same."

She shook her head. "I think he does, if you want to know the truth. I have seen the way he looks at you. It is not that I am worried about."

"What then?"

She pressed her lips together as if trying to find the right words. Then she looked up at me. "Oh, Eileen, I would never say this if I didn't love you both, you must believe me."

"Of course. Go on."

"Well, since I've been back to the island I've noticed that Richard is different somehow. He seems rather withdrawn, as if he's in his own world most of the time."

"Perhaps it is just the many responsibilities of the estate he has taken on."

She shrugged. "I don't know. It seems more than that.

After all our stepfather died some time ago. Richard's been running the estate for three years. I do not think it is that that is weighing on him." She looked at me oddly. "I do not think it is anything so simple."

A tremor started within me, and I tried to remain calm as I said, "Do you mean that you think something less tangible than overwork is troubling him?"

She nodded, eyeing me shrewdly, waiting for me to take her meaning. I might as well say it then. I was tired of everyone hinting at Richard's instability yet not coming straight out with it.

"Nannette, do you believe there is something wrong with Richard? That he is crazy?"

I could see the moistness gather in her eyes, and I could tell that she cared a great deal about her brother. But she nodded.

"Yes. Oh I don't know how to explain it, Eileen. It's just that he seems so distracted lately. There is a strange look in his eye sometimes, almost as if he doesn't recognize me. Of course you wouldn't notice it. It's been so many years since you've been around him."

I didn't want to tell her that I had noticed it myself. It was frightening the way Richard seemed to be with me one moment, and then not himself the next moment.

"I don't know," was all I said. "I admit that sometimes he does seem distracted. But he has always been a rather private person, Nannette. There is the possibility that he has something on his mind that he has not told any of us about. He may be worried about something. You are right to be concerned, and we must try to coax his concerns out of him. It can do him no good to keep them bottled up inside of him."

I had clenched my fists in my skirts as I said it, feeling the remorse and anger swirl within me again. *Dear, dear, Richard,* my mind cried silently. *Please don't let there be anything wrong with you.*

Aloud I said. "If Richard is troubled perhaps all he needs is time. He may confide in one of us, if we are patient." Then a new thought occurred to me. "Have you spoken of this to your mother?"

She shook her head. "I've thought about it. But when he's with mother, he seems more himself. I have not wanted to bother her with it."

Her eyes grew wide again and she reached for my hand. "Oh, Eileen, I feel so much better talking to you. I wanted to help him, but I didn't know what to do." Her eyes fell. "I'm still not sure."

I squeezed her hand. "I'm sure we both want to help Richard. But I think the best thing we can do is wait and show him our affection." I reddened slightly speaking aloud of my feelings. But Nannette did not make me feel embarrassed about it.

Still, when she raised her eyes, I could see a new concern coming into them. I raised my eyebrows, waiting for her to speak.

"If you love him, Eileen, you must be careful." She bit her lips together.

Her words caused my heart to skip a beat, but I tried to smile reassuringly. "Don't worry about me, Nannette. I'm sure I can take care of myself. And Richard would never hurt me."

She looked at me, then said slowly, "No, perhaps he wouldn't. Not on purpose."

Our conversation had left me unsettled, and yet I was glad we had confided in one another. Still there was a dull ache of remorse in my heart, the more I admitted to myself just how far my feelings for Richard had gone. If he had some weighty concern that he would not share with me there was little I could do but stand by and watch him resolve it.

But if it were something deeper, some trouble of the mind or spirit, I felt entirely helpless. I loved him, I knew that, but I did not know if my love could give him peace.

Nannette stayed into the afternoon and then made me promise to return the visit the next day. She and Lettice were making plans for the party to be held at the end of the month, and they wanted my suggestions.

I agreed that I could take a day from my efforts here, and perhaps it would do me some good to be around the others for a while. But as I saw Nannette off on the mare she had ridden over, I knew in my heart the real reason I had so easily accepted her invitation.

I had begun to miss being near Richard. I wanted to see him to try to reassure myself that whatever his trouble was that I could somehow share in its resolution.

Chapter 14

I had Riggin saddle Gerty, one of the dappled mares with my old side-saddle, and dressed in my claret riding costume. I left early and went at an easy walk, enjoying the sound of Gerty's hooves in the sandy road, and the call of birds in the distance. There was a breeze, and the leaves of the palmetto palms rustled in the pine flats as I passed.

When I arrived, I took Gerty to the stables, then I went into the kitchen where Marta was chopping vegetables on the counter. She looked up and wiped her hands on her apron when I came in the screen door.

"Hello Marta," I said. "Is Mrs. Blakemore in the house?"

"My goodness, Miss Eileen, we didn't expect you so early. The family's gone down to the beach while the tide's still low. Mister Menasce insisted on searching for unusual shells to use in the scavenger hunt he's got planned for the party."

"I see." This was the first I had heard of a scavenger hunt, but I supposed plans for the party had progressed in my absence. "Then no one is at home?"

She shook her head. "Master Blakemore is in the

191

study. Said he had some work to do and not to disturb him."

"I see." If he was busy working it would be a bad time to break in on him.

"I'll wait in the parlor for everyone to return then."

"All right, Miss. Can I bring you anything?"

"No thank you, I'm quite all right for the moment."

I left her to her tasks, and peeling off gloves and hat, walked to the hallway to leave my things on the stand. As I passed the study, I paused. The door was ajar, and I couldn't help glancing in. My heart quickened at the thought of seeing Richard, though I hadn't meant to interrupt him.

But what I saw made me stop where I was and my heartbeat race even faster. Richard was behind the desk, flipping through papers and muttering to himself. I saw him throw a ledger aside with a curse, run his hand through his already mussed hair and pull open a side drawer in agitation.

I swallowed, trying to tell myself that I had just caught him at a bad moment. He had obviously misplaced something and was annoyed at not being able to find it. He pulled open more drawers, rummaging in them and tossing part of the contents on the floor.

I saw him move his lips and snort in disgust, and his agitation shocked me. Feeling suddenly guilty that I had not knocked first and suddenly fearing that he would look up and find me spying on him, I silently tiptoed down the hall.

I felt light-headed as I stepped into the parlor and sat down gratefully on the sofa. All my fears came flooding over me at the sight of Richard's unusually agitated appearance. Gaius's words came back to me. He had

192

suggested that Richard took things without knowing it. Was it more than mere absent-mindedness?

Suddenly the pressures of all that happened here were too much, and I felt the tears well up. My shoulders shook, and I pressed my hands to my face. All my resolve seemed to melt in futility, and I felt the last thread of my determination slip away. What if there was something more wrong with Richard than I knew? Something that I could not fix no matter how much I cared?

There were matters of the mind that were far beyond me, and though I wanted with all my heart to believe that loving concern, a sharing of thoughts was all it took to ease a troubled mind, I knew that there were other maladies that sometimes struck a person, things our present knowledge did not know how to address. If such a thing was happening to Richard, and if I must stand by and watch him become the victim of such abberration, I was not sure I could bear it.

It was in such a state of discomposure that Lettice found me. I had been too involved in my own turmoil to hear anyone come in, and then I heard the rustle of her skirts as she crossed the parlor.

"Good heavens, my dear what's happened? Not another accident, I hope."

I shook my head, trying to wipe the tears with the back of my hand, while she dug in her pocket for a handkerchief. "No, no, nothing like that." I had no idea if news of my spooky skeleton shadow had reached her, but I was not going to bring that up now.

"I'm sorry," I snuffled. "I'm afraid I just started thinking of everything at once and it seemed rather too much." I blew my nose. "I'm all right now."

She patted my shoulder. "Of course, my dear. It's

understandable." She rose to slide shut the double doors to the parlor so we could be alone. I blotted my eyes and shook my head.

Lettice studied me from where she was, her hands folded in front of her skirts. She uttered a deep sigh.

"You've been under a strain, Eileen. I am sorry that your homecoming had to be so unpleasant."

I shrugged. "I'm not sure what I expected."

She arched an eyebrow. "But you certainly could not expect the things that have happened to you."

Her skirts swished softly as she crossed the room again and came to sit next to me.

After a moment, she said, "Eileen. Have you considered leaving the island?"

Her question startled me. "Leave? Why no."

"You are determined to stay then?"

"Of course. It is my home."

She sighed slowly, her eyes taking on a contemplative quality. "But not a home in the normal sense."

Her words made me uncomfortable, but I knew that Lettice was not one to mince words. I ought to appreciate her straightforwardness, for I had not asked to be pampered. What good were false reassurances that led nowhere near the truth?

I straightened and faced her. "It does not seem to be. But then what could I expect? I am the only person from my immediate family that is living. It may not be a happy home in the sense that some people would want, but I still feel my roots very strongly. I feel I owe it to my father to carry on."

She smiled sympathetically. "Were you very close to your father?"

I cocked my head to the side.

"Not close in the way that a mother can be to her daughter of course. And I'm afraid that in my adolescence I was rather caught up in my own life, and I can see now that I did not give him the amount of thought I should have. But we kept up a regular correspondence while I was at school, and he always sent money to cover all my needs, plus extra when he could, to make sure I could satisfy a caprice now and then. I believe he was a very good man."

She lifted her chin slightly. "Yes. In the few times I saw him, I believed that too."

I fidgeted. Somehow I knew that she was thinking of her late husband, Jasper. I did not know what to say next, and so I fiddled with the wadded handkerchief.

Her musings seemed to find words, and she looked at me. "I know it may seem strange to you, but I don't believe that your father, James, and my husband, Jasper, were so very different."

I could only look at her to explain what she meant.

She settled back in the chair, and I listened curiously, for this idea certainly did not fit with what I knew of either of them.

"I know," she said, "that many people blame Jasper for his harshness, but he was not like that when I first met him."

I watched her silently, able to follow her thoughts back to a time when she was not so much older than I was now. I could almost see the pictures in her mind as she began to talk about that time.

"Nannette was two and Richard seven when Jasper Blakemore first stopped into my hat shop in Jacksonville. He wanted to buy a hat for his mother, who was still living then." She smiled at the memory. "He seemed to admire my skills as a milliner, which I had cultivated after my first husband had died, leaving me to support the two children. I thought what a strong, handsome man he was, and he seemed so out of place in the small shop with the flowered hats and long bolts of material for veils. I helped him select a proper bonnet for a woman his mother's age, and he left. I thought I would not see him again.

But he came back the next season when the family was again vacationing at the National hotel. By that time I had enlarged my shop, thanks to the wealthy northerners who came south for the winter months.

"Jasper made more purchases for his mother, and I began to believe that she did not need as many things as he bought. I saw then that he was not a happy man, and I wondered if he had an unhappy marriage. He told me he was not married, and I guessed perhaps that there had been an unrequited love affair or perhaps trouble of another sort."

She shrugged. "He never told me what troubled him so, but he did talk about the sponge-fishing business, which by that time he was engaged in. Still I believed there was something else he was not telling me."

She looked at me directly as if surmising I would understand.

"When a woman loves a man, she knows much about him that others do not see or that he himself does not know he has revealed."

She went on. "He was a hard man in business. That I could see, ruthless with his competition. But he was always kind to me." She sighed. "Perhaps I was a little too blinded by love. I knew that Nannette and Richard never cared for him, and this frustrated him. Whatever it was that had troubled Jasper when he married me only seemed to deepen as time went on. It was my bitterest disappointment, that I could not heal him with my love."

I shrank inwardly. Had I not harbored that very thought about Richard? It was ironic that Lettice should speak of something that troubled Jasper when I found myself in a similar situation with Richard. I shivered slightly. There was the difference of course that she had already been married to Jasper. She had no choice but to be loyal to him.

"Did you—" I paused. "Did you ever find out what it was that disturbed him so?"

She shook her head slowly, and a veil of sadness seemed to draw over her. "I never did. I speculated of course, over the years. But at the last, it seemed to be the business that consumed him. He spent most of his time at the docks and on his boat. I knew he must have made enemies. And then there was that accident with one of the hooks. It wounded his leg, tearing clear through the muscle."

I winced, remembering the accident. It was just before I left for boarding school.

"It was not too long after that that he died, was it not?" I said.

"Not very long." She looked at me. "I believe he knew it was coming. It was an awful death."

I swallowed instinctively. I had been away from home by then. I remembered my father's terse letters. *Your cousin Jasper has been killed in an accident. He was aboard his boat when it burned. We had hoped that he had had time to escape, but the remains were found.*

My stomach twisted at the thought of a death by fire. I always hoped that the fumes had suffocated him first, so that he had not had to feel the pain of his burns.

197

I made myself look up at Lettice, who was gazing at her hands in her lap. "I never believed it was an accident."

"You mean you think someone set the boat on fire."

She nodded and looked up. "Yes, I think it's obvious. By that time he had much competition. He was not liked. It was a shame he could not have worked with the sponge-fishing community in a more genial way. I do not believe his profits would have suffered that much. But he had changed by then. Something drove him. The business was everything. All he could think of was making it pay.

"For what? I sometimes asked him. The farm here was not doing badly. We had enough for our needs. But he kept saying it was for the future. For the children. And so I did not question it." She shook her head. "But look where it got him."

I rose and paced the room, unable to stand the tension I felt both for Lettice and for myself. There were parallels between her story and mine, subtle as they were. I finally stopped and faced her.

"Were there any profits then, after the boat burned I mean?"

She shook her head. "No records were found, and it was assumed they burned with the boat. A little money had been put into an account at the bank. But it was not the profit he had hoped for." She spread her hands before her. "And so it all came to nothing."

"I am sorry."

She shook her head gently. "It is all behind us now. Eight years have passed. I try not to dwell on it."

She seemed to return her thoughts to the present, and I was not certain why she had chosen this moment to share her thoughts about Jasper.

"You have your own burdens, Lettice. I hate to add

198

mine to them."

"I consider you part of my own family, Eileen. I want to share your concerns."

I frowned, beginning to see what she was getting at. "And you question my wisdom in deciding to make a home here," I said.

I could see the regret in her eyes. Yet suddenly I could see something else there too. She might tell me she considered me part of her own family, but a mother's firstborn could not help but take first place in her heart. I saw in her eyes the protective instincts of a mother for one of her own.

"I am not sure it is wise for you to be here at this time."

I frowned. "Why not?" I was determined to press her for her reasons.

"Why for your own welfare of course." Still, I sensed she was holding something back. I moved to the sofa and sat near her.

"And for Richard's?"

She jerked her chin up, and an opaque film seemed to veil her eyes. I knew I had guessed. While the others had been surreptitiously trying to warn me against spending time with Richard, Lettice, his mother, suspected that I was not good for him. What I could not understand was why.

"Lettice, you have said that we would share our womanly thoughts. Please do not withdraw from me when it comes to Richard. Surely you must know that I only seek his welfare. You must tell me your thoughts."

She seemed to sink further into the chair, and I thought that some of her resoluteness of a moment before wilted. She fingered the upholstery and looked at me absently. Then she seemed to gather her thoughts anew and make the decision that she could trust me.

"If it is true that you care for my son, Eileen, and I believe my instincts are correct in telling me that you do, you will not press him."

I could not help the resentment that flared within me.

"Whatever do you mean?"

She clasped her hands nervously in her lap. "Richard has many responsibilities."

"Oh come now, Lettice. A man's responsibilities are not what keeps him so distracted from his family that one should discourage social intercourse."

I began to fear that Lettice too suspected there might be something seriously wrong with Richard and wanted to keep us apart to minimize the heartbreak, but I had to communicate my feelings to her. For it was too late for such strategy.

I lowered my gaze in embarrassment, the memory of Richard's touch flooding over me and bringing with it all the sensations that I felt when I was with him.

I said in a low, hoarse voice, "Lettice, I do care for him. I don't know if you can understand that. Please don't try to protect him from me. You've no cause."

I wondered crazily if she thought I would hurt him somehow, or if I would only add to his trouble.

She sighed. "I know you mean him well. And in normal circumstances I could wish for nothing more than to have you as my daughter-in-law, but I am not sure Richard is ready for marriage." Then she gave me a penetrating look. "I know only too well where two hearts can be led if marriage is not the question."

My face flooded with embarrassment. So, she had

guessed our passion. I felt hideous and foolish, knowing that a woman in my position never let a man's natural instincts lead her as far as Richard had led me. It was only that I believed in him so. Why would Richard be the way he was with me, so sincere, seeming to fill himself up with me, if his intentions were not honorable?

Unless, and the horrible thought only struck me then, he was betrothed to another. I looked at Lettice with rounded eyes, moving forward on the sofa, spilling out my question.

"Lettice, you are not trying to tell me that he is meant to marry someone else. You must tell me if he is, for he has said nothing."

She shook her head. "No, nothing like that. I just feel that Richard needs to resolve certain problems of his own right now, and that the distractions of romance may not be for the best."

Rather than clarify her thoughts to me, she had only left me more confused. I tried to read her eyes, to see if I could see meaning behind her words. I had thought Lettice truly liked me. Now I felt as if she were trying to tell me I was wrong for her son, and that she disapproved of my feelings for him. I could hardly know what to think.

We sat in silence for a moment. Then I said, "Do you yourself know what these problems are? Do you truly think Richard is imbalanced?"

Her mouth was drawn in a straight line, and she did not look at me. "I would prefer to say that he is preoccupied, and that some people might not understand him."

"Lettice, I understand him. At least I would like to. You must believe me. I would never hurt him in any way."

The rapport I had felt so often with Lettice had deserted us, and I felt the same distance I sometimes did with Richard when he seemed to withdraw into his shell. It was enough to threaten my own sanity. How could I live among these people if they continued to shut me out? I simply could not believe this was happening.

She sighed then, and I imagined a little of her old self returned to her. "Perhaps it is just the curse of this place. Perhaps no one who lives on Calayeshi Island is destined for happiness."

I clenched my fists. "I am sorry you feel that way, Lettice. And you may be right. It would be a sad thing indeed if there is no happiness at all to be found here. I suppose I refuse to believe that such a curse is irreversible. I think that is why I stay. For one generation, surely, the tragedies must stop."

I believe I had some notion about good confronting evil, the way I had felt upstairs the day I had been threatened by a shadow, but I could not quite put it into words, so I explained in the best way I knew how.

"I suppose I am stubborn. I don't know why, but there is something in me that will not let some unknown threat get the best of me, Lettice. Have you never felt that way?"

A faraway look came into her eyes, and her lips relaxed into a half smile. "I have felt that way," she said. "But it was a long time ago."

I pressed my lips together. I did not know what else to say. She thought it best I leave the island, and when she had entered the room and found me sobbing I would have agreed with her. But that was in a moment of trauma, and already I felt my strength returning.

No. There were matters here that needed sorting out, and I would stay to do the sorting. I would find out what evil demon had possession of Richard's soul; what spirits could not rest for want of wrongs; who among the living harbored me some grudge.

And until all that was done, I would not go.

Chapter 15

As I left Lettice and passed into the hallway, I ran into Ian, who greeted me with a cheery smile.

"Ah there you are, Eileen. We've just been looking for you."

He looked dapper in his white flannel trousers and white shirt with sleeves rolled up, and his face was tanned from the time he had spent outdoors. At least one person on this island seemed to be living a carefree life.

"We're just going to plan the scavenger hunt," he said. "And we need your help."

"All right."

Just then Nannette joined us, looking equally cheerful and pretty in her blue and white dotted swiss. She smiled a welcome to me, and it seemed that the concerns that had been heavy in her heart when I had last seen her had been pushed to the back of her mind. I was still confused over my interview with Lettice, but perhaps it would do me some good to join Ian and Nannette. It took only half my mind to listen to their chatter in any case.

They led me into the dining room where we would have more room, and Ian produced a pad of paper and pencils so we could make our lists.

"I don't think I've ever planned a scavenger hunt before," I said, not sure how much help I would be to them.

But Ian waved away my objections. "It's not a job that requires any experience." He winked at me. "I know you have a rich imagination, and that's all we need."

His remark and the flirtatious way he delivered it to me made me blush. This was the Ian I knew, frivolous, unaffected by the deeper matters of the day, pleasure and good humor being his main pursuits in life.

I shook my head in irony. Such gaiety and light-heartedness had once attracted me to him. And who would not be? For in Ian's presence one felt that happiness might be within reach. But I knew now that his grasp of life was only superficial. And from the admiring glances that he was casting both in my direction and Nannette's, I knew that I had been fortunate not to pledge my heart to him, for his fidelity as the years passed was likely to be only as reliable as his capacity for serious thought.

I studied Nannette. She returned Ian's glances and laughed at his every remark. Surely she was too intelligent a girl to fall under the spell of Ian's superficial charm. I wondered if I should speak to her, warning her about becoming involved with such a man. But she might not appreciate my interference, thinking that I was jealous.

There was probably nothing to worry about. Nannette too liked to have a good time, and though I thought that once given, her loyalty was unbreachable, it was not lightly given.

"Now," said Ian. "The beauty of a scavenger hunt on this enchanting island is that we can send our guests after exotic and unusual things. What do you suggest, Eileen?''

I frowned. "We'd better not make them too unusual or send them too far. There is always the danger that someone would meet with a mishap in the woods, and I should think we should send them no farther than the near end of the beach.''

"Yes, the beach," he said. "That will be part of the fun. To see what glorious shells they might bring back.''

Nannette gave him a teasing look. "As long as there's nothing alive in the shells they choose to bring back.''

Ian gave her a look of distaste, and I had to laugh. Ian might be fascinated with the exotic setting of the island, but he was a city boy at heart. Still, he rallied.

"But what about the things that wash up on shore? Did you not both tell me of the machete you'd found from a Spanish wreck.''

"Yes," I said. "But that does not happen very often. We're more likely to find only old jars or rusty chain.''

"Ah, yes," Ian went on. "But wouldn't it be astounding if someone really did come across something of value. Some old family jewels that had been hidden away for so long that everyone's forgotten them, or some such.''

Nannette dropped her pencil and I blanched. I had not told Ian about the missing family jewels, and from Nannette's startled expression it was plain to me that neither had she. Was it just coincidence that made him say such a thing?

"Where did you come upon such an idea?" I asked, trying to recover.

Ian laughed and observed us both. "Why," he said smoothly. "All mysterious islands have some sort of buried treasure, don't they? After all, it was not so far away that a pirate hid his hoards on Captiva Island? Mightn't he have scattered some of it among all the coastal islands, in case he needed to make a quick escape and come back later for his ill-gotten goods?"

I tried to smile good-humoredly. "If there was anything like that here," I said. "I would think it would have been found long ago."

"Oh? Why?" There was a note of goading in Ian's voice that I tried to tell myself I was just imagining.

"Because every inch of the island's been gone over," said Nannette, and I shot her a quick glance, but it was too late.

"Has it now?" said Ian. "That's curious. What was being searched for?"

I don't know why I hesitated to bring up the family jewels. They were not a secret. But I had never mentioned them to Ian, for some reason. I shrugged. Nannette seemed to be waiting for me to speak, and so I explained.

"There are some family jewels that were lost here," I said. "That is, they were stolen. But the thief most likely got them off the island and sold them on the black market."

"Most likely? You mean the culprit was never caught?"

"I'm afraid not."

I could see the interest in his eye and was sorry we had brought it up. His imagination was kindled now, and there would be no stopping him.

He frowned. "When was this?"

I rose and paced toward the window, my arms folded across my chest. "Shortly after my sister died."

"Ahhhh."

I had told him about that tragedy, neglecting to mention that the jewels disappeared at about the same time. I turned to see that he was scratching his head, a faraway look in his eye.

"Then you don't know who stole them?"

"No. Only that they were discovered missing."

"By whom?"

"My father. They were kept in the safe," I hesitated. Why did I always feel so obligated to explain every detail to people who pressed me for questions? I closed my lips. I had said enough. I knew that Ian's curiosity was not likely to be satisfied with this brief explanation, and I was right.

And of course accompanying his questions were the humility and charm that I could see by now enabled him to wheedle his way into every situation he wanted to be in. I was getting further annoyed with Ian, and though I was perhaps being selfish in not indulging his fancies just now, I was not in the mood to answer his questions. I decided to leave Nannette and Ian to discuss it.

"Nannette can explain how it happened," I said. "I believe I'll go see if there is anything I can help Lettice with."

I could feel their gazes following me, and I paused just around the corner in the hallway long enough to hear Ian question Nannette once again.

"Rubies set in gold," she was saying. "Two bracelets, a necklace and brooch. They were handed down in the family for generations before my grandfather settled here."

I shook myself, thinking it was a bad omen to be discussing the jewels after all that happened to us so far.

As I was standing there, Gaius came down the stairs above me. He paused and I turned, realizing it must look as if I were eavesdropping on the two in the dining room. Not that I owed Gaius any explanation, but his curious glance made me feel ill at ease.

"Hello," I said. "Nannette and Ian and I were just planning the scavenger hunt for the party. However I failed to come up with any good ideas. Perhaps you would be better at helping them."

He came down the rest of the way, resting his hand on the railing and smiling easily at me. I noticed how impeccable he looked, his blond hair combed neatly away from the part on one side.

But he ignored my suggestion that he join the other two and moved toward me. Since I had told him of my feelings at the picnic, Gaius had not pressed himself on me, and I appreciated that fact.

Now looking at him, so confident, so considerate, I wondered if I had made a mistake in refusing his attentions. I liked a man who was solicitous of a woman's feelings, and after the conversations of the morning, Gaius's apparent stability seemed tempting.

I blushed slightly at my own thoughts and lowered my head. Gaius moved toward me, touching my elbow with his fingertips. His words were low, spoken just inches from my ear.

"Would you like to sit with me in the parlor for a few moments?"

"I—" I looked up at him, about to protest, but the gentle look in his eye made me reconsider. I felt as if the events of the morning were propelling me toward Gaius as a last resort. All I wanted at the moment was to be with someone who accepted me. Someone without problems of their own.

He led me to the parlor where I had so recently been with Lettice, but once we were there, I had nothing to say to him. He seemed to read my thoughts and understand that I did not wish to discuss anything serious.

"I have a hankering to do some fishing," he said. "I learned from one of the tenants that the largest tarpon taken by rod and reel weighed one hundred eighty-four pounds."

"I don't know," I said distractedly. "I suppose that is correct." While my father had taught me to fish, I found I never had the patience to wait for the fish to bite. "Will you take a boat out then?"

"I believe I shall. I purchased a large straw hat and some fishing equipment in town to try it out. It would be something if I could come back with a good catch to present to our hostess."

"Yes. I'm sure Lettice would appreciate that."

He smiled gently, coming up beside me, touching my arm. "Alas, I can see that these sporting activities do not hold your attention today. Since my only wish is to please the lady I am talking to, pray tell me what subject of conversation would fascinate you?"

"I'm sorry, Gaius. I'm afraid I am not very sociable today. I hope I do not seem rude."

"Far from it. It's just that I sensed that you carried some concerns on your shoulders today, and I hoped that I could lighten your load by distracting you with some frivolous topic."

"I appreciate your attempt, honestly I do. But I think I have had enough conversation for now." I tried to smile my thanks. He had said he would be my friend, and he seemed to be making every effort to live up to that promise. "Will you excuse me?"

"Of course, my dear. Just don't forget me for those times you do need a listening ear."

I thought that for someone who had pressed me so ardently so recently, he was making a great job of settling for friendship. But as I looked at him I could still see the shrewdness in his eyes that I had sensed when I had first meant him. Perhaps by offering me friendship when I needed it, he hoped to win me still. I had to admire his patience.

I was at a loss as to what to do with myself. I was being no help with the party plans, and I did not know if Lettice would be particularly receptive to my help. The only thing left to do was to return home, wishing I had never come this morning at all.

I headed toward the back of the house, and as I passed the study, the door opened. I stepped aside, startled as Richard appeared.

He had an intent look on his face, and I was immediately reminded of the image of him searching so desperately among the papers in the desk this morning. I shrank backward inwardly.

He stopped suddenly, and we stared at one another for a moment, while I waited for my breathing to even. His eyes, which had seemed dark and piercing in this light, seemed to mellow as he looked at me.

"Eileen," he said. "I didn't know you were here."

"I—" I stammered. "I was just leaving. I had promised Nannette to come help with the party. But she and the others are doing very well without my help."

He lifted an eyebrow as he closed the study door behind him. I watched him extract a key from his pocket and turn it in the keyhole.

"I didn't realize you kept the study locked," I said in surprise before I even thought about my words.

He gave me a sharp look as if it were none of my business. But he said nothing. Instead, he touched my waist and we moved on down the hall.

I was surprised when he led me into the kitchen where we found Lettice and Marta busy making batter. Lettice had an apron tied over her dress, and her hands were covered with flour up to her elbows. She looked up as we came into the kitchen, and Richard walked over to her to place a kiss on her cheek.

I clasped my hands awkwardly, and stood there, but her glance toward me was calm, if not as open as I would have liked it to be. I felt truly desolate that I had lost her love. And here I was with Richard as she had not wanted me to be. But he seemed not to notice any strain between Lettice and me, and in fact the smile in his eyes was more clear than I had seen in him for some time.

He rubbed his stomach as he teased Lettice. "I hope whatever that is will fill a man's stomach at supper. I plan to work up an appetite in the mangrove swamps today."

"The mangrove swamps?" asked Lettice.

He nodded. "I have had reports of sunken logs that have trapped some of the fish in the bayous. I'm going to take the rowboat and go see if that's true."

Then he looked at me. "That is, after I've seen Eileen home."

"There's no need," I interjected. "I rode over on one of the mares, and a leisurely ride home will be just the thing."

But the look Richard gave me halted further protests. I was not ready for so eager a look from him, and I thought that he must be teasing me.

"Nonsense," Richard said. "I have time to escort you part way."

I barely nodded my assent, and then going up to Lettice I paused, hoping my nervousness did not show. But as she met my look, I thought I saw something like regret in her eyes. Something caught in my throat, and I believe that had we been alone we might have said reassuring words to each other, and I believed that perhaps our relationship was not so hopeless after all. I sighed. There were so many things to be untangled here, not the least of which were the human emotions that made us say and do things that we were not always in control of.

However, Richard was ready to whisk me away, and so I kissed Lettice and hurried out with him.

Instead of heading toward the stables, Richard turned to me.

"I'm going to row around the north end of the island. come with me, Eileen."

My heart skipped a beat, and I looked at him questioningly. He had never asked me to accompany him on his rounds of the estate and I was surprised that he was asking me now. But it would be a chance to be with him, to talk to him, and to try to fathom our situation.

My hesitation must have showed for he said, "Of course if you don't want to . . ."

"No, I do. It is just," I paused. "That I thought I might be in the way."

He lowered his gaze to me and my heart lurched again, but this time not because of fear, but in response to the interest I saw there. Then he said, "If you must know, I would enjoy the company."

I nodded. "All right, if you wish, I would like to go."

Already I could feel the strange intimacy between us

forming, and had I had no other concerns, there would be nothing I would want more than to row out among the bayous with Richard. But now all the insinuations of Lettice and the others clouded my mind.

Would it not be foolish to go with Richard alone to an isolated part of the island? I could change my mind now, I thought as we walked along to the path that led through the trees to the dock where the smaller boats were kept. But no words formed in my mind to make a sudden excuse. I wanted to be with Richard. I wanted to have the chance to speak to him about his behavior. Perhaps I was foolish, but I harbored a hope that he would say something to me that would explain everything.

He helped me into the boat, and I sat in the stern while he took up the oars and pushed off. I let the sun wash over me, feeling calmed by the balmy breeze and the sound of the oars dipping in the surf.

We rounded the island to the western side, and the beach slid by, as Richard rowed quite steadily. I don't know how long we journeyed in silence, but finally Richard rested the oars, letting the current carry us toward the northern tip.

We passed the bluffs and he rowed again as we came to the long fingers of the bayous that reached out into the water, forming an intricacy of inlets and waterways that comprised the mangrove swamp.

Soon he turned the boat, and we glided into an inlet that I would not have seen, so hidden was the entrance by the thick growth of oak, cypress and mangrove. We left the sunlight behind as the boat glided along the seemingly motionless water, the moss and leaves overhead nearly blotting out the sky in places. Tall reeds and wild dandelions lined the banks. A stirring in the reeds caught my eye, then a swamp rabbit looked up at me and skittered away.

There was a stillness, almost an airlessness about the place. Suddenly I felt a big warm drop on my cheek and looked up to see that a dark cloud had formed above the trees.

Richard lifted the oars and sniffed the air. Above us, the trees had become loud with birdsong, noisier than usual. I looked at Richard.

"A storm's headed this way," he said. "Don't worry. We're not far from the chapel. If it rains, we can take shelter there."

I nodded. I did not mind a little rain. And storms often blew up so quickly there was little way to know ahead of time. Richard headed between the cypress and willow trees to a waterway that led away at a right angle, leaving the mangroves behind. I had been to this part of the bayous with my father before, but I did not know this maze of inlets as Richard seemed to. And I had not penetrated this side of the swamp with Ian the day we went sketching.

The rain seemed to let up here and we came to another narrow stream. Richard took it, letting the boat drift.

The birds had stopped their cacophany, and silence lay about us now like a blanket of sleep. But the silence in a mangrove swamp seems oddly to contain a mysterious sound, something I could almost hear, but not quite. I could tell that Richard was straining his ears, focusing his attention on what we both seemed to sense. I held my breath.

The ripples in the water glided outward from the skiff and broke soundlessly on the mudbanks. Then from a distance a red-winged blackbird called his raucous notes.

Richard relaxed his pose and looked at me.

"It's beautiful, is it not?"

I nodded. His eyes were clear, and again I felt that he and I shared the beauty of the island as few other people could. I was entranced by the setting, and though I might have felt uneasy being here alone, I felt safe with Richard. He seemed in no hurry, and I wondered if his plans to search for sunken logs were merely an excuse to come to this part of the island. But I seized the opportunity to question him about what was on my mind.

"Richard," I said, "You said that you thought there were spirits about the island trying to tell us something or make things happen. Are you sure there is not some human menace?"

He smiled as if to himself. "Why do you ask."

"Well," I grew bolder. "I passed by the study this morning and glanced in. It seemed as if you were looking for something. I couldn't help but wonder what."

I had braced myself for his anger, but instead he laughed at me. "Spying on me now, is that it?"

"I didn't mean to be spying."

But he shook his head. "I'm not angry, if that's what you're afraid of. And I will answer your question since you seem to have such an inquisitive mind."

I waited, only slightly annoyed at the way his words made it sound as if he were treating me like a child.

He looked at me as if examining my reactions. "I do believe someone on this island is looking for something. I do not discount the work of the spirits of our dead ancestors, but yes, you are right, it is probably a more human threat we face."

My spine tingled. "Then you, too, think there is some danger?"

He had not missed my slip. "I too? Who else thinks there is danger?"

"Well, Lettice, of course. You heard her say it."

But he was not satisfied with that. He raised a brow, leaning slightly forward. "And who else?"

I sighed. "Everyone, I suppose. After my accident I believe everyone dreamt up their version of who or what was disturbing our paradise."

"Hmmm. And tell me, did any of them suggest that you might be in danger from me?"

My quick glance downward gave me away. But then I raised my eyes slowly to him as he watched me, his eyes taking on the eerie glow of the swamp half-light.

"Richard," I said. "How could I possibly be in any danger from you?"

He let out a breath and the tension seemed to drain out of his body. "I had hoped you would say that."

He picked up the oars and dipped them into the water. I ducked my head to avoid an overhanging branch. Richard let the boat drift, then it stopped again, bumping into a knotty cypress knee that jutted out of the water.

We moved on, passing more cypresses, sweet gum, cottonwoods. A cat squirrel ran along a branch and hurdled the stream, landing on a tree on the opposite bank. The sky was a solid gray mass of clouds seemingly swollen with an odd light. Then I drew in a breath. High on the bank to my left lay the skeleton of a skiff like the one we were in. Only the hull and a few boards with rusty nails remained. The sight made me shiver.

"Whose boat was that?"

Richard shook his head. "Poachers most likely."

The water here was greenish, reflecting the swamp life above, like a mirror image. Richard stuck an oar upright into the water. Halfway down it stuck in the mud. The soil was only a little way beneath the surface of the water, just as water lurked only a little way beneath the ground that supported the trees. The swamp was neither solid nor liquid, rather it was both earth and water mixed thickly together.

The sky grew grayer. Two great blue herons streaked by overhead, their wings practically brushing the tree tops.

A peal of thunder sounded, then a few raindrops bounced off the surface of the water. Richard steered us beneath some protective branches of cypress, then to an embankment where he secured the boat around a low-hanging tree limb growing almost horizontally over the water. He climbed to the bank then held the boat steady so I could disembark.

I stood carefully, took his free hand and stepped onto the bank where he directed me. From where we stood, I could not imagine that there was any way through the dense woods, but Richard reached for my hand and led me forward.

Soon I saw we were on a narrow path that had been cleared. The rain rustled through the trees, and even with the branches forming a roof above us, I could feel drops of rain through my clothing.

I knew that these rain storms seldom lasted long, but came and went with the passing clouds. But as we made our way through the forest, the cloud above us did not break up and move off. The branches on either side of us dipped and swayed in the pelting water. A thick mist rose around us now, heavy and wet.

Then the path widened, and we came out on the sandy road, now sluggish with the rain. The trees parted, and I glanced at the sky. A strange glow pulsated through the clouds, and a distant rumble rolled toward us. A green chameleon slithered past my foot, and I saw its body turn a dull brown as it crawled along a branch that had fallen. Then it changed green again as it jumped off into the wet foliage.

I was beginning to get soaked, my clothes clinging to me, and water running into my mouth.

"The chapel's just ahead," Richard shouted into my ear. "Can you make it?"

I nodded and we sloshed on, all thought of appearance given up, our main objective simply shelter.

Then miraculously before us the chapel loomed, its ivy covered stone walls a haven from the downpour. We stepped onto the slippery flagstones, and then we ducked through the arched doorway and into the chapel.

Richard shut the wooden door behind us, and I shook myself, the water dripping at my feet onto the stone floor.

"Heavens," I said. "I wouldn't have expected such a storm."

Richard looked at me strangely. "This is no storm," he said.

Chapter 16

The word *hurricane* hung between us unspoken. The solid chapel walls blocked all sound. Richard took my hand and led me up the stone steps to the gallery above the nave, where we walked along the south wall and paused to look out an arched window. The sky in the south had turned a deep yellow. Then I heard an eerie sound.

"What is it?" I asked.

"Herons," Richard said, "and blackbirds and ibises."

I listened to the cries of all the birds together. They had changed unmistakably. These were no mating cries, nor flight notes such as those heard from a flock on wing. Instead, the birds were all calling at once, many species, making a sharp sound like a wail. The collective noise seemed almost human, like a voice wavering on hysteria.

I had forgotten the change in the sound of bird cries before a hurricane strikes.

Richard pulled the shutter closed. "Come," he said. "We'll need to get out of our wet things."

"Into what?" I asked.

"There are blankets and candles stored in the sacristy for just such emergencies."

We passed on along the gallery and took the stairs that led down behind the altar and into the small sacristy. Richard opened a cabinet and just as he had said, brown wool blankets lay folded. From another cabinet he pulled several white linen towels, which he handed me.

"Thank heavens," I said, beginning to dry my hair.

Richard removed his coat, and I glanced around to see if there was anything to undress behind. He had toweled his head dry, and as he was unbuttoning his shirt he saw my dilemma.

"This is no time to be modest, Eileen," he said. "Get out of that dress or you'll catch pneumonia."

I must have given the appearance of a woebegone drowned dog, for Richard sighed and turned his back. I fumbled with my hooks and eyes as embarrassment added to discomfort built into a feeling of frustration, and suddenly, foolishly, I thought I would cry.

"Let me help you."

I felt fingers at the back of my neck and then he undid what I could not reach. My embarrassment receded with the relief I felt as Richard pushed my dress over my shoulders and it fell to my feet. I still stood with my back to him and so could not see his expression, but I knew I could not stop there. My petticoats and underthings were also wet.

I untied my petticoats, letting them fall. Then I felt the towel drape my shoulders and Richard's hands massage them. I looked sideways, and he let go of me so that when I turned slowly, I saw that he had stripped out of his clothes and wrapped a blanket around his torso, one end tucked under his arm. His hair was roughed from the toweling and the linen towel was draped over his shoulders.

He frowned. "You'll have to take off those under-things," he said. "Here." He draped a blanket around my shivering form, then he turned his back again.

I wriggled out of my drawers and camisole and pulled the blanket all the way around, letting it hang to the floor. The rough wool started to warm me, but I still shivered.

"All right," I said. "You can turn around."

"That's better," he said, with an approving glance. He stepped to me and patted the blanket with both hands. "I'll rub you dry," he said softly.

I nodded numbly as he used the blanket as a sort of giant towel to blot and chafe my cold skin. I supported myself with my hands on his shoulders as he worked his way down my body, but already I could feel my circulation returning.

He rose, his arms still around me, and I felt the added warmth of being in the circle of his arms. A sense of embarrassment filled me, but Richard put me at my ease. What else was there to do but get rid of our wet clothing?

Richard picked up the extra blankets. "We might as well find a place to wait it out," he said.

We made our way into the shadowy chapel. I looked at the unadorned altar in the chancel with stained glass window behind, dark now without sunlight to light the colored glass. The chapel was arranged with shallow rows of pews on three sides, and we sat on the south side.

I had lost my sense of time. There was nothing to do but wait, and my thoughts turned to what we had been talking about before we took refuge from the storm.

"What were you looking for this morning in the study?" I asked, for he had never answered my question.

He had been looking at the roof and walls of the

building as if assessing the strength of the structure. But he tilted his head at me and answered.

"A clue, you might say."

"A clue?"

"I told you someone on the island is looking for something. I was looking for something that might lead me to it first."

"But in order to find a clue, wouldn't you have to know what it is that someone is looking for."

He looked at me, his eyes penetrating mine. "I believe I do know."

I felt my skin prickle as I stared at him. "You know? What then?"

He laughed silently, his mouth curving in a smile that was not altogether pleasant. "What else would be worth looking for on this island but the missing rubies? The family jewels."

I shook my head. "Is that old mystery never to be laid to rest. Is greed that powerful, Richard?" I had taken his arm. "Just because they've never been found, they seem to enchant everyone to foolishness. Richard, surely you cannot believe it."

He gazed into the darkness of the corners behind the pews. "But I do believe it. I think someone knows they are hidden here. That the jewels never left the island. And that person will do anything to find them.

"That is why you are not safe, my dear." His look frightened me as he went on. "It is why I brought you with me today. I do not think it is wise to risk your being alone until this matter is settled."

I was shocked. "I? But I know nothing about them. Why would I be in danger? I least of all even believe they are anywhere to be found. Surely if someone is mad enough to persist in looking for them he or she will realize that I cannot help them."

His eyes softened as he put his persuasion before me.

"Think. The jewels were originally kept in the safe in your father's study. It was there that he discovered them missing. You are the only member of your immediate family still living. Perhaps you have a clue you are not aware of. Or perhaps the clues or even the jewels themselves are hidden in the manor house. Whoever wants them is desperate, Eileen. You may be standing in the way of their search."

He raised a dark brow, gazing off again as if thinking. "No," he said. "You are not safe from someone obsessed with finding them."

I was shivering, and not from the cold. Gaius's words came back to me. He had insinuated that Richard himself was a thief and did not know it. My throat turned dry in ironic counterpoint to the wetness that surrounded us. How did I know that it was not Richard himself who wanted the jewels and who would do anything to get them?

My head started to spin. I wanted to move, but what would be the purpose? If I stood up, where would I go? I could only close my eyes and cry silently. *Oh Richard*, I thought silently, *Tell me it is not so.*

He must have noticed my distress, for his arm came around me and he pulled me nearer his body.

"Come now," he said in a gentle voice. "Are you cold?"

He kissed my cold temples, but I found little comfort in his solicitations. I tensed and sat up straighter, struggling for something to say.

"I feel thirsty," I said. "I don't suppose there's

anything to drink here."

He removed his arm from my shoulders and rose, extending a hand to me. "Ah, but there is, if you don't mind drinking some of the communion wine."

The thought seemed to amuse him, but I was thirsty, and I knew the wine would help warm us.

"Do you know where it is kept?" I asked.

"Of course. I make sure the stock does not run out."

Richard fetched two small gold chalices from the sacristy and returned with an uncorked jug of wine. Then he knelt to set the chalices on the stone floor and pour the wine. He handed a cup to me, and I sipped.

The tangy burgundy that slid down my throat brought welcome relief and did something to sooth my nerves. Richard drank and then refilled his cup. Then he rose and walked toward the side door of the chapel. I followed him to where he opened the door to look out.

From here we could see the graveyard behind the chapel. Moss torn loose from the trees blew across the cemetery like torn pieces of the gray sky above. The noise of the birds had broken into separate choruses again, shattered and then as we stood there, they quieted. The grass glistened as the sky turned a sort of copper color. Then the wind started again.

It came in a gust from the west, fluttering the leaves and bending the grass and trees. The second gust was longer, and the interval that followed it was shorter. With the third gust came the rain again. I knew enough about hurricanes to know that high winds accompanied by heavy rains ushered in the most treacherous part of the storm. Moss bounced in the trees and small objects, bits of birds nests and twigs blew across the churchyard.

I was frightened by the storm, and when I looked at

Richard I saw that his face was flushed, and his eyes glittered as if in fever. I knew that animals and humans were often thus affected in the face of a hurricane, as if the body were making itself ready to protect itself from the oncoming danger. Frightened as I was, I began to feel the same strange excitement.

We shut the door and latched it, listening to the wind rise outside. Then we checked the opposite side door to make sure it too was latched. Then we went up to the gallery and made sure all the shuttered windows were fastened. Even within the stone structure I could hear the violent gusts of wind, and wondered in a moment of fear, if we would actually survive the storm. I could hear the rain as it hissed and lashed like whips of waters through the trees outside.

Then I cried out, clasping my hand over my mouth. In the corner of the gallery, two pairs of eyes gleamed at me. But as I accustomed my eyes to the shadows, I saw that it was only a raccoon huddled there.

"What is it?" Richard darted to my side.

I sighed and pointed. "Only a raccoon. It must have come in for shelter."

The furry creature darted away, more frightened of us than we of him.

"At least he's harmless," Richard said. "He'll curl up and wait out the storm. As we should do."

I glanced at him. He stood near me, his eyes translucent as he gazed down at me. Again I was stirred by his nearness, but I fought it.

"Do you think we'll be all right here?" I asked.

Richard glanced at the sturdy stone walls surrounding us. "The place is strongly built. We are in no danger."

The wind was an endless shriek, rising and falling.

Every so often something hit the roof and in spite of its sturdiness, I felt as if the whole chapel shuddered on its foundation. It was as if some invisible rage had unleashed itself outside. I thought of the wild creatures outside, wondering how they found shelter in such a storm. Not many had sought shelter here, as had the raccoon.

A tree limb struck the roof in full force like an earthquake, and I jumped. Richard put his arm around me to steady me. Wind screamed in the half dark. A burst and a loud shattering of glass told us that something had shattered the stained glass, though I knew the window would not break all the way through, the leaded designs being too strong for that.

Richard's contemplative look told me he had thought of something, and he turned to me. "I want to take a look out of the bell tower."

"The bell tower?"

"Yes. The circular stairs lead up there."

"Of course."

How many times I had climbed those stairs as a child, though I had been forbidden to do so. But the bell tower, which was on the level with most of the trees gave one of the best views of the north end of the island.

I followed him up the curving steps, and when we reached the top we could hear the wind gusting at the wooden door. Richard unlashed it, and it flew back, the wind knocking us against the walls.

The bell had been removed, though I didn't know why. Perhaps it had been damaged and had been taken in for repair. But we could see beyond to the shapeless dark mass of water that was the bayou, all waves and whitecaps now, never seen here in normal weather. And the mass of water was approaching the chapel. Now I knew what

Richard had come to see.

The water was rising, and would soon envelope us. Already the near line of palmettos were in water halfway up their trunks. It was as if the swamp were growing around us, nourished by the hurricane's fury, and I wondered if we too would be hurled into the water. I thought of our boat, broken up on the bank somewhere. Would it too be a reminder of two lost lives, stranded in this desolate part of the island?

I watched transfixed as the churning water came toward us through the trees. Debris scraped against the stone walls below, as if the swamp were clawing at the chapel. Then a big oak that had once shaded the church-yard snapped and fell. In the deafening wind I did not even hear the tree fall, but watched it slowly sink to earth and lie across the church steps.

Again I seriously wondered if we would die here. Richard put his weight against the door to the bell tower, and it slammed shut. He latched it, but I felt we had only momentary respite from the elements. How could a stone chapel withstand a storm that had so easily uprooted the huge old oak tree that had grown beside it for a hundred years?

We returned down the steps and to the sacristy. The stone floor was already wet with muddy water seeping in from outside.

"Here," Richard said, grabbing the remaining blankets. "We'll take what we can and go up to the gallery."

He rooted among the supplies and put the wine bottle, cups, candles and a lantern into the blanket. Then he searched vainly for matches. I thought that if he found them, they might already be too damp to light. Finally he located a box in the corner of a cupboard along with several boxes of communion wafers. We took these and made our way up the stairs.

We climbed to the gallery and sat on a sturdy pew away from the shuttered windows. There was nothing else to do but wait, hope and pray. Glancing at Richard's stoic demeanor, I wondered if he felt any of the fears I did. Even if the walls should hold, a new dread occurred to me. I was frightened not only of the flood, but of snakes that would climb to this height to avoid the encroaching water.

Then suddenly, the gale stopped. The calm was unearthly, and I did not know what to make of it. Richard rose and unlatched a window, pushing the shutter aside. The wilderness outside was still and soundless. Nothing moved, no trees swayed. The lake of water still surrounded the chapel, a glittering maze of broken branches, leaves and pieces of earth. It was a scene of silent devastation, the water speckled with drops of water falling from the soaked trees. The rain gutter to our right had broken off and stuck out from the corner of the roof.

We had had to shout to each other to make ourselves heard above the din before, now I could hear Richard's breathing.

"We're in the eye," he said.

Chapter 17

The second half of the storm would be as bad as the first, I knew. And it was with an odd feeling that we waited for the wind. I stared out at the false sense of peace that had settled over the swamp and gazed at the jaundiced sky.

How long we stood there, I do not know. There was no chance of trying to run with the eye, as it was moving in the opposite direction from home, and even if we had wanted to try, we had no method of transportation now. We stood tensely, waiting.

At the first gust of wind and splatter of rain, Richard pulled the shutter closed. I returned to our pew, pulling my blankets around me, and as the wind outside mounted again, he joined me.

"How long will it last?" I whispered as he pulled me toward him. This time I did not resist, but nestled against him, his strength seeming a great comfort in the dark, cold, drafty place.

"I don't know," he said. "We'll have to spend the night here at least. Don't worry," he said, kissing the top of my head as I folded into him. "We'll be all right."

All other thoughts except those of survival had fled. I

230

knew not the mysteries of the island or how Richard fit into them. He was my strength and comfort, and I was thankful that I was not here alone.

We clung to each other as the wind mounted again, shrieking its fury. I closed my eyes only to envision the water rising farther and tried not to think of all the creatures who, like us might seek shelter here. I thought of the raccoon, hoping he had found some dry rafter, but I dearly hoped that nothing more frightening than that would crawl toward us over the damp stone floor.

The tension the storm brought was almost unbearable, but Richard held me tightly, and I could hear his heart beat where my ear was pressed against his chest. I was barely aware that his hands were gently massaging my back and shoulders and that my arms had slid out of my blanket to encircle his waist. I did not question that we sought to comfort each other thus, and the warmth that my body felt was a blessed relief to the dampness and terror I had had before.

His hand found my jaw, and he caressed my cheek with his thumb. I turned my face toward his and saw the clear, lucid expression in his black-green eyes. His mouth was open slightly and then I saw the tiny light in his eyes as he brought his mouth down over mine.

My soul leapt up in response to his kiss, and I felt myself a willing vessel for the outpouring of tension between us. I did not stop him as his arms went around me and he pressed his body against mine. Our kiss deepened and I felt a great sigh escape me when he lifted his lips and kissed my jaw, then my ear lobe and further down at the base of my neck.

Suddenly I was eager for his embraces. I had the irrational thought that if we were going to die, why should I hold anything back. I knew now that I would not rest until the passion I tasted with Richard was satisfied. I had known nothing of what passed in such manner between men and women until Richard had held me the day of my accident. But once I had been shown the depth of that emotion I knew I wanted more and more of it.

I almost prayed that the storm would last forever, so that what Richard was doing to me now would never stop. This must be true bliss I thought as I began to move in his arms. For his kisses on my cold skin and his hands feeling my body through the thickness of the blankets brought me pleasure such as I never knew existed. I pressed closer to him, wanting every inch of my body to find a niche against his.

"Richard, Richard," I moaned against his hair, for his mouth was on my collar bone and with every impression of his lips and tongue my heart flew to a higher plateau of sensation. I arched against him, knowing in some dim part of my mind that what I was doing was wrong, that in normal circumstances I wold never have permitted such embraces. But here in the storm, the conflicts of desire that wrestled with rightness were buried. The howling of the wind only seemed to carry me to a further frenzy.

The blanket had slipped off my shoulders and Richard raised his head to look at me. His eyes were lit with passion and with the fever pitch of the elements outside. He must have felt as I did, and I knew we were lost in each other.

His lips were parted, and he whispered hoarsely, "Eileen, my love. You should stop me. We should not be doing this. Surely I cannot stop myself."

And with that his mouth came down on mine again, and his tongue probed deeply against mine. We clung to each other, our bodies on fire now, demanding, desiring.

He drank me in, his hands tangled in my hair, still damp as it splayed behind me. Then with his hand supporting my back he laid me back on the church pew, made softer by the extra blankets we had spread beside us. He knelt on the floor beside me, his chest raised over me as his hands began to work their magic on my skin again.

I entwined my fingers in his dark hair unconsciously pressing his head against my breast where his lips and tongue were making tiny circling motions. I gasped when he lowered the blanket still further and cupped my breast with his hand. Then he placed his mouth over the nipple, and I gasped, for I had never experienced anything like the feelings that coursed through me.

His hand moved lower over the curve of my hip and thigh. I felt defenseless and vulnerable with my leg exposed to his caresses, and yet I was burning inside, unable to stop him.

He moaned, his head pressed against me. "I want you, Eileen." He raised his head to kiss my jaw, my lips.

"You're so much a part of me," he said. "You've always been a part of me. I want it always to be so." He kissed me again, and I clung to him, his words swimming in my mind.

Yes, I was part of him. I belonged to him. I could not explain it any more than I could explain the island's claim on me, on both of us. But being with Richard was somehow right, though I knew that others might call it a sin. I knew I loved him and could love no other man. Whatever he would do with me, show me, I wanted with all my heart.

Outside, the storm raged on, and Richard's embrace

became more fervent. He lifted me off the pew, then with one hand pulled the blankets down to the stone floor where he knelt. Then he lowered me to the floor as well, where he could lie down beside me, the full length of him against me.

"Richard, Richard," I moaned as I wrapped my arms around him and gloried in the length of him against me. "I am yours, truly."

I felt his surge of desire, and his mouth found my ear, while his hand curved over my buttocks, pressing me toward him. The fire deep within me surged as I felt him against me, and our mouths opened wider as we tasted of each other. Then his hand came up again to massage my breast.

"Richard," I said, breathless. "I don't know what to do. I've never . . ."

"Do not worry, my sweet, my delicious love. I will show you. I will be gentle. Let me love you as a man loves a wife, for that is what you are to me."

I thought my heart would burst right out of my chest and fly skyward at his words, and I kissed him more ardently. "Show me," I said, mad with love and want for these new things he was revealing to me. My last hesitations were gone, for I felt the commitment between us. I knew that what we did here was a symbol of what we were to each other, whether or not it had been sanctified by a ceremony. This would be our ceremony as we would bind ourselves to one another, our hearts beating as one, our bodies to become one.

He took my hand and kissed my fingers. Then he guided my hand between the blankets that still separated us. I reached eagerly down his strong, smooth torso, and when I hesitated, he guided me further until I contacted the taut evidence of his desire. He showed me how he wanted me to caress him, and though I could not look him in the eye while I was discovering this new intimacy, I delighted in the feel of him.

He lay back, his eyes closed, his lips opened and moaned in pleasure. I could feel the throbs of pleasure emitting from his flesh. Then he rose on one arm again, and pinned me back, his eyes devouring mine.

"Eileen, my dearest. You are mine. You belong to no one else."

He moved on top of me and, as the blankets slipped from between us, we eagerly explored every part of one another's body. It did not seem vulgar as I was led to believe from the little bits I had heard about this from my girlfriends in school. Instead what we were doing seemed very private, something between us only, but something of which I was not ashamed.

My eyes had grown accustomed to the dark, and I could make out the outlines of his masculine features, my hands moving over his chest, entangling my fingers in the hairs on his chest.

I sensed that he could wait no longer, and when he raised himself above me, I moved to accommodate him.

"The first time, it will hurt," he whispered in my ear. "I will try to be gentle."

My fingers dug into his back as he guided himself in and I drew a breath at the tightness and pain. But I tried to relax, learning the new lesson of movement back and forth. I arched to him, and soon became accustomed to the rhythm, although my insides ached.

He gasped deep breaths, and I could tell that he was holding himself in check. Finally my pain numbed and I seemed to be moving more fluidly with him. He sensed my readiness and gave way to the tension that had built up in him. Even in the newness and the dull ache, I thrilled as each thrust seemed to go higher and higher in me, and I only pulled him closer, wanting all of him.

Finally, he shuddered and moaned, then lay against me, spent. I held him to my breast, willing that we would never part, knowing with all my being that no matter what befell us I never wanted to be parted from him. I did not care whether he had committed other crimes, I would stand by him. And if he were sick, I would take care of him. So deep was the love I felt, so heightened my emotions.

Gradually, my heartbeat slowed and my ears again became aware of sounds other than our breathing. It seemed that the storm had not let up, but the walls of the old chapel seemed impregnable, and for that I was thankful. Richard held me tightly, rolling onto his side, and we tucked the blankets around us, huddling in the dark. I reached up to fold a towel for a pillow under my head, and tried not to listen to all the strange sounds of water gurgling or wonder what other creatures swam in the water that covered the floor below. We were in the driest place we could find, and here we would wait out the night.

I did not know if I would actually sleep, but gradually, as I soaked in Richard's warmth, my breathing evened, and as I listened to his steady heartbeat, I fell asleep.

Chapter 18

I awoke stiff from sleeping on the floor of the gallery, but immediately the memory of what had occurred the night before overcame me and I felt a rush of warmth and embarrassment. As the fingers of light seeped in from around the shutters and poured through the damaged stain glass window, the strange intimacy Richard and I had shared the night before came back to me.

I felt the weight of his arm across me and as I moved, he murmured beside me and pulled me closer. I turned to face him, and he kissed me, waking up my heart.

"Good morning, my love," he said, and I gazed at his sleepy eyes, the night's growth of beard on his face, knowing for the first time what it was like to share a night, albeit such an uncomfortable one with a man.

A wave of nervous hysteria came upon me and I felt the urge to laugh. Part of it came from the relief that the storm seemed to have abated, and the sun shone. I struggled to sit up, still shy of facing Richard after what we had done. Many thoughts crowded my mind, for surely such an act changes a woman forever. I did not even dare to think of how what we had done would affect my relationship with Richard.

Such thoughts were too overwhelming, so I concentrated on small details.

"Look how the light comes through the windows," I said, pulling my blanket around me. "Let us open them and look out."

He stretched and pulled me back down beside him. "Time enough for that," he said, nuzzling my ear.

I laughed, taking pleasure in his nips and kisses, then once again I struggled out of his grasp. "Richard," I said. "I must get up. There are certain private things I must attend to."

"Very well. Wake me when you are through." And he pretended to fluff up the towel pillow and go back to sleep.

I laughed as I pulled the blankets around me and got to my feet. I had not seen Richard so playful before. I looked down at his form in a mock sleeping posture, swallowing a lump in my throat. It seemed the intimacy between us grew when we were alone, creating our own world. But what would it be like when we returned to the company of the others?

I went to open the shutters, and the sun streaming in nearly blinded me. The water had receded some, but still overflowed the banks of the bayou. The trees were tangled, with limbs and refuse strewn everywhere, and the birds were shouting and fluttering about, busily starting to rebuild their homes.

Thinking of homes made me wonder how the rest had fared the storm, and I was suddenly anxious to return. Though I was certain that the manor was strong enough to withstand the storm except for minor damage, I wondered how the cottage had withstood the gales. I prayed that the oak timbers had held to their foundations.

Downstairs in the sacristy I found that our clothes were still wet, but if our matches were still dry and we could find anything dry enough to burn, we might be able to start a fire and dry our things. I surely did not want to make my appearance in a blanket with Richard dressed likewise.

I ran my fingers through my tangled hair, but without pins or combs had no way of fastening it up, so I turned to looking for matches.

When Richard came down, he approved my idea. He broke up an old chair for firewood as everything outside would be too wet, and I found some paper for kindling. We carried our fuel to the stone steps in front of the church and set to work. Our crude survival efforts made me feel very much like the Indians that used to inhabit these parts. I was also aware of a feeling of warm pride that came from working side by side with Richard.

"Do you think the road will be clear enough?" I asked.

"We'll have to see. But the water looks like it's gone down enough that we'll be able to pass. We'll have to walk of course."

"I don't mind. I suppose our boat got broken up by the storm."

He nodded. "I'll see if that is the case, but I don't hold out any hope for it."

Soon we had a fire blazing and held our clothes over it long enough to get them passably dry. By the time we had dressed and eaten all the communion wafers for our breakfast, the sun was high. We would be a long time reaching home, and I could imagine that Lettice was quite worried by now.

The going was difficult, for there were many branches in our path. What we could not move out of our way, we had to climb over. My ruined gown became torn in a number of places, and mud caked over much of our costumes.

After a few hours of such torturous progress, I had to rest. I didn't think we were far from the manor now, and my thirst was great. I sat on a tree stump, the trunk of which had broken and fallen in the road, and caught my breath.

Richard surveyed our wild surroundings and I could see the melancholy steal over him again. I almost regretted returning to civilization, for with it came the weight of his concerns. Something tugged at me, and I felt the strange fear creep over me again. Was that how it was to be then? That I would only know Richard for the person I knew he could be when we were isolated from the rest of the world? Was there some reason that he had to withdraw into himself when we met with others?

I tried to push such thoughts aside and rose to plod onward. There had to be an answer to this dilemma. If the missing jewels or whatever mystery Richard was so preoccupied with obsessed him so, then the only answer was to solve the riddle. I felt a great sinking feeling in my heart when I contemplated this solution. I would help him solve it if I could, but I scarcely knew where to start, or indeed if he had identified the meaning behind the mystery.

By the time we came out of the woods and could see the drive that led to the manor house, my limbs ached and my mind was too numb to think. We dragged ourselves the last step, and when we approached the house, Henrietta ran out.

"Thank heavens, Miss, you're all right." She was quite distraught and she rushed forward, taking my hands. "We feared you were dead. Riggin rode over to the cottage this morning to see how the family fared, and when they learned that you weren't here, it set them in a state. Thank goodness."

"I'm all right, though a little worse for wear," I said. "Master Blakemore and I took shelter in the chapel."

"Oh, bless you, Master. Your mother was not sure you had set out together, but she'll be relieved to hear what happened. Come in now and get out of those clothes."

She continued to mutter prayers of thanks as we started for the steps. Richard followed me and Henrietta led him to my father's room where I knew he would find something that fit well enough to change into. I gratefully shed my clothes and gave them to Henrietta to burn. Then I asked her to draw me a bath, I soaked in the porcelain tub.

After a night in the wilderness, the neat, clean appointment of the bathroom with warm water, soap and clean towels seemed a greater luxury than I had ever appreciated in the past. I took my time, and after I had washed and toweled my hair, I rose and donned my dressing gown. After wrapping a dry towel turban style around my head, I made my way back to my room.

As I approached my father's room, I felt a surge of warmth. I half wondered if Richard would step out of the room, see me in my dressing gown and follow me into my room to take me in his arms again. Such thoughts of intimacy reminded me of what was between us now, but I tried to school my fantasies, trying to give priority to the many details that must be seen to.

241

But as I passed my father's room, I saw that the door was open and no sound came from within. I had my hand on my doorknob, but instead of turning it and entering my own room, I tiptoed across the hall to look in. The door to the wardrobe was slightly ajar, but there was no one there. Richard must have dressed already and gone downstairs.

I returned to my room and pulled the bell pull. When Henrietta came, she helped me dress as I asked how they had faired the storm.

"Sounded like the roof was comin' down round our ears, it did," she said. "But these old walls have been through worse than that."

"Yes." I thought suddenly of the storm in which Erin had died. "Was anyone hurt?" I asked.

She shook her head. "Sally and I were in the house, and Riggin saw the storm comin'. He came back, and we secured everything we could."

"Are the animals all right?"

"None of the horses got loose, though they was frightened I dare say."

"And is there much damage?"

"The garden shed clean blew away, and there's tools and branches and the like scattered all over. We'll have a job cleaning it up. But we got the shutters closed, so none of the windows broke. Except for the French doors in the music room. They blew in, and there's glass all over that room."

The music room. We had just begun to fix it up, and it seemed as if we would have to start all over again.

"I'll have the glass replaced right away then. Anything else?"

"We dragged most of the iron lawn chairs to shelter. Riggin's out lookin' things over now. It'll be a day before we see what's what."

"Well then you've done very well. I'm grateful."

"Just doing my job. I didn't sleep a wink all night what with the howling and shrieking, and us worrying about you."

"I'm sorry I worried everyone. When we set out there wasn't a cloud in the sky. The storm came up so fast."

She nodded. "That it does sometimes."

I finished dressing and started downstairs after her.

"Is Master Blakemore downstairs?"

She shook her head. "No, Miss. He changed into a suit of your father's clothes and said to thank you. He was anxious to get over to the cottage to let the family know you were both safe, so he borrowed one of the horses."

"I see. Yes, that's quite all right."

I could not help the disappointment I felt that he had gone without saying good-bye, but I could not let it show. Of course he would be concerned about his own family. And I'd rather he faced them first. I knew they would be relieved that he had brought me home safely, but I wondered if any one of them would guess what had occurred during our night together.

I blushed, keeping my face averted from Henrietta. Already I was feeling the embarrassment that came from contemplating what I had done. Not that I regretted it, but so little had been said on both sides, I merely wondered how it would affect us now.

"Thank you, Henrietta. I am rather starved. Is there anything to dine on?"

"Yes, Miss. If you're ready for luncheon I'll serve you some roast chicken and cream of mushroom soup. I made it up for anyone who'd been out working after the storm."

"That sounds wonderful."

I let her serve me in the dining room and made quick work of the meal, which my body appreciated. But I ate so much it made me sleepy, and since I had not slept as comfortably as I usually did, I decided to retire for a nap.

Upstairs, I lay on my bed, fully clothed, images fading in and out of my mind, until I dozed off.

I was not aware of how long I had been asleep, when footsteps in the hallway and then a knock on the door awakened me. I yawned.

"Come in."

The door opened and Gaius entered. I felt surprised, for I had not expected to see him.

"Hello, Gaius," I said, sitting up.

"Please don't get up," he said, crossing to the bed and seating himself on its edge. "We were so worried about you. Thank heaven you are all right."

I lay back on the pillows I had fluffed up behind me, still clearing the cobwebs from my mind. "Yes, I'm just a little tired. I'm sorry I worried everyone. Does Lettice know I'm quite all right?"

"Yes, poor woman. I sat up with her nearly all night, watching her pace the floor. She was sure you and Richard had been caught in the storm and were drowned. I must say we all had a rather terrible time of it."

"I'm awfully sorry. I wouldn't have worried Lettice for all the world."

I could imagine that Lettice must truly think I was a bad omen for her son. Even though I did not cause the storm, she probably blamed for me luring him out in it, although it was the other way around. Already I feared having to face Richard's family, and I pressed my lips together in anxiety.

Gaius took my hand and gave it a squeeze. "She is just relieved that you are all right. We all are. Leave it to Richard to be the hero and bring you home safely."

I lifted my chin. "You've seen him then?"

"Oh yes. He rode up as if nothing in the world had happened. Gave a brief explanation about your accompanying him to the north end of the island when the storm hit and taking shelter in the chapel. I'd say you were lucky there."

"Yes, we were lucky."

He tried to make light of it, neither of us dwelling on the question of what we might have done if we'd been caught in the wilderness with no place for shelter.

"Still, I can't imagine you were very comfortable in that drafty place with no food."

"We made do. There was some wine and a few wafers from communion."

He raised his blond brows. "So you dined on communion wine and wafers." He threw back his head and laughed. "That's a good one I must say. I shouldn't feel so sorry for you after all."

I smiled at the humor of it. "It wasn't so pleasant though. We were soaked, and the water rose around the place. We took refuge in the gallery."

"Ugh. I can't imagine anything worse than being cold and wet." His smile turned into sudden seriousness and a troubled look passed over his eyes.

"Oh it was all right," I said to reassure him. "We found blankets and got out of our wet things—" I suddenly realized what I was saying and shut my mouth, my eyes round. I glanced away in embarrassment. But it was too late.

He was silent for a moment, then when I risked a glance at him he was gazing at me as if putting two and two together. "Blankets. Oh yes, so you could get dry."

I nodded, looking at my hands. I still did not know if he would suspect anything. Was this how it was going to be. How would I be able to face anyone? They would all want to know what had happened to Richard and me in the storm. Must I feel like everyone would read my thoughts if I told of our refuge? It was my own guilty conscience of course, telling them half the truth but not telling all of it. I could feel my ears burn.

But I tried to assume a normal expression and smiled reassuringly at Gaius. "And how did you all fair at the house?"

He was still studying me, that look of puzzlement in his eyes, but then he seemed to come back to the present and took on the broad gestures that I had grown used to seeing in him.

"We had an exciting time of it. We did what we could to secure the house and stables and brought in the wicker furniture from the verandah and grounds. Then we lit a fire and gathered in parlor. The water came only as far as the edge of the garden, so we were in no danger from the flooding. I looked out several times and saw the wildlife skittering all over in search of shelter. It was quite an experience."

"Then you've never been in a hurricane before?"

He looked at me sharply, and a pained expression passed over his face. I drew in my breath, feeling as if I'd said something wrong. But he shook his head, rising and pacing across the room, his hands in his pockets.

"No, I haven't. I wouldn't say as I'd care to experience it again."

I was struck by the sudden bitterness in his voice. Truly Gaius could be a paradox. One moment all braggadocio, the next perplexed and anxious. I narrowed my gaze at him. Richard had suggested that there were things about Gaius Amundsen that he did not know, and I wondered much about him myself. I knew whatever it was that made him act the way he did, he would not confide it in me, though something just forming in my mind made me wonder if there might not be a way to get him to do so. I shook my head. In some ways, Gaius was as curious a person as Richard himself.

I glanced away and smoothed the coverlet beside me, the familiar anxiety beginning to churn in my stomach. Was this island such a place of secrets then? Who else had secrets that I did not know? And why? Even I had my own secret now.

I clenched my fist. There had to be a way to sort this out. I made myself relax and smiled at Gaius. I would begin by winning his confidence. He had offered friendship. Let him prove himself. If he felt affinity for me, perhaps he would grow closer to me if I were kind to him. I did not mean to be scheming, but it was the only way to find out if Gaius harbored some secret that I should know. I had to win his trust.

"And the others?" I asked. "Are they all right?"

He nodded. "Lettice would have come to you immediately, but there was much to do at the cottage. I offered to come and relay her concerns. She and Nannette will come to you tomorrow."

"That is kind of them. But I know there will be much work at both our homes to do in the way of repair. They should stay where they will be needed."

"My thought exactly," he said. "That is why I offered

247

to come here to help you. Lettice has Richard and that fellow Ian, though I'll be dashed if I know what good he'll be."

I grinned at his reference to Ian's uselessness when it came to work of any sort, but Gaius continued.

"You've only Riggin, and I know a couple of extra strong arms would help."

I thought of the heavy iron lawn furniture that would have to be dragged back into place and of the construction work that would have to be done on the doors that had inevitably blown off their hinges. And the garden shed would have to be completely rebuilt.

I cocked my head and looked at him. "You really wouldn't mind doing some heavy work?"

He shook his head. "Not at all." Then he snorted. "I wasn't raised a pampered gentleman, remember. My father is in manufacturing and I had to work my way up. He couldn't give me everything on a silver tray."

He seemed to stop and gaze at me as if he'd suddenly revealed more about himself than he wanted. But I nodded. It did seem that I might be able to get to know Gaius better, especially by allowing him to remain here and work with me.

I had to admire his sportsmanship. He did not seem in the least wounded since I had refused his amorous advances. I thought shrewdly to myself that perhaps his confessions of love for me were not quite sincere. Was it twice then that I had been pursued by young men who in a few weeks time were so able to forget their ardor. Was I so forgettable?

I hardly knew what to think, but I would not dwell on that now. I swung my legs over the bed and rose.

"Are you any good at carpentry?" I asked him.

"Passably. I can hold a saw and hit a nail with a hammer."

"That will be good enough. I think Riggin will appreciate your help."

He seemed pleased to be of service and I sent for Henrietta to make up a guest room for him, since he would be staying on here while we worked on repairs. Then we went down to supper.

I looked forward to an evening's conversation with Gaius. Perhaps I would find out more about him, and about his friendship with Richard. I sifted over the various things he had said to me, and as we left the table to have our coffee in the parlor, one thing stood out.

He had said his father couldn't give him everything on a silver tray. He had made it sound like it wasn't simply a matter of choice, in which case his father would have wanted him to work his way up, so that he wouldn't become a spoiled heir. If that were the case Gaius might have said his father *hadn't* given him everything.

But Gaius said he *couldn't*. I wondered why not?

Chapter 19

The next day Lettice and Nannette came to see me, and they did seem greatly relieved that no harm had come to Richard and me. Lettice was more her old self again, though once or twice I caught her gazing at me with a speculative look. I told them all Richard and I had been through, leaving out of course what we had done. That was for us alone to know.

I thought I was beginning to get used to facing society with my new secret knowledge and not feel guilty. It was a strain, however being with my cousins, for I wondered how much they sensed. The visit had gone off fairly well, with Nannette making faces every time I mentioned our fear of snakes or other creatures that might have accompanied us to the gallery.

"And the poor little raccoon," she said, when I had finished my narrative. "Did he stay dry throughout it all?"

I grinned at her, knowing her fondness for friendly animals, especially helpless ones. "I think he did, though I confess we did not see him in the morning."

As they rose to leave, Nannette gave my hand a squeeze. I met her gaze and she looked deep into my eyes.

I felt for an instant that she could see my soul, and that she must read my secret. But the next moment, she gave me a bright smile and kissed me on the cheek.

"We're so glad it turned out all right. If we'd known Richard was with you, we wouldn't have worried."

Over her shoulder I glanced at Lettice, but she did not give away any of her thoughts.

For the next several days we worked to repair the damage, much of it outside. I heard nothing from the cottage, knowing that they had double work there, for not only must they repair what the hurricane had done, but must start getting the house and grounds ready for the upcoming party, which was only a little over a week away now. I wanted to hurry and finish my work here and go to the cottage, as I had offered, to be of assistance for the party preparations.

Nannette and Lettice had told me of the foodstuffs that were planned. And of course we must see that there were enough lanterns and decorations for the grounds and go over Ian's scavenger hunt list. Nannette and I were afraid that if we left it to him, he would send the players after things they might never find, and we would lose all our guests. We would select things they might find either about the house or the grounds, in the gardens or the near beach.

True to his word, Gaius was a big help to me at the manor house. He rolled up his sleeves and set about tasks that Riggin assigned. In fact he kept himself so busy that I had little chance to talk to him except at meal times, and often our conversation then turned to practical matters. After supper he was usually so tired from the extra exertion that he went up early.

Though the work progressed well, sometimes a sense

of uneasiness overcame me. I would feel frightened for no reason, and I wondered if I were losing my reason. Was that part of the island's curse, that whoever dwelt here came under a spell and one's mind was touched with evil?

Sometimes a look from one of the servants or from Gaius, who I suspected watched me when I had my back turned, or a dark cloud passing over the sun would suddenly bring a feeling of depression over me. But there was nothing to do about it except wait and see what the future would bring.

Richard had warned me against being alone with Gaius, and I wondered if he approved of Gaius's helping me. I felt a momentary spark of resentment that it was Gaius and not Richard who had offered to help me. But of course Richard had his own estate to look after. And I did not feel that I was alone. Henrietta and Riggin slept in the servants quarters above, and a single bell pull would wake them.

And though I was suspicious of Gaius's motives, he behaved as a gentleman, and I could not believe I had anything to fear from him.

One evening, to amuse myself, I went along to the music room. We had been lucky enough to get glass from town, and the glazier had replaced the panes. While the room was not decorated the way it would be when I was finished with it, it was usable now. A craftsman from Tampa had done a good job on the piano, so that now when I touched the keys, a bright, musical sound came forth.

I lit the candelabra that sat on the piano as well as two wall sconces, and sat down to play. The music I played from was old and yellowed, but as I turned the pages I remembered the melodies as my mother had played them.

I played the soft, beautiful strains of "Für Elise," the way my mother had showed me how to play it, and I thought if she could hear it, she would be pleased.

Then I searched through the stack of music, pulling out the ballads and sing along pieces I thought I would take to the party at the cottage for everyone to enjoy. I came across a favorite of my mother's, a piece I had not thought of or heard in a very long time. It was a sad little song about a mother whose child had gone and never returned. It had a haunting melody with words by an unknown poet.

I began to read the music and stumble through the notes. But it soon came back to me, and I almost imagined I heard my mother singing the words the way she used to do after Erin died.

I knew I should not allow myself to sink into the melancholy such memories were bound to cause, but the music drew me on, and soon I was whispering the words softly to myself. It was an odd little song, stranger than I remembered. I suppose I had never sung the words before, but now as I half whispered them, half sang them to myself, a picture of the woman in the song began to emerge.

Her daughter was gone, she cried. She looked upon the meadows, in the forests, everywhere, but the child was not to be found. Finally, she waited by the empty tomb, but fruitlessly, for the child did not even return home to die.

By now I was caught in the spell. Yes, I could see how my grief-stricken mother could pour her heart out by playing this haunting melody. I almost imagined my mother instead of myself sitting here, her hands on the keys, not mine. She would play it thus. I launched into the piece from the beginning, giving way to the emotion I expressed both on the keys and in my soft soprano voice. I was carried away by the woman's desperate search, felt the anxiety she felt, pressed the keys harder, poured forth more emotion. For a moment I imagined it was my mother playing and not me.

Horror seized me, and I lifted my hands from the keys suddenly. For a moment the music seemed to carry on, then drifted silently away.

No, I screamed silently as I stood, knocking the piano stool over behind me. My hands were on my face and I whirled around half expecting to see my mother's apparition standing behind me, hands clasped as she sang.

But there was no one there. Still, my overwrought imagination felt a presence near, and with every muscle tensed, I stepped to the center of the room, afraid to breathe. I could swear someone had been there with me, urging me onward.

"Who is it?" I asked half aloud. I don't know if I expected an apparition to answer, but I could not just stand there numb. If someone had come in to listen to me play, why would they leave when I stopped?

I went to the doorway, but there was no one in the hall. The candles in the wall sconces fluttered, and I stared at them, feeling the fright building.

I fled down the hall, reaching the main wing. Then I forced myself to slow to a walk, went to the kitchen and told Henrietta I was finished in the music room.

"I thought I would return there, but I've decided not to," I said. "Would you mind extinguishing the candles?"

If she thought anything odd about the fact that I had left the room with the candles still burning, she said nothing. I left her and headed toward the stairs.

At the bottom of the stairs, I rested my hand on the newel post, pausing to slump my shoulders and let out a breath. There was something wrong with this place. Why did I insist on staying here? I dragged myself up the stairs and moved down the hall toward my room.

Before I turned into my room, I gazed curiously at Gaius's room. Then I walked toward it and put my ear to the door. From within I heard snoring. I frowned and turned back to my room. Gaius might have decided to come downstairs and listen to the music. But that would not explain the odd sensation I had had that my mother had actually been there herself. A trick of the imagination I suppose, but the feeling that she had been trying to communicate with me was strong.

I got ready for bed and sat brushing my hair in front of the mirror. A feeling of discouragement poured over me as I stared at my face in the mirror. What if there were no way of solving the many dilemmas that faced me here? How could I ever tell if the dead wanted to speak to me?

Again I felt the battle between determination to remain and see things through and the helplessness that came from not knowing what to do. Perhaps I should leave it all as I had considered once before. But as I lay the brush down slowly, gazing at my long, brown, wavy tresses, I thought of Richard's fingers entangled in my hair.

My heart beat wildly at the memory. I could not leave the island now, for love held me here. I had not known love before, but I knew it now. Love was wanting never to be parted from the beloved. Love was chafing to be with him again, wondering how he had spent these last days. Two miles between us was too much. How would I survive living in another place far distant, always wondering about Richard.

That I had had no word from him worried me. I tried to still the thoughts of self doubt, telling myself that Richard would not want a clinging, dependent lover. If he admired me for anything it must be for my fortitude, my willingness to guide my own life. That must not change.

I thought of how my mother had become a ghost of herself after Erin had died, and had seemed to depend more and more on my father. While I knew James had loved his wife, surely he had felt suffocated by her failing health and weakness. I would not be like that. I thought of myself as a strong person, though in moments like this, when my spirits sank, I was hard-pressed to live up to all my bold assertions.

If I had wondered why Gaius had so suddenly lost his ardor for me, I was soon given a clue. He was driving me over to the cottage, when he told me that a guest would be arriving today. A young woman he had met at the town picnic.

"Her name is Anna Coleman. She seemed rather lonely, so I prevailed on Lettice to invite her to our festivities. The dear girl has been staying with her aunt in Coral Springs. And since she seemed to have little to do except keep her old aunt company, Lettice generously invited her to come a few days early so she could have a taste of the outdoors life."

"Oh."

So Gaius had a new interest? Of course it could be like he said. Perhaps he did take pity on lonely looking young women. Then again perhaps he had sought her company after I had refused him. Still, until I met this Anna, I would reserve my judgments.

I had noticed that Gaius had seemed a little distant and perhaps this young woman had been occupying his thoughts after all.

As we turned into the drive, I felt the nervous anticipation overcome me. I had not seen Richard since we had come back from the storm. Hope mingled with uncertainty, and I was even more self-conscious about seeing him again than I would have thought.

As the house came into view I could see that not only had the lawn been freshly mowed and any refuse removed, but the hedges had been clipped, and there was a fresh coat of paint on the shutters. All in all the cottage looked quite gay, and it made me hope that this festive weekend gathering would be a success after all.

The horses clopped merrily up the shell drive as if they knew that feed bags awaited them at the end of the journey, and both Gaius and I were in good spirits as we approached the house.

Nannette came out to meet us, looking very pretty in eggshell colored muslin.

"Welcome," she said as Gaius reined in. She flew around the carriage and I got down without waiting for Gaius's help.

"You look well," I said to Nannette, who was all laughter and smiles.

"Why thank you. It's just that we're having such a time getting ready. I had forgotten how exciting it could be to have a house party. We haven't done it in ever so long. And our first guest has already arrived."

I glanced at Gaius, who raised his brows and looked toward the house.

"Is it the girl you were speaking about, Gaius?" I asked.

"Her name is Anna Coleman," said Nannette. "And she's been visiting an aunt in Coral Springs. A quiet, shy girl, but very nice. From the looks of her pale complexion and thin face it ought to do her a world of good to be here. Lettice invited her to come early so she could get a taste of the out-of-doors."

"Yes, Gaius told me." I wondered if there were another reason the girl had come early, but time would tell.

"Well, come in," Nannette said, dragging me by the hand. Gaius followed more slowly as Charlie appeared to take the horses.

Then as we were coming up the stairs, the front door opened and Richard came out. I stopped in the middle of the steps and he gazed down at me from the porch. Our eyes locked and I felt the warmth flow between us. My heart fluttered in my chest, but I tried to keep an even demeanor. I thought I saw the flicker surge briefly in his eyes, and his mouth, which had been drawn in concentration, seemed to relax.

Gaius and Nannette had passed me and were already on the porch, and I gathered my skirts to take the last steps.

"Well, here we are, back from our hard labors at the manor," Gaius was saying to Richard, who appeared to only half-listen.

Nannette opened her mouth to speak, then glanced

from Richard to me and seemed to change her mind. She turned and hooked her arm into Gaius's elbow, pulling him toward the door.

"I do believe Anna is upstairs, but then you already know her, don't you? You made her acquaintance at the picnic. Why didn't you introduce her to everyone . . ." And her voice faded as she led Gaius down the hall.

"Hello Richard," I managed to say when we were left alone. "Has everything been all right here at the cottage?"

A formal businesslike expression replaced the hint of interest I had seen before in his eyes. "Yes, quite all right. And you? How has it gone at the manor?"

"Very well, thank you. Gaius was a great help."

I regretted saying it immediately. I wanted to say that I would have rathered it had been Richard staying in the room across the hall from mine; that I would have thrilled to see Richard with shirtsleeves rolled up hammering nails, or squatting to take measurements where the new garden shed must be built. But I could not say any of those things.

The corner of his lip twitched as he said, "I'm glad."

I swallowed, feeling we were getting off on the wrong start. But then what had I expected? For him to take me in his arms and kiss me for all the world to see? The longer we stood there, so close and yet not touching, the more anxious I felt. I suppose I had harbored hopes of a more romantic meeting than this.

I lowered my head, not knowing what to say. Richard crossed to the square pillar next to the steps and braced an arm against it.

"The tenants suffered some damage from the storm, of

course, but not as bad as I had feared."

"Oh, that's lucky."

I began to feel foolish. Here I was thinking only of myself, when I should have realized that Richard would have had everyone's welfare to think of. No wonder he had not come to see me. His responsibilities would have come first. Still there lurked the suspicion in my mind that he was jealous of Gaius. But how could I know unless he told me? What could I say to show him there was no reason to be. Surely after what had passed between us . . .

But then a worse thought struck me. Richard had told me not to trust Gaius. And yet I had let him stay in my house with no one else there except the servants. Could Richard possibly think that I had been wrong to do so? That I had not considered my reputation by doing so? In the throes of trying to manage after the destruction wrought by a hurricane, such trivial thoughts had been far from my mind.

Richard seemed tense, and I could think of nothing to say. And so we stood there. I was about to go in, when he turned.

"Eileen."

I stopped and turned.

He was gazing at me with a pained expression in the depths of his eyes, which were luminous but dark.

"Yes. What is it?"

He stepped nearer and took my arm, guiding me along the verandah until we reached the railing at the end. He lowered his head, his voice little more than a whisper. He dropped my arm.

"Eileen," he said again, then he looked me directly in

the eye. "What happened at the chapel. It shouldn't have happened. Don't blame yourself. Please let me apologize."

I stood there completely stunned. I had expected him to say anything but this. As my heart constricted, and the pain seared through my chest, reality struck me. Of course we had both known it had been wrong. We had been carried away with passion, fear of the storm, and the unusual circumstances of having to spend a cold night together with nothing between us but blankets.

But I swallowed hard, the tears coming to my eyes as I looked away. Yes of course I knew it had been wrong, but my love for Richard had justified it. I had hoped that he had felt the same. But standing before me so stoically, not making a move or gesture to show that he harbored any kind feelings for me, it was obvious that he did not feel the same. He had lost control of his passions, and now he was sorry.

My shame overwhelmed me, and without a word I turned and fled into the house and up the stairs, praying I would not meet anyone and have to explain.

I heard him call my name from the foot of the stairs, but he did not come after me. It would have done no good. No further explanations were necessary. He did not love me, and I had cheapened myself by letting him have his way with me. I supposed that now he might feel that at the very least he should offer to marry me to make an honest woman out of me. But I would not have that. No matter what I had done, if we told no one, I could still hold my head up in society. I would not marry him out of obligation.

In the room I had occupied while I was here, I shut the

door, latched it and threw myself onto the bed, burying my sobs in the pillow. I wanted to go to sleep and never wake up. I felt pain such as I never knew existed. What had I done? I had thrown myself at Richard, foolishly given everything of myself to him.

But great love has its price, for when it is lost, in its place comes great pain.

Chapter 20

Some time later there was a tap at the door. I sat up and rubbed my eyes. Though my limbs were numb, and I didn't want to face anyone, I realized the awkwardness of my position. I could hardly stay cooped up here, for it would arouse too much suspicion. I would have to find a way to bury my feelings until I was alone. I would have to put on a cloak of normalcy for everyone else to see.

For if everyone saw how heartbroken I was, they might guess my secret.

"Come in," I said to the second knock.

I hastily splashed water on my face from the basin on the highboy and turned. Nannette came halfway in the door, a worried look on her face.

"Come in, Nannette," I said, moving to the dresser to smooth my hair. "I'm just freshening up."

I did not for a moment think I could hide my upset from her. But the routine movements helped me assume a pose.

She came to stand behind me, peering at my red eyes in the mirror. For the cold water had not been able to hide their puffiness.

"You've been crying," she said.

I jerked my head in acknowledgement. "I had a sudden outburst. It's all over now."

She put her hand on my shoulder, and the gesture of sympathy made me feel worse. But I struggled not to burst into tears again. I met her gaze in the mirror.

"Do you want to tell me about it?" she asked.

My lips trembled. "I don't know." I turned sideways, putting my face in my hands. "I feel so awful."

She directed me to the bed where I sat down and leaned back on the pillows. A few moments helped me restore my normal breathing, and subdue the threatening sobs.

"Now," she said gently. "Tell me what's happened. It's something Richard said, isn't it?"

I clenched a fist and thumped it on the bed. "Oh, Nannette. I feel so humiliated. I don't know how I can show my face."

She smiled gently. "Come now. It can't be as bad as that. He's said something to hurt your feelings, is that it?"

I clenched my jaw and gazed at her. "I'm afraid it's more than that."

The seriousness of my problem caused a shadow to cross her eyes. "Oh, I see. You have had a misunderstanding." She shook her head, wringing her hands. "Oh, Eileen, I was afraid of this. I tried to warn you."

"About Richard, you mean?"

"Yes. I could see that you were coming under his spell." She bit her lip. "I knew no good would come of it."

I frowned, the emotions still churning within me. "How could you know?"

She shook her head, picking small pieces of lint from the coverlet. "I can't say I knew anything, it was rather that I was more afraid. Afraid for you."

"But why?"

She shrugged. "Call it intuition. I know my brother. That is there are things I don't know about him, but I do know this. He keeps to himself alot. He doesn't seem to let anyone become truly close to him. Oh I don't mean to say he isn't a good brother. He takes very good care of us. But I was always afraid that when it came to love . . ." Her words drifted off.

"Yes?"

"Well, I can't explain it exactly. I just knew that it would be very difficult for him. Not that he doesn't have the usual male desires. I think he's normal in that way. But I was afraid for the woman who might love him. I was afraid he would end up hurting her."

I blushed, looking away when she spoke of his male desires. Didn't I know too well what she meant by that? "But why can't he let someone love him?" My words choked off in a little cry, and she took my hand.

"Oh dear Eileen. I'm sure that if he could love anyone, it would be you. Perhaps he does love you. Only he doesn't understand himself yet."

Again I pounded the bedspread with my other hand. "But why can't he experience love? What is there about him that everyone keeps thinking is so strange? Is there no way to find out the cause?"

I was at my wit's end and knew I sounded rather hysterical. My pride had suffered, and I could not have felt lower. Still my words poured out in desperation. But Nannette only shook her head, gazing at me pitifully.

"I wish I could tell you, Eileen. It's just that all my life I've sensed that he didn't lead a normal life. Normal in the sense of other carefree young men. But you must understand the responsibility he has here." She lowered her eyes. "And the guilt."

"Guilt? What guilt?"

She looked at me. "Well, you know how he and Jasper never got along. When Jasper died, Richard seemed to feel it was in some way his fault."

I frowned. "I don't understand. It was an accident on Jasper's boat. Richard never went to the docks, did he?"

She shook her head. "No, he didn't. At least I don't think he did." I could see the doubt in her eyes and it made my spine tingle.

"Nannette," I said, leaning forward. "You aren't telling me that you really do think Richard had something to do with Jasper's death. That he might have had a hand in it?"

She shook her head, the color leaving her face. "I don't think so. I think it's more complicated than that."

Then she looked into my eyes helplessly. "That's what I mean, you see when I said that Richard carried a great weight. If he feels somehow responsible for Jasper's death, he's got to make peace with himself. He's got to learn to live with himself before he can live with anyone else."

I sat back, surprised at Nannette's wisdom. She had done a great deal of thinking for a girl who appeard to be so flighty and fun-loving. But then she had had many years to contemplate her brother's character.

"Thank you, Nannette," I finally said softly. "I begin to see."

She smiled sheepishly. "I don't mean to tattle. I just thought it would help you understand. I don't know what's happened between you and Richard, and I don't need to know. It's just that if—" she paused, embarrassment flooding her face now. "If you've shown your love for him in any way, it's just that he might not be able to accept it for what it is."

I felt much calmed by what she said. Not that Richard hadn't hurt me, but I began to see that there might be reasons why Richard couldn't always open himself up to me.

"He isn't always so shut off, Nannette," I said. "There have been times when he's been quite—" I struggled with my feeble words. "When he's seemed to share things with me. Only briefly, it is true."

Then I dropped my eyes shaking my head. "But I can see what a fool I've made of myself."

She shook her head sympathetically. "Don't worry about that. And perhaps he does have feelings for you. Poor Richard, if only he could see." She sighed deeply. "I have prayed that someday Richard's burdens would lighten. Perhaps they will. Perhaps he will see that you love him. Maybe you are right, Eileen, it will be your love that heals him."

I smiled gratefully, appreciating her great concern for both of us. "I don't know. I can't offer him any more than I have."

I had to glance away for a moment. Then I looked up again. "I won't throw myself on him anymore. He's made it plain that he regrets what has happened between us." I tried not to blush as I said it, only implying that perhaps Richard and I had exchanged a few romantic gestures. "I'll have to let him come to know his own mind."

"Yes, if only he can."

"Yes," I repeated, the sadness dragging at me. "If only he can."

She rose from the bed. "Shall I leave you alone?"

"No. I must freshen up. I can't hide from everyone. Does anyone else know what happened?"

She shook her head. "Gaius went directly to speak to our guest. I was the only one who heard you come in and run up the stairs. I'm sure no one heard whatever words passed between you and Richard on the verandah."

"Thank goodness. Then I'll come down." I walked to the mirror again, then turned. "And Richard?"

She shook her head. "He went off after you came up. He saddled a horse. I don't know where he's gone."

"Then I shall not have to face him until supper," I said more to myself than to her.

"Well then," she said. "I'll go find Mother and tell her you will be down shortly. We'll have tea if you'd like."

"Yes, that would be fine."

I freshened up as best I could, changed and went down. Hearing voices in the parlor, I went that way.

Lettice glanced up from where she sat and when she saw me, she rose.

"There you are, Eileen. Come meet our guest."

A thin, plain-looking young woman sat on one end of the sofa with Gaius on the other end.

I walked into the room, and the young woman's gray eyes fastened on me.

"Miss Anna Coleman, this is Eileen Blakemore."

The girl's eyes rounded slightly, and she stood to take my hand.

"I'm glad to meet you, Anna," I said. "Gaius has told me about you."

Her hand felt cold in mine, but she curved her lips upward in greeting. I noticed that her eyes had a sunburst of green in them, but they lacked luster.

"How do you do?" she said.

I took a seat in the wing chair, and Anna resumed her seat on the sofa.

"I understood you have been visiting your aunt in Coral Springs," I said.

She nodded, her eyes still fixed on me. I glanced at Gaius, who was leaning casually against the corner of the sofa. He was watching with a half smile on his face, and from his expression, I could not fathom whether he was merely being polite or whether his interest in entertaining this girl went beyond mere sympathy.

She did seem a little pitiful. Her homespun check gown with its prim white collar was neat, but not fashionable. Her hair was pulled back and tied at the base of her neck with a ribbon. She had fine, even features, but her face was gaunt, as if she'd lived a hard life. It made me curious.

"And your own people?" I asked. "Where are they?"

Her eyes rounded slightly, and she said, "My parents died when I was very young. I've lived in an orphanage most of my life. It was only recently that I discovered my aunt, and she sent for me to come visit."

"Oh. I didn't know." That would explain her gaunt look. My heart went out to her. No wonder Gaius had invited her here. She looked as if she'd had little enjoyment in her life.

"Well," I smiled warmly. "I'm glad you're here. I'm sure we all want you to make yourself at home."

She seemed to respond to my warmth with a brighter smile of her own. I thought I saw moisture glistening in her eyes and was surprised. Had it been that bad? Was she so unused to people offering kindness?

Lettice smiled her agreement and just then Martha entered with the tea tray, which she placed on the low table between us. I glanced up to see a flicker in Gaius's eye that I could not decipher. It was almost a look of displeasure, though there was no explanation for it.

Lettice poured, and we busied ourselves with our cups. Lettice handed Anna her cup, which she balanced uneasily. She seemed rather nervous, and after taking a sip, her cup clattered noisily in the saucer. She seemed to be watching all of us, and I felt a little sorry for her. If she'd spent her life in an orphanage, she probably did not quite know what was expected of her in society. I smiled to put her at ease.

"Is this your first time visiting the gulf waters then?" I asked, though from her sallow complexion, the answer to that question was obvious.

She nodded, and I continued. "Then I shall take you for a walk along the beach. I think you'll enjoy the varieties of shells and the plant life."

"I'd like that, thank you," she said shyly.

So interested was I in our new guest that I had almost forgotten about Richard. Almost, but not quite. I sat back a little as Lettice took up the conversation and Nannette came into the room with Ian, whom I had not seen in some time.

Nannette introduced him to Anna, and then he bowed over me.

"It's good to see you, Eileen. We were afraid you'd been eaten alive by swamp creatures, but old Richard kept you safe and sound."

Ian's typical frivolity made me smile briefly, but the pain followed. Still, I accepted his solicitations, for he could not know how painful any mention of my night with Richard in the chapel would be.

"And how have you been, Ian?"

"I've been kept very busy, thank you. The storm was quite exciting here, though it was lucky there was no serious damage. It was something to watch the water coming in, though I must say it left quite a mess behind, and I was put to work helping clean it up."

Everyone began to chatter at once. Gaius offered Anna more tea, which she accepted. I chatted with Ian, who took a seat on an ottoman at my side, and for a quarter of an hour I felt my spirits lifted by the company.

Ian turned to tell Nannette something funny, and her bright laugh punctuated the conversation. Lettice seemed at ease and glad to have me back in their presence. Altogether, the mood seemed quite light, and I found myself wishing it could be this congenial always.

I cast my mind back to the gay little get togethers I had always enjoyed in the Van Nuys's parlor in New York, and I realized that we had not really had many such relaxed, gay times here.

But happiness here seemed like a thin veil lying over a deeper menace that plagued us all, a menace that was only biding its time. It made me wish that life could be more normal.

But then, thinking on it as I watched the group enjoying themselves, would I really trade my island, my home, for the spurious gaiety of the Van Nuys's parlor, for Ian's flirtations, for Millicent's cooing.

No, I thought not. Of course now that Richard had humiliated me, thoughts of fleeing the island were again brought forth in my mind. But where would I go? There was no place else that would claim me? In spite of Richard, this was my home. I belonged here as much as he did.

We had finished our tea, and the sun was on the

271

western horizon. I felt the need for some sea air, and I thought I would offer to take Anna to see the sunset, which was always spectacular and always different. She seemed to respond to the idea with alacrity, but then Gaius intervened.

"Now, Anna, you promised to walk with me."

Anna's eyes showed her confusion as she said, "Oh yes, so I did." She seemed to gaze at me in disappointment. "Perhaps we can go another time."

"Yes, of course," I said. Her look puzzled me. She seemed as if she would have preferred to go with me rather than with Gaius.

My curiosity rose. Were Gaius's attentions not being returned then? But then, looking at him, I really could not judge what his motivations were in entertaining this new girl.

I smiled at her, and the uncanny sense that we were exchanging an understanding that needed no words passed between us. I liked her, and I wanted to warn her of Gaius's fickleness. But something about the way she held herself belied her outer appearance of weakness. She might not have been blessed with a privileged life, but she gave the impression of having an inner strength that I wondered if she were even aware of.

Of course all this was intuition on my part, for I had only just met the girl. Still, when I crossed to her and pressed her hand again, her eyes gave off a luminous glow.

"There are many places to see on the island," I said. "I will show them to you with pleasure when Gaius is otherwise occupied."

Again there was a flicker of surprise in her eyes.

"Thank you," she said, squeezing my hand. "I did not

expect so warm a welcome."

Gaius touched her elbow, and I sensed his impatience to be off. I stepped back and watched them depart. As they did so, I saw Anna glance up at him.

It caught me off guard, and I found myself watching them as they moved into the hall and Gaius opened the door for her. He was not looking at her, and there was something about his look that puzzled me. It was not the look of a young man about to take a stroll with a woman whose company he fancied.

I was standing at the double doors of the parlor and evidently my perplexed expression was evident on my face. Lettice came to stand beside me and followed my gaze.

For a moment, we were silent, then she said, "There's something about her. Some quality . . ." She let it drift off.

I had felt it too and was not surprised that on such brief acquaintance, Anna Coleman had found her way into Lettice's heart as well.

"Well," said Lettice. "We must see that she has a pleasant stay."

"Yes," I said.

Nannette and Ian came up, and Nannette hooked her arm through mine. "Ian and I are going for a stroll too. Won't you join us?"

I protested. "Oh no, that's all right. I'll be all right here."

"Nonsense," said Ian, who was on my other side propelling me out the door with them. "You've been cooped up in that musty old mansion of yours. The sunsets can't be as beautiful from there as they are here."

I glanced at Nannette, and for a brief moment

wondered how much she'd told Ian. Not that she would ever betray my trust, but she might have put a word in his ear that I needed company, for now I felt him leaning on my arm, pressing it with his other hand as I was drawn along with them. It seemed I was not to miss the sunset after all.

Chapter 21

We walked down the path leading through the garden and the woods to the beach. Gaius and Anna were well ahead of us, and I could just see their figures as they descended to the beach. I had a great curiosity as to what they were talking about.

"We've finished the list for the scavenger hunt, Eileen," said Nannette. "Ian was so impatient to do it."

"But you must look it over," he said quickly. "See if you approve."

"I'm sure it will be fine."

I was hardly listening. I felt suddenly lonely, the odd member of this gay little group, and I couldn't help but wonder where Richard had gone. I tried not to think of him. Indeed I tried not to think of anything at all, rather to let the soothing sounds of the island evening wash over me.

The sky was pink streaked with blue and gold. It struck awe in us all, and we stood for some moments watching the colors move across the canvas of the sky, working their magic.

Finally we moved to return, and as I glanced over my shoulder I noticed Anna and Gaius some distance down the beach. She was seated on a tree trunk that had fallen and been bleached by the sun. Gaius faced her, his back to the sunset, and they seemed rather deep in conversation.

Then as if he sensed that they were being watched, he turned his head and looked at me across the distance. I quickly averted my gaze, feeling guilty, of spying on them.

We went in for supper. I dreaded entering the dining room, knowing Richard would be there. But I was determined to hold my head high and let none of my emotions show.

All the same, when I passed under the arched double doorway into the dining room, and saw him standing at the far end of the room, sipping on a glass of sherry, my heart seemed to fall to my feet.

I quickly accepted a glass from Ian, who came my way, and again I wondered if Ian had really missed my company or if Nannette had put him up to being chivalrous on this occasion. In either case, I appreciated his attention, for it helped me save face.

Lettice entered and we all took our places. I was at the far end of the table and would not have to face Richard, since he sat at the head of the table, with his mother at the foot. I did chance a brief glance at him as Ian held my chair for me, and saw that he held his jaw rigid. His expression was fixed, and he gave away nothing.

I did not know how I would be able to go through with the meal, but luckily the others kept up the conversation and I was not called upon for much comment. My eyes drifted to Anna, seated next to Gaius, who was across from me. Her eyes were a little brighter from the wine, and more round as she listened to everyone.

"So, Anna," asked Richard during a lull in the conversation. "What do you think of our island so far?"

Her chin snapped up as if she were surprised that he would address her. But she said, "It is very lovely. It is as I had imagined."

"You must make yourself feel at home here," said Lettice. "Please let me know if there is anything you want during your stay."

Anna's eyes flew to Lettice, at the other end of the table. "Thank you."

"Do you ride?" I heard myself ask her. I had promised to help entertain the girl, and doing so might help me keep my mind off my own problems.

She shook her head and lowered her eyes to her plate. "No, I never learned."

"Then I shall teach you. If you'd like, that is."

She looked at me with that expression of gratitude I found so endearing. "Do you really think you could teach me?"

"Why of course—"

"But Anna is afraid of horses, aren't you?" Gaius interrupted me, and I stopped midsentence.

Something sparked in Anna's eyes, but she held my gaze. "I don't really know. I've never been around them. I think I am rather afraid. But it's just that I don't know what to do around horses."

I smiled at her, resenting Gaius's interference. "I can show you. We have some very gentle mares. Would you like to try it tomorrow?"

She hesitated, looked sideways at Gaius, but then seemed to decide for herself. "Yes, I'd like that."

"What a splendid idea," said Nannette. "Eileen is a very good horsewoman."

Gaius was eyeing me speculatively, and I was afraid he would speak out against our plan, but then his demeanor seemed to change, and he said to Anna, "Yes, that does sound like a good idea. You should be in capable hands."

"Well, that's settled," said Lettice. "Ladies, shall we retire to the parlor? The gentlemen will join us after they've had their port."

There was a rustle of skirts as we rose and the men stood. So we were going to engage in this old custom of allowing the men to their port without female companionship. I could see that with guests coming, Lettice chose to observe all the formalities.

I did not intend to look at Richard as I passed him, but when I reached his chair, I glanced up. He was watching, and I was surprised at the expression of anxiety in his eyes. Then he quickly tore his eyes away from me and reached for his glass.

I almost stumbled. Perhaps he was feeling guilty over his treatment of me. Well, I didn't mind if he suffered a little on my account, I thought resentfully. I was certainly suffering enough.

In the parlor, we seated ourselves around the room and made idle chatter. Anna sat next to me, and we began to talk of books we had read, finding that we had a great many in common.

"Eileen, dear," Lettice finally said. "Why don't we have some music. The men will be along shortly. If you play, perhaps Nannette and Anna will sing."

It was a very gentle way of inviting Anna to perform without embarrassing her in case she was not skilled in music. I went to the piano, and Nannette rose and reached for Anna's hand.

"Come now, you must sing with me," said Nannette.

"My brother simply can't stand it when I sing, so I don't do it very often."

Anna smiled shyly, and did not refuse, so with me seated on the piano stool, and the other two behind me, we picked through the music until we settled on "Carry Me Back to Old Virginny." I began the piece, and then Nannette and Anna came in with the words.

Anna had a very clear, melodious voice that delighted my ear. I concentrated on getting the accompaniment correct, and by the time we finished, a burst of clapping came from the door.

We all turned and found that the men had come in in time to hear us finish.

"Do go on," said Ian, settling himself on the sofa beside Lettice. "That was splendid. Do another."

"Yes, do," said Gaius.

Richard was staring at Anna in a puzzled way, and then when he caught my glance, the muscles in his face tightened. I daren't look at him any longer, but turned back to the piano.

We began a ballad, and gradually I heard Nannette's voice die out so that the second verse was sung by Anna alone. She knew the song, and I played to emphasize her singing. Her voice lilted on the melodic line, and I was astounded that such a beautiful voice could come from such a plain-looking girl.

We reached the end, and I let the last chord die away. This time there was no applause, but rather when I looked at the faces watching us, they all were caught with entranced expressions. Truly Anna's voice had transported them.

Nannette, who stood near was the first to recover. "That was very lovely. I can see that you two don't need my help at all."

"Oh now, please," said Anna, her sallow cheeks now tinged with pink as she was obviously embarrassed to suddenly find herself the center of attention.

"You have a lovely voice," said Lettice.

I could tell that she wanted to say more, but was obviously unsure of her ground. Was such talent inherited? But one did not ask that of an orphan. Had Anna studied music at the orphanage? Perhaps I would be able to ask her these questions when we were alone.

I turned back to shuffling the music, and then saw that Richard had taken a seat at the card table where he could see me directly over the top of the piano. My mind went back to the last time I had played for this gathering and the passionate looks that had passed between us. I fumbled and dropped the music and leaned over to get it. Richard rose from his chair and came to help me.

He said nothing, but when we reached for the music on the floor at the same time, our hands touched. I started to pull away, but his hand went around mine. I looked at him, my eyes wide.

He said nothing, but held my gaze as if trying to read my thoughts. My face reddened, and I thought his gaze would sear my skin, so hot did it feel. Then we both rose.

"Your music is very lovely," he said finally.

I mumbled a thank you, still not looking at him.

I chose another piece that we could all sing along, and Nannette coaxed Ian and Gaius to participate. Richard poured himself another glass of port and continued to sip it for the rest of the evening. He looked troubled, and gradually I felt my resentment slipping away. The music, the wine, and the warmth of the room must have made me a trifle light-headed, for I caught myself looking at him more often than I intended.

And to my surprise, some of the old warmth seemed to communicate itself between us. I did not know what to think. He had humiliated me, then said he regretted what had happened in the chapel. He had ruined my reputation, that is if anyone ever found out what we had done, and I had every right to hate him.

But alas, I could not hate him. Was I his prisoner then? Was there no avoiding the spell Richard Blakemore had cast over me? By the end of the evening, his looks in my direction were quite deliberate, and when I quit playing, complaining that I was too tired to play anymore, he rose.

"I'll see you up," he said simply after I had said good night.

I could hardly refuse him in front of everyone, and so leaving the others to the game of cards they had started up, I moved stiffly to the door.

He followed me silently, and again I remembered that other night when I had gone up, wishing he had accompanied me. Now I was not sure what to think.

When we reached the top of the stairs and made our way to my room, I turned.

"Thank you, Richard, good night."

I put my hand on the doorknob, but he stopped me from turning it. He grasped my hand in his and made me face him.

"Eileen, I fear I've hurt you, and I want you to know I'm sorry."

I felt the grief well up in me and the tears gather in my eyes, but I would not cry in front of him. I raised my chin defiantly.

"I don't blame you if you hate me after what I did," he

continued. "But I simply cannot live seeing you so hurt. Is there any way I can make it up to you?"

I could hear the self-disgust in his voice and it threw me off. I looked at his face. Could it be possible that he felt as much shame as I did?

I could see the remorse in his eyes, and some of my anger died.

"I don't hate you, Richard," I mumbled, taking a deep breath and struggling to keep from crying.

Still he stood there, studying me. I could feel his eyes on my face, and I hated myself for the old longing I felt. Then I burst out at him, "You can't possibly understand."

But his hands came up around my shoulders, and he pressed his lips to my forehead. "I think I can understand, my pet. I think I can understand. If only you can forgive me."

The emotion in his words confused me. I had expected him never to want to set eyes on me again, I had not expected compassion. But I did not want compassion from him.

My sobs were out of control now. How could I tell him that it was not my reputation that I cried for, rather the humiliation of loving a man who did not love me. But I was choking on my tears, and could not say anything at all.

"Come, come, my pet. Please don't break my heart by crying." And he pulled me against his chest, pressing his lips in my hair. "It is right for you to care about your reputation, but you need not fear for that. I will kill anyone who dishonors your good name."

I clung to him, still sobbing, more confused than ever, and yet surging through me was the comfort of being held in his arms. Arms I thought never to be held by again.

"You don't understand," was all I could mumble, but he continued kissing me and holding me until I stopped crying. Finally, after a great gulp, I raised my head.

"I'm sorry," I said. "I did not mean to make such an awful show. I don't"—I stammered—"I don't usually cry."

"I know, my pet. I know."

He kissed my cheek, then fingered my hair, and I looked up at him, at the warmth in his eyes. Eyes that reflected the light from the candles in the wall sconces.

I could see my reflection clearly as I looked into his eyes, and I knew that he must see in my face what I saw in my reflection in his eyes. How could he not know I loved him?

I felt the emotion gripping me. I did not resist when he brought his mouth down on mine for a kiss. I sank against him for a moment, but then I fought him.

I pushed back, and he released me. Then he grinned, lifting a finger to my jaw. "You are right, my pet. I must control my baser instincts for now."

Then he grasped me in his arms and pulled me closer to him, looking me in the eyes. "But only for now. You do understand that, don't you, my love? We cannot be together yet. Not yet."

And he pulled me against his chest as he gave a great sigh. Then he set me from him, his expression masked, and I knew that he had again put on his formal expression with which he dealt with life in its exigencies.

"Good night, Eileen," he said. He opened the door for me, and I stepped in, staring at him.

"Good night."

With that he turned and went back downstairs.

I watched him go, touching my face with my palm. I did not understand what had happened at all. Perhaps

Richard could not stay away from me, and was struggling with his baser instincts as he put it. But that still explained nothing.

I had not expected such an apology. Was it possible that I had misjudged him? But I shook my head as I made my way to the dresser. He did not have a heart of stone then, for he did care something about my feelings. But the knowledge of his compassion still did not heal my wounds. He was sorry for what we had done, and he admitted he still wanted me. But where did that leave me?

He had said he would control himself for now, but only for now. Did that mean that he intended to use me again? Was he planning to make me his mistress? I sat at the dresser, my head in my hands. Judging from my own reactions to him, I wondered if I even had the strength to deny him what he wanted. I seemed to be so drawn to him that I would give myself to him under any conditions.

I sighed and sat up. That was not the kind of life I had planned. Richard said he would defend my good name, but one cannot defend a wrongdoing if one has truly done it.

I unpinned my hair, got undressed and climbed into bed. A wind had come up outside and began to howl around the eaves. It was a shrill howl, rising in pitch and then falling.

But being a child of the island, I had grown used to it and in fact the wind often lulled me to sleep. As I lay in the darkness, drifting off to dreamland, thoughts entwined themselves in my mind. The wind still rose and fell, and the last thing I thought of before I let sleep claim me was of Anna's beautiful voice.

*   *   *

The next morning I dressed in my claret riding habit, and went down to breakfast. Only Nannette and Lettice were eating as I took a helping of potatoes and eggs from the sideboard.

"Goodness," I said, "am I that late?"

"Richard went out early," said Nannette. "And Anna came down early in anticipation of your ride. I offered to let her wear one of my riding costumes. I doubted she had one, and so I told her that I expected she had not brought one along because she wouldn't have known she would need it."

"That was thoughtful of you, Nannette."

She gave a dimpled smile and shrugged.

I finished breakfast quickly and then went out. Not seeing anyone about, I started for the stables. As I rounded the corner and approached the door to the stables I heard voices from inside, and something made me pause.

"I'll be all right," I heard a woman's voice say.

"Don't be fooled by her." That was Gaius, for I recognized his baritone. "Remember, I warned you." Then I heard the shuffle of footsteps.

I straightened, hummed a tune, and scuffed my boots as I approached the door, for I didn't want to make it seem like I had been eavesdropping.

When I entered the shadowy stables only Anna stood there in front of one of the stalls, looking at the horse within as if she were trying to discover how best to pet it.

I stopped, smiled, and said, "Good morning."

She looked very neat in Nannette's tailored riding costume, her hair pulled up in a bun under her cap.

"Oh good morning," she said, smiling shyly. "I was just looking at the horses. Do you think they'll like me?"

Just then Lady Jane, the mare whose box she had been standing next to, nudged her shoulder and Anna nearly lost her balance.

"Oh my," she said, reaching up to touch the animal's nose.

"I think you have your answer," I said, laughing. "Here, she wants some sugar." I handed her some lumps, which I had brought in my pocket.

She looked uncertainly at the lumps I put in her palm, so I explained. "Just put your hand out, she'll take them from you."

Anna did as she was told, and Lady Jane ate the lumps, then shook her head in thanks.

"There you see?" I said. "I think you have a natural affinity for them. Have you never been around horses then?"

I remembered Gaius saying that Anna was afraid of them, but from what I had just seen, this did not seem true.

"I don't know," said Anna. "That is I was not around horses often at the orphanage. There was little time for leisure. Mostly it was just hard work and school. When I got older I taught the younger children, you see."

I nodded. I did not want to press her into talking about her life as an orphan, but if she wanted to share it with me, I was interested.

"I imagine you were a very fine teacher."

Her cheeks tinged slightly. "I did like the children. Being one of them, I suppose I wanted to do whatever I could to help them."

I cocked my head to one side. "You said you weren't sure about the horses."

She became uneasy then and turned to watch the

mare. "I don't remember what my life was like before I came to the orphanage. There may have been horses where I was born."

"I see."

She didn't seem to want to talk anymore, so I went to ask Charlie to saddle two horses for us. I decided Anna's lessons might as well start now, so I had her watch him do it.

"You see the strap he's pulling," I pointed out after he had hoisted the side-saddle onto Lady Jane. "That's the cinch. He has to pull it very tight or else the saddle will slip off."

"Oh dear."

"Don't worry. You develop a feel for doing it, though sometimes horses will try to trick you by bloating their bellies with air, then later when they let the air out, the cinch loosens.

Charlie led the horses outside to a step up where we could mount. I got up, then demonstrated how to hold the reins and how to guide the horse. She looked dubiously at the side-saddle, but I encouraged her.

"Don't worry," I said. "Lady Jane is the gentlest of mounts. Even if you forget how to steer her, just hold the reins loosely, and she'll follow my mount. She'll bring you home safely, no matter what."

Finally Charlie helped Anna mount, and she picked up the reins as told.

"Try just going around in a circle in that clearing there," Charlie directed. Charlie led Lady Jane out to the circle, and then let her go.

I watched Anna, whose seat was good. She held the reins firmly, and seemed to show no trace of nervousness.

"You can talk to your horse," I said. "Horses understand a lot more than most people realize."

Anna smiled and nodded. For a beginner she was catching on very quickly. I could hardly believe she'd never been on a horse before.

I led the way toward the road. I thought we would ride over to the manor, for she might like to see it, and it would give me a chance to see how things were going on there.

It was a glorious day. The sun was warm, but not too warm, and the sky was a clear blue.

We ambled along at a walk, and felt little need to talk. I pointed out the sugar cane fields and the palmettos, and Anna seemed to take it all in with great interest.

We turned at the fork in the road and soon came to the drive where the live oaks and pine dappled us with shade.

"It smells wonderful here," said Anna.

"Yes, there's nothing like the fragrance of pine."

Finally we turned the last bend, and the manor was visible.

"I thought I'd show you my home," I said.

"The manor house?"

"Yes. It's a big, drafty old place. Much too big for me alone, but I'm doing my best to make it a comfortable place."

I glanced at her and was surprised to see that her face was frozen in an expression of mixed curiosity and apprehension. I stared at her. Had she already heard the horrible tales of things that had happened at the manor? I ground my teeth. Perhaps that was what Gaius had been trying to warn her of. Again, I puzzled at Gaius's relationship with this girl. I did not know what it was, and it had seemed to spring up so suddenly that it made me wonder. But I would have to make an effort to keep her from being frightened of setting foot in the old place.

I tried to speak lightly. "Has Gaius told you of the place?" I asked.

Her eyes fluttered to me, and she seemed to try to gather her thoughts. "Yes, a little. I mean he just told me that you had inherited it."

"Yes. My father died just prior to my returning home."

She was silent, and when I again glanced at her, her face was so white I was afraid she might faint and fall off the horse. Some sort of trepidation passed over me, and I slowed my mount, making sure I rode beside her as we reached the house.

She said nothing, but as we passed beneath the allee formed by the overhanging oaks, she began to look to her right and left, and I thought that perhaps she had gained control over whatever it was that had so frightened her. I frowned, thinking I must question Gaius about what he had told her. Of course someone else could have dropped hints that the manor was haunted, or mentioned the family tragedies that had taken place here. I supposed that such tales might be enough to frighten any visitor.

But I did not like the prospect that all visitors to my home would come thus apprehensively. It made me want to bring life back into the place more than ever. I did not want everyone who came here to consider this a place of death.

We passed down the drive and rode around to the stables. No one greeted us, but then they were not expecting us. I dismounted and led my mount to the water, then after she had drunk, wrapped the reins round the fence. Then I led Anna's horse to the block where she could get down. I gave her the reins, and she too led Lady Jane to where she could take a drink, then patiently led the horse to the rail, where she could be tied.

As we walked toward the house, Riggin appeared from the barn.

"Hello Riggin," I greeted.

"Oh, morning, Miss. You've come over from the cottage then?"

"Yes, just for a ride. This is Anna Coleman who's visiting from Coral Springs."

He doffed his cap.

"I'm pleased to meet you, Mr. Riggin."

"We'll be leaving again in an hour, Riggin."

"Very well miss. I'll take care of the horses."

We went round the house so that Anna could see the front entrance. I was rather proud that the manor was beginning to look more presentable, for we had painted the shutters, and the hedges had been trimmed.

Henrietta opened the door for us, and we stepped into the front entrance hall. I introduced Anna, and Henrietta seemed pleased that we had a visitor.

"The parlor's just been dusted, Miss," said the housekeeper. "You'll be comfortable in there."

Again, I had the sense that Anna was extremely nervous, her eyes darting around the room quickly, as if she were afraid to look at any one piece of furniture for very long. She rubbed her arms as if she were suddenly cold.

"I'll show you the rooms then we can have a cup of tea if you'd like."

"I—" she hesitated, then swallowed.

I thought quickly that perhaps this was a mistake

erhaps to show her a house of such grandeur, or otential grandeur anyway, might make her feel even orse, for she would probably never live in such a place erself.

"Of course we don't have to see the house. Perhaps ome refreshment would be better."

"No, I—" she paused. "I want to see it. Please."

I began by showing her the dining room, then went cross to the library. "My father had a study as well," I aid. "But he liked this room with its many books."

She stood in the center of the room, staring. Then she oked at the portrait of my father, her eyes round.

"That is my father, it was done just a few years ago."

She nodded and walked hesitantly to the big oak desk the center of the room, where some old photographs ood. She seemed almost afraid to touch them, so I lifted p a picture of my mother. Then I thought that perhaps nna's discomfort came from being in a house with so any family memories, when she had nothing to ompare it to herself. And I was right.

She took the photograph in her hands and stared at it r a long time. "How fortunate you are," she finally aid. "To have had such attractive parents."

From the strain in her voice I could tell that she wished ne had known her own parents, and my heart went out her. I took the picture back and led her to the door.

"Yes," I said. "Of course I miss them."

"Yes," she said, swallowing.

"We can see the upstairs another time," I said, eciding it would be best to sit down for tea in the parlor, ut as we came to the entrance hallway again, she glanced p the long flight of stairs with its polished banister. Her ok of curiosity was so strong I thought that perhaps she wanted to have a look at the upstairs rooms after all.

But then she seemed to think better of it and followed me to where I was standing at the parlor doors.

"That will be fine," she said.

We went in and took seats in the parlor where Henrietta brought the tea. Anna's eyes were drawn to the portrait of my mother over the fireplace.

"That was made shortly after she was married."

Anna stared at the painting for a long time, saying nothing, and again I wondered if showing her a house so full of family tradition made her feel awkward, having no family herself. After I had poured and we sat back to drink, I tried to think of something else to say.

I wanted to question her about Gaius, but I was afraid that would seem too presumptuous. So instead I turned to idle chatter.

"I've just begun to work on this place," I said. "So many rooms were closed up for a long time."

"Yes," she said, looking around the room as if trying to accustom herself to being here.

"There's the music room. I've just been renovating in there." I was watching her carefully for her reaction, feeling more and more sure that Gaius had put ideas into her head about this old place, though for what purpose could not fathom.

But she only looked at me and smiled. "That's nice."

"Anna," I finally said, setting my cup down and leaning forward slightly. "Forgive me if I seem over curious, but I wonder if I could ask you something."

As she looked at me, I could see the change in her face, her eyes narrowing slightly, her mouth tensing as if she needed to prepare herself for my question.

But I wasn't sure what to ask. Just what was he

lationship with Gaius? How had they met? And yet what right had I to ask such questions. She was a guest in my home, it was my duty to entertain her.

Then I shook my head. "I'm sorry. It's just that I had a feeling . . ."

She watched me, and for a moment I felt as if the tables were turned and it was she who was scrutinizing me.

I rose. I could not place my finger on my feelings. "Shall we start back? If we want to return by luncheon, we'd better go now."

She seemed relieved to be on our way, and as we left the room, she cast one glance backward at my mother's portrait.

I informed Henrietta that we were leaving, and that I would be back day after tomorrow to prepare for the party as my room at the cottage would be needed for the other guests.

"Very well, Miss. And Master Richard, did he find what he came here for yesterday?"

I stared at her. "Richard was here yesterday?"

"Why yes, Miss. He told me it was all right with you if he looked in the study. I hope that was all right."

"Yes," I said, recovering. "I had forgotten." Richard was here yesterday? So this was where he had gone when he went out for his ride?

I met Anna in the entrance hall and we went out the back of the house and round to the stables to get our horses. I was more and more puzzled by this chain of events and did not know what to make of them.

We mounted up, and Anna seemed nicely in control of her horse. Then we started back down the drive. As we passed under the live oak allee and then passed into the shady road, I felt the air of oppression leave me. Perhaps it was true that there was something about the manor house that affected people strangely. A curse? A demon? Oh how hard I was trying to exorcise it, if only I knew what it was.

We left the sugar cane fields behind, and approached a stand of pines. Suddenly an explosion rang out from the woods. My heart went to my throat, and my horse, startled by the sound of gunfire, reared. I struggled to bring her under control, but Anna's horse bolted.

"Hang on," I shouted. She had barely got her seat, and I was afraid that if the horse ran into the woods, she would lose it.

I struggled to turn my horse, and finally making her obey the bit, kicked her into the woods after Anna, ducking to avoid oncoming branches.

Suddenly I heard shouts from behind, but I could not turn to look. My heart was pounding and I was nearly torn from my saddle with each low branch, but I tightened my hold and managed to keep my seat. But where had Anna gone? Surely she wouldn't be able to control a runaway mount.

We came out of the woods, my mare's flanks heaving, and we pounded across the beach, sand flying behind us. In the distance I saw two riders.

Anna's horse was still flying along the sand, but now someone else rode out of the woods and gave chase. I tugged on my reins and slowed. Then I turned to see Richard riding up behind me. He came up to me, a stricken look on his face, and we both reined in.

"Are you all right?" he asked, looking over me to see if I'd been scratched anywhere.

"Just out of breath. There was a shot. It scared Anna's horse and it ran away."

We both looked into the distance to see the two riders. Anna's rescuer had stopped her horse and they were turning now.

"It's Gaius," I said. Then in the next breath I turned to Richard. "Who was shooting?"

He pulled his mouth into a grim line. "I don't know. But when I find out I'll deal with him myself. Someone could have been hurt."

"Who would hunt so near the house?"

"Only a fool," he said. "And no one hunts without my permission." His tone was angry, and I had no doubt he would see to the matter personally.

Gaius and Anna neared us, and I rode up to her.

"Are you all right?" I asked.

She nodded, though her face was white and her lips a grayish color.

"She's had a fright," Gaius said. "But I daresay she'll get over it."

I still wondered how she had managed to keep her seat. "It could have been worse," I said, and then regretted it, for from the look of fear in Anna's eyes, the thought of anything worse happening seemed to frighten her even more.

"But we're all right now," I said. "Come, let's go back."

Not a word had passed between Richard and Gaius, and I felt the tension between them as Richard threw him an open glare, then turned to ride beside me.

Chapter 22

We rode back to the house in silence. Clouds were blowing up, and by the time we dismounted and saw to the horses, drops of rain were beginning to fall.

The accident seemed to have cast a pall on everyone and I began to wonder just how festive our weekend party would be after this. But when we went in Lettice was speaking to a young married couple who had just come from the mainland. She introduced us to Opal and Henry Schnier, and though I tried to make polite conversation with them for a quarter of an hour, my mind wasn't on it.

Excusing myself, I met Ian, who had come in from sketching because of the rain.

"Drat this rain. I had such a good spot too."

Evidently he had not heard the shot, so I didn't bring it up. "And how are the sketches, Ian?" I asked to be polite.

"Rather good if I do say so myself. By the way, you don't happen to know where Miss Coleman is, do you? I thought I'd like to do her tomorrow if the rain quits."

I shook my head. "I don't know. She was with us a few moments ago, but she might have gone to her room."

"Well then," he said. "There's nothing I can do at the moment. Might just finish reading the newspapers that were sent over this morning, since we're cooped up here."

We went upstairs together, and as I paused at my door, I turned.

"Ian," I said.

"Yes?"

"Do you hunt?"

"I've popped a few partridge in my time, why?"

I shrugged. "I just wondered."

I went into my room. Who could have been shooting this morning? Ian had been sketching. But then if someone had been carrying a gun and didn't want anyone to know about it, he could have left the gun in the woods. I hoped Richard would find it.

The rain did not let up until just before supper. I had tried to rest in my room and read, but could not concentrate on the printed page. I went to Lettice's sitting room and tried to write a letter to Millicent, whom I had neglected all this time. But by the time I had finished it, I was not at all sure it was what I wanted to say.

I decided I would visit the horses in the stables just for something to do, and in order to have a change of scene. I went down to the kitchen and pocketed sugar cubes to give them, then went out.

The rain had left everything glistening, and there were a few puddles by the house, which I had to avoid. But the scent of rain was refreshing.

The stables were dark and cool, and I felt comforted by the presence of the animals. Going up to Gertie's stall, I reached out a hand, and she came to me.

"That's a good girl," I whispered, rubbing her soft muzzle.

She whickered, and I petted her, finally reaching into my pocket for the sugar.

"So, you are an expert horsewoman, I see."

Gaius's voice startled me. I turned.

"I didn't hear you," I said.

"I'm sorry, I just wanted some air after being inside all afternoon."

"Yes, so did I," I said, leaving Gertie and moving on to the next stall.

"But it's too wet to go far."

"Yes. Luckily the rain stopped, so the guests arriving will have an easier time of it."

"Quite." He followed me as I went to all the horses, talking to them and feeding them their sugar.

"I see you have quite a way with the animals," he said.

I nodded. "Yes. Growing up here the animals become a part of one's life."

"Even the wild ones on the island."

"Yes, I suppose."

I had started to move on, when he caught my shoulder, causing me to turn toward him.

"Eileen, I admit I saw you coming in here, and I followed. I wanted to speak to you."

"Oh? What about?"

He frowned. "I don't mean to alarm you, but I've become genuinely worried for you."

"For me?" I couldn't help it if my tone was mocking. I was beginning to feel as Richard did about Gaius. I didn't trust him.

"For your safety," he said and looked at me seriously.

I shivered slightly. "Why would you say that?"

"Oh come now, Eileen. The things that have happened since you've been here. Any fool could see that you're not safe."

I lifted an eyebrow. "Accidents do happen."

"Yes, but not so many in so short a time."

"What is your explanation then? That someone is trying to do away with me?"

He lifted a blond brow. "I wouldn't have put it that way, but you might be in danger."

I narrowed my gaze, watching him. "From what, do you suppose?"

"I don't know. That is what concerns me."

"You may be right. But until I know who wishes me harm, there is little I can do about it."

"And if you did know?"

I patted Lady Jane's nose and gazed at Gaius shrewdly. "Then I would ask him why."

Gaius met my gaze, then the corners of his mouth curved upward in a smile that did not meet his eyes. "Are you sure it is a man? What if it is a woman who wishes you harm?"

"That's ludicrous."

"Why? Do you not believe that women can carry out evil schemes?"

"I'm not saying they couldn't, but there is no reason. And there's only Lettice and Nannette."

"Well yes, but now there is Anna, and the other guests arriving."

"Oh come now, Gaius, are you trying to tell me that someone like Anna, whom I've just met has been lurking about the island, appearing in storms on the other side of my French doors at the manor house and carrying a white cat into the woods to frighten my horse and firing a gun this morning? I think you might come up with a more reasonable explanation than that.''

He raised his hands in protest. ''I'm not accusing anybody, I'm just saying it's possible.''

I faced him squarely. ''Gaius, why are you telling me this? Why this sudden concern?''

Something struggled in his face, and then his eyes took on a vulnerable expression that I almost believed was sincere. He reached out to touch my arm, then dropped his hand self-consciously.

''Eileen, I made no secret of my feelings. But when you told me how you felt I did not press you. I have tried to be satisfied with your friendship, but surely you must realize that I cannot stop caring so abruptly. If anything were to happen to you—'' his words were choked off and I was startled at his emotion.

I looked down. ''I appreciate your concern Gaius.''

''Well. Enough said. I just don't want you placing yourself in any unnecessary danger.''

''I'll try not to.''

Just as we started to leave I thought I heard the clink of metal on wood and glanced toward the tack room. Gaius followed my gaze and frowned. But we walked out into the sunlight, which had appeared as suddenly as had the rain, and we made our way to the house.

Gaius left me in the kitchen, and I paused by the window, gazing out. In a moment, Richard emerged from the stables. My heart hammered in my chest. Had he been in the tack room listening to my conversation with Gaius? Why? And why had he not made himself known?

The next day was bright and sunny. Ian had gotten

Anna to agree to pose for him, and when I came down to breakfast, they met me in the hall.

"Oh, there you are, Eileen. Anna and I are going out, and we wanted to know if you would join us."

"That's very nice of you," I said, "but I wouldn't want to interfere."

To Anna I said, "Ian's got enough sketches of me in that book of his. It's you he wants to do today."

"Oh no, please," she said. "You wouldn't be interfering. I would enjoy it."

From the sincere looks on their faces, I decided perhaps I should go. I was still feeling confused about Richard, and being with Anna and Ian might cheer me up. Remembering what had happened yesterday, I thought we should not go too far from the house.

We walked down to the beach and after Ian found an appropriate spot, he posed Anna. She was self-conscious, but he arranged her so that he could make the best use of the background. I was glad it was she and not I who would have to sit patiently while the artist's pencil flew over the page today.

For myself I was content to sit and gaze at the scenery and draw pictures with a stick of driftwood in the sand. When I got tired of sitting, I strolled along the beach a ways watching the waves lap over each other.

When I returned to take my seat again, Ian threw me a curious glance, and I thought perhaps he wondered where I had gone.

"I hope you're not wearing Anna out," I said.

But she smiled from where she sat, and it looked as if she were enjoying herself. She was much more at home out in the open than she had been at the manor house yesterday, and I decided that things of nature must interest her more than musty old mansions full of bad memories and dubious occurrences. I returned her smile.

"Oh, Ian," she finally said. "Can I move now? Surely you've got quite enough of my left side."

He looked at the picture for some seconds and then glanced up, but when he did he looked at me. Anna and I were both smiling at him, but his gaze fixed on me in an odd way. I wondered if he were comparing the picture he had just drawn with the one he'd done of me on the bridge.

"Well," I said. "Which of us is the better subject?"

"I'm sure Ian has many better subjects for his sketches than I," said Anna, getting up.

I laughed. "I'm not sure he has any subjects but us at all."

Ian rose, dusting off his trousers, his contemplative mood seemingly replaced with the teasing mood we had struck. "But I'm not finished. If you two ladies will accompany me, I saw the most intriguing setting, just a little distance down the beach. It would be the perfect place for two portraits done together."

"Oh, Ian," I admonished. "This is supposed to be a holiday, and you're making us work. It isn't fair."

"Don't be too hard on him," Anna said, coming to his defense. "I think it's very dedicated of Ian to want to do the sketches."

"Yes, I do strive for a good likeness, and that unfortunately takes time," he said.

We walked along to the spot he had selected, though we took time to admire the shells along the way. Then suddenly a dark shadow crossed the sand, and I looked up. Richard's hawk.

We stopped to watch as the hawk descended gracefully. Then Richard came in sight and called the hawk back to him.

"How fascinating," said Anna.

"Yes," I said.

We went along to meet Richard, who showed Anna the bird. I said nothing, but watched how patient he was in answering all her questions.

But I could see that Ian was anxious to be on his way. We were about to move off, when Richard stopped me.

"Won't you walk with me, Eileen?"

I turned to the other two, but Ian assured me they could do without me.

"I'll be along shortly," I said.

I turned to accompany Richard in the other direction. We walked silently, and I did not know what he expected me to say or do.

"Did you find out who was shooting yesterday?" I finally asked.

"No," he said.

"Do you think," I hesitated. "That it was an accident?" He glanced at me, and my heart twisted inside. "No, of course not," I said. "Nothing on this island is an accident."

I couldn't help the bitterness that had crept into my voice.

We plodded on through the sand, and I clenched my fists as we walked. Finally I stopped and faced Richard, making him stop. The hawk spread her wings and danced on his wrist.

"How long must this go on, Richard? Is this the way of life on Calayeshi Island then? Have I come home only to find that someone stalks me?"

My anger turned into hurt and grief, and I felt tears

threaten to spill down my cheeks. But my torrent of words rushed on.

"How can you stand to live here, Richard, knowing that some unknown evil lurks? And knowing that some think you're the one who wants me off the island or worse. I thought it wasn't true, but I don't know anymore. I don't understand you Richard. Sally said you'd taken Pericles from the manor house. That cat keeps frightening me. What were you doing with it?"

I was sobbing now, my hands on my face as I shook my head. I could hold nothing back now. What did it matter? Nothing seemed to help. I knew no more than the day I had come here. What did it matter if I made a fool of myself?

"I thought you cared for me, Richard then I thought you hated me. But you could never hate me enough to kill me. Oh tell me it's not true, Richard, tell me."

I heard him move away to find a branch on which to set the hawk. Then he returned.

"Eileen," he said, taking my shoulders in his hands. "Look at me."

I lowered my hands and looked up at him through tear-stained eyes.

He wiped the tears away with his fingers, then shook his head. His eyes were gentle, and I felt my heart melting.

"Eileen. I would never hurt you. Never. I was afraid I had, in the chapel." His look was so full of emotion that I felt my knees weaken.

"No, no," I whispered into his shoulder. "It cannot be you."

He held me until my hysteria passed, and still I clung to his strong shoulders. Why couldn't we have met somewhere else and fallen in love like normal people with nothing to stop us from loving? For whatever it was that seemed to come between us I hated it all the more because it was unnamed.

"I took the cat from the manor house when Lettice complained of mice," he said. "We thought old Pericles might make short work of the rodents."

"When was that?"

"It must have been in June. We were having a lot of rain then."

I exhaled in relief. When Sally had told me about seeing Richard with the cat, I was too startled to even ask when it was. How stupid of me. Then I had hated to bring it up with Richard for fear he would think I didn't trust him. Only my emotional outburst brought my questions out, and I saw now that it was for the better. Surely more communication between us would have helped.

"I know how it must be for you, my pet, I know." His voice was soothing, my ire receding. "Soon it will be over."

He reached into his pocket for his handkerchief and gave it to me to blow my nose.

"What do you mean it will be over soon?" I asked, when I had regained control of myself.

He jerked his chin up, not looking at me. "It is a feeling I have."

"Richard, if you know something I do not, please tell me."

He frowned in concentration, then shook his head. "I'm sorry, I cannot. It's nothing definite. Let us just say I have my suspicions."

I supposed I would have to live with that. Still, I resented the fact that he would not share his thoughts with me. Richard fetched the hawk, and with his other hand took my arm, and we walked back through the trees toward the house.

I was not in the best of moods and did nothing to hide my sullenness. I was tired of all my doubts, annoyed with myself and annoyed with Richard. I did not want to act like a spoiled child, but all my romantic notions were not bearing out. Richard said he cared for me, yet I still could not penetrate the shield he kept around himself. I cursed myself for falling in love with such a man.

We stopped at the mews, and I said, "Thank you for seeing me home," and turned to go in.

"Wait," he said.

I paused while he set the hawk on its perch. Then shutting the gate he came to me again, looking into my face, but he said nothing.

"What is it?" I asked.

But he only frowned and shook his head. "Nothing."

I turned again, too impatient to see him through his mood, for my own temper was nearly out of control. My heart sank when I remembered how close we had felt, trapped by the storm in the chapel. Was it only in adversity then that we could find intimacy? I bit my lip, hoping no one would stop me as I ran up to my room.

When I came out of my room for supper later, Ian stopped me in the upstairs hall. He had changed for dinner, but he still carried his sketch pad.

"Eileen," he said, as I started down the hall.

"Hello, Ian. How was your sketching today?"

He had a rather intense look on his face as he caught up to me. "It was rather revealing if I do say so myself. In act that is what I wish to talk to you about."

"Oh?"

He glanced about us then said. "There's not enough ight here. Could we go down to the parlor?"

"Why of course."

I followed him downstairs, only mildly curious about what he wanted to show me. I knew that all artists had to be humored, and I did not mind spending a little time admiring Ian's sketches. And the likenesses were getting rather good. I could see his improvement since the drawings I had seen in New York.

We went into the parlor where he lit one of the kerosene lamps.

"Here," he said, pointing to the sofa next to the lamp he had turned up. "Sit there."

He sat next to me, placing the sketch pad on his knee. He opened the pages, stopping only briefly at the sketches he had done of me two weeks ago. Then he went on to the ones of Anna. Some were only half finished, as if he had started them, but then was not pleased with the result.

Then he came to the later ones he had done after I had left them alone. There was very little background, but he had concentrated on her face, which in the drawing, looked quite attractive.

"Aha," said a voice.

We looked up to see Gaius standing at the double doors. Other guests were coming down now, and Lettice was bringing them into the parlor. Another couple had arrived from the mainland, Rhoda Hamilton and her beau, Garrett Duncanson.

We greeted the newcomers, and as we were forced to chat with them for a while, Ian started to close his sketch

pad. While we were talking with Rhoda and Garrett
Gaius picked up the pad and carried it over to the lamp. I
glanced at him watching him turn the pages, pausing first
at some of the better ones Ian had done of me, and then
going on past the others to the one of Anna that Ian was
about to show me.

I was trying to keep my mind on the conversation I was
having, but for some reason my eyes were drawn to Gaius
as I watched him study the pictures. He was only half
turned in my direction, so I could not read his
expression. However, he finally closed the pad and
returned it to the sofa beside Ian.

"You have quite a hand," said Gaius by way of a
compliment.

"Thank you," said Ian, glancing up at him. "It is a
hobby only. A mere pastime."

"Still," said Gaius. "You have some talent."

Something about the way he said it sent a warning up
my spine. I did not know exactly, but I had the feeling
that Gaius had not liked what he had seen.

My throat had become dry. Was Gaius at the bottom of
all the odd accidents that had been occurring here? I had
no proof, but somehow I sensed it was so. But if so, why?
And because he had not liked Ian's pictures, and I was
sure he hadn't, did that mean that Ian was now in danger
as well?

I could hardly keep my sociable smile in place as my
mind rushed on to contemplate the possibilities. Gaius
knew something the rest of us did not know, I was sure of
it, unless Richard had guessed Gaius's secret or what he
was after. For I knew that Richard was not telling me
everything he suspected.

I remembered that Gaius had been keen on our

family's history and had been curious about the family jewels. Was that it? Had he become obsessed with finding them to the extent that he would stop at nothing to get them? But why? Evidently his family was not poor. No, there had to be more reason than that.

Lettice came to announce dinner, and we went in. Gaius offered me his arm, and I did not want to refuse him in front of everyone, so I calmly put my hand on his arm.

Gaius Amundsen, I thought as we walked sedately toward the dining room. You are not what you appear to be.

I vowed to find out his true reasons for coming to Calayeshi Island.

Chapter 23

We were fourteen at dinner, and it was a pleasure to see the table laid from end to end with flowers arranged in its center while the chandeliers blazed on our silks and satins.

When Richard came in, I felt my heart flutter, he looked so handsome. Once again, he caught my eye from his place at the head of the table, causing my cheeks to brighten.

We took our seats, and throughout the soup course, served by two young waiters Lettice had engaged to help with the weekend party, I chatted with Garrett on my left and Ian on my right. But through the din of dinner conversation and the flow of wine, I did not forget my earlier resolve.

Gaius sat between Lettice and Karla Lottingham, a friend of Nannette's from the mainland, and though he politely listened to the conversation of those around him, he cast several glances in my direction. He did not look at Anna that I could see, and I wondered why. They had been so friendly before. I did not think it was just the fact that he was acquainting himself with the new arrivals. No, it was not as simple at that. For I decided that

310

verything Gaius Amundsen did was coldly calculated.

I glanced up and caught Richard's eyes, and I felt as if e read my thoughts. Somehow I knew that both Richard nd I thought Gaius was guilty. But guilty of what? Was hat what Richard was trying to ascertain? He had not een lying to me on the beach today when he told me he lid not know anything for certain, that he only had vague uspicions. I could almost understand it now. For I felt he same. We could hardly ask Gaius to leave the island ecause we suspected him of trying to cause accidents nd frighten me. We had to have proof that he was doing o.

I sat back, having eaten more than I intended. The adies rose to retire to the parlor, and the gentlemen tayed over their port.

Once in the parlor, I felt less obligated to participate in he chatter, but listened with half an ear. Several other oung ladies in this gathering played the piano, so I was lso spared that task. Rather, I took a seat in a wing chair n a corner from which I could observe. I could use the rowded occasion to ruminate over what I knew, and as he ladies formed themselves into groups to talk or to get p a game, I simply watched them as if they were a ackground to what was going on in my mind.

I looked at Nannette, who was gaily chattering, her air in exquisite curls and her gown of blue silk, shot vith silver threads flattering her natural good looks. I did ot feel that Nannette was part of any subterfuge. Her ace was too open to hide anything, and I believed that er anxiety for her brother's welfare came from the eart.

I watched Lettice, moving around the room, poised as ver, her congenial expressions controlled, too controlled. She too was concerned for Richard's health and sanity, but there were things she knew or suspected that she had not told me. I sensed that she kept many secrets to herself. Not that I blamed her, for she probably had reasons for doing so.

And now there was Anna. Did Lettice too wonder about her relationship to Gaius? Who was Anna Coleman? Where had she really come from? And what did she want here?

The gentlemen came in, but still I remained in my distant state of mind, watching, observing. I saw Richard take a seat across the room with an expression on his face not unlike my own.

Then Lettice brought in a large box in which she had written the names of all the gentlemen. Since we were an equal number of men and women, the ladies would draw names to see who would partner them on the scavenger hunt tomorrow night.

"Who will draw first?" asked Lettice, holding the box which she had wrapped in colored paper, leaving an opening at the top for us to reach in.

"Let Eileen draw first," suggested Nannette.

"No," I said and smiled. "I would prefer to go last and let the other guests enjoy their surprises."

"I'll draw first," said Karla, laughing. "I hope I draw a very handsome partner." She reached in and drew the name of one of the other gentlemen with whom she was acquainted from the mainland.

The other two ladies drew names, then Nannette drew Ian's name. Anna drew, her eyes rounding as she looked at the piece of paper.

"Who's name did you get?" asked Nannette.

My pulse throbbed loud and steady, for there were

only two men's names that had not been drawn.

"Why Richard, you are to be my partner," said Anna, looking at him with wide eyes.

"Ah," he said, and bowed his head to her very politely.

I met Gaius's eyes as he stood slouching against the wall on the other side of the room, his hands in his pockets, and I did not think I imagined the mockery in them as I reached in and pulled out the last slip of paper, opening it for all to see that my partner would be him.

The next morning, we all gathered around breakfast, and then I went riding with some of the guests. By afternoon I was tired, and decided to rest in my room. The scavenger hunt would take place after supper, and we would all be provided with lanterns. Lanterns had likewise been strung from the house to the beach and to the edge of the woods as well, marking our boundaries.

Dressed in high laced boots for walking about outside, I met the others in the parlor where there was much excitement. Nannette and Ian were the guardians of the lists to be given out, and made a great deal of keeping them hidden until the hunt was to begin.

"Are you ready for the game?" asked Gaius, coming up behind me. His voice was low and had an edge to it that made the hair on the back of my neck stand on end.

"Why yes, I am."

He raised his eyebrow at me. "Do we intend to win then?"

My nerves tingled. The way he said it gave me to believe he was talking about more than just the game. But I tried to give him an even smile in response.

"We might win," I said, "since we do know the island

313

somewhat better than the others."

"Except your Richard, there," he said.

My Richard? I did not respond.

Finally Nannette came around with the lists and Gaius and I bent over it. The first item we had to find was a shovel.

"A shovel," he said, frowning. "I'm stumped there. Do you know where we ought best look?"

"I think there might be a shovel in the tool shed, the newly rebuilt one."

"Very well," he said, gesturing that I should lead the way. He followed me out, and it was no trouble to walk along the shell path to the new tool shed. I held the lantern while Gaius fiddled with the latch. Soon we were inside, rummaging about for a shovel.

"Aha," he finally said, holding up a small one. "Will this do?"

"I think it will," I said.

"Then let us make haste."

We were the second couple to return to the house. Our prize was accepted and then Nannette gave us our second assignment. We needed to bring back a conch shell. For that we would need to go down to the beach.

I looked at Gaius, who nodded, thinking the same thing, and we started out. I told myself I had no cause to be nervous. There were lights everywhere, and couples moving about within hailing distance. Still, I felt my old apprehension about being alone with him.

We had passed through the garden and were just entering the woods when suddenly our lantern went out.

"Oh, drat," said Gaius, fiddling with the wick, but to no avail. "I'm afraid I haven't any matches."

"Neither have I," I said. "But we can return to the

house and get some."

I turned to go back, but he did not move.

"It will slow us down if we both go back. You take the lantern and get us a light. I'll go on. See, they've lit the path well enough to see by. Just give a call when you come back this far. I'll see your light. And by then I may have found what we need."

"All right."

I wasn't going to argue. I didn't really care that much about the game. And I preferred returning to the house with the light than accompanying Gaius in any case. I turned back up the path.

Once in the house, I took my time about getting a new light. Nannette saw me come in and thought we had returned already with our prize.

"No," I explained. "My lantern burned out. I've got to get some matches."

"Oh, I see," she said, looking over my shoulder. "Where's Gaius?"

"He went on to the beach to search alone. I hope that's not against the rules."

"No, no. It's all right."

Just then Anna came in.

"Hello," she said. "I'm afraid I got separated from my partner. I'm sorry. I got confused about which lantern was his, and in the darkness I got a little frightened." She pressed her lips together.

"It's all right, Anna," I said, putting my arm around her shoulders. "I'm rather tired of the game myself. And I'm afraid I've lost my partner too. Why don't we have some refreshment instead? The men can do just as well without us for the moment."

"Well, perhaps you're right."

She seemed worried about it, but I succeeded in luring her to the punch bowl in the dining room.

She drank her punch, then sat it down and raised her head to look at me.

"Eileen, I must tell you something," she said nervously. "I must warn you."

I set my punch cup down so hard it sloshed over onto the lace tablecloth. "Warn me about what?"

"Richard, Gaius, oh," she bit her lip. "I don't know."

I clutched her arm, rather hard, for I saw her wince. "You must tell me. What is it?"

She would not meet my eyes, but she said, "I cannot tell you everything, Gaius would—" she hesitated.

"What! What would Gaius do?"

Then she looked up, entreating me with her eyes. "We must find them," she said. "Gaius means to do something dreadful, and I think Richard knows it. Or at least he suspects it. And if Richard tries to stop him, Gaius will kill him."

I let go of her. She had said enough. Without stopping to pick up the lantern, I ran out of the house. One way to keep an eye on Gaius was to stay with him. I didn't stop to think logically, or even to sort out what Anna was trying to tell me. All I knew was that if Richard found Gaius and I was there as well, at least Gaius would have the two of us to deal with instead of just one.

When I got all the way down to the sandy beach, the trees behind me hid most of the lanterns, even the lights from the house. A sliver of moon hung in the sky with stars that twinkled far overhead, but the trees hid all else.

The wet sand sucked at my slippers as I walked along the edge of the water. I muttered a curse, holding onto my skirt to keep the hem from getting wet. Not finding anyone, I turned to find my way back to the path.

A figure stepped in front of me suddenly, and I screamed, then clapped my hand over my mouth.

"Gaius," I said, after gasping two quick breaths. "You startled me."

My eyes had grown accustomed to the dark, so that I could see his eyes glinting at me. He had not moved, and I took a step back, my foot sloshing in the cold water that raced up to claim my heel. As I stepped back, Gaius came forward.

"Forgot the light, did you?" His voice was strange, evil.

"Gaius, what's the matter? What are you talking about?" I said, moving sideways. I could go no farther backward or I would be in the water.

He muttered something I could not hear, and I raised my voice. "Gaius, come back to the house with me. I want to talk to you."

But he only came toward me muttering. Gone was all pretense of playing a game. Something had happened since I had left him, for he was behaving very strangely now.

He still walked toward me, and though he spoke to me, I wasn't sure it was me he saw. "At last, my father will be avenged," he finally said. It was as if he didn't really speak to me, but only to images in his mind that he believed to be enemies.

Panic rose in my throat as I stumbled over a piece of driftwood at the edge of the water. Surely he wasn't going to force me into the water. I finally got my balance again and spoke with all the intention I could muster.

"Stop there, Gaius, and tell me what it is you want."

He stood still, but he was clenching his fists at his side.

I was shaking as I realized he meant to kill me. Even if I could raise my voice loud enough to be heard, he could push me in the water and hold me down long before anyone could reach me.

I tried to sidestep him, for the water had reached my ankles now, and the tide was coming in, wave after wave sloshing over my feet, the sound churning in my brain.

He muttered again and reached out, grabbing me by the arms, the sudden movement frightening me even more than I already was.

"You who had everything when I did not, now you will pay," he said.

He squeezed my arms and I cried out. Then he let go of me so abruptly that I stumbled over my hem and fell to the sand, gulping air as I tried to get to my feet again. I was angry then. Even if he had become deranged, it angered me that he would not tell me why he was doing this.

"You've no reason to harm me, Gaius. Tell me why you want to do this."

He stood still, staring at me as I scrambled up and got a secure footing on the solid, dry ground. But he moved toward me again, the moonlight catching his face. I saw the odd twisted look.

"You know where the jewels are. You must. My father meant them for me, you see. You should have shown me where they were. It would have been easier."

I struggled for breath, this time talking to him in more even tones, trying to reason with him.

"Gaius, whatever are you talking about? If it's the family jewels you're after, no one knows where they are. I've told you that, time after time. And why should

318

you have claim to them anyway? They belong to the Blakemores."

I tried to ignore the wild beating of my heart. I had to get him to talk. Even if I couldn't believe any of what he was saying, I had to get as much out of him as possible.

"Go on," I said. "Tell me why you think you deserve them."

He raised his face as if he were looking through me, and I knew he was only seeing the pictures in his mind. "He hated you all. He told me he did."

"Who?"

"My father, Jasper Blakemore, of course."

I gasped. "Jasper?"

He nodded. "You couldn't guess it, could you? You didn't know I'm his flesh and blood. So you see that is why the jewels should be mine. He wanted me to have them all the time."

My mind was spinning at this new revelation. But it still made no sense. "Even if you are Jasper's son, why do you claim the jewels? They'd been handed down to my father for safekeeping."

So that was it. That was why he hated me. I shook with fear. Even if it weren't true. Even if in some perverted way Gaius thought he was Jasper's son and had become obsessed with the jewels, thinking that they would have been left to me must have made me seem like his enemy.

But I still could not believe it. He was grinning down at me now, a terrible macabre grin. I should have screamed, but I was too frightened. Surely this was my end. He was going to kill me. I saw it in his eyes. My strength gave out. I could not fight him anymore.

But from somewhere within me a new idea formed. It

319

might not be too late to reason with him.

"Gaius," I said, attempting to hold him off. "Listen to me. I can help you. We can both find the jewels. We can still share them."

The mention of the jewels made him hesitate. I knew I had gained a tiny margin of advantage, and I pressed it. "You should have told me that was what you wanted. We could have worked together. We can still work together. I might be able to remember things I had forgotten. Don't you see? It's not too late."

I kept talking, trying to distract his attention. Finally he was listening to me. But I was still not safe from him, and the look that darkened his face now proved me right. It was too late for my reasoning. He had gone too far.

"No," he growled. "Why would you want to share them with me?" He laughed a hideous laugh. "I don't need you now anyway. For I know where they are."

"How do you know?"

He grinned at me, his eyebrows raised. "Aha. Greedy are we? But of course your fine family would like to know where they are. No, I've worked too hard to figure it out, and it's my secret now."

"Oh really. So you've discovered the island's secret after all."

I was angry now. If he was going to kill me I might as well tell him what I thought of him. I didn't yet know how, but all my dilemmas were in some way connected to him. Whether or not he was Jasper's flesh and blood I did not know, but he believed himself so. And that had been his justification for coming here to try to ruin our lives.

I saw now how he had tried to turn me against Richard. If Richard was mad, then Gaius's evil had driven him so. Hate filled me, and though I knew that my strength could

320

ot possibly best this deranged man before me, I wanted
o make him pay for his deceit.

I shivered. My feet were wet, and the night air was
enetrating my limbs. He gripped my arms, pushing me
oward the water, but I summoned the courage to laugh
arshly.

"You think you can rid the island of its curse that
asily, Gaius . . . whoever you are? Perhaps this island
oes not wish to give up its secret. You will be doomed if
ou disturb its secrets. You will not live to enjoy the
poils you so greedily desire."

I don't know where my words came from, but I flung
hem at him even as he gripped me harder. Something of
vhat I said impinged on his mind for a second, for I could
ee the flicker in his eye.

But then rage filled him again and he clamped his arms
bout my shoulders, pulling me toward the water. I
creamed, but he clasped his hand over my mouth. My
ingers tore at him, but he had dragged me into the water,
vhere we struggled. Farther and farther out he pulled me
s the tide lapped all around us.

Then from a distance I heard my name being called.
aius heard it to, and it made him hesitate. The sound
ame again, nearer. It was Richard. He must be looking
or me.

Gaius hesitated. If someone was coming this way, he
vould not be able to hold me under the water long
nough to drown me and still run away. He would be
aught.

"Eileen," Richard's voice boomed from the trees.

Suddenly Gaius dropped me and I sank into the surf,
he weight of the water on my clothes pulling me down. I
puttered, going down on my hands and knees in the wet,

321

sandy bottom. But Gaius was sloshing through the water now, getting away.

"Eileen!" came Richard's cry.

I coughed and choked, trying to answer. Finally I was able to pull myself to my feet and make my way to shore.

"Here," I cried in a weak voice that I was sure was not loud enough to carry even half the distance up the shore.

But Richard must have heard me, for I saw him now running across the sand and plunging into the water to reach me.

"Eileen, are you all right?" He reached me and swept me up in his arms. Then he hoisted me up and carried me the rest of the way to the beach.

I was still coughing and spitting out water, and when we reached the shore, he took me up to the dry sand and set me down.

"I'm all right," I finally managed to get out. "Gaius . . ." And I pointed in the direction he had gone.

Richard glanced in that direction, but he seemed more concerned for my welfare. "Can you walk?" he asked.

"Yes, I'm all right."

"I'll take you to the house."

Chapter 24

Lettice met us at the door, but at a look from Richard, she merely stepped aside so I could go upstairs and change. She could hardly miss my wet skirt and my disarrayed hair. Her face was drawn in concern, but she said nothing.

As I started up the stairs, Richard said a few low words to her, and she nodded, glancing after me. But evidently he had satisfied her, and she did not follow me.

I changed into a dry gown, and hastily did up my coils again. When I went downstairs, one of the other couples returned, and Nannette was giving them their next assignment. I heard her tell them that the remaining objects must be found within the house. When the couple turned their back to begin their search, her eyes flew to me, and her look of social congeniality turned to a look of fear.

Ian was talking quietly with Anna in the corner. Opal and Garrett came in. Lettice came in and came over to where I was standing. She kept her voice low and her back to the other guests.

"Richard told me what happened," she said, the dread showing in her eyes.

"Where is he now?" I asked, looking over he
shoulder.

"He's gone to look for Gaius."

Fear stabbed my heart and I unconsciously clutched
Lettice's arm. "Lettice, he won't be safe. Gaius is mad!"

"He'll be all right."

Her commanding tone stopped me from running ou
into the night after them again, but I still searched he
eyes, unbelieving that she could stand there so calmly
knowing that her son faced a madman.

For that is what he was. I saw it clearly now. Gaius had
been behind all the threats, trying to lead me away from
Richard. Trying to come between us by insinuating that
Richard was mad and by befriending me.

Our voices were low and strained, for we did not wan
the other guests to know anything was amiss. All th
same, I could feel the tension in the room, as if everyon
were aware that something was about to happen.

"Lettice," I whispered. "Gaius wants the jewels, th
ones that were stolen all those years ago."

"Many people have wanted the jewels."

"I know, but he thinks he was meant to find them. It'
what drives him. He thinks he," I hesitated, not wantin
to hurt her with what Gaius said. After, it was probabl
completely unfounded, and I had no idea how he had go
the notion he was Jasper Blakemore's son.

She turned and took my arm. In a more normal voice
she said, "Let us get some punch, my dear." And we wen
toward the dining room, nodding to the final pair wh
had come into the parlor carrying a wagon wheel.

I felt relieved that everyone was in the house now, an
that Nannette was keeping them there. Everyone, that i
except Gaius and Richard.

324

As if reading my thoughts, Lettice said, "Don't worry bout Richard. He can take care of himself. He knows the sland well, better than anyone else, even someone who hinks he has had enough time to explore."

I had to put my faith in her judgment, still I felt uneasy s we came to the punch bowl. She ladled a cup for me, which I took. But the fruit punch tasted bitter on my ongue.

"Now tell me what it is that Gaius thinks," she said. She had drunk her punch, and stood straight, as if prepared for what I might tell her.

I swallowed. "He thinks he is related to the family." It was as close as I felt like coming at the moment.

Her eyes narrowed as if she were thinking of omething, and then she nodded, and her eyes cleared. "I ee," she said. "That explains many things."

Again I felt the knot in my stomach. How could we just tand here under the pretense that we awaited the utcome of the scavenger hunt, when in reality a far more deadly search was going on?

"There is something else," I said. "Anna warned me bout Gaius."

Lettice looked at me evenly, and again I could tell there were thoughts going round in her head that she was not evealing.

"Yes, Anna," she said.

She started to move toward the doors again. "Come," he said. "It is getting late. The game must be over soon. hall we congratulate the winning couple?"

I followed her into the parlor where Nannette was waiting for someone to come in with the final object of he scavenger hunt.

"Who do you think will be the first to find a piece of

china with the words 'Home Sweet Home' on it?" she asked to no one in particular.

No one answered, so I said. "Someone is sure to find the platter on the dish rail in the kitchen."

"Yes, probably," she agreed.

Then the front door slammed back. My heart contracted, and I flew across the room to the hallway. Richard stumbled in the door, and the sight of him made me shriek and stumble toward him.

His shirt was torn, the sleeve ripped from his shoulder, and his face was streaked with dirt. But before I could reach him, he turned and bent over, dragging a heavy looking, carved wooden box behind him.

At first I could not conceive of what it was, then he gave it a shove, so that it slid to the center of the entry hall, where we all stood now, for everyone had been drawn by Richard's sudden return.

"There," he said, straightening and running his hand through his tangled dark hair. "This is the prize we've all been looking for."

"What," said Henry Schnier who, with Opal, had just descended the stairs and did not realize what was happening. "Is the game over?" He stopped on the stairs, looking down at Richard.

"Yes," said Richard, meeting his curious gaze, and then slowly looking around the room at the rest of us. "I'm afraid it is."

I had been staring at the short, carved wooden box that he had brought in, and as I stared at it, the dread that had been with me all evening rose to a dizzying sensation as it finally sank into my mind what I was staring at. Then I looked horror-struck at Richard, for I could not believe he had done such a ghastly thing.

"Richard," I said, nausea and fear gripping me so that was aware of nothing else. "What have you done?"

He took a step toward us as I withdrew instinctively, ne reaction coming from a fear beyond my own control.

"Why?" I gasped then pointed at the object in the enter of the room. "It's Erin's casket."

"What?" asked Ian, stepping around Lettice and unkering down to examine the thing more closely. "A asket?"

There were several other gasps in the room, and I felt s if I stopped breathing. But I nodded, my head starting o spin. I had been very young when it was put into the ault, and I'm not sure I would have been able to describe , but seeing it here, there was no doubt. I knew what it as, the abhorrent symbol of Erin's death.

But Richard bent down and picked up one end of it, noring my distress.

He nodded in the direction of the parlor. Ian took the ther end and they hoisted it into the parlor and set it on ne gaming table.

"Richard, what can you mean by this?" Nannette had ome up beside her brother.

"You'll see," he said. "We'll all see."

And to my shock and horror, he fingered the latch and nen opened the lid. All eyes were on him as he turned it oward us so we could see the contents.

I stared as he reached in and lifted out a canvas rawstring bag. He placed this on the table and then ulled open the bag. From it he withdrew a long, blue elvet box.

My heart was hammering now, but the nausea had ettled and the perspiration on my forehead had cooled. or even before he had the box opened, I knew what we

327

would see.

There was an intake of breath as the clasp on the box was opened and the dark red rubies set in polished gold picked up the gleam from the overhead chandelier.

"Oh my," said Anna, moving closer to the table.

"Then it was true," said Nannette, staring at her brother. "They've been here all the time? How did you know?"

But my attention was now drawn back to Richard himself, and I saw that a cut on his forehead had started to bleed.

"Richard," I said, going to him at last, my hands flying up to brush back the hair from his face. "What has happened? Where's Gaius?"

"Trying to escape, no doubt," he said. "He would have taken this with him if I hadn't followed him."

"How did you know where he would go?" I asked Richard. I had fished in his jacket pocket for a handkerchief, which I now used to carefully blot his wound.

"I didn't know, exactly. But he had gone to the north end of the island."

"And this?" I indicated his torn clothing and the blood on the handkerchief.

His look was ironic. "I followed the path along the bluffs. Then I saw him, heading across the island, and knew where he was going."

"The cemetery," I said.

"He was trying to get into the vault. So I waited. He must have been there before, because it didn't take him long to get the vault open. Then he took out the casket."

Richard grimaced, and I began to worry about what his struggle with Gaius had cost him.

"Then what happened?" asked Nannette, her eyes wide.

"He didn't give it up easily," said Richard. But he did not elaborate.

Feeling slightly dizzy, I closed my eyes and opened them again. I held Richard's arm, and he had tucked my hand against his side, but whether I was supporting him or the other way around, I did not know, but we seemed to lean on each other for mutual support.

He gazed down at me then, and though I was anxious to attend to his cuts and bruises, I saw something in his eyes that made me almost weak with relief. He looked at me as if his words were only for me, though I knew he spoke for the benefit of the others as well. But the old mask was gone. He looked at me clearly, directly, and there was emotion in my eyes that started a tremor deep within me, though I dared not give it the name I wanted to.

"Where is Gaius now?" asked Lettice, still amazingly calm for all that had happened.

Richard shook his head. "At the dock, most likely, trying to find a boat."

"Oh," my head fell, disappointed that the thief would get away.

But Richard's words brought my head up. "He won't get far." He looked at his mother. "I took the precaution of setting the boats adrift and sending for the police from Coral Springs. They'll find him and bring him back."

"Is that a good idea, to have Gaius brought here?" I asked.

Richard looked deeply into my eyes. "I thought you might have some questions for him. I believe we all do."

"Yes," said Lettice. "You did the right thing."

His face was beginning to look pale, and so with my

hand firmly under his arm, I said, "Let me tend to your scratches. You'll need to change, and," I paused in embarrassment, "see if you have any bruises."

He managed a weak smile at me and we moved toward the stairs. Lettice sent Martha to bring some cloths, water and bandages, but she met my gaze and said she would remain downstairs with the guests.

I got Richard to his room upstairs, he took off his coat and sagged onto the bed.

"I'll be all right," he said. "I'm just a bit stiff."

I shook my head in agony over his evident struggle with Gaius. I dipped the cloth in the water and Martha bathed his forehead, while he closed his eyes.

When I was finished, he grasped my hand and brought it to his lips to kiss it. I blushed in embarrassment, and if I weren't concerned about his bruises, I would have put my arms around him and held him against me, but I satisfied myself with the look in his eyes.

"Thank you," he said.

Then he took off his shirt, wincing as he did so, and I examined his back.

"Only a few scratches," I said. "I'll dress them."

When I finished with my ministrations, he took a clean shirt out of his wardrobe and he put it on. Just then we heard a commotion downstairs, and we looked at each other.

"They've found him," I said, and we went out of the room.

Downstairs, two stocky-looking men had led Gaius into the parlor and sat him on a chair. His hands were handcuffed behind him, but the sneer on his face told me he was not bested yet.

"So," said Richard, going to the cabinet to pour

himself a badly needed drink. "Here we have the grave robber, the petty thief. You're bound for jail where you belong, Amundsen. I only brought you here for one reason. I thought you owed it to my family to explain just how you ascertained the whereabouts of the coveted rubies. In fact I think we would all like to know who told you about our little family secret in the first place, for it was evidently that which lured you here. Am I right?"

Gaius glared at Richard. "I owe your family nothing. In fact it is rather the other way around. Your high and mighty family owes me something it never paid. That is why I came here to claim the jewels."

I looked at Richard curiously. "Do you mean to say you never mentioned the jewels to Gaius when you were at school?"

"No," said Richard. "I never did."

My gaze flew to Gaius, who though perhaps beaten, had given up none of his arrogance.

"And how did you know where to look?"

He stared at me, his eyebrow raised, the malice communicating itself to me across the room. Then his eyes slid to the left.

"Your sister told me."

My heart had stopped beating. No one spoke as Gaius looked at Anna, whose face seemed to change color. I could feel Richard's gaze on me as I stared at the mysterious girl who had come into our midst so unexplained.

"Yes," said Lettice, sitting down on the wing chair near where she had stood. "I thought as much."

I took a few steps toward Anna, but found no words. I too sat down, as I began to feel the floor give way beneath my feet. But the girl facing Gaius looked at us all.

"The resemblance," said Ian, stroking his chin. "It was what I was trying to tell you last night, Eileen."

I looked at him dumbly.

"The drawings, I was showing them to you when—"

"When Gaius interrupted us," I said. Then I pinned Gaius with my gaze. "I see," I finally said. "It's beginning to fit."

Was I then the only one not to guess? The last person to know that the young woman I knew as Anna Coleman was not Anna at all?

I shook my head, looking at her. "Can this be true? But Erin . . ."

She looked at me, her lower lip trembling as she took two small steps in my direction, still unsure of what I thought.

"No," she said softly. "I did not die as a girl of four. I am your sister, Erin Blakemore."

Chapter 25

I did not now whether to laugh or weep, or whether I was truly losing my mind this time. But she was not a figment of my imagination, and as she came toward me, I remembered the affinity I had felt for her when we'd first met but could not explain.

"Erin?" I said, through my tears. "Is it really so?"

She nodded, and then we fell into each other's arms. Our tears mingled until we both looked at each other again. Finally she spoke.

"It's true," she said. "But I was afraid you wouldn't believe me. Not after what I've done."

I blew my nose on the handkerchief Lettice offered me, and Richard came to put an arm around my shoulders. Everything was happening so quickly I hardly knew what to think. But I hadn't forgotten the culprit in our midst.

I glanced at Gaius. "How? . . . ."

She lowered her eyes, wringing her hands in front of her skirt. "I can't hope that you'll forgive me. I agreed to help him, but now I see that I was wrong. It was Gaius who told me who I really was, and that he'd help me get back what was rightfully mine, for the family had wronged me too."

"But Erin," said Lettice. "If you really are Erin. No one knew you were alive."

"I know. When I got here, things were different than Gaius had led me to believe. I tried to see it the way he did. But I couldn't. You were all so good to me, I—" The rest of her words were choked off by her sobs.

She held her face in her hands, but I reached around her shoulders. "It's all right. Sit down. Take your time. We want to know everything."

She took a seat on the sofa next to me, and when she again had control of herself, she began to speak, and as she did, we were taken back with her to that night when the hurricane struck fourteen years ago.

"You had all left on your holiday," she said. "All except Cousin Jasper and me. Then the ferryman came, bringing news that a bad hurricane threatened. I don't remember that of course, but I do remember my nanny getting me ready to travel, even though I had a fever. We couldn't stay on the island. It wouldn't be safe.

"Cousin Jasper had come to the manor house to fetch us. He ordered all the servants down to the docks to take the launch to the mainland. Nanny put me into the carriage, but I got out again. I wanted to go back for my dolly. Then I don't remember what happened next, but . . ." she cast a direction in Gaius's direction.

"I must have stopped in the entry hall. I do remember looking into the study where Jasper was doing something at the safe. I could see him from where I stood. I wouldn't have known what he was doing, of course, but he must have thought so."

She sat more rigidly, remembering. "He got angry when he saw me, and he ran past me, shouting at those in the carriage to go on to the launch. He would bring me in his boat. I heard the carriage leave, and then we were left alone."

I pressed my lips together, spellbound by her story, as she continued.

"The storm was heavier then," she said, "and after getting my dolly, I waited for Cousin Jasper to take me to the dock. It was pouring rain. I remember how the water hit me in the face as we got into the wagon. But when we got to the dock, the others had left. We had only the rowboat. Jasper put me in the boat, and we put out into the churning waters.

"I started crying. I was shivering with my fever, and the water kept dousing me, but we got to the dock on the other side."

I stopped her. "Then the boat never overturned at all?"

She shook her head. "I was wet and cold, but it was only from the rain and from the water that splashed up on me as Jasper rowed."

Again, I felt a sense of unreality as I realized that the images I had conjured in my mind explaining how Erin had drowned were all fabricated. It was unsettling.

"I was crying when we got to the dock, but Jasper pulled me out and dragged me along the street. I don't know exactly what happened then, but I remember him bedding me down in the back of a wagon. I must have fallen unconscious for a time, for when I woke up I was in a warm bed in a small, dark room. I was hot, and I didn't know where I was, but I was too frightened to make any noise.

"Instead, I got out of bed and went to the door. I could hear voices downstairs. But I went back to bed, ill with my fever. The next day we traveled by rail, but I don't remember much. I slept as much as I could. Then we came to the orphanage, and Jasper turned me over to Mrs. Potter, who I didn't like very much. She told me my cousin had left me there and gone to look for my parents, that she would take care of me until I was better.

"It was weeks until I got well, but no one came for me until one day, Cousin Jasper came back, looking very sad. He told me my family had all perished in the storm, and that he had to leave me at the orphanage for a little while, but that he would send money to see that I was well taken care of."

She shook her head, moisture appearing at the corners of her eyes. "I was too young to do anything but accept this as true. And so I grew up in the orphanage, thinking that my family was dead. I always remembered images of my childhood home, but I didn't know where it was. And no one at the orphanage had ever heard of Calayeshi Island."

I reached over to squeeze her hand. I remembered the storm that had passed us by where we were vacationing on the Halifax River, where our family went for a month every winter.

Still holding Erin's hand, for something in me told me she was speaking the truth, I faced the others.

"I remember how Jasper showed up at the hotel, grief-stricken because the boat had capsized." I knew the others remembered the story Jasper had told as well. "Though he dove and dove, he could not find Erin. For she had drowned."

We were all silent for a moment, and I glanced at Gaius, who was stone-faced, as if he weren't even listening to us.

"Apparently Jasper went to such great lengths because

rin caught him stealing the jewels from the safe," said
Richard. "A child of four might remember what she had
een and talk indiscriminately." Then he strode to where
aius sat.

"What I want to know is why? Why did Jasper think
e had a right to the jewels?"

Gaius averted his head, but then Lettice rose and went
o stand in front of Gaius. Her voice was firm as she said,
Gaius thinks he came to us unknown. But that is not
rue. I know him. I have seen him before with Jasper."

He jerked his head around to scowl at her.

"At the sponge docks," she said in a quiet, even voice.

He made a movement as if to rise, but his handcuffs
eld him back. His face turned a deep shade of red and
hen quickly drained.

"Are you sure you want to hear any more?" said
Richard to his mother. He must have guessed the truth
nd wanted to protect her, but Lettice remained firm.

"It's all right. I believe I know what he is going to say.
Only I want to hear it from his own lips as do the rest of
s."

"All right, Amundsen," said Richard. "You might as
ell tell us."

Gaius thrust his jaw forward. "I will tell you," he said.
If you'll give me something to wet my throat. And take
hese blasted things off. I'm not going anywhere."

He glared at the two officers standing at the door. He
as clearly outnumbered, and from the way his
houlders slouched, I could tell that he knew he was
eaten.

Richard glanced at the policemen. "Your men are
osted outside?"

"Yes sir," the biggest one nodded. "We'll take him in

337

when you're ready."

"Very well," Richard. "Cuff one of his hands to the chair. I don't trust him." Then he poured a glass of sherry from the decanter on the side table and handed it to Gaius, who was rubbing his wrist with the hand they cuffed to the arm of his chair.

He frowned, but took the glass and swallowed his drink. Then he leaned back, crossed his legs and set the glass down.

"Yes, why not tell you all the truth? If I cannot vindicate my father, at least I can tell you how he really felt. You were too good for him, you see. At least that's how it was when he fell in love with my mother."

He sipped from his glass, giving us all his arrogant stare. "The woman my father loved was from the wrong side of the tracks," he said. "She had no money and no family. His father didn't approve of the match and prevented the marriage. That didn't stop him from loving her, however. And even when he got my mother pregnant, the Blakemores would not allow him to marry her. Oh, they paid her well enough to keep quiet. To go away so that Jasper could marry someone with better breeding."

I glanced at Lettice, but her face was passive, and I was again struck with the idea that what Gaius was saying was not entirely strange to her.

"He was crushed of course. Offered to go with my mother, but she wouldn't let him. She took the money for it was her only alternative, and left. She went into service with a family who was kind enough to hire a pregnant woman. She told them her husband had been killed, of course. And so I grew up below stairs in a house on the Hudson River. It wasn't such a bad life for a boy. I

layed outdoors a lot. Became friends with the family's
only son and heir.

"But there are certain things a servant's son doesn't do
in society. I resented it, and I told my mother that one
day I would be rich too, so that no one could ever look
down on us again. That was when she told me who I really
was.

"She got sick, and when she couldn't work anymore,
she told me to go to my father. That he would do
something for me. I was only ten when she died. But I was
determined to find my father. I packed all my earthly
belongings in a bag and made the journey to Coral
Springs. I found my father all right. He knew who I was,
and he was glad to have me. He told me he'd teach me all
he knew about the sponge fishing business and that he'd
take care of my schooling.

"He never let me down. He sent me to boarding school,
and in the summers I worked for him. We were very
close, my father and I, for he never felt like he fit in with
the rest of the Blakemores. But he told me not to worry.
He'd take care of me. He said he had a plan. That one day
he and I would go away where we could live together and
start life over. We just had to wait a little while until he
could get his hands on something that would make it all
possible."

I looked at Richard, who was shaking his head. What a
horrible life Jasper must have led. What a bitter man he
had become, and then he had passed his bitterness on to
Gaius.

I didn't know what had happened all those years ago to
make Jasper feel he was such an outcast. My father
thought Jasper was a hard man to get along with, but I
had never heard the story of Gaius's mother. And I could

not know what kind of prejudices existed then to prevent him from marrying her if he'd really wanted to.

Of course the story as we heard it might have been perverted. Perhaps Jasper had been smitten by a woman he could not stay away from, but one he himself did not want to bring into the family. No matter what he had told his son, we would never know the truth.

"When did he tell you about the jewels?" asked Richard.

Gaius took his time answering, indicating that he wanted his glass refilled. When that was done, he set it beside him and continued.

"He didn't at the time. But he got his chance to do what he'd been planning to do. But Erin caught him in the act. He had to get rid of her. He wouldn't have killed her, but the storm provided him with an excuse to say she had drowned. It was all he could do, for she might let his secret slip someday.

"When I was sixteen, he had an accident with one of the hooks. While he was recuperating, he feared that worse threats lurked. He had competition. He wanted me to know everything in case anything happened to him."

"So that was when he told you what he'd done?" I asked.

Gaius nodded. "He told me then how he had faked Erin's death and returned to the island. He never told me where he had concealed the jewels, for he thought he had enough time. We would come together to get them. But he told me they were in a place where no one would ever look."

"I remember how Jasper went to visit the cemetery," said Lettice, still sitting rigidly, her hands folded in her lap. "Of course we all thought at the time that he went night after night to keep a silent vigil. For wasn't he trying to purge himself of the remorse he felt at having lost the child out of his very own hands?"

Now the bitter irony found its way into her voice. I could see her jaw clench as she rose and paced in front of Gaius.

"And so we left him by the vault at night to pray. When he knew none of us were watching, he must have opened the vault and the empty casket and hid the jewels in their secret place. I can see it now. What fools we were."

Gaius curled his lip. "But he knew there was no safer place. He kept them there, an investment in our future."

Then rage showed on Lettice's face, and she slapped him. I heard the smack of her hand on his cheek. He sat there, stunned. I gritted my teeth and held onto my chair, for I too felt the violence course through me. I wanted to knock all his arrogance out of him. But it would be no use. I knew you could not fight pain with pain.

Lettice turned her back, and Richard put his hands on her shoulders.

"It's all right," she said, taking a deep breath, and wiping away the tears from her eyes. "I'll be all right."

Then she walked to the end of the room.

I rose and approached Gaius. "Then Jasper made it look like Richard stole things." I looked at Richard. "Don't you see? He had planned it that way so that one day the guilt would fall on you." I shook my head, disgusted at the length to which the evil had gone.

But Gaius had no sympathy for us. "I watched helplessly at the dock as my father perished in that fire," he said. "None of the rest of you saw that."

"Stop your self-pitying drivel, Amundsen," said

Richard. "Jasper Blakemore was the kind of man to mak[e]
enemies. I knew him, don't forget. I don't know anythin[g]
about your mother, and believe me, I am sorry if she wa[s]
wronged. But you seem to hold us all accountable, whe[n]
we knew nothing about it. But I had many years in whic[h]
to see Jasper Blakemore turn into a hard man. If he ha[d]
enemies, it was at least partly his fault. We didn't ki[ll]
him."

"Go ahead, defend yourself," said Gaius. "It's what I'[d]
expect of you."

"Then that is why you befriended me at school," sai[d]
Richard. "All that was part of your little plot."

"I took the money my father had saved for me, passe[d]
my exams and enrolled at the college he told me to go t[o.]
He said all the Blakemores went there, and I should g[o]
there too."

"So you bided your time at school until you m[et]
Richard," I said. "But what about Erin? Did Jasper te[ll]
you where she was?"

Gaius's gaze rested a minute on Erin, and I thought [I]
saw something like regret flash through his eyes befor[e]
she averted her head so she would not have to look [at]
him.

"She was sixteen. I found her, told her the truth abou[t]
who she was. I told her that together we would lay clai[m]
to what was ours. For we had both been cheated by th[e]
Blakemores."

"But you are wrong, Gaius," I said. "We would hav[e]
welcomed Erin to us. She didn't need you."

Erin faced me, a determined expression on her fac[e.]

"He made me think I needed him. I know it sound[s]
twisted, but he made me feel obligated to help him. H[e]
made me fall in love with him."

From what I knew of Gaius I could see how easily she could have fallen under his spell. He had a charm that had been difficult for me to deny when he had used that charm on me at first.

"I understand," I said.

She pressed her lips together, looking at me regretfully. "I know now I was wrong. But once I married him, there was little else I could do. He was my husband."

"And then he brought you here to find the jewels."

"Yes. We still didn't know exactly where they were. Gaius came to find out what you and the others might know, to search the island for clues. But then I got here and oh—" she broke off in a sob.

We waited until she had collected herself while Gaius, angry at the way things had turned out, downed the rest of his sherry. I felt sorry for her, vulnerable and misled by his twisted tales.

"So you tried to frighten me," I said to Gaius. "But why? I knew nothing."

"How was I to know that? I thought you needed a little help to jar your memory. And I thought maybe you'd come back for the same reason I had, to claim your inheritance and leave this place."

"But it goes further than that," said Richard. "When you decided you could manage finding the jewels on your own, you needed to distract us from sending the authorities after you once you were gone. We couldn't call the police in to fight our own ghosts. And if you had to kill any of us who stood in your way, you would have done so, isn't that true?"

Gaius faced Richard then, and I had never seen such rage and hatred. But Richard continued to confront him, as all the evil passed between them in a contest of wills.

Finally Gaius looked away.

"I wouldn't have let him," said Erin, more courage coming into her voice. "I didn't know how obsessed he was. I was frightened, terribly frightened. I couldn't tell you for fear you'd blame me. But then tonight I knew Gaius would do something awful. I had to warn you."

"It's all right, Erin. It's all over now."

"Yes," said Richard, turning away from Gaius at last. He signaled to the policemen, who came and replaced Gaius's handcuffs and led him away.

I sat down again, relieved that he was gone from our midst. Richard came to stand behind me and placed his hand on my shoulder in a gesture of comfort. We all seemed to try to gather our wits about us and then one by one, all eyes fell on Erin, who still sat in the corner of the couch, clutching her hands in front of her.

"I know what you all must think of me," she said, not looking at any of us. Suddenly I didn't see a strange young woman before me, but a frightened little girl, eyes darting here and there when a bird had startled her.

"Oh Erin," I said, but she wouldn't look at me.

"This is all partly my fault," she said. "I'm an accessory. I'll have to go away at the very least."

"No," I said. "You don't have to go away, Erin. You are my sister. You belong here."

Then I looked at Lettice and Nannette, for I could not speak for them.

Lettice rose slowly and walked over to stand before the girl shrinking at the end of the couch. "Whatever happened has not been entirely your fault," she said. "Gaius was fighting enemies who were not really there. He took advantage of your position and lied to you. You are welcome in my house."

344

"Oh yes," said Nannette. "I'm glad we've found you. It will mean so much to Eileen to have her sister back."

Then we were all crying and hugging each other. I wiped my tears away and looked at Richard, who smiled benevolently. Even Ian seemed moved by the emotional scene. He had gone upstairs to get his sketches and now returned. He poured a glass of sherry and came to sit beside me.

"You see," he said, opening his sketch pad. "I knew there was a resemblance. The differences between you are superficial really."

"You're so clever, Ian. None of the rest of us saw it."

"You weren't looking for it. But see here." He pointed to one of the sketches. "The bone structure is similar. Your round and healthy cheeks may not look like Erin's gaunt ones. Your proud carriage and her hunched shoulders are simply a result of the different lives you've lead."

I was amazed. In the lines of the charcoal Ian had seen the resemblance. He had felt it in his hand.

"I tried to tell you last night."

"Yes, I remember. Gaius interrupted us. He must have known what you'd come upon."

Erin came to look at the drawings.

"You may keep them," Ian said to her.

She looked at them and then at him. "I shall treasure them, Ian. Thank you."

We all sat together speaking words of relief and piecing together what had happened. Richard had stretched out in the wing chair by the fire, putting his feet up on the ottoman. He followed our conversation for a while and then gazed quietly into the fire.

I knew he must have been thinking about Gaius, how

he too had been duped by friendship at first. And then how Gaius betrayed him by trying to make it seem as if Richard were mad.

I moved to the ottoman, and sat down. In spite of it all I thought I had never seen Richard look so relaxed. Gone was the harried look that came from knowing something was wrong but not being able to spot its source. With truth came relief.

"It's all over now," I said, looking at the bright orange flames that danced in the fireplace. "Are you very hurt that your friend turned out not to be what you thought?"

He smiled sadly. "Life is full of disappointments, but in times of danger, one finds out who ones friends are."

I looked at him, and all the love I had longed to see since he had held me that night in the chapel returned to his eyes.

"Oh Richard," I said.

One by one everyone said good night and went upstairs until Richard and I were left alone. The lamps were turned down low, and the firelight flickered behind us.

He slipped his arm around my waist and pulled me close to him. "I'm glad you've found your sister," he said.

"Yes," I said. "The manor house will not be so lonely now."

He lifted my chin to study my face, and then he said. "The night is balmy. Come outside with me."

I followed him onto the verandah. All was dark before us, but in the shadows of the moon I could make out the palms rising like sentinels by the drive. Somewhere in the woods an owl hooted. Richard stood close to me, and we were so silent that I could hear his breathing.

"This is our island after all," he said.

"Yes."

"You have no desire to leave it then?"

Mixed emotions churned within me. I would have no desire to leave it if I knew Richard loved me, but his next words satisfied that need.

He turned to me and took me in his arms. "Marry me, Eileen. I love you. The island would not be the same without you."

For an answer I put my arms around his neck and raised my lips to meet his. His kiss was deep and loving. Then he lifted his head and I rested against him.

"I never want you to feel trapped by the memories here."

"I don't feel trapped anymore," I said. "Now that we know the truth. Oh Richard, you've made me so happy. I belong here with you always.

Chapter 26

Two days later Richard and I stood on the dock seeing Ian off. He came up to me and took my hands.

"Good-bye Eileen. I'm glad things are settled at last."

I smiled at him. "Yes, they are. I'm sorry you are leaving so soon."

He shrugged. "I too have experienced the spell of the island, but I don't think I'm suited to island life after all."

I laughed. "Missing society at last?"

He blushed. "I suppose I do get rather restless in all this peaceful tropical beauty. But you Eileen. You will be happy here." He dropped his eyes. "I do want your happiness. I mean that."

I squeezed his hand and raised up to kiss his cheek. "I know that, Ian. Thank you."

Then he turned to Richard, who stood a few paces off. "Good-bye, old man. And may I add my congratulations."

Richard's eyes flickered to me. "You may."

We had announced our engagement the night before.

Ian kissed Erin and then Nannette, who strolled with him down to the launch. Then he got in, and as the ferryman pushed off and jumped into the boat, we all waved.

He took a seat in the stern and waved his straw hat at us. "Come and visit," he shouted. "All of you."

We waved him off, then I went down to stand beside Nannette. "Will you miss him?" I asked.

She smiled and shook her head. "I'll miss his gaiety, but that is all."

I felt relieved, fearing that she might have fallen in love with him. And thought Ian was a good friend, I could not say that his heart was true. Though someday when he was older, he might settle down with someone like Nannette. But she was safe from his fickle heart for now.

We walked back to where Richard and Erin stood. Erin's cheeks had a rosy glow that she had not had before. Her hair was done up in a neat chignon, and she wore a gauze gown that Nannette had presented her as a welcome gift.

I took Richard's arm as we followed the two girls to the new carriage and got in. We settled ourselves and Richard picked up the reins. We drove past the sugar cane fields, the breeze, and the bright sun refreshing us. We turned down the road that led to the manor, and then turned again into the live oak allee.

The manor looked cool and shady, and when we pulled up, Nannette and Erin jumped down and went inside. Richard helped me down and we stood looking at the stone edifice.

"Are you sure you won't mind living here?" I asked, as he came around to slip his arm around my waist.

"Not if it is what you wish," he said. "Though I have offered to build you another mansion if you want it."

"No," I said, my heart full as I stood with him in the sun. "We've banished the ghosts, haven't we? I vowed to bring life to this house when I returned here. And now I know I will."

"Yes," he said, a devilish gleam in his eye as he gazed at me. "You will do just that if I have anything to say about it."

He started to kiss me, but I stopped him. "Not out here, Richard, where everyone can see us."

"Well, then take me inside woman, to a more private spot."

I laughed and he followed me in, and then I led him into the parlor, which at least afforded us a little more privacy.

"There," he said, closing the parlor doors and coming toward me purposely.

"Won't the others wonder what's happened to us?" I said.

But he took me in his arms again. "I don't care what anyone else wonders right now," he said, lifting a dark, quizzical brow. "I want to kiss my wife-to-be."

DISCOVER DEANA JAMES!

CAPTIVE ANGEL   **(2524, $4.50/$5.50)**
Abandoned, penniless, and suddenly responsible for the biggest tobacco plantation in Colleton County, distraught Caroline Gillard had no time to dissolve into tears. By day the willowy redhead labored to exhaustion beside her slaves . . . but each night left her restless with longing for her wayward husband. She'd make the sea captain regret his betrayal until he begged her to take him back!

MASQUE OF SAPPHIRE   **(2885, $4.50/$5.50)**
Judith Talbot-Harrow left England with a heavy heart. She was going to America to join a father she despised and a sister she distrusted. She was certainly in no mood to put up with the insulting actions of the arrogant Yankee privateer who boarded her ship, ransacked her things, then "apologized" with an indecent, brazen kiss! She vowed that someday he'd pay dearly for the liberties he had taken and the desires he had awakened.

SPEAK ONLY LOVE   **(3439, $4.95/$5.95)**
Long ago, the shock of her mother's death had robbed Vivian Marleigh of the power of speech. Now she was being forced to marry a bitter man with brandy on his breath. But she could not say what was in her heart. It was up to the viscount to spark the fires that would melt her icy reserve.

WILD TEXAS HEART   **(3205, $4.95/$5.95)**
Fan Breckenridge was terrified when the stranger found her near-naked and shivering beneath the Texas stars. Unable to remember who she was or what had happened, all she had in the world was the deed to a patch of land that might yield oil . . . and the fierce loving of this wildcatter who called himself Irons.

Available wherever paperbacks are sold, or order direct from the Publisher. Send cover price plus 50¢ per copy for mailing and handling to Zebra Books, Dept. 3860, 475 Park Avenue South, New York, N.Y. 10016. Residents of New York and Tennessee must include sales tax. DO NOT SEND CASH. For a free Zebra/ Pinnacle catalog please write to the above address.

THE ROMANCE OF LORDS AND LADIES
IN JANIS LADEN'S REGENCIES

BEWITCHING MINX (2532, $3.95)

From her first encounter with the Marquis of Penderleigh when he had mistaken her for a common trollop, Penelope had been incensed with the darkly handsome lord. Miss Penelope Larchmont was undoubtedly the most outspoken young lady Penderleigh had ever known, and the most tempting.

A NOBLE MISTRESS (2169, $3.95)

Moriah Landon had always been a singularly practical young lady. So when her father lost the family estate over a game of picquet, she paid the winner, the notorious Viscount Roane, a visit. And when he suggested the means of payment—that she become Roane's mistress—she agreed without a blink of her eyes.

SAPPHIRE TEMPTATION (3054, $3.95)

Lady Serena was commonly held to be an unusual young girl—outspoken when she should have been reticent, lively when she should have been demure. But there was one tradition she had not been allowed to break: a Wexley must marry a Gower. Richard Gower intended to teach his wife her duties—in every way.

SCOTTISH ROSE (2750, $3.95)

The Duke of Milburne returned to Milburne Hall trusting that the new governess, Miss Rose Beacham, had instilled the fear of God into his harum-scarum brood of siblings. But she romped with the children, refused to be cowed by his stern admonitions, and was so pretty that he had the devil of a time keeping his hands off her.